'A remarkably powerful, moving, assured and beautiful ... ing the debut of a major writer. I couldn't be more impressed' Robert Drewe, author of *Swimming to the Moon*

'*Testament* is a masterfully composed and ambitious novel that really grips its reader — intense, full of hard-researched detail and vivid, original language. It is a remarkable first book that avoids the trap of many Holocaust books by understanding the idea of responsibility beyond the original trauma' George Szirtes, International Man Booker Prize-winning translator of *The World Goes On*

'In her astonishingly assured debut novel, Kim Sherwood explores how we remake ourselves and learn to live with the secrets of the past. But she also reminds us that every portrait of British people is a portrait of the world. A moving, elegant meditation on identity and the masks we must all sometimes wear' Christopher Fowler, author of *The Book of Forgotten Authors*

'Every now and then there is a first novel that stops you in your tracks. *Testament* is one such. It enters dangerous territory — the Holocaust — but does so not only with humanity but a startling control of language . . . Here is a novelist born whole and entire' Christopher Bigsby, author of *Remembering and Imagining the Holocaust*

'Interwoven with the darkness Sherwood dropped little glimmers of hope, of redemption and of love . . . Stunning' *My Bookish Blog*

'A thing of beauty . . . Where Kim Sherwood will really see you undone is in the small acts of kindness that are candles held against a storm. Those were the moments I had to lower the page and take a breath' *Van is Reading*

Kim Sherwood was born in Camden in 1989 and lives in Bath. She studied Creative Writing at UEA, is now Senior Lecturer at the University of the West of England and teaches prisoners with Mass Observation Archive. Her pieces have appeared in *Mslexia*, *Lighthouse*, and *Going Down Swinging*. Kim began researching and writing *Testament*, her first novel, after her grandfather, the actor George Baker, passed away and her grandmother began to talk about her experiences as a Holocaust Survivor for the first time. It won the 2016 Bath Novel Award.

Praise for *Testament*

'Achingly powerful, Sherwood's impossibly beautiful prose captivated me from first page to last. *Testament* tells a fractured history as if it were an intimate memory. A work I won't soon forget' Guy Gunaratne, Booker-prize longlisted author of *In Our Mad and Furious City*

'Kim Sherwood's poetic fiction looks at history's impact and the morality of forgetting . . . Her writing is elegant and highly effective. This novel explores big ideas – some of the biggest ideas there are – but its power as a work of fiction lies in the personal . . . Sherwood pulls the threads of her narrative together with great skill to deliver a sad and beautiful book' *Irish Times*

'What a writer. I was totally captivated. A compelling, moving and ultimately uplifting story that delivered on its promise to fill the void left by loss' Heather Morris, author of *The Tattooist of Auschwitz*

'Powerful and moving . . . Hugely poignant, beautifully written' *Independent*

'Moving and vivid' *Sunday Times*

'Sherwood writes with a beauty and bravery that befits Holocaust remembrance and honours the strength of the human spirit' *Press Association*

'What is exceptional about Kim Sherwood's compassionate, poetic and deeply researched novel is the way she interweaves the twisted threads of the story . . . Sherwood has taken on the major tragedy of the twentieth century with a psychological insight rare in a writer who is not yet thirty . . . Unbearably poignant' *Jewish Chronicle*

'A rare thing – could easily be a third or fourth novel, so fluidly and gorgeously does it read. Sherwood's characters are finely nuanced and her poetic prose is every bit as exquisite . . . Stunning' *Skinny*

'This ambitious debut novel sensitively grapples [with] the effects of trauma through the generations' *Literary Review*

'A sensitive and searching novel about Holocaust survivors and their families, it scales a mountain of repressed emotion and feels drawn from life' *Sydney Morning Herald*

'Startling, raw and intense, this is a novel which compels you to read it, almost daring you in its quiet delivery, to look away. It is unputdownable and it is beautiful' *Literature Works*

'A truly heartfelt, stunning debut' *Saga*

'An extraordinary book; sad but optimistic, that enshrines the human spirit. I was so moved by the way it shows blessed creativity thriving even in the depths of hell' Patrick Gale, author of *Take Nothing With You*

'I am absorbed by the delicacy, even the beauty, with which she writes of the trauma of history . . . It's a real pleasure to see Sherwood approaching this theme – to do with how we discover, read, and reread our past – with subtlety, playfulness, and elegiac sadness' Amit Chaudhuri, author of *Friend of My Youth*

'*Testament* is ambitious, beautiful and brave. A vital act of remembrance of the Holocaust, it's also a deeply involving story that reaches across generations to speak to our own troubled times. How many debuts are actually important? This one is' Polly Clark, author of *Larchfield*

TESTAMENT

Kim Sherwood

riverrun

First published in Great Britain in 2018 by riverrun
This paperback edition published in Great Britain in 2019 by

riverrun

An imprint of

Quercus Publishing Ltd
Carmelite House
50 Victoria Embankment
London EC4Y 0DZ

An Hachette UK company

10 9 8 7 6 5 4 3 2 1

Typeset by CC Book Production
Printed and bound in Great Britain by Clays Ltd, Elcograf S.p.A.

For my grandparents

No. 1. The number on your tattoo

No. 2. Your registered number

No. 3. Name

No. 4. Date of birth (year, month, day)

No. 5. Place of birth

No. 6. Occupation

No. 7. Last address

No. 8. Location of ghetto

No. 9. The first stop en route to your deportation

No. 10. In which camps were you interned (from, to)

One

One

only his body

THIS IS THE LAST conversation we will have.

Silk: 'Where did it go?'

'I didn't go anywhere. I'm right here.'

A half-smile – he is king of the half-smile – a patient grandfatherly smile that tells me I am not interpreting him correctly, but that he has the time to teach me how to read him.

'Eva. My girl. Did it know I loved it?'

'Yes. I know.'

Birds perform evensong in the horse chestnut outside his bedroom window, inviting me to escape through the half-drawn curtains from one scene to another, leaving Silk's deathbed backstage. We used to do that together: clamber in and out of ground-floor windows, trailing mud and paint. *Never use demarcated exits*, he'd tell me; six years old, no idea what 'demarcate' meant, but swearing suspicion against all maps and signposts. I look over my shoulder at the tree. *Don't take this exit*, I want to tell him. *Stay with me*. But I can't – not when the Silk I know has been forced to surrender pronouns and poetry and can no longer implore me: *Eva, only a selfish love exhorts a man not to go gentle into that good night.* The horse chestnut is weak, holding up rain-soaked leaves. I think of the pink blossom Van Gogh painted from the window of his madness; I hear the trill of wood pigeons and remember a line from a nature documentary. When the birds stop singing, that will be the sound of extinction.

Whistling pierces the bedroom, inside our walls. It's Silk, his cracked lips pursed. He does it again, a brief wood warbler, a party trick for summer picnics that is so loud and so sustained by the silent house it is like the ringing of crystal glass.

Silk plucks at my hand.

I don't want to understand. It might be the last thing he ever teaches me, apart from how to manage death.

But after another nudge I inflate my lungs for an off-tune bastardisation of the roundelay outside. He laughs, does it himself, pitch-perfect. I copy, once, twice, until finally I am good enough and he folds his lips together, shutting a suitcase.

Then follows the procedure of medicine, blankets, pulling curtains to shut out pockets of polluted dusk, pockets I release at his protest, before finally burrowing my hand into his ready fist: goodnight. A creaking floorboard tells me that I am walking away from him, and as with every time I leave him, I think: this could be it.

'I love you.'

In the dark, he might have been winking.

THE STAGE MANAGEMENT OF loss. You think you will remember separate moments: a final breath, the weight of morning light across his legs. But the script changes. Loss does not keep to its moment; there is a keenness about grief, a sharp greed to it, hungering inside you. I do not remember if it really was our last conversation, our last touch, our last lesson, or whether when I went back to him that night – fearing death had infiltrated the scars and sores of his body, old and new, which I had discovered in these last weeks' intrusion into his privacy – whether we exchanged a joke, a story, a word of thanks, before he left.

But I do remember this: the birds did not sing again in his lifetime.

GRANNY ROSEMARY HAD PASSED away in a hospital. I was only sixteen then. I made tea and held Silk's hand; I watered her allotment; I cried. There was no time for crying now. There was his body, heavy on the bed. I phoned Dr Pinney, who said I should call the coroner because he hadn't seen Silk for over two weeks. It counts as unexpected, he said. The coroner arrived with a kind of ambulance. I leant against the granddaughter clock, called that because it stood less than four feet, as I used to, tapping Silk's knee in search of its wooden hinge. The brass second hand thrummed against the small of my back – *you've-grown you've-grown he's-gone he's-gone* – as three men heaved Silk from the bed. The sheets snagged on his wayward foot, his amputated toe a red stump. They took him too quickly, and I was left with a silent house, and the smell of panic.

The minute hand urged me to call John and tell him: your father is dead. To call the press and tell them: Joseph Silk is dead. But I couldn't tell the world before I told John, and I couldn't tell him at all. So I called Mum, waking her up in Melbourne.

'I've got to tell you something he's gone he died in the night – can you call Dad I can't.'

After long minutes Mum called back; she couldn't get through to John's mobile, and there was no answer at the house in Provence.

Then Silk's phone buzzed: John ringing. I hung up with Mum, following the smudge-swipe of Silk's thumb over ACCEPT.

'Joseph? Hello?'

'No, it's me. It's Eva.'

'Oh. I couldn't get through on your phone. Your mother's calling me – doesn't she know how expensive it is to receive calls from Australia?'

'I need to tell you something.'

'Then tell me. Getting your mother to act as a go-between is fucking ridiculous. *Melbourne* is not between England and fucking France. It's six in the morning here.'

'I know it is. Listen. It's happened. He's gone. Silk is gone.'

A punch, a scuffle, like the sound of a microphone taped over a failing heart and ripped free – and then silence.

'Dad, I can't hear . . . Are you still there?'

'Gone where?'

'What do you mean?'

'I mean, did it happen in the hospital? At home?'

'Home. He was talking about how much he loved us. He wasn't in any pain.'

'They said he'd recover.'

'They weren't sure after the second stroke. I told you that. I tried to tell you that. To come here.'

'You should have tried harder.'

8

'We've got to tell the press.'

'What the fuck does it matter?'

'It's important, there's going to be people wanting details . . . Hello? Are you still there?'

'I've got to go.'

'Wait . . .'

'Bonjour, Eva?' It was Liset. 'John is very upset, what is happening now?'

'His father is dead.'

I BUMPED THROUGH THE house to my flat upstairs. Sat down at my kitchen table. Looked out at Hampstead Heath, the second pond burnished by sun. I fiddled with the frayed strap of my camera bag. When the phone rang I thought it was Mum, but it was BBC Radio. Silk's agent had said I would talk to them – hadn't Winston got in touch with me? No, he hadn't. Would I talk? Yes, I would.

I told them Silk had passed away quietly in the night. Below, two swans challenged each other on the pond, their great wings beating. I picked up my camera and pressed RECORD as I agreed that, yes, Silk had enjoyed an unusual longevity in his career, popular since his late twenties. I told a story about Silk painting in a derelict lido where the loudspeakers still worked, how he filled the empty tank with 'The Blue Danube'. The swans thrashed. They could fill my lens with blood. I told them Silk was very proud to adopt Britain as his homeland.

'You're studying documentary filmmaking, Eva – making a

documentary about your grandfather, is that right? He's shied away
from personal narratives in the past.'

'I am . . . we were doing something together. A short film.'

'Will you finish it?'

The swans locked – they could not separate.

'Yes,' I said. 'I will.'

At some point the phone call ended, the swans mutely surrendered. I'd moved into the top floor of the Fitzroy Park house in the
second year of my Film BA. Silk needed help; I needed somewhere
affordable to live. Mum had already moved to Australia, thinking
I would follow. I still hadn't. My flat watched me now: the wall of
postcards, Cary Grant and Charlie Chaplin, the sagging bookshelves.
After Granny Rosemary died, I inherited Silk's nighttime language:
the groan of Victorian floorboards, the tumble of broken china in
the sink, Silk pacing each room, shouldering into doors. Nightlights
marked his route: he had a terror of the dark. I set my clock to his,
keeping him company, until he seemed to agree to some unspoken
proposal, matching his time to mine, presiding over dinner parties
with my friends, teaching us to waltz and jive in the living room.
When I began my Documentary MA, I suggested we collaborate.
The documentary was supposed to show more than his paintings, to
show his life, but we disagreed on what that meant.

My laptop waited in front of me. With just a few keys I could
summon Silk back to life, return him to his easel, his silver hair
brushed back in a thick wave, a smile waiting in the lines of his
mouth, his six-foot-four frame refusing to bow to old age.

Friends from university fiddle with lighting and sound. I am
behind the camera, and begin as if we have never met.

'When and where were you born?'

Silk straightens, touching the extinguished Allies Club tie at his throat. 'I was born in London in 1945, eighteen and already a man. I was born to the sound of Big Ben regaining his voice and the Thames regaining her lights, a thousand blackout blinds thrown down. That's where I was born: to blue, cloudless skies, the signature of warplanes scrubbed free.'

'Are you going to give me a real answer?' I ask.

He eases back on the stool, squinting at me. 'What was the question?'

'When and where were you born?'

'I suppose you'll be wanting my middle name and star sign, too.'

'Are you saying where you were born is incidental?'

'You're going to make this harder than originally promised, aren't you?'

'Then tell me, why London? Why did you choose London as your birthplace, or rebirthplace?'

'My *rebirth*?'

I move around the camera. '*You're* going to make this harder than originally promised, aren't you?'

'Ha. Why London? Someone once said – I don't know who – that in a time of crisis Londoners fly into a great calm. That's why London. Because it is a city served and shaped by a tidal river; a city in which people are *supposed* to come and go. It's the only way the city will stand. That's why these clowns banging their drum about Britishness and immigration grieve me. To paint a portrait of Britain is to paint a portrait of the world. That river comes and goes. Look out. Feel the tide turn. Who will be on the next boat? Maybe you,

Eva Butler, chasing the world. Maybe me, arriving in England one fine autumn day, Ill-prepared for tea with cold milk, and the many words I would need to talk about the weather.'

A small silence.

'I guess some of that's usable . . .' I say.

The room laughs. Silk loosens his tie.

I kept the laptop closed; I kept my eyes closed. I was woken by my alarm, by my own voice on the radio – 'Yes, people always tied him to Abstract Expressionism, but as a painter he didn't like labels . . .' I rushed into my bedroom, slamming the antenna down. My phone began to parrot, another kind of alarm, friend after friend: *Silk-is-dead Silk-is-dead Silk-is-dead.*

WE TURNED THE KITCHEN into The Joseph Silk Funeral Office. The long table he'd sliced illegally from a giant lime tree after the storm of 1987 almost disappeared under paper. Olivia, Silk's lawyer, and his agent Winston bartered in competing volumes about the changes Silk made to his will without telling anyone, addendums in Caran d'Ache pencil, replacing John's name with my own.

'It's what you deserve, you know,' said Olivia. 'And need. Silk was so worried about jobs, housing. *And* John hasn't come home for a decade. But there's a lot to sort out. Silk's daubs, for one thing.'

Silk liked Olivia for her disdain of fine art. It didn't make me laugh – it barely penetrated. I was full up. A letter had been sent to John informing him of Silk's decision. I waited for his call, his arrival, his ice storm. And waited. I didn't sleep. Mum would arrive in eight days. I made invitation lists and recycled sympathy cards.

Somebody asked why Silk hadn't kept a Life Book detailing what insurance to cancel, where to find his birth certificate and marriage licence, what bank accounts to close.

'Tell them to watch *This Is Your Life*,' I said.

Winston shook his head. 'The number of times Silk asked me why that couldn't be kept off YouTube . . .'

The death certificate was easily found: the coroner had given it to me briskly, like a voided receipt. The full name of the deceased and any other name he once had proved harder, because I had to look up the spelling. Joseph Silk and József Zyyad sat side by side, contained in their boxes.

Pension: tick, received from the Royal College of Art.

Spouse: Rosemary Silk. Deceased. Occupation: dance choreographer. I wanted to add wrangler, confessor, stabilising wheels, patient muse. But that was hard to fit in a box.

Children from current or most recent marriage: one, son.

Any other spouses: no.

Any other children: no.

That was one of Silk's inexplicable prides. Friends had brought home news of mistresses they couldn't give up, of second families, awkward sharing arrangements. Winston remembered an argument between Silk and Rosemary, Silk insisting, 'My mind may have strayed to painting when it was needed for homework, and my attentions may have strayed when my mind wasn't watching, but my love – my love never went anywhere, and no strays ever followed it home. You've got my heart housebound.' Rosemary's retort: 'I can't tell if you'd rather be praised for knowing how to put on a rubber, or knowing your way around a sentence; but if it's sentences we're talking about, I refuse this prison sentence for what I took on in good faith.' Winston smiling as he recalled it, telling me he'd never known a couple like them, a couple who'd chuckle at each other's rejoinders. Theirs was a negotiation where turn of phrase mattered more than outcome. 'It's what kept them on the dance floor.' But sometimes I would wonder why Silk and John were allowed immovable natures, and the women around them only the disappointing gift of compromise.

Silk's date of birth: 02/05/1926. Olivia said she'd call the registrar to explain that there was no birth certificate. There were no records, no Life Book, no committed memory.

'None of it can have survived . . .' Olivia said, slowing down as she picked up her pen. The verb underwent a transformation on the page, becoming a noun, becoming weighted: *survivor*. 'I'll call them and explain.'

Messages from the funeral director haunted my inbox: what would you like on the menu? What would you like on the grave? Post-it notes littered odd surfaces: the bathroom mirror, an antique ottoman. Some were inscribed with headstones, some blank; some buried Joseph Silk, others József Zyyad.

Silk's body was gone, but only his body. He continued to watch me from family photographs and Polaroids of art crowds from the sixties – they went out and came back in the form of magazine articles and Sunday spreads, all pre-empted by Facebook and Twitter. Footage of him painting took up the entire BBC homepage, with a link to Arts & Entertainment.

He was on TV too. The evening news said Silk was one of Britain's last twentieth-century art giants. The initial authors of history described his peculiar eyesight, the derangement of colour. They identified him as British, before adding in the second paragraph that he was of Hungarian extraction, and in the third that he was Jewish. But then began a slow shift, so that by day three 'the Holocaust survivor and artist Joseph Silk, also called József Zyyad' was to be buried in Highgate Cemetery, sharing the ground with Karl Marx, that other un-Jewish Jew.

Silk had always rejected being defined as a survivor, or as Jewish, but now the columnists and art editors realised: he isn't here to roll out an ironic *oi vey*. They compared him to R.B. Kitaj, another settler-artist, but one who held up his Judaism, table-banging in his manifesto: *I've got Jew on the Brain. Jews are my Tahiti, my Giverny, my Dada, my String Theory, my Lost Horizon. The Jewish Question is my limit-experience, my Romance, my neurosis, my war, my pleasure-principle, my death drive.* Expert psychologists demolished Silk's would-be rebuttal with one sub-clause: '*As a survivor*, Joseph Silk claimed his work did not stem from the Holocaust . . .' The Jew doth protest too much.

My Great-Uncle László died ten years ago of a heart attack. Silk and László used to see each other once or twice a decade, László living in Tel Aviv, Silk giving monthly donations to Free Palestine. László was a short, cut-off man with pride built for a father, but only given to me. I was eight when I first met him. He arrived at the house with a cardboard tube under his arm. I thought it was a present for me, a map or a poster, but he unfurled the scroll for Silk. It was an attempt at a family tree. I remember the shuttling sound of cardboard and paper as Silk's arm flew out, knocking the thing from the table. I remember the shock on his face, as if he hadn't been aware of raising his hand. The brothers went at each other like bulls. Shouting brought Mum and Rosemary running into the room. Someone picked me up, carrying me upstairs, where I listened to the belt of accusations, burning with an understanding I felt the adults around me didn't possess. This rage: it was terror. He's afraid. My grandfather is afraid. Afterwards, I found Silk alone in the Blue Room. He was trying to paint but his hand was shaking. I remember pulling at the tangled threads of their argument: 'Aren't you English like me?' When he didn't respond, I pressed: 'Where are your family?' He turned away. 'What's a camouflage Jew?' There was exhaustion in the rise and fall of his chest, in the tremor of the brush. I closed my hand over his fingers. We applied the brush to the canvas together, and blue bled in a slow river. I thought he was crying, but didn't look up into his face, just stood within the shelter of his body, sheltering him.

shake loose the earth

COMFORT EXHAUSTED ME: MAKING cups of tea, making jokes. Solicitations of honesty exhausted me. I retreated to the bathroom like someone seeking a hurricane room, balancing a teacup brimming with twenty-year-old port I'd found at the back of a cupboard – the dishwasher shaking every glass in the house, the recycling gleaming wine-bottle green. I lay back in the empty bath and looked at my blank phone. John had been an orphan for four days and was yet to return to his childhood home and his daughter, with only the narrow sea to cross.

John never liked Fitzroy Park. He called the house an ice locker, always glaring. He hated growing up here, hated the Heath, the elm avenues butting up against our garden gate. He hated the floor-to-ceiling windows Silk installed after he and Rosemary inherited the house through what amounted to diligent squatters' rights. The constant white glow kept Silk in comfortable confinement in the Blue Room, his studio occupying the stubby end of the L-shaped house, so that if you were washing up you had a diagonal line of sight across the garden to Silk's workroom with its beaten path to the Heath. If you were watching late-night TV in the living room, you were asked to endure the fluorescence of the studio's un-curtained panels. If you were going down to the cellar, you were forced to tiptoe past the sunken door. John called it a panopticon of escape routes. I saw the windows as a gift to Silk: the colour spectrum for his lonely vision. Light was Silk's language, and, in that, John was mute.

Catching myself wide-eyed with fear and loss in the black screen, I tapped CALL and jammed the phone against my ear, imagining John seeing my name and trying to decide: accept, decline, accept, decline . . .

Decline: the ringtone spooled out into the bathtub, circling the rings of dirt left by Silk's experimentation with pulp. I sat holding the phone after it had gone to message, giving John eighteen seconds of the house and me breathing. I tapped END.

'So that's that,' I told the conch shell on the bath rim. John hadn't answered, and wouldn't answer – now that Silk was gone, the strange umbilical cord that connected us was cut, and I was free of it.

I sat back. I had loved bath times at Silk's house, playing Batman and Robin figurines with Mum. At home – wherever home was then – the slosh of tidal waves was unacceptable, John studying town planning, and Mum never with time to play, getting dinner ready. Here, Mum used to balance a flannel on my forehead, keeping shampoo from my eyes. The flannel was cooler than the bath water, and sometimes I would bet which of two lukewarm drops would drip to my chin first, while Mum told stories of a red desert childhood.

Now I picked up the shell and put it to my ear. No ocean, just the suggestion of blood. I set it back, remembering the months we'd stayed with Silk while doing up a new flat; one morning stepping into this bath, pulling the brass lever for the shower, and looking down at my new teenage stretch marks to see red. The surprise of it made me release clenched muscles and more blood came. I shut the water off and stood, just looking.

Mum and Granny Rosemary weren't in, just John – then still called Dad – and Silk. No one to call. I switched the water back on and washed the blood away, then climbed out shivering and picked up my pyjama trousers. They were spotted red too. The bathroom cupboards offered no help, and I ended up perched on the toilet lid in my towel. I felt like crying, and did not know why.

I stayed in the bathroom for nearly an hour, until Silk knocked. The door was broken – we used a paintbrush to turn the mechanism – and he let himself in as I told him I was fine, I mean, something has, but I don't . . . His eyes swept the room: me swamped in a towel, my pyjamas on the floor, the red splotches of blood that would have seemed grey to him. All the light of the house couldn't restore the balance of his vision.

'You've been in here a long time.'

'Do you know when Mum's coming home?'

'No,' he said, closing the door a little so that John – whose tread I could hear on the stair – would not see into the room. 'Did your father upset you?'

I said nothing.

Silk's attention returned to my stained pyjamas, but his expression remained calm, and I thought he didn't understand why I was blushing, something he called itchy or prickly, familiar with the sensation but not its colour. But he understood enough.

19

'You'll get a cold like that. Get dressed and we'll go out, just you and me.'

We went to Louis' Deli, a Hungarian patisserie that serves devil's puffs and floating islands for which Silk was prepared to compromise his British identity. We stopped at a chemist on the way because Silk said it was the only place that sold the car sweets Rosemary liked. He talked me through the different sanitary towels quietly. At the counter Silk introduced himself to the chemist and asked for two boxes of ibuprofen to help his swollen joints; he said it was hard to hold the brush. The chemist was so eager to help he didn't once glance my way, saving me the inquisitive look I felt certain would make me die from embarrassment.

I had my first ever coffee that day, a double espresso with no milk or sugar, a drink fit, he said, for a young woman such as myself.

Did your father upset you?

Your father, never *my son*. A performance of separation he and John had already torn through, rabid and impatient; a performance I would now quietly finish.

He understood enough.

ACCEPT: 'EVA, IT'S LATE here.'

'Here too. Don't you think we should talk about this?'

'About what?'

'You must have got the letter by now.'

'You're welcome to it.'

I set the cup between my legs: the whole room seemed to shrink to that clink of china, the wobble of port inside. 'Is that it?'

'That's it. And while you're at it, you can deliver the eulogy. I'm not coming.'

'You can't mean that.'

'You can count the fucking ways in which I mean it.'

The line went quiet. I stared at the screen. Something stuttered up my chest and into my windpipe and came out as a laugh. How do I love thee? Let me count the fucking ways.

I stood up so fast I knocked the cup over and port sloshed down the pale surface, bloodied again. Don't slip. No Mum to catch you, no Silk at the door. I climbed out holding on to the edge.

A RECENT UNFINISHED PORTRAIT of me waited on an easel in the corner of the Blue Room. Or some version of me. At that moment, I didn't know which of us was more real. Eva Butler, twenty-four, red hair and green eyes – the ambivalence, a boy once said, of changing traffic lights – Australian freckles waiting to happen, the cheekbones of Eastern Europe, an unassuming nose, a chin ideal for the gentle grasp of Silk's hand as he painted my face on my sixth birthday. Or Eva Butler, the canvas ageing me until I mirrored Silk, my hair a grey swathe, a glimmer of laughter turned contemplative in the underdrawing of my eyes – this lurking pentimento that managed to cast me as its poor reflection.

I turned the spotlight away. The room glimmered and winked. On the shelves, the concertina British Colour Council Dictionary flashed its silk scales like rainbow trout. Silk's collection began in the fifties when his friend got him a job as a cleaner for the British Colour Council. In the illicit lamplight of night shifts, Silk had carried out his own eye tests. Medici crimson and Kenya red were grey to him. But cerulean, firmament, heavenly blue, azure – they consumed him until he could smell clear sky. The Blue Room was born.

Now, journalists and art historians wanted to force meaning onto the Blue Room, an archive, a way to un-mix the *miscellany*, a word Silk – who wrapped his tongue around his chosen language with the fervour of a first kiss – would tell them came not only from Latin for mixed, but Middle English for mischief, itself from the Old French meschief – a bad result – comparable with the Spanish word menoscabo: diminution, loss. So what was the Blue Room: a great solid mountain of goods, or a hollow mine, whose very size reflected loss on an un-categorisable scale? What mattered here: the glorious pile of looted furniture, or the dust it would leave behind after removal men carted it out?

Sotheby's had hosted a ten-day auction for Andy Warhol's thrift collection. The Centre Pompidou had reconstructed Brancusi's studio, dust and all. Winston, plotting what to do with the Blue Room, asked me to draw up a catalogue.

How to begin counting the milk caps and postcards of seas and rivers and ice fields, the cloth picked from British Rail train seats and Chelsea FC shirts – spit on their name – and toothpaste tubes and torn Levi's and pipes of steel that caught the light in a certain way, the milk of magnesia bottles I found in Camden market, the minerals and dried-up ink and pressed forget-me-nots and sapphires and peacock and honey bird feathers and glasses and jugs and vases and Fortnum & Mason tea tins, the mess china from nineteenth-century naval ships and my childhood Captain Planet figurine, pages torn from books about the Blue Rider group and a Kandinsky most people thought was a copy but I knew better and a Hasselblad photo of the Earth rising over the lunar horizon in 1969 and food cartons from companies that no longer exist.

All this he experienced as a miracle.

What do you do with a miracle when its treasurer has abandoned the bank? Put it in storage, throw it away, make a permanent installation? Let it stay here and patina with dust? Keep earning that pocket money. Keep dusting. Take Silk and Rosemary's lives apart like an archaeologist packing up a find: shake loose the earth. Pack it up and ask John what he wants – pack the whole house up and ask John what he wants: the cufflinks, walking sticks, records, the giant impractical lime table yanked from its roots.

What shall we do with *us*, John? Now that our melodrama is done and I didn't even tell you what I think of you, just a pathetic, *You can't mean that*, and I am maddeningly still left with room for doubt.

No. Dig for something else. I moved shaking hands across Silk's desk, a diviner summoning lost property. But what I had lost would not be found here, would not be found at all. Silk had left me in the middle of a conversation, and I didn't know the next line, only that the cue was his.

My hand froze on a thick envelope. A stiff weave, the kind he used for birthday cards. Maybe he had left directions for me. A map charting a way forward, a way through, a way out. I turned it over. My shoulders dropped. The name on the back, next to *If lost*, was Dr Felix Gerschel.

The letter was from the Jewish Museum in Berlin. I'd brought it to Silk months ago. Cleaning palettes, spotting 'Jewish' and 'Berlin' on the envelope, he told me to throw it away.

'It could be something interesting,' I said, and opened it. The muscles in his jaw bunched as I read aloud, the impact too quick to take the words back: 'It says that the National Relief Committee for Deportees in Hungary interviewed you in 1945 about your . . . experience. They asked you a selection of over three hundred questions. The Jewish Museum in Berlin has found your testament in their collection and wants to use it for an exhibition they're putting together, about survivors, survivors who went on to be artists, and artists who didn't, um, survive. This researcher, Felix Gerschel, wants you to come and see the testament, and then to interview you. Or he can come here . . .'

'Three hundred questions? Never in my entire life have I been so interesting. Rip it up. I can't go to Berlin. Not now. Don't they know how busy I am?'

The plastic brush knocked against the lip of the palette as he chipped at the acrylic. I slipped the letter back into the envelope and left it on top of a Eurostar offer to senior citizens, one way for just £39.99.

Now the glue was matted with pollen and hair. How many times had he read it?

Silk never discussed the war. The little I did know of his experience came from newspapers and art books and conversations with Great-Uncle László. Silk left Hungary as a refugee in 1945 after the deaths of his sister and mother in unknown circumstances, and his father in Auschwitz. He was settled in London, where he met Rosemary, and had John six years later, in 1951. That was it. Everything I knew about Silk's life began in London, 1945.

I sat down, skating the letter this way and that over my knees,

24

listening to the rasp of paper on the stubble of my unshaven legs. *You can deliver the eulogy.* You can have the house, the canvases, this Gordian knot in your stomach, the grief that forces your eyeballs to the back of your skull to watch the world continue without him. This *in medias res* fucked-up entrance to the history of your grandfather: a disputed legacy and the father that legacy stunted and these questions, so many questions, the first of which has to be, how do I stand up without you?

I picked up my phone. Entered the area code, and listened to the strange ringtone.

'Gerschel. Hallo? Ist jemand da?'

'Is that – I'm looking for Dr Felix Gerschel.'

'You have found him. Me. This is my home number, though, and I am out of office hours—'

'You put your home number at the bottom of the letter. You said he – we – could ring anytime?'

'Who is this?'

'I'm sorry, my name is Eva, Eva Butler. I'm Joseph Silk's granddaughter.'

'Jesses. Excuse me, I am surprised to . . . I mean, I am so sorry. I was a huge admirer of his work, I did my PhD—'

'It made the news out there, I guess.'

A pause, then a small laugh, one of sympathy. 'All over the world, I imagine.'

'Right.' I clamped my spare hand under my armpit, the damp patch warming my fingers. 'I'm calling because I wondered if Silk – if Mr Silk – ever got back to you?'

'He did.'

'What did he say?'

'You say you are the granddaughter of Joseph Silk?'

'Yes.'

'And your full name, please?'

'Eva Butler. It's my mother's surname.'

'I see. I am sorry to – it would be a great honour to be speaking with Joseph Silk's granddaughter, but without any proof that you are who you say I cannot give that sort of information.'

'But what are you going to do with his testament?'

'I am very sorry, I cannot discuss—'

'Do you still have it?'

A rustle, and then the sound of typing. I imagined him googling me. 'Frau Butler, I really . . .' The voice obscured now, as if the phone was pinched between shoulder and ear. Two hands: one typing, one moving the mouse. Perhaps he'd found my blog, *Picture Show*, reviews of films Silk and I watched together. Maybe he was scanning over my write-up of *The Lion in Winter*. After his first stroke, Silk reassured me: *I'm not scared, darling. Smile, darling. There's no need to be scared.* I gave him the smile he wanted, borrowing Henry II's gambit: *What kind of courage have you got?* He delivered Philip's reply lightly: *My courage is the tidal kind. It comes and goes.* It was his favourite line. *I'm no Henry*, he'd say. *My life, when it is written, will not read better than it lived.*

'Mr Gerschel,' I said. 'Did he ask you to destroy it?'

The typing stopped. 'Yes.'

I stood up. The letter slid to the floor. 'Did you?'

A long silence. 'No.'

I paced to the window. My bedsheet-white reflection stared back. 'Why not?'

'Herr Silk called again. He asked me to bring it to London.'

'Why? To destroy it himself?'

'I think he wanted to read it.'

'Why?'

'Perhaps he had forgotten its contents, I do not know how his memory was, but really—'

'No, I mean, what makes you think he wanted to read it?'

'I do not know. Something in his voice.'

'Why didn't you come?'

'I was going to. I had a flight booked. Then I saw on the news, he had a stroke. I called his agent but no one got back to me. Listen, I really should not have told you this . . .'

'He had two strokes.'

'Yes. I read this also. I am very sorry—'

'Can I look at it?'

'Pardon?'

'If I got on a plane tonight, tomorrow, could I read it? I can bring my passport, his passport, everything. If you'd just meet me.'

A long silence. I rocked up onto my toes and stayed there.

'Of course, Frau Silk, this would be the museum's pleasure.'

I lowered to the floor, inch by inch.

BUY A PLANE TICKET, wiping out more than half your bank account. Do not call your mother or text your father. Do take two wallets and two passports.

I was following stage directions written in somebody else's hand, somebody who could close the door on Fitzroy Park and follow the Thames out. The lane was quiet, as it always was. Some of the cottages still possessed their original cob and thatch. Our house was first Georgian, then Victorian, then Bauhaus, Silk would claim. You could convince yourself that you were in the countryside, standing here. A past that never ended, a future that never arrived. You could convince yourself nothing had changed.

I heard Silk ask: Do I have the keys, Eva?

No, Silk, I do.

you are here

'Lᴏsᴛ?'

I jumped, finding a woman in a ragged parka at my elbow. 'No – yes.'

'Jüdisches Museum?'

I took a step back. 'Yes.'

I didn't like being identified as Jewish here. It was the first time I'd ever thought anything like that.

The woman pointed, further into west Berlin.

Blushing, I said, 'Thank you,' and hurried down the street.

It was 10.30 a.m. I wasn't meeting the curator until three. I walked through housing blocks and past small shops, whose owners watched me from their doorsteps. A red signpost pointed down an alleyway, and I was turning the corner as I stepped over a bronze plaque that appeared to have melted into the cobbles.

HIER WOHNTE
MAX LASKE
JG. 1903
ERMORDET
11.8.1942
IN SACHSENHAUSEN

I knew that ermordet had something to do with death. I knew the meaning of 1942. I took my phone out and swiped up for record, capturing the tips of my toes and the sun winking on the bronze. A playground ran down one side of the alley, and I was jolted by the smack of a ball against the fence. The children playing were mostly Turkish or black, which surprised me, stupidly. I wasn't thinking right. Max Laske, 1942.

I didn't want to know what the museum knew. Outside of Great-Uncle László there was no engine for remembrance in my family, no drive to articulate history, and Silk always kept us *outside* of László. I knew the facts, knew place names and numbers like anyone. But I was suddenly very afraid of knowing more. I slowed, watching the back-and-forth of the ball.

If you don't want to know, what are you doing here? Why see the testament at all?

Because he's in it. Because he's here. Because he wanted to destroy it or save it. Because he would not leave the decision to strangers. Because it might explain the silence that eclipsed John's childhood, and the silent rage that strangled mine. Because I don't know what to put on his gravestone. Those forcibly neat words given to Max

30

Laske – I don't know what those words are for Silk, and the engraver keeps calling for an answer. Because he left me too soon.

The alleyway opened onto a wide street overshadowed by two giant buildings. One baroque and certain, a courthouse implacable to post-war concrete. The other a massive blue bulk – oxidising zinc, I realised – scarred by slit windows and contorted edges, twisting back on itself. I knew both buildings made up the Jewish Museum, but couldn't tell how they connected. I crossed the road, feeling the breeze of a car brushing my calf. Watch out, little Eva. I walked up the ramp to the older building.

The security was like an airport. I opened my overnight bag before the men could ask; they hardly glanced at its contents. If you offer yourself up, people will leave you alone. That's one theory, anyway. Collecting my belongings from the conveyor belt, I joined the queue for tickets. I told the woman behind the counter who I was there to meet. She checked the computer.

'Dr Gerschel has put your name on a list.'

I raised my eyebrows and waited for a flicker of shared irony, but received a smile so wide I wondered what I'd done right.

'Enjoy the museum.'

'Thank you.'

The entrance hall hummed. I picked an audio guide, scrolling through the options: Chinese, English, Hungarian, Japanese, Yiddish . . . Silk had never taught me the languages of his homeland or abandoned religion. Osip, an old friend of Silk's, once took us to a Yiddish cabaret at Hampstead Synagogue. The stand-up comedian delivered a twenty-minute routine without a word of English. It was the first synagogue I'd ever been to, and the last Silk said he had attended, aged nineteen. He said the service hadn't been so funny then. He'd accepted the invitation because it was Osip. *Don't refuse old men their pleasures*, he told me. Osip wasn't much older than he was. Every minute or so the whole hall laughed. I hated sitting there blushing and silent – 'What an English rose you have for a granddaughter, Silk' – so I laughed with them. Later, I asked Silk what the jokes were about.

'Bagels,' he said, expressionless. 'And the end of the world.'

I replaced the audio guide and chose a map, unfolding its pages. Three words told me, YOU ARE HERE.

The Jewish Museum stretched across the old and new buildings, bound and separated by a line made up of underground passageways and bridges. A line labelled the Void. I felt lost before beginning. Silk used to draw maps for my first forays into London alone, sketching the lions, hot and quizzical, in Trafalgar Square; the light-box letters of Prince Charles Cinema; the neon scrawl of Bar Italia. He connected each destination with blue wandering feet, detours and about-faces. Handing the map over, he'd say: *Here, get lost.* Mum would sigh – *and who will be picking her up?* – as she turned the paper over, drawing insistent arrows, telling me, *the bank will be on your left, a church on your right*, telling me, *find your landmarks, make your map.*

On the museum's map, a red arrow slipped through the ground I stood on, bumping down the stairs and bashing itself against the sharp corners of the new building. I stood at the black mouth of the staircase, of the Void.

My eyes were closing. I felt like I was falling forward, the map growing around me.

I needed to sleep. I could go to a café, even find a hotel for the day. I had money now. Silk's money.

But I didn't leave. I felt the thrust of that red arrow, grasped it like a bannister, and descended, remembering Mum reading *Alice in Wonderland* to me. *In another moment down went Alice after it, never once considering how in the world she was to get out again.*

THE HERMETIC SEAL OF the new building was punctured by these zigzag steps: concrete slabs and solder lines. Gleaming walls snatched and scattered my reflection, tumbling it down the stairs. I faced a long passage intersected by three axes with letters on the walls, saxe blue capitals spelling EXILE, HOLOCAUST, CONTINUITY. I took the route that made the most sense to me, thinking that in Silk's story this came before exile, this thing summed up in one sentence: FLOSSEN-BÜRG MAUTHAUSEN RAVENSBRÜCK BUCHENWALD CHELMNO BELZEC THERESIENSTADT AUSCHWITZ LUBLIN-MAJDANEK TREBLINKA SOBIBOR BERGEN-BELSEN. Had Silk been deported to one of them, even more than one? There were no stories. There was no shared memory. I would find out at three o'clock.

János Zyyad died in Auschwitz. Silk's father. Now I thought about it, I realised I'd never heard Silk say it himself, not directly, or in interviews. But still it existed as a fact, in books and PhD theses, on Wikipedia, reduced to gossip, footnotes citing 'General Sources'. Anything, I realised, that Silk couldn't edit.

I squeezed through the crowds, peering over shoulders and phones at nobody's heirlooms, glazed bowls and postcards and silver candle-sticks. I stopped at the Kozower family photographs. Children at the dinner table. They looked back at me with such strong gazes they seemed safe in this sepia stillness, inextinguishable. I had not found any pictures of Silk's family or his childhood in Budapest, going through filing cabinets and pine boxes and envelopes in the sleepless hours of the last week. Maybe nothing survived. Maybe he destroyed it all, or gave it to a museum anonymously. I had found a file of every postcard I ever sent him when I was away, every birthday card I made him as a child, every nonsense poem.

Raised voices made me duck my head. A Spanish family arguing. I kept my head down, finding relief in weightlessness, watching flip-flops, bare feet, sandals, a teenage girl loosely holding a grey-haired woman's hand, four fingers looped around her bent thumb.

Did I comfort Silk in that way? Or, in his last years, when honesty might have ripened, did I rush to muffle his words, insisting he had only ever been a good man?

Close your eyes. None of the languages make sense, not even English. They are soft echoes. A baby cries: no, no, no.

One of the cases protected an ink drawing. Clandestine art, the caption read. In 1941 Bedřich Fritta was deported to Theresienstadt, a 'model camp' just outside of Prague where cafés and shops created the illusion of normality for the Red Cross. Fritta was forced to work first as a draughtsman for the walls that would keep him, and then as a graphic artist for propaganda. At night he and other artists became witnesses, documenting prisoners wailing and dying and waiting in black ink. Some of the pictures survived, hidden in walls, smuggled out, rolled tightly in tins. Bedřich Fritta was discovered and sent to Auschwitz in 1944. On permanent loan from Thomas Fritta-Haas.

I leant into the sketch, my breath glossing the glass. A demonic film camera shone its light on an old man. The wall behind him hid a skeleton. *Film and Reality.*

A museum guide – a host, they were called – watched me, checking perhaps that I was OK. *I am not OK.* The hair on my arms stood up; one of the letters described body lice standing stiff as hairs. I looked at Fritta's urgent strokes.

I want to save Silk from belonging to this history.

Leave now and you'll never have to know.

Did the museum plan to put Silk's work next to Fritta's? I wasn't sure when Silk began painting – his answers were always contradictory. He described his mother as an artist. But it was something he came to later – and never utilised to protest or expose, to exercise that kind of will.

When Silk was in his mid-twenties he accompanied an actor friend from Yorkshire to see a speech therapist. The actor wanted to learn the Queen's English. Sitting outside the office, Silk shaped his mouth to those new vowels. To me, he sounded like a born north Londoner. His bookshelves were stuffed with English literature, which he'd read to me, W.B. Yeats's 'He bids his beloved be at peace', T.S. Eliot's 'Marina':

> Living to live in a world of time beyond me; let me
> Resign my life for this life, my speech for that unspoken,
> The awakened, lips parted, the hope, the new ships.

Setting the book between us, he said, 'This to me is being an immigrant. I resigned Hungary, the past, for this life. I am two people, one left behind, and one I see in your face now. Of the boy I was, there is no trace. It comes down to memory. And I remember nothing.'

I had hidden from Silk's expectant look, which told me he wanted my assent, looking instead at the yellowed page curling from a tired spine, where the same phrase appeared four times in one stanza: *meaning Death, meaning Death, meaning Death, meaning Death*. It seemed that exile reverberated down our family line, casting my mother back to Australia, my father to France, and me here, to the Axis of Exile and its jumble sale of new languages, as if it were me, this time, who had fled. As I had fled. LOS ANGELES, STOCKHOLM, SANTIAGO DE CHILE. I stopped in front of LONDON. In 1945 a mail and cargo carrier had let Silk curl up amongst its sacks, lifting off from Switzerland and setting down at London Airport. It was raining, Silk told me. *And I thought:* this *is the Mother Country?*

I pushed out into the Garden of Exile, with its off-kilter door, slick green and sea grey. The blue of the sky was sudden, like the trough of a wave. The ground was uneven: a slanting plane of grey columns striking upwards at unpredictable heights, like a foreign skyline, like chimneys. On top of the columns, oleaster trees reached across to meet each other. I listened to birdsong. Competing pips of small lungs. The rusty jabber of crows. This discordant peace might have been the first clear sensation to hit Silk when he reached London in 1945. He would have liked this garden, its impression of an ocean, if he were with me now.

Three years earlier I had helped install *Mariner*. He chose to exhibit it at the RA because of the scale of the walls, erecting a twelve-foot stained-glass box glowing with Vari-Lites, onto which he projected footage of his paintbrush, each stroke mimicking the crash of a wave. When the deep ultramarine hit the blue the room glimmered, rocking with my recordings of Land's End, as if we'd been sunk. Silk leant on his walking stick in the middle of the installation – a sight familiar to friends since he was a young man – and gave a small nod.

'You know what Picasso said? If you haven't got any red, use blue.'

Why did he need a walking stick all those years? Another accident, he said, never telling me more.

I am aware, here, of your ghost. And it doesn't want me to ask questions.

I FOLLOWED THE AXIS of Exile into the diaspora of history, past headstones and suitcases and an incongruous Christmas tree, clinging to bridges that looked down into weathered towers, until I reached The Memory Void. It smelt of stone wet by rain. Windows high above cast light onto thousands of steel faces filling the long concrete shaft, faces an inch thick, punctured and wailing like the drawings of a child, reduced to eyes and mouths. A low sea wall kept them from the door, and as I approached, a boy sitting there with his girlfriend said, 'You're supposed to walk on them.'

The girl said, 'What?'

'The faces. You're supposed to walk on them.' He had an audio guide pinned to his ear with his shoulder, leaving both hands free to circle her waist. I wanted his arms to shield me.

'We can't do that,' the girl said firmly.

Some of the faces had no mouths, only the outline where a punch might make contact. I knelt down, soothing the nearest face; it sang.

I remembered Great-Uncle László beating the table with his fist on his final visit: 'Are we not to have a homeland? Are we not to have a home?'

Silk had looked calmly about the kitchen: 'What do you call this?'

László told him he wouldn't be free until he gave voice to his suffering. Silk shook his head. 'Who says I'm suffering? I have a right to forget. A right to build myself a new life, a right to be happy. Your insistence that I talk, these calls to *remember*, they are a threat to my being: the man I am now, the man I have been since 1945. I won't allow it.'

'Don't you think I understand what it costs? Don't you think I have nightmares for weeks after I give my talks at schools? When I attend memorials? When we celebrate liberation? When we sing kaddish?'

'That's your choice.'

'It's not a choice,' László said. 'What's a man without memory?'

Silk told him: 'Happier.'

But László wouldn't drop it, and Silk's face purpled as he spat, 'What are you, then? Memory without identity, memory alone, and alone you are, but *not* because of me – I've never stopped you searching, so stop – stop forcing—' until his throat closed up. The doctor said he was allergic to shellfish, but he'd never been allergic to it before, and never was again.

I moved into the silence of The Void, following the common gravitation to the edges, hands trailing along cold concrete. It was the silence of strangers joined together at a cathedral or a terminus. A little girl walked face-first into the corner and buried herself there. A man hovered nearby, arms pinned around his chest, as if waiting for his part in some vigil.

I asked Silk once why he never returned to Hungary. He told me, 'I stayed vigilant.'

As I watched this stranger bristling now in his vigil I thought he was alert to the necessity of doing so. It was the only gesture of resistance in a place such as this – the resistance of being alive.

The shutter release of a camera. A bald man with a big bag slung over his chest, and behind him two girls, one with streamer-pink hair. I squeezed out of the way as the man marched past, hurrying to get to the faces, his quick gait slowed by the undulating floor. The girls held to the wall, fingers skirting the concrete.

The sound of the faces being walked on was the smash of plates hurled across a kitchen; it was crystal ringing, scaffold falling; it was a headache building behind my eyes. The ache of stories, a broken dam.

I released a long breath. The end of the tower was clogged with darkness.

I crept forward, into other people's photos, sliding my own phone to record. I looked down and saw Silk's feet instead of my own, picking their way over mud and stones.

Silk shrugging as he said: *It comes down to memory. And I remember nothing.*

I sat down in the dark and forced breath into my chest. It did not help. Tears gathered in my throat, and something else, breathlessness, *stuckness*. People could sit here for hours, I sensed, and no one would wonder at it. People could come apart here. I opened myself to the Babel voices, a faint chanting, the squeak of a hinge – and was dismantled, breaking up, fumbling for nothingness, with Silk's voice calling me on.

No. 14. What were the first anti-Jewish measures and when did they come into force

No. 16. Who executed the orders and by what means

No. 17. Was the rule on wearing yellow stars strictly enforced

No. 19. How did the Jews in your location react to the measures

No. 21. How did people of other faiths in your area react

No. 23. When did German troops occupy your place of residence

No. 26. When were orders for ghettoisation issued

No. 39. Did the local Hungarian community try to smuggle food into the ghetto

No. 45. Did you try to escape

No. 50. Were there any deaths in the ghetto, and what were the causes

No. 51. Who died

Two

anything but what I am

POSSESSIONS FIRST. BOOKS AND spoons and watches on the floor. József has nothing left to give this new flea market. A soldier at the station already took his money, claiming it in exchange for the pea soup that made everyone in the locked freight cars shit the length of the motherland. Cooked with laxative, the others said, forty or fifty men whose skin he feels he has climbed into. German and Hungarian soldiers, fellow Magyars, shout at him now, at all of them, for the stink of it. This is the first time he has gone beyond the borders of his birth. He thinks he might shit himself once more from fear alone. A rifle butt pushes him further into the darkness of the shed.

Armbands. He wears a yellow scarf, sewn by his mother, around the arm of his father's second-best coat. These are the rules of labour service. Despite being attached to the German army, no military dress is permitted. Change of rules, a soldier says. No civilian dress either. He drags József's coat off, jerking the armband loose and tossing it back into József's hands. Shirts off. The replacement is thin cotton, too big for him, with a giant yellow star stamped front and back. The paint is stiff. He buttons the star up, uniting its angles, and wonders if it will resist the rain beating the metal roof. He binds the yellow scarf around his arm again, carefully.

Line up. This way. That. Stand straight. Are you looking at me? A Magyar soldier swings his rifle at a man's head.

The servicemen crowd together, crushing József, and he goes down under the force of it, skull hitting concrete. A boot buckles his ribs. He stays down, trying to curl around it, but the boot shakes him off and stamps harder, again and again, kicking a boil of blood into József's body, flashes bursting in his vision, the man screaming in Magyar with such fury it is a shock when it stops. József gasps at the soldier's feet, the soldier no longer looking at him, but at the crabbed form of an old man.

Close your eyes.

Thud-smack, the soldier's rifle coming down, the old man crying, so close his pain bores directly into József's ear, noise that bites and blares and brawls. No. Stop. The soldier's knee is in József's back, using him to get closer to the old man. The point of contact is enough to feel the pullback of muscle, the swing, the follow-through, once, twice, three times.

The rifle clatters to the floor. The noise stops. The wet disintegration of the old man's silence touches his fingers. Blood, bone, hair. He thinks he is next and keeps his face pressed to the concrete, but the soldier pays him no attention, just sinks down over József's body, tired.

*

46

BREAKFAST IS A HALF-EMPTY tin of sugary coffee and a slice of stale bread. The men around him take two bites that last for long minutes and pocket the rest, but József is too faint to follow them. As he balloons one swollen cheek with the last of the coffee, a man opposite with teeth like muddy cobbles gives a heavy sigh. Another man sitting to his left, wiry hair sprouting in the grooves of his face, asks in Magyar, 'You arrived yesterday?'

He swallows. 'Last night.'

'From where?'

'Budapest.'

'Has the city been emptied?'

'Evacuated? No. The bombing isn't that bad yet.'

'*Emptied.*'

'No – why?'

Another long sigh.

'How old are you?'

'Eighteen last week.'

The man with the bad teeth lifts a grey eyebrow at József and says: 'Mazel tov.'

József tries not to blink under the man's look, but to return it, suddenly angry that this broken-down horse assumes he is green from the city. József has seen more than enough to make him a man before now: his father return from labour service so undone József's little sister Alma mistook him for a beggar at the door; his brother beaten by children who used to be his friends, 'Jew rat' written in his books, and the teacher crying, telling József between chokes she'll find some way to protect them. But after a minute he realises the man's gaze is not contemptuous, just empty.

47

He asks them both, 'What are we doing here?'

A one-shouldered shrug. 'Mines. Copper. Train tracks.'

'Are they – what happened last night, does that happen a lot?'

József wants them to look at his face and offer sympathy. But neither says anything. It is another man who leans in and tells him, 'All the time, since Marányi.' The name draws the whispers of those around them, comparing the command of Lieutenant Colonel Balogh with Lieutenant Colonel Marányi, telling him that though Balogh said he hated Jews, when he was in charge no corporals took food from our rations, and when it rained he took blankets from the guards and gave them to us. You think he was so angelic, tell me why did he let them destroy our mail? This argument is knocked aside by the word Marányi and with it everything Marányi has done, stealing money and sending it home to his wife, truss-ups every Sunday, ignoring the doctor, who tells him the weaker ones will die hanging above the ground like that by their thumbs, spinning, but Marányi doesn't care if they do. There are executions too, disappearances, starvations, stopping the local Serbs giving us eggs and milk – we would have died by now without the Serbs, and we'll die now they are kept out.

The man with the teeth leans across the table, bringing his smell closer. 'You know how Marányi began? Gathered us all together in the square, told us: *I am not pro-Jewish. I hate them.* And he hasn't let us down. Whatever kind of torture he can come up with, he'll make us suffer.'

The knot of men comes loose as a guard approaches, a German by his uniform, though not army, József's bunkmate had explained, but Todt, paramilitary men charged with running the Bor mine for the SS. The German grips the shoulders of the toothy man opposite, easing him back into his seat, all the time studying József, his bruises. He says something József does not understand.

The man in his grip whispers: 'He asks, how did you like your food?'

József nods.

The German laughs, claps the man on the back, and moves on to the next table where men with different armbands bend over tin cups – all except one who has turned around, watching the table of Magyar Jews where József sits. A solid man, his thick shoulders hunched, a man who would be difficult to knock from his chair.

'Are all the Germans so . . . ?' József trails off, unnerved by the flicker of a smile from the man watching. It is not a friendly smile.

The toothy man takes a full minute to speak again. 'Marányi is Magyar. The guards are German. What the fuck does it matter?'

The man at the next table has returned to his coffee, showing József the hillside of his back.

REGISTRATION IS AN HOUR standing in the early morning heat. József does not spend long looking at the blocks or the barbed wire or the gate; his gaze is fixed on the wooden scaffold. Ropes move in the breeze, a series of loops: puppet strings waiting for puppets. There is no noose for the neck; instead there are braces to hang men by their hands and leave them dangling. He has never stood more still or more straight, despite the too-small wooden shoes. He can smell the corridor and stairs of his apartment block; he is standing with László on guard at the door with its iron embellishments, playing Emil and the Detectives.

By the time they set off up the mountain his body has swollen and seized. The surrounding foothills are dense with fir, thick like the hair on his father's forearm, as if he is in his father's arms; but when did he last receive a touch from his father? József scrubs the sting of salt from his eyes. Ferns border the road, and he tries to stay in their shade but the column won't let him. Birdsong clamours in alarm. The clogs are crushing his toes. He watches the guard ahead, deciding finally that the man won't turn around, and tries to get one shoe off while still walking, but the first hop on the spasming muscle is enough to make him double over. A man behind swears at him, and somebody else snatches his elbow. József jerks away but the grip is too strong.

'Arrive without shoes and they'll put you on report.'

József just stares at the man, pulled along. He remembers his steady gaze from the next table at breakfast. No yellow star glares from the man's shirtfront, but he is speaking Yiddish. Before József can show he understands, the man releases him and shoulders through the column, gone.

József limps on. His breath is a metal ball in his throat. The army health check in Budapest cleared him; he is robust next to some of the men around him, but feels he might collapse on the road, and they are not even there yet, wherever 'there' is.

He obeyed the call-up signs posted in the streets only after his mother's pleading turned to red-faced screams, telling him that if he didn't go they would come for him, and it would end badly, *badly*. He reported to the Palace of Invalids, as his friends called it – Invalid House to the army, barracks built for veterans of the many back-and-forths with the Ottomans. After the health check József was given his pay book. It contained his company, a photograph ringed in stamps, and the date, 1944.VI.I. On the front was a large black 'Zs' in permanent pen. *Zsidó.* Jew. The registration certificate was folded neatly into the tin rectangle of his dog tag, which swings away from his body with every forward step, returning with the resistance of the mountain.

The hills open up to a plateau, and the column finally stops. There are hundreds of men up here, thousands, filing in from every direction. Below, the steppes drop to poppy-covered plains unravelling like rolls of silk wallpaper to the Carpathian Mountains. At the heart of the plateau, mineshafts burst from the red soil like black sores.

More shouting. More lines. More numbers.

József is assigned to the Durchlass – German, he knows, but he can't remember what it means. As he queues for the entrance to the mine his fear becomes unswallowable.

File forward.

What if they are fed down the throat of the mountain and never let out? Explosives litter the ground, coils of wire he doesn't understand. He is given a pickaxe.

File forward.

A few steps and he is in the dark. The ground drops, steep and burrowing deeper. He fumbles for purchase. The walls are wet soil and rock with a metal rail, rusty to the touch. The earth beneath his feet is so sheer he thinks he will fall. It tips him down, unstoppably, and panic makes him gulp the air, but there isn't any, just the hot choke of gunpowder. Echoes of wooden shoes on rock tumble down before him. Madness, this is complete madness, he can't see anything, the man behind won't let him out. Breathe. Whatever is in the air, breathe. There is a spot of light. Gas lamps throb in József's vision like spots of solar flare on a photograph. They draw him on, through the rising water that is now around his knees, so cold he can feel nothing beneath the surface of floating debris. The tunnel branches and he follows the man before him – dead end.

An old Magyar whispers to him, 'Be careful how you strike the ore, the gases in the air are explosive. One spark and . . .' But the Todt foremen venturing into the dark shout, 'Schnell, schnell.' The old man tells him it will last eleven hours.

Only the water they stand in to cup and drink.

No light, no air.

Stomach barbed wire.

Swimming with László and Alma on Margit Island, pointing to the Danube through the chain-link fence. *Look, Alma. Say water, Alma.*

The kitchen of their apartment, the crackle of cheese and potato blackening in hot fat, his mother looking off, shaking hands dusting the air with flour. The tallow candles painting her reflection over the waves of the windowpane.

His father in Ukraine, thinking about his children, wondering if they've been taken and where.

Keep breathing.

Dig.

'DO YOU UNDERSTAND ME?'

The question pulls József out gradually, like a knotted towel tugged through a fist. He is watching his clogs pick their way down the mountainside, his clawed, hobbled feet wet and bleeding inside;

52

he is holding his arms by the elbows, creating a sling for muscles and bones shocked by the vibrations of the pick; his hands are wet with burst blisters. He lifts his head. It's the man who warned him about the shoes. József tells him, 'Yes,' in Magyar, then replays the man's question and realises he isn't speaking in József's first language but in the language of his grandparents, and says, 'Yes,' again, this time in Yiddish.

'You're Magyar?'

József nods, a single fall of the head.

'And it was Magyars who kicked you around last night?'

Another nod.

The man smiles. 'Now you know how we've felt for the last four hundred years.'

From the man's accent József guesses he's Yugoslav, and says nothing.

They walk on, the muscles in the man's jaw moving like marbles sifted in a trickster's palm.

'Don't listen to what those fools told you this morning.'

'It wasn't true?'

'It was. What I understood anyway, your bat-shit language.' The man shrugs. 'Still. Don't listen to it.'

József drinks sweat from his upper lip. 'You don't wear a yellow star.'

'Why should I?'

József tries to think of the reason but the words won't come out right. He closes his eyes, and when he jolts awake he finds he hasn't fallen because the man's hand is back at his elbow.

'You speak Yiddish,' József says.

'I could tell you to keep out of what doesn't concern you in German, Italian, maybe even Magyar. Doesn't make me anything but what I am.'

József says nothing. Below, town squares map themselves by tiny flags and terracotta roofs, clustering around the bronze flash of the Danube, his way home walled in by mountains, bloodied by the last thrash of sundown. He feels the river's surety, its stirring bulk expanding in his chest, pressing on his heart, as the man next to him gently takes his arm.

What Did You Do in the War, Daddy?

THE MUSEUM GARDEN WAS fenced off from Berlin by the courthouse on one side, the new building on the other and sentry-like trees all around. It was ten past three – the curator was late. I watched a sprinkler twist amongst the russet leaves of an acacia. Away from the spray, old men and women slept in deckchairs. Drooping newspapers rose and fell on stomachs. Children played, hitting low branches with sticks.

'Frau Butler?'

I looked up. A man took a step closer.

'I am Felix Gerschel. You are Eva Butler.'

'Yes.' His confidence was both reassuring and ridiculous. 'I am.'

'That is a relief. I am sorry to be later than intended.'

He was tall, with thick eyebrows and curly blond hair that would be brown in winter. Big eyes like swimming pools, Clark Kent glasses, a light beard. He wore sandy chinos and a red-wine T-shirt over broad shoulders and a thick body, half muscle, half stomach, a man who worried about the gym in university but now, in his late twenties, had given it up. He bounced a little. He was wearing flip-flops.

'Let us sit in the shade, where we are less illuminated.'

I followed him to a picnic table beneath a canvas of Virginia creeper. He remained standing, another lift on his toes.

'You have eaten lunch?'

This sounded so little like a question that it took me a moment to say I hadn't.

'I will buy something. Staff discount. You have allergies?'

'Oh – no.'

Another bounce. 'Lucky you,' with a grin. He turned and marched back towards the building, head down. I hadn't told him what I did or didn't want, but it seemed awkward to follow, so I just waited. He returned after a few minutes with a wobbling tray.

'You are English so I got you tea with milk. But then it is hot so here also is some orange juice. I have three baguettes, this cheese, this tuna, this chicken.'

His eyebrows were fixed high on his forehead. He didn't seem to be breathing.

'Which one is for you?' I asked.

'I have this salad. I am gluten-frei.'

'Then we seem to have a surfeit of sandwiches.'

He grinned. 'I forgot to ask what you wanted. I am very anxious to meet you.'

I wasn't sure if he meant eager or scared. I picked the sandwich closest to me and he finally sat down. 'Thank you for agreeing to see me. I have my passport.'

'Hard to get here without one, I would think.'

'You wanted to see it.'

'Oh, yes.' He flooded red beneath his beard. 'Thank you.'

I pulled free my red passport and Silk's wrinkled blue one. I slid them over. 'I feel like we're in a Bond movie,' I said, to say something.

'Then you would have to assassinate me as a representative of the old Eastern bloc,' he returned, a rush in his voice as he opened my passport to the back.

'Does that make me James Bond?' I asked.

'But of course. Your picture is very nice.'

'Ha. Thank you.'

He held Silk's open for long seconds, so that when he passed it back his thumbprint remained above Silk's face. 'It is an honour to meet you,' he said.

'Thank you. You too. I mean, it's nice to meet you.'

He gave me another grin. 'Now shall we talk about the weather?'

'We already did. This is less illuminated.'

'You are correct.'

'Whenever possible.'

'When did your plane arrive?'

'Early. I went around the museum.'

'Ah.' He speared a chunk of cucumber. 'What did you think?'

'I don't like it.'

That surprised us both.

'I mean, I think it's incredible, how it's done. It just made me feel . . . more than I wanted to.'

'This is often the way. I am sorry.'

I shook my head. 'What's it like, working here?'

'You stop noticing it. It is only when I take friends around that I notice.'

'You're a curator?'

'Curatorial Assistant. A lowly curator. They brought me in a year ago for this exhibition, where your grandfather's testament will now appear.'

'Might now appear.'

His fork paused in the air. 'Yes. Helping with an exhibit is like doing a two-year internship – then they hire you, or not.'

'Are you an art historian?'

'I did my MA in curation and design in Berlin, and my PhD on Joseph Silk's work at the Sorbonne in Paris.'

'Wow.'

'Oh yes, so eminently hirable. I am now master of the internship.'

'Why did you choose Silk for your PhD?'

'He has always been my favourite artist.'

'But you're German.'

I spoke before thinking, and we both considered each other in the silence it left.

'What I mean is, what drew you to a Hungarian-British artist?'

'I am German,' he said. 'I think that is what you mean. German and not Jewish.'

'You're not?'

'Most people who work here are not Jewish.'

'Oh.'

'But, as context . . . my grandparents lived in Sopron, northern Hungary. My grandmother was German, my grandfather Hungarian, like yours. After the war, the German citizens of Sopron were made

58

to leave, to go home, even if they had been living in Hungary for generations. It was so in the Czech Republic and other places. My grandparents were not very forward thinking, and settled in East Berlin. You might know the rest of the story.'

'Yes.' I knew I should apologise but said nothing. I was thinking about that old film, *What Did You Do in the War, Daddy?* He must have known, because he continued firmly:

'My grandfather worked for the Hungarian railway. He was not taken into the army because he was old. On their own, the Nazis managed to deport twelve thousand Hungarian Jews. With help from Hungarian Gentiles like my grandfather – you should know that there is no separate word for this, Magyar means Gentile, at its root – it became 437,000 in a few months. By the end of the war, half a million Hungarian Jews were dead. My grandfather was a signal operator and an anti-Semite. My grandmother was an anti-Semite. My mother is not. My paternal grandfather was a German soldier and an anti-Semite. My paternal grandmother was not. My father is not. I am not. With every generation, evolution leaps forward. I am most at home with my opposable thumb.'

I swivelled my teacup. 'I don't know what to say.'

'You could laugh at the joke.'

'It seems too late now.'

'I like a joke that works the room.'

That did make me laugh and he smiled, wiping his forehead. 'I am sorry,' he said, 'to leap at you, only I kept thinking about how and if I would explain this to you, and that was not what I imagined, but there it is. It is like – do you ever go to academic conferences? If you do, and they are the kind I go to, everybody starts sentences with, "The white heteronormative Western male . . ." and you wish you were anything else. As my paternal grandfather joined the Nazi party, couldn't my father have sabotaged the Stasi? If I have to be German and Hungarian, couldn't I also be Jewish, or gay, or work with orphaned children? No. I am just me.'

'I'm settler-Australian on my mum's side, and half British on my father's.'

He grinned. 'Then I feel much better. You should be ashamed of your nations' pasts, young lady. To answer the question you asked when you still thought me normal, I went on a school trip to London in 2000. We saw Joseph Silk's solo show at the Serpentine Gallery. I fell in love with *Harvest Sun*.'

'He painted that when I was born.'

The curator turned his salad box a quick three hundred and sixty degrees. 'That is not in the books.'

I looked up at the museum. 'Have you read his testament?'

'Yes.'

I wanted to ask what it said but didn't want the answer. I plucked at my watch. 'What do you do, exactly, in the museum?'

'Much of the collection that was first gathered *still* has not been catalogued. So I am going through unlabelled box after unlabelled box looking for items that could be of use to the new exhibition.'

'Which is about artists?'

'Oh yes, yes, about visual artists and writers: prose, poetry. The curator is shaping it to be quite, ah, disparate, quite broadly representative. We have tried to find an artist from each nation or situation. Twelve in total.'

'Will judgement be made about what the survivors *did* with their art?'

'What kind of judgement?'

'Whether they should have been . . . duty-bound to talk about their experiences. If they confronted anti-Semitism.'

'As Joseph Silk did not?'

'Yes. Is the museum planning to pass judgement on him?'

'I cannot say. It is up to the curator. But I am not planning to do any such thing. I will look after him. That is why they hired me.'

'How are you planning to exhibit his paintings? The estate won't lend you any.'

'Aren't you the estate?'

I wanted to tell him: *No, I'm me*. But I said, 'Silk would have said no to any request.'

'The Tate Modern has agreed to lend us two, maybe three paintings.'

'Don't they need my permission for that?'

'They own the paintings.'

I pushed my hair back. 'And what about this testament? What if I don't want the museum to keep him, display him?'

'Don't you mean *it*?'

I looked at the curator, my neck rigid, and then relaxed into a small smile. 'I'm very tired.'

'If you do not want us to have the testament, we will of course give it to you. That is a family member's right.'

'You've read it. Will it change the way people think about him?'

He shifted from side to side. 'Such things always do.'

'How did you find it?'

61

'It was in one of the unlabelled boxes. It is not normal for our museum to have anything that is not German, but a Berlin couple, Max and Alena Rosenzweig, bequeathed us their belongings, and I found it amongst their artefacts.'

'Why did they have it?'

'I do not know. The questions were asked by the Hungarian Committee for Attending Deportees – DEGOB in Hungarian. There are other testimonies like it, in the Jewish Museum in Budapest.'

'Have you told them you found it?'

'Yes, when we were checking its provenance.'

'Did they ask you for it?'

'Yes.'

'What did you tell them?'

'I told them it is the property of the German state.'

'Is it now?'

His Adam's apple bobbed up and down. 'Yes. Legally. Unless you want it. You should have seen – when I found it, saw his name, I put it on the desk the way you might lay a baby down and then fled from the room, washed my hands, paced the corridor, washed my hands again . . . I could not believe it.'

'Don't you know never to leave a baby alone?'

The curator dimmed.

'Have you told anyone else?' I asked.

'Only my supervisor and the director. And my mother.'

'Have they told anyone?'

'This is beginning to feel like a real James Bond interrogation.'

I flipped my watch face around. 'I keep a gold-mounted laser in my handbag. It could get worse.'

'Then I beg you to spare me, and in return I will buy you ice cream.'

I was going to say no but his smile made me smile back and he took that as a yes, bouncing off again. Maybe he'd return with all the flavours available.

I was almost right. He had two glass bowls, one with a single scoop of sorbet, the other piled to the top.

'There's no way I can eat all that.'

'There are worse problems. I will learn to ask what you like.'

'Do you really think our relationship will last that long?'

He gave me a look. 'We will see. Dig in.'

I took the spoon from him. 'Thank you very much. So, what other artists and writers are you planning to show?'

'Paul Celan. Primo Levi. Bedřich Fritta, whom you will have seen in the Holocaust Axis. Miklós Radnóti – he is Hungarian. An incredible story. He was shot into a mass grave, his body exhumed after the war. Locals told the officials where to look. They dug him and twenty-two others out and found a notebook completely intact in the inside pocket of his coat. It was filled with poems he had written on the march. He was, in fact . . .'

'Was what?'

'Let us speak of this later, once you have read . . . It is not so much lunch conversation. So you don't like pistachio ice cream. I will remember that.'

'Did you really think pistachio was your safest bet?'

'I never go for safe bets. What is it you do, please? You are a student?'

'Sort of. I got halfway through my MA, but had to put it on pause. Silk needed full-time care.'

'You looked after him by yourself?'

'Yes. But this is not lunchtime conversation either.'

'No. What were you studying?'

'Film and documentary, with a particular love of British cinema.'

'You were making a documentary about Joseph Silk?'

'We hadn't got very far. I wanted to take him to Budapest, see where he grew up, but he said it wasn't relevant. I tried to explain that it could be relevant to me. He said family trees were designed that way so they could be cut back when a branch grew diseased.'

Silence. Then: 'I found your blog, *Picture Show*. You write about films you watched with Joseph Silk.'

'And Granny Rosemary. Thursday Night Films. They'd introduce me to their favourites. It started when Rosemary stopped being able to walk. I had to track down a video machine for some of them. We used to watch Hitchcock constantly – *North by Northwest*, Rosemary and me for Cary Grant, Silk for Eva Marie Saint. *Marnie*: that long shot of Tippi Hedren walking down the railway platform, the yellow bag. He loves that.' Loved. Felix remained impassive. 'Grey, to him.'

'Were you named after Eva Marie Saint?'

'How did you know Silk chose my name?'

'I didn't.'

I scraped at the ice cream with my spoon. 'It's Hebrew. It means life. I looked it up once.'

'So that was why?'

'If it was, it might be the only thing he ever did in Hebrew in his life.'

'Why did he choose your name?'

'My mother asked him for ideas, as I wasn't getting their surname. My father refused to come up with anything.'

'That seems strange.'

'Not really. He never wanted children. He had some kind of a breakdown when I was born . . .' The curiosity and concern in his eyes left me suddenly claustrophobic. 'What was I telling you? My blog. I put in Silk or Rosemary's memories of a film. Like Silk going to the premiere of *From Russia with Love*. An actor friend gave him a ticket. Silk could do a great Sean Connery impression.' I blinked, heaved a deep breath. 'I can't, though. Don't ask me. And if I have any more ice cream, I'm going to run in circles and then collapse, and you'll have only yourself to blame. Shall we get this over with?'

'You know, you don't have to read it.'

'And have the whole world know and not me?'

'Then you are planning to let us exhibit it?'

'He wouldn't want me to.'

'Perhaps you should wait before you make decisions. You could come back when things have a different perspective, call this just a nice break in Berlin. After all, if you are feeling too much—'

'This isn't me. I'm still in London. This is somebody else. Who, I have no idea. You're just the unlucky man standing in the firing range.'

'I don't feel so unlucky.'

THE ARCHIVE WAS ACROSS the road, in what I had taken to be a warehouse undergoing demolition. Felix said it was once a famous flower market, and when the building had gone up for sale the museum decided to step in and save it from being knocked down. They needed extra space, anyway.

'The archives are off limits to the public and to most of us museum staff. It is a carefully controlled atmosphere and they do not want to risk contamination.'

It sounded like another hermetic seal, no room to live. Inside, everything was battleship grey. Books lined one wall, and a desk took up the other, where the curator now spoke quietly to the archivist. She looked at me with unmasked interest and then nodded, moving away through a door that locked electronically behind her.

'We can wait here,' Felix said, pointing to a table. 'She will bring the testament to us.'

I nodded, sitting down to hug the bag on my lap. Two tables away, a white-haired man peered over an open document. A man in his forties sat with him, perhaps his son, anxiety stamped on his face.

'Do you know what he's looking at?' I whispered.

The curator shrugged. 'There is always someone here, looking.'

The old man's eyes moved over the pages like a patient in recovery surveying a broken picture frame they don't want to pick up; considering the pain it would cost to bend down that far.

'Take a breath.'

'What?'

'You look like you need to breathe.'

'Oh.' The old man did not look up but still I felt I'd ruined the chapel silence around his bent shoulders. 'I'm sorry.'

'That is the way with this room,' said Felix.

'Maybe you should paint it a different colour.'

'What would you recommend?'

'Larkspur.'

He nodded solemnly. 'A good blue.'

The door whispered open, and the archivist emerged. She was carrying a plain folder. I felt tense with sudden politeness, thanking the woman, looking at the folder now in its tray in the same way I looked at the spread of available coffins. When I made no further movement, Felix reached across and opened it. Two pieces of paper spread out in front of me, thin as onion skin and rigid with typed sentences, Silk's story, which I did not know, and could not read — apart from the dates.

'This isn't him,' I said.

Felix pinched his lips, the way you might while waiting for someone to catch a Freudian slip.

'It isn't,' I said. 'This says he was born on the second of May 1925. He was born in 1926.'

'This, I'm afraid, is not true.'

'He was eighteen when he got to London.' The son raised his head. I tried to box my voice. *Eighteen and already a man.* 'This is the wrong József Zyyad. This is a mistake. It's all a mistake.'

From the shadows, Silk told me that *mistaken identity* meant that the facts of a person, unchanging and determinative, had been wrongly taken.

'He names his parents and his siblings,' Felix said stiffly. 'It is not a mistake. Joseph Silk was twenty when he reached London. He – he misrepresented himself.'

The question, *Why would he lie?* and the assertion, *He wouldn't lie to me.* Both tried to be said first, and I said nothing.

Felix touched the edge of the testament. 'Perhaps he wanted to undo what was done to him.'

I followed the nudge of his fingers, thinking, for a moment, that the words were resistant because of the tears in my eyes. 'I don't – I don't know any Hungarian.'

Felix nodded, reaching into the leather satchel he had pinned between his feet. 'I prepared an English translation, in advance of this problem.'

He put a typed sheet next to the original document, no cover, no moment to prepare as I met my own language and its meaning in the same instance.

Name: *Zyyad József*
Date of birth: *2nd May 1925*
Place of birth: *Budapest*
Occupation: *Heaver*
Last address: *18 Károly krt*
In which camps were you interned: *Bor, Mauthausen,*
    Gunskirchen

I read on, heart quickening. Halfway down the first page I became aware of Felix's hand in the corner of my vision, offering me a tissue. I kept reading, trying to find Silk's voice, but this had no humour or grace: it was like hearing a tired manifesto or a song recital no one cares for anymore, the words rigid and halting, a litany. The interviewer's questions kept coming; somehow the awful things emerging from Silk's mouth did not stop them. Finally, the questions shifted into the present tense, and the answers became blunter, and it was done.

68

I closed the testament. 'You're not showing anyone this.'

'Eva, please, just consider—'

'I'm taking it with me. I'm taking him with me. Now. This is everything he didn't want to be remembered for.'

'You can't.'

'You said—'

'Please, lower your voice. I need the consent of the Director, and she has to convene with the curator and the head archivist. Please. Tomorrow. We can give it to you tomorrow.'

'If you're saying that because you think in the meantime I'll change my mind—'

'I'm not. I promise I am not. Please.'

I stuffed his translation into my bag. 'I'm taking it with me tomorrow. Tell her to have it ready.'

'I will.'

'Good. Thank you. I'm leaving now.'

'Wait—'

But I was already striding past the old man, saying sorry to the ground at his feet, swinging through the heavy door and running past empty plant pots and out onto the street, blue sky lapping at me, the zinc building opposite burnished with its colour. I set off the way I'd come, back down the alley, back onto the street with its apartment blocks and listless men, heading towards Checkpoint Charlie, towards a wall through which I could tunnel, and leave this behind me.

up there scurrying time

'I'M HERE.'

'József?'

'Here!'

Of course, it is Dragan who's come to find him, squeezed into a corner of the tunnel. József can barely see his friend approaching: just a threadbare outline against the brown-black, as if Dragan is only half real.

'Where have you been, öcs?'

Öcs: little brother, the only Magyar Dragan has learnt. With a younger sister and brother in Budapest, and four small cousins, József has never been anyone's little brother, but he takes Dragan's hand now, squeezing the bones.

'I can't see anything,' he says.

'It's just the dark.'

He wants to tell Dragan that he is used to the mine's darkness, after a year of the labour battalion. The mine is not the bruised black of thunder or the red-lined char of a burnt body; not the total black of his mother's eyes. It is the emptiness of his stomach, drawing in;

it is glimmering copper and false gold; it is the channels and streams of the Danube tugging at his legs. But now he sees no false gold, and no way out. He sees nothing at all.

'József, come on. Don't make me shake you like a little girl.'

József wipes his nose. 'Just you try. I'll knock you on your backside.'

'Keep telling yourself that.'

Dragan wrestles him from the earth and they sidle together into the main passage. He is a child again, chasing his mother's rabbit coat through the Great Synagogue – before her clothes were motheaten and damp, before they lost their house. Time seems fragile. He must always remind himself of its true nature, its violence; it is the rifle butt driven into the back of his head that morning; it is the congeal of blood and bone.

Dragan's steady gait pulls him on. The first fragment of sunlight feels like a trick. But it surrounds József, drawing him out of the mine and onto the mountain platform where the February wind lifts his cotton shirt. Bright, glaring. József knuckles his eyes, looks again. The same unreal tone. The umber soil and green scrub of the hills blur together. The ring of white-capped mountains is a line of smut. The sky is blistering, blue over-spilling.

Dragan asks, 'Öcs, what's wrong?'

'My eyes, I can't see . . . it's too much. Too much blue.'

'Hold on to me. Don't let them know.'

SPRING, DISTURBED BY BOOTS and refused by barbed wire, passes stubbornly: trees still flourish, flowers still strive. The sky is brighter than anything in József's father's warehouse. Their world was cloth, once: his great-grandfather a travelling silk merchant, his grandfather the proprietor of a blue-dye workshop, his father the owner of a textile factory. Before it was all confiscated, József would press rare woad between his palms, listening to his father recite tones: *Prussian blue, French blue, this here is more brilliant than lapis lazuli — you ask your mother what she'd prefer: a precious stone or a shawl in this colour.* If they were the Goldbergers, they might still be free. Leo Goldberger owned the biggest textile factory in Budapest, his name inscribed on the building front without fear. Mr Goldberger hadn't been sent to the Ukraine. But neither had he bought a failing arts journal to please his intellectual wife, and renamed it *Küpa* after the indigo well that dyed Hungary's most famous cloth. Mr Goldberger had not taken this great Magyar art and leant its name to a socialist rag. Why did János do this? Pride? To please Emmuska? What made his father believe he too could use words to stamp himself on the world, that he could talk, seduce, persuade, joke, lull a person into agreeing with him, into seeing the world his way? His father would have no word for the blue sky József sees now, its blinding glow interrupted by clouds that dissolve in neat lines: waves in no hurry.

József has been assigned to the quarry, a miracle, he tells Dragan, that proves God can still hear him and has saved him from the darkness of the mines. Bribes are more effective, says Dragan, appearing on the quarry rota the next day. He is afraid József's sight will slip completely, leaving him lost in the mountains. He might then be sent to Lager Rhön for 'medical care', or be accused of slacking and sent to the penal camp with the Russian prisoners and supposed saboteurs.

You only have to look at the way those men hold their bodies to know the pain worked into them at night.

József bows to the sky and pushes the metal wagon. It carries rocks cut bigger than his head, and even with Dragan on his left and the Italian POW on his right the wagon lumbers along the track like a dying animal. The Italian wears a shirt and flat cap. He looks like a gentleman farmer and it would make József laugh if each push didn't wrench his back. Dragan has shared a few jokes with the man, snatches of language from the Mediterranean coastline, and more than that, winks and raised eyebrows; Dragan can make anyone mirror his rueful smile, as if he somehow knows the secret of the world and everybody else knows he does too. Dragan is a Serbian convict. József is yet to summon his nerve and ask him: *convicted of what?* And, more than that, a quieter question: *are you Jewish, secretly, in your heart?* An Orthodox cross bounces free of Dragan's shirt with every push of the wagon, but his Yiddish is as good as József's.

The Italian man talks across József, and Dragan draws a quick breath to translate: 'Some Magyar artists have crash-landed in our midst. We're to have cultural readings on Sundays. Who needs food, eh?'

József laughs, shaking sweat out of his hair. Damn this sun. Fuck shit curse to hell with this sun. Breathe. Sip the sweat. Push. Who needs food? Who needs water, when there is poetry in the world? His mother used to give him old issues of *Nyugat* to read. He wishes he'd listened properly to her fervent whispers of revolt, to the whispers of the friends she would gather in when János was at work, when he still had the factory. They talked about the latest books and news from Germany and America and his mother played the piano, whose keys stayed dormant when his father was home. She was a lot younger than János, and the difference showed when she played.

Afterwards, Emmuska would straighten her crumpled skirt and fix her hair and wait for her husband, perhaps arriving home on time, perhaps late, smelling subtly of a different house with different flowers and perfumes and soaps. Then they'd have dinner, Alma and László eating in the children's room, József promoted to the adults' table where he'd watch the level of wine in his father's glass, as if being the custodian of its volume might give him some control. Their home was two in one: the nouveau-riche businessman living in Pest, and the revolutionary girl born wealthy in Buda. József would watch closely for signals of love between these two houses, trying to learn their language, he who was praised as the linguist of the family. Magyar, Yiddish, some Serbian and German, even radio English, when they were allowed a radio. But the syntax of his parents was unknown to him, their exchanges lacking any rhythm he understood, sometimes listless, at other times resounding, the sudden slamming of doors, the scrape of a bureau across the floor as János pressed Emmuska against it . . . It seemed to József that his father drank mercury, and his mother enjoyed the taste on her lips.

József has only kissed one girl: Livia Schiff. His mother passed by the open doorway as their tongues touched, and there was no more kissing. János had come into his bedroom late that night. He'd been working cash-in-hand for the local tailor, a man whose cloth he once supplied. He gripped József's chin, making him flinch at the coldness of János's fingers.

'Always jumping, József! I have a son who forgets his father's face. Your mother spoke with me, about the Schiff girl. She wants you to know, you only kiss the girl you marry.'

József's gaze was fixed on his father's cracked lips. How many women had he kissed besides his wife? His mother's closest friend, János's mistress, was the only woman József knew about for certain.

'How can I know if I'll marry her?'

His father's laugh: 'How else? By kissing her, József.'

They have reached the end of the line. József sags into the wagon, resting his forehead on a corner of warm rock. Dragan plucks the back of József's shirt to pull him upright, creating a sudden pocket of cool air against his sweat-slick skin.

'Come on, Fleischer is watching.'

József climbs into the wagon and passes a rock the size of a baby into the Italian's waiting hands, just as he had passed baby Alma back to his father when Emmuska arrived home from the hospital. The Italian's collar is black with sweat, and standing in the midday accusation of the sun, József sees his father burnt black with sweat and decay, clearing minefields with his hands in the snow – if he's alive. If he's still alive.

JÓZSEF IS LATE FOR the reading and catches what seems to be the final lines of a poem. Stillness has gripped the closely packed bodies, and no one will let him through to find Dragan, so he clamps his bleeding hands under his arms and waits. Sundays are a day of rest, which means performing labour around the camp rather than the mines. He repaired the barbed wire fencing today without gloves

75

or tools, and is unable to clap when the silence of the room breaks. Without hearing the poem the applause seems dislocated, as if the men are clapping for the stone walls, the metal roof, the soldiers in the doorway, guns hanging idle at their crotches. One of the guards is clapping too.

In the break of movement József fights his way to Dragan at the front. With no Magyar, he wonders why Dragan is bothering; but looking around in the grey candle spurt, he sees Italians and other Yugoslavs too. He finds the poet, bent down, talking to another man who is getting a violin from a peeling case. The poet looks like a faded film star: dark hair swept back from his forehead, shaggy sides showing how long it has been since he touched civilisation, and more, revealing the thinness of his cheeks, how disproportionate his face is. The man has the collar of his trench coat up, and wears a tie too, as if this were a train station, and he were collecting coins from a ready-made audience while waiting for the next departure.

'Who is he?'

The man next to him whispers: 'Miklós Radnóti.'

József watches the poet retreat to the edge of the room as the violinist steps up. Miklós Radnóti. His mother loves this man's poetry; she says he's part of a new movement, the next Petőfi to lead a revolution. But all József sees is tiredness as Radnóti leans his head against the window and breathes out, slow, his body collapsing: a circus tent folding under the pressure of a storm. József hopes it is only his eyesight; he hopes no one else in the crowd realises this man is almost on his knees.

The violinist starts: a series of quick plucks that rouses the audience, has them scrubbing their faces, smiling. József taps his toes, copying Dragan's movements until they are competing for speed, and across the room Radnóti laughs. József grins at the poet, receiving a nod back. A sudden gust: the doors have opened, more guards slipping in, and the laughter stutters, but they just stand and watch, some tapping steel-toe-capped boots, drowning out the wooden clogs of the prisoners. The violinist gives them a quick bow and keeps his hands moving.

'This is why I came,' says Dragan in József's ear.

'The music?'

'No, öcs. Your ears. This poetry, this music, this is the sound of your country.' Dragan covers József's eyes with cold fingers. 'Listen. You can still see the world.'

József straightens. He forgets the guards at the door as colour drops into the black loneliness, bright scales climbing inside him, so that he can see the room better than ever before: there are no walls that matter, no barbed wire, only the truth that what once filled his mother's living room can still exist here, no matter how the world inverts itself.

The music stops. The man bows, sweeping his instrument in an arc that takes in the whole room, and then urges Radnóti forward again. The poet steps reluctantly into the light.

His armband is white, a Jew converted to Christianity.

He links his hands, as if considering prayer. 'I wrote this poem before my first labour service in Romania.' Radnóti clears his throat, eyes fixed on the drumming roof, and begins:

I lived but as for living I was shiftless in my life, knew always
    I'd be buried here when all was done,

that year layers itself upon year, clod on clod, stone on stone,
that in the chill and wormy dark the body swells,
and cold, too, lies the fathom-deep and naked bone.
That up there scurrying time is ransacking my poems,
That down, down, down, my mortal heaviness must drive;
All this I knew. But tell me – did the work survive?

Nobody claps. Nobody smiles.

SUMMER BREATHES THROUGH THE camp, ripening the stench of sweat and waste. József leans against the wall with his shirt in his lap. Ahead, a man has been trussed up and hung by bent thumbs in the square. Sitting with Dragan, József does not try to bring the man's twitching yellow star into focus, but studies the sky. The velvet peacock of a woman's scarf. His hands throb, as if he is the one tied up, like last time. He tears into his bread. The growing drip of blood beneath the man's dancing body is grey to him.

He has learnt there is no limit to what a man will do. A Magyar guard might shoot him in the head to check a rifle is in working order; Dragan would take the bullet. He does not know why. Yesterday Warrant Officer Eichel promised that no Jews would return home from this place. It could happen at any time. So József swallows and asks abruptly: 'Convicted of what? Why are you here, Dragan?'

A small pause. 'Of what did they convict you?' says Dragan.

'Nothing. They called me up for service.'

'Why _this_ service?'

'Because I'm . . .' József plucks at his armband.

'There is no *because* that invites rational explanation. Change the subject.'

'Tell me why you're here first.'

Dragan cups József's cheek, redirecting his stained-glass gaze. József realises he has been talking past his friend's ear. 'Just be glad I am, öcs.'

RADNÓTI CHANGES POSITION ON the bunk, hunching closer to the notebook. József squints, picking out the details: the poet is writing in a staggered block with one deep crack down the centre, as if weighing two columns of words for their worth.

'What are you writing?'

The pen trembles, ink smudging, and then slips on.

József says, 'Sorry,' and lies back.

They have been moved to Lager Berlin, Bor's central camp. The march was a passage of insanity: fast-running feet tripping over each other in haste, over already finished bodies, past blistered country, ruined homes, dead trees, the dead eyes of strangers. They now await German orderliness, the imminent separation and selection for wherever they will go next. Until someone decides, József has wrapped his bleeding feet in his shirt and is content to never move again. Dragan said there was a train station nearby: they'll most likely be taken there. Anything but more walking.

The Red Army is coming. It terrifies the Germans. You can see it in the way they run, too, always looking back over their shoulders. Shells are exploding somewhere: the English, the Americans, the Soviets? *Run, Adolf, run* . . . Where did he hear that? An illicit snatch of BBC World Service back in Budapest. *Run, Adolf, run, Adolf, run, run, run, now that the fun has begun, gun, gun* . . .

Next to him Radnóti is bending so close to the notebook József can see the bulge of his nape straining to hold his head up. He remembers the poet reading: *The pilot can't help seeing a war map from the sky*. The ground rumbles. He pictures the Allied plane dipping its wing into the sky-currents, like Alma skimming cold water with her toes. Does the pilot know what is happening to those held inside the buildings stretched beneath him? Or is he humming *Now that the fun has begun gun gun* . . . ? He tries to place his family in Budapest, bombs blinking in and out of his vision, the building blazing, flattened, his family hiding in a basement, his mother reading *Stars of Eger* to László and Alma as the fire spreads: *Chapter One: Where Do Hungarian Heroes Come From?* He cannot think of the first line. He cannot keep the peace in his mind. Radnóti seems to have come to the end, the pen lifting away hesitantly. *Write, though all is broken, on the sky*.

The notebook is a small brown thing, like a schoolboy's, 'Abana 5' printed on the front. Dragan told József he'd seen a Serbian gardener give it to Radnóti through a fence in Camp Heidenau. The exchange took place with no words: the gardener approached the wire, forced the thick pages to curl like a snail's shell, and pushed it into Radnóti's waiting hands. József has talked enough with the poet to hear about his three tours of labour service: winding back the barbed-wire border of Romania, the sugar factory, nailing ammunition cases, the beatings, his books stolen, his head shaved, made to perform star jumps in the tufts of his hair.

The shelling is getting closer. It wakes Lorsi in the opposite bunk, but the musician closes his eyes again. He tucks his violin beneath him.

'Do you think it's the Red Army?' József asks Radnóti. 'Some say they will free us before Rosh Hashanah.'

'If they do, I hope they bring some ink.'

The doors swing open and they all sit up, but it is only Dragan, autumn leaves caught in his stride; a burning stench follows him. For a second József sees flames eating László and Alma's beds. Dragan pulls him from the bunk. Standing in the lee of the bigger man's body, József whispers, 'What are they doing?'

'Destroying papers. We're leaving.'

THE LABOUR SERVICEMEN ARE divided into two groups in the owl light. Demands to see armbands, dog tags, identification. They are sent to opposite sides of the square: those on the right will march out tonight; those on the left will help dismantle the camp and march out two days later. Lieutenant Fleischer paces up and down, a clip-board in his hand, a rifle slung over his shoulder. József is gripping Dragan's shirt when Fleischer reaches them. The German jabs his finger into Dragan's chest.

'You, to the left.'

József tries to focus on Dragan's face, but cannot. Their hands meet: trailing fingers, bumping knuckles. There is no time to say anything. Dragan is gone, merged with the line of men on the left who will wait two days before leaving. It happened too quickly; he meant to say goodbye, thank you. Fleischer hauls him forward. To József's eyes the man's uniform looks like it is spotted with mould, as if he is wearing rotting flesh.

'To the right, Jew rat.'

József's hand is empty: nothing to grip, no one to steer him. His steps are uncertain. He urges the phosphorescent stars to spotlight Radnóti. A guard has put the poet into the right-hand column, promising it will mean quicker help for his tooth. Lorsi has gone with him, and József tries to find the violin shape amongst people's smuggled bags and coats. He cannot make out the poet or musician, and hears laughter before he bumps into the hanging tree. He is righting his cap when Fleischer smacks him round the head with his rifle butt. Blood explodes from his forehead.

He expects another strike, his last strike, when a strong hand takes his. Dragan has broken ranks and drags him, insistently, painfully, to the right-hand side. Fleischer takes two steps after them, then leaves them be, turning back to his original task. They join the column of men who will leave today.

I wrote my name on the sands

A FADED RED SCRAP WITH a hammer and sickle, and in large print next to it: THE LAST KREMLIN FLAG. A smaller sign told me it was not really the last communist flag. The genuine article had grown soot-stained from passing traffic and was now kept inside the checkpoint museum. I stood blocking the doorway to Starbucks at a busy crossroads with a military hut at the centre, where two German men dressed as American soldiers mooched in the five-foot space, calling, 'Good morning, take photo, souvenir.' I couldn't figure out how to get to the centre of Berlin. The place names on the map were jumping. A man shouldered into me as he hurried to McDonald's. Next down was Checkpoint Curry, whose emblem seemed to be Coca Cola. YOU ARE LEAVING THE AMERICAN SECTOR. If that was true, there was no evidence of it. I wanted to leave. I just didn't know how.

A hand grasped my shoulder. I almost dropped the map. It was Felix, red-cheeked from running.

'Where will you stay?' he gasped.

My heart was kicking. 'I'm going to find a hotel.'

'I have a spare room.'

'Excuse me?'

'I don't think you should be by yourself.'

'You don't know me. I'm fine. I'm fine on my own.'

'I am certain you will be. But you do not seem accustomed to it yet.'

I stared at him. I was aware of tired sweat pooling at the hollow of my throat. I wasn't breathing properly.

'I live with my mother,' he said. 'She will be there too. I promise, I am a safe person.'

'I'm not letting you keep the testament.'

'I know. I would like to do this service for you.'

'Why?'

'You wouldn't be here if it weren't for me.'

'I'm here for Silk.'

'Then I would like to do Joseph Silk a service. This makes sense, yes?'

I began to smile. 'None whatsoever.'

WE GOT THE U-BAHN and changed onto national rail. I told him I'd never been to Berlin before and he offered to show me one of his favourite places on the way home, a park, and I said OK. We exited a small station onto a long avenue lined with faded apartment blocks and bursting allotments. The setting sun turned windows an embarrassed pink. I felt like we had left the city entirely.

'I once found Joseph Silk's street,' Felix said. 'On a trip to England.'

'Why didn't you knock?'

'What do you mean, please?'

'He wouldn't have minded. Students used to turn up all the time.'

'Oh, I could not do that.'

'You didn't want to interview him for your PhD?'

'It is not that I did not *want* to, but . . . my supervisor advised against it.'

'Why?'

'Impartiality.'

The housing stopped, and the road curved into a forest. Tall firs, purple-black against the twilight, smelling like mothballs. He said nothing more, so I asked what made this park special.

'Spree Park. I used to play here, before the Wall came down. There is a theme park ahead. It closed for rejuvenation when the city came back together. The new owner imported big model animals over from South America, for children to play on. The models were filled with drugs. The owner is in prison now, and the park remains shut. There is no better metaphor for the rush of capitalism in those days.'

'So it's closed now?'

'Yes. But there is a gap in the fence.'

A Tyrannosaurus reared above the trees. I stopped walking.

'Do not worry,' he said. 'It's asleep.'

'God, that's weird . . .'

'It gets more weird. Come.'

A gate circling the beasts was hung with signs I could not read, beyond *Achtung*. We walked close to the chain link, the curator pointing out a woolly mammoth missing one tusk, a diplodocus with its neck peeled of plastic, revealing fragile chicken wire.

'This whole thing is abandoned?'

'Mostly. No one takes care of the animals.'

'Apart from you.'

'That is right. Here is my door.'

The fence was pulled back, a man-sized hole so obvious it looked deliberate, even legitimate, and I ignored the Gothic signs nearby, stepping forward onto a railway. A toy railway, the tracks the width of my hips. I stared down at it, rusted copper in the last light. The curator joined me, hopping between the slats.

'I used to play on this train,' he said. 'My mother has pictures.'

He walked ahead, both of us in single file, as if playing again, me a rear carriage ready to detach, the translation of Silk's testament in my bag.

Felix said, 'The best bit is just ahead.' I trailed him through a thicket of trees into increasing darkness. A giant Ferris wheel took up the next clearing. It was yellow, blotched with rust and spray paint. One of the cars was scrawled with the word 'HAPPINESS'.

'Are you responsible for the artwork?'

He grinned. 'Some.' He led me to a picnic bench and we sat down. The surface was scarred with penknife mementoes, a kind of Braille: lovers, crossed hearts, countless professions of *being here*.

'I'm giving the eulogy,' I said.

'At the funeral?'

'Yes.'

'Not your father?'

'No.'

'He gives neither baby names nor father eulogies?'

'No.'

86

'Do you know what you will say?'

'There's a poem I've been thinking of since I first spoke to you. It's called "Testament". There's a line in it . . . *Time will come again at the Flood, though I wrote my name on the sands when the Tide was out.* Silk liked that.'

'His paintings were the name in the sand?'

'Maybe. In the second half, the speaker says, *Do not think when you think of me as a ghost that haunts the lamenting sea* . . . He wasn't looking for anybody to mourn him. Silk. He was ready to go. He didn't want people sentimentalising his life, covering it in words . . .'

I fell quiet. Next to me, the curator traced knife-cuts with his thumb. He seemed about to speak when there was a colossal creaking, metal expanding, or falling apart, and above us the Ferris wheel began to move. Yes, with some speed now, the Happiness climbing, and I looked around for someone controlling it before realising it was the wind. It was ghostly and wonderful, the wailing of mourners. We sat watching it together, as if witnessing some kind of miracle.

I wanted to see Felix's face. Night was on us, blocking in the trees and the wheel with deep indigo as the minutes passed. I could just make out his smile. He glanced my way, and then leant towards me, until our shoulders were touching. I relaxed into his body. It felt comfortable and safe, as he had promised, out here amongst the dinosaurs.

Then someone shouted: 'Achtung!'

We both twisted to find the voice, and a torch beam hit me in the eyes. I put up my hand, bringing into focus a man wearing black shorts and a black shirt, a badge stitched onto his chest, a bicycle on the ground behind him. Rapid fire of German. Felix raised his arms, and I couldn't tell if he was surrendering or defending us. A pit of terror dug itself so quickly within me it was sickening.

'He's a security guard,' Felix said, and I stepped forward so that I was shoulder-to-shoulder with him.

'We're really sorry,' I said, 'we thought it was OK.'

'Signs,' the guard snapped, 'there are signs.'

More quick German, the curator talking in urgent tones. The guard moved his attention to me. In the torchlight, I could just make out his eyes. The flatness shocked me. He was yelling about money.

'Thirty euros then you go,' he said.

'What?'

'Fine. Pay me fine or I call the police.'

'Look,' the curator said, 'I'm not a tourist, I'm not falling for that,' before switching back to German.

'I am calling the police.' The man unclipped a phone from his belt and pressed two buttons, and held it out to Felix. 'Fifty euros or I dial last number. You are trespassing. *Schnell, schnell.*'

The curator snapped something in German, something that rocked the man, made the phone wobble in his hand. They stared at each other.

I reached out, hooking my fingers into Felix's jacket. Tugged gently. 'Let's go,' I said. Then to the guard: 'We're going to go. We're very sorry.'

The guard shook the phone, as if wanting us to take it. 'I will dial the last number. Fifty euros and cameras. You have cameras? You take picture? Trespassing. Cameras and fifty euros.'

'We're going now.'

The Ferris wheel groaned. I could not hear anyone else nearby, no human sounds but our own breathing, no light except for the guard's torch, which ran over my body, feet to head. I stared into it unblinking. The man's eyes remained flat. He closed his fingers over the phone. He said: 'Run.'

I turned, pulling Felix after me.

WE COLLAPSED TOGETHER IN the forest, my back against a tree, Felix wheezing so badly I asked if he was OK.

'I'm sorry,' he said. 'That's never happened before.'

'It's fine.'

'I told you I was safe. I'm so sorry.'

'Security has told me off on Hampstead Heath a hundred times. Never quite so terrifyingly, but still. Don't worry about it.'

'It's not fine.'

I reached out, finding his shoulder. 'What did you say to him?'

'I told him no ex-Stasi rent-a-cop could scare me anymore. I think rent-a-cop is what you would say.'

'Ex-Stasi?'

I felt him shrug. 'Let's go, OK?'

THE APARTMENT WAS A hybrid, the rooms half the size warranted by such tall ceilings, a once spacious home truncated. The place smelt damp. Felix's mother was cooking, a small woman whose hands moved quickly under the halogen strip, which baked her joints brick red. The curator explained in German who I was. I swayed from hip to hip to relieve my tired feet; the soles of my shoes sucked warped linoleum from the floor. Felix's mother glanced at me, asking a question he translated with a snort:

'She asks if you are a difficult eater too.'

I smiled. 'Nein.'

She paused, knife halfway through a carrot. 'Sprechen Sie Deutsch?'

'That was it, I'm afraid.'

She laughed. 'I am Marlene, my son so rude he does not even say.'

'I was going to—'

'Like Marlene Dietrich,' I said.

'Just so.' Marlene laughed, turning back to the carrots. 'Just so.'

'I'll show you the room,' said Felix.

I followed him down a short hallway. The bedroom door had a poster of Pippi Longstocking, my childhood hero. Inside, there was a loft bed with riggings that seemed halfway between a tree house and a pirate ship.

'My sister's room,' he said. With one shoulder up to his ear, he looked like a shirt sliding down its hanger. 'It's half-term.'

'Did you build the bed?'

'With my father. When he still . . .'

'She stays with him in the holidays?'

'Yes.'

'I would've loved a bed like this.'

'Well, it's all yours.'

'Thank you.' I put my bag down. 'What does your mum do?'

Felix cleared his throat. 'She's a cook. I'm going to get her a nicer apartment. I'm applying to the council. My father isn't paying child support and my mother . . . I'm only living here for now. The internships I've been doing don't pay enough, so . . .'

'I just meant what does she do. That's all.'

'What does your mother do?'

'She's a lawyer.'

'And your father?'

'I'm not really sure. Can I see your room?'

'Oh, um, it's kind of messy.'

Marlene appeared in the doorway. 'It's nice, your room. Are you ashamed? Show her.'

I followed Marlene out, Felix's arguments losing speed as she hustled me inside.

'I understand if it seems strange to you,' he said behind me.

The walls were stacked with bookshelves. A quick tally gave me Silk's name in fifty-two different fonts and colours. The desk was recognisable only by its legs, covered by books and magazines, showing *Tributary II, 1972*; Silk as a young man standing behind Hepworth and Moore; *Men's Pond, 1960*; Silk's face, so close his smile and greying hair were out of focus, leaving only his eyes crisp. I traced the leak of brown and green from his irises, pigment escaping from black holes. *Harvest Sun, 1991*; *Sar-e-Sang*, named for the mines in Afghanistan that birthed ultramarine; *Coniston Blue II*. Silk's first girlfriend in England was a nurse, he'd said, who took him on holiday to the North. *She was Cumbrian. Her accent was so thick I only understood every sixth word, but that was enough. She wore white stockings. That was enough too. The Cumbrian word for girlfriend was mott. Strange, the things to stay with you. I first learnt the word blue as blea because of her. I told friends, all I can see is blea. My cheeks itched, how much they laughed at me.*

91

On the floor, old newspapers formed a brittle carpet, the freshest on top, *Le Monde*, *Tageszeitung*, with arts supplements pulled out. I picked up the *G2*, the cover showing Silk's Saturday salon. I was in the background. I dropped the newspaper onto the curator's bed, looking up at his clip-frame posters: Silk's *Opticks, after Newton*, and *Laguna Veneta II, after Turner*. 'Something wrong with Van Gogh?'

'Please?'

'Never mind. You must know more about Silk than I do.'

'I don't think that's true.'

I looked him up and down, from his feet curling inward to his tangled hands. 'I guess we'll find out.'

I LAY AWAKE STUDYING a cartoon map of Europe tacked to the wall. The Danube pushed its way through the land, stubbornly shrugging off cities. I imagined following it. The bag containing the translation of Silk's testament sat in the groove between mattress and bed where the curator's sister kept her diary and a box filled with small rusted keys. The diary itself was locked, and I supposed one of the keys opened it. The wise precaution of a spy, I thought. I used to do that kind of thing, making up secrets to keep so that I had some to call my own, aware of Mum and John and Silk and Rosemary hoarding jealous and angry silences above my head, a silence ready to ignite.

I tried to put myself in the Blue Room with Silk when he called Felix, to feel his heart thump. Did you call him to save it, or destroy it? Budapest looked down at me from the map, the Danube stitching it together. I pictured Silk leaning on his walking stick in the Jewish

Museum, cast into shadow by his own words, blown up across the pale walls. I saw his stick tremble with the effort. I told myself: He no longer exists. He no longer exists. But if he doesn't exist here, how can I?

I lay awake, caught between the fear that I was losing all equilibrium, that the self was a sheet of ice far thinner than I had known, and I was now falling through it without resistance, with terrifying speed into the depths below, swallowed by a cavity in my mind that had no bearings and no light, but that I had always been aware was waiting for me; and a fear that I was simply following a script of mourning, that these feelings were exaggerated, momentary, and that I would soon lose even the absence of him.

'WE CALL IT A Berlin Breakfast.'

Standing on the balcony, I tried to match the energy in Felix's voice. 'Enough for all of Berlin, I imagine.'

'You cannot mock me when I know the English version. Here there is something called *fruit*.'

I considered the hope in his eyes. 'I wouldn't mock you.'

The plastic table was covered with small plates offering hard-boiled eggs, chopped apple, cheese, toast (gluten-free and otherwise), jams, coffee, avocado, bacon, pastries – I didn't know where to start, and did not argue when the curator began to arrange my plate. I looked out at the woods bordering the flat.

'Are we still in Berlin?'

'No, I have whisked you to Bavaria.'

'Ah, I suspected as much.'

93

Felix's glasses magnified the grey skin beneath his eyes. He looked like he hadn't slept either.

'I can't let you have the testament.'

He gave me a small smile over his coffee. 'Ah,' he said. 'I suspected as much.'

I CLIMBED INTO THE plane with Silk's original testament in my bag. When the engine pulled the wheels from the earth my fingernails left half-moon dents in the postcard of *Harvest Sun* I'd bought in the airport. The shop had a whole series of his paintings, rendered six by four and glossy.

Well, look at me, as famous as Nelson.

Why Nelson? I asked my translucent reflection.

The first British hero to have a state funeral complete with memorabilia. See to it I have plates with my face on them, won't you?

You think you're a hero?

You've read my testament. You know exactly what I think of myself. You always have.

Yes, I've read it. It says your vision, the way you paint, is because of your labour service. It says you are responsible for the death of a man named Dragan Ivanovic. It describes things you would never want anybody to know about: for your own dignity, your privacy, your self.

Why did you buy that postcard?

You painted it the year I was born.

I did. But you own the original. You know who died that year?

Sándor Márai, the Hungarian writer. Put a gun to his head in San Diego.

Did I ever tell you I considered killing myself, after I heard the news? Struck by the ease of it.

You didn't tell me. But I know anyway.

How?

You told my mother.

And she told you?

She said you wanted to live to see me born.

An awful lot of pressure on you. Right up to the end. I told you I lived for you, after Rosemary died. I shouldn't have said that. An ugly and selfish truth, like all my truths.

Don't ask for sympathy and don't give any, Silk. Not now. I'll cry on the plane in front of all these people.

So cry.

No.

I slipped the postcard into the folder with Silk's testament and looked out over the Rhineland.

a foul death blows overhead

I T'S HARD TO FIND any potatoes left to sever from their roots, and the crunch and choke of people eating them raw gnaws at József. They sleep under open sky. Furtive fires burn against the soldiers' orders and József tries to absorb their glow. It is Rosh Hashanah and he is bound on all sides by prayer, by the piyyutim, by repentance. He mouths the words, trying to force his thoughts inside them, but thought and word will not align. A shofar horn sounds – smuggled in with someone's 550 grams of bread, which is meant to last until Belgrade – and József thinks: for what should we repent? God is not listening.

They have been marching for two days. Two kilometres of running feet: at the front, baptised Jews, Radnóti somewhere among them; Jehovah's Witnesses and Seventh-Day Adventists; a dozen different companies, prisoners from across Europe; and finally – at the rear – the Jewish inmates of Bor. On Rosh Hashanah a man's fate is written down in heaven, ready to be weighed on Yom Kippur. Then, on Hoshana Rabbah, it is finally sealed. Starved, exhausted, József believes that God will paint him into darkness tonight.

The wind carries the bark of a dog with it, and words from the Gospel: 'Give us this day our daily bread. And forgive us our trespasses, as we forgive them that trespass against us.' This supplication sounds the same as the piyyutim. Catholic evocations, Orthodox oaths, Adventist promises of Jesus returning: prayers floating up with the ghostly sparks of flames amongst the heave of tears and vomit.

His skull is cleaved open by the drunken laughter of the guards. The fire is a silver flash, nothing more. Forgive those who trespass against him?

Dragan squeezes his hand in the dark.

THE COLUMN IS THREE kilometres from Belgrade when József hears the order to stop. The word is a miracle, and he bends over, laughing.

'This doesn't make any sense,' says Dragan. 'We must have run over two hundred kilometres from Bor to get here. Why stop now? We could be in the city by mid-morning. I can see the Statue of Victory.'

József follows Dragan's pointing finger. A pencil-thin column stands out from the fortress on the banks of the Danube. The emerald brilliance of the water grips him.

'My father used to take me to the fortress,' says Dragan. 'We beat the Ottoman Empire, once. We beat the Austro-Hungarian Empire. My father fought for our liberty then. Now the Nazis use us as their testing ground, and your Magyar countrymen help them.'

József touches his arm. 'Come on.'

They trudge with the column into a stubby cornfield. The sky is polished steel but the heat belongs to mid-summer. A storm coming. Eventually a cry goes out: 'Line up for water.'

József looks at Dragan. 'Do you think it's a trick?'

'Why march us across the width of Serbia to shoot us in an open field?'

So they line up: a thousand men clutching rusted containers. The queue is restless, some collapsing, others fighting to get to the front. József pictures jugs, vases, glasses, cups, troughs, from which he might drink. Palatinus Strand, Széchenyi Baths, Gillért. *Say ship, Alma. Say water, Alma. Say water.* After two hours József and Dragan have only advanced by ten metres. Dragan sleeps on József's shoulder.

'Look at that,' says a man behind them.

In the next field, guards eat soup. The closest man wags a chunk of bread at them, as if inviting someone to try and get it. József looks away.

It takes four and a half hours. When they finally drink, the water is enough to make József cry with relief, and Dragan grips his wrist, holding the tin back.

'Not all at once.'

'I can't . . .' József covers the tin with his open hand. 'You're right. What are we waiting for? Why not march on now?'

A man lying nearby turns over, opening one eye. 'Haven't you heard? There are trains waiting nearby, ready to take us to Budapest. The soldiers told us. The war is nearly over. They're beat. They're done with us.'

'Budapest?'

'Don't listen to him, József,' says Dragan. 'Typical Magyar, all your delusions. I know why we're waiting, and it's not that.'

'How would you know?' says the stranger.

'We're waiting because they don't want to march us through Belgrade in the daytime. They think people will try and help us, as they have in the villages. When we reach Hungary, they won't need to take such precautions. Your countrymen won't help you.'

'Stop,' whispers József.

Dragan turns on him. 'Well, they haven't helped you, have they, öcs? Your government will give the Germans every one of you by the end, and none of you Hungarian Jews have done anything to stop it. No one's helped you but me.'

'I know, but . . . No one knew this was going to happen. How could we?'

'I knew.'

'You knew they'd arrest you?' asks József.

Dragan just shakes his head. 'We're all fools.'

THE COLUMN MARCHES TOWARDS Belgrade as stars stretch over the skyline, the train home to Budapest someone's joke. It is black when they reach the city limits, and the soldiers force them to run. József trips over the rubble of bombed buildings, but Dragan keeps him upright. He thinks he can hear the Danube splashing its banks, but then the soft sound is swallowed by sudden gunfire. Lights flicker on inside the houses: a growing grid of yellow. Windows open. Voices shout from above.

'What's happening?' pants József.

'The people are asking who we are, what's happened to us.'

Shouts go up: we're from Hungary, Italy, Croatia. Help us. Dragan begins to yell in Serbian. Gunshots interrupt him: the guards are firing into the column. The servicemen spill into a large square, and now doors are opening, and József can see hazy figures surrounding them.

'Dragan, what's happening?'

'Come on, this way, they'll help us . . .'

But then the glare of headlights falls across them. German soldiers have come to support the Magyar guards. The crack of bullets fills the square, chased by screaming. The column is forced on. József follows, running down the middle of the road. Kübelwagen drive down the pavement, stopping the Serbs in the houses from reaching the prisoners. A gap opens as József stumbles past an open door. The light is on and he sees a woman clasping her son to her chest with one hand and offering him a jar of water with the other. He realises she is crying. He brushes the glass with his fingertips before a gunshot makes him duck and scramble on. Looking back, József thinks he sees the boy turn the jar over in his pudgy hands, before it falls and smashes.

They run without stopping to a bridge crossing the Danube. Boots echoing on stone. The water winks below, a thread of magic. He wants to jump in, but next to him Dragan is retching.

'I can't,' he gasps. 'I won't . . .'

József puts his arms around Dragan and hauls him across the bridge. They are marched through a field to a compound. Lights turn on somewhere and József can make out squat buildings surrounding a tower. Gates close behind them. Walls and trees close in. The Danube and the Sava are so close but he cannot see or hear them. They are herded towards the spiked tower.

'What is this place?' he asks.

'Sajmište,' whispers Dragan. 'It used to be the trade fairground.'

'Used to be?'

They are crowded into the central square where broken glass and bricks litter the dead grass. Shouts to stop. József drops to his knees, then collapses onto his back and pants at the sky.

'This is where it happened,' says Dragan.

József swallows spit. His throat is burning. 'Where what happened?'

'They killed them here. I heard about it in prison.'

József is cold, suddenly, right down to his bones. 'Jews?'

There is no answer. József hugs himself, pressing chin to collarbone, trying to disappear inside his own chest, as if he were both the baby and the mother he had passed, and could clutch himself to safety.

THEY ARE KEPT IN the arena for two days, until Yom Kippur, when the ground hums with prayers. József sits back-to-back with Dragan, slotting his spine into the Serb's knotted bones, and looks up at the ocean-blue sky.

'I joined the partisans when the Germans invaded.'

József stiffens.

'That was April. By September we'd taken most of Western Serbia back. My job was to disrupt German train lines around Belgrade so they couldn't send reinforcements. My wife wanted to help but she was pregnant, and I begged her to remain in Belgrade, in hiding.'

'Did she have to hide because you were a partisan?'

'She had to hide because she was Jewish.'

'But you're . . . ?'

'Not. But I loved her. Jelena. When they arrested me, the words they were using . . . rat-lover, Jewish-whore-lover . . . I understood. They didn't know I'd blown up their trains and killed their soldiers. For that I would have been shot on sight, and I would have been proud. Instead, they sent me to Bor.'

'What happened to Jelena? Dragan?'

Behind him, Dragan straightens. 'Quiet. Something is happening.'

Across the arena, men are standing up. Soldiers surround them, rifles pointed. Dragan rises and József follows, his eyes darting over the buildings, destroyed by air raids, the concrete pale and peeling like wasted flesh, the barred windows missing glass. József tries to hear over the nearby Yom Kippur service – the devout are actually fasting – and finally catches one word: parade.

They line up, stiff-boned and tight-stomached. They march. Back and forth. The sun beats them. Blue sky bleeds into his eyes. Soldiers strike them as they pass. An hour in, Dragan says to József, 'They are selecting people.' After another hour one hundred men are taken away. The soldiers making the selection pass by József and Dragan without giving them a glance.

When the parade is over, József and Dragan lie with their bodies touching from shoulder to knee, so that when József starts to laugh the shaking in his bones wakes Dragan up.

'What? What is it?'

'Yom Kippur,' says József. He is laughing so hard he is crying. 'We are going to be spared. We were weighed and spared.'

'So you believe in God, still?'

The laughter lodges in József's throat, and, without it, he can hear screaming. The men who were selected are being tortured, and he is heady with relief that it is not him. He tries to make that feeling harden into something like armour, let this love of being alive protect him.

How can I abandon God?

What if He were to abandon me?

JÓZSEF RUNS, HOLDING DRAGAN'S arm. The older man has slowed down since the fairground. They are going to stop at the brick factory in Cservenka, a small town breaking up the endless ruined fields ahead.

'The Germans are on the run, Dragan,' says József, his breath curling ahead of him, winter's first sign, and he is still dressed only in his cotton shirt.

Dragan grunts.

'You've seen the convoys coming through here – they're even taking oxen with them. They are scared it will soon be them with not enough to eat. They can't keep us marching like this forever, and they can't kill us all at once. There are thousands of us. They can't.'

'They will. We can either wait at their leisure or choose our own time to die. Those are the choices. And I'm not waiting anymore.'

Before József can respond the column jerks forward and his boot comes down on something that is not stone or mud. It is a notebook, with 'Abana 5' printed on the front. He opens it. There are five cramped messages in the front, in five languages: Serbian, German, French, English, Magyar.

> Please forward this notebook, which contains the poems of the Hungarian poet Miklós Radnóti, to Mr Gyula Ortutay, Budapest university lecturer, Budapest, VII. Horánsky u.1 I thank you in anticipation.

'See?' says Dragan. 'He understood, this poet of yours. We're not getting out alive.'

JÓZSEF SWAYS BETWEEN DRAGAN'S shoulder and the shoulder of the old man next to him. The brick factory veers, shit-coloured smears of roof and walls growing dimmer. The officer is coming closer, his whip in his hand. There have been selections before, but none like this.

When they arrived, the guards locked the gate. The air smelt of fire, like coals warming beneath their feet. A new company of officers took over. Dogs dashed about their boots. Dragan seized his elbow, whispering: 'SS.' Two days of parades followed, two nights squeezed into an attic used for drying bricks, five hundred of them lying on top of each other, until today, Hoshana Rabba.

Form up in companies.

József had grabbed Dragan, trying to control the sobs that threatened to crack him open: 'It's happening, it's happening, God is sealing our fate.'

Dragan closed a fist around József's wrists, and tore the yellow armband off. 'Not yours.' He pulled him towards the Serbs.

Now, clutching Dragan's forearm, József watches the SS officer approach. He cannot breathe. He cannot think. He is going to be selected.

'Your name is Željko Jokić,' says Dragan.

'What?'

'Listen to me. Your name is Željko Jokić. If they ask. You are a Serbian thief. You're Serbian. Gentile. Do you hear me?'

'Yes. But Dragan . . .'

A torch spits light at him and József ducks, his eyes searing.

The soldier barks a question, full of rage, actual hatred that strikes József more than the words do, stuns him into silence. Are any of you Jewish? Speak now, it will be worse later. The officer takes another step towards him.

Dragan's hand is at József's wrist, there is a delicate tug, and Dragan eases in front of him, shielding him from the man. Dragan says something in German, and the officer grabs him by the shirt. József tries to hold on to his wrist, tries to speak, to cry out, *wait, don't*, but no sound emerges, and Dragan is torn away by the officer, all of Dragan torn away. József stands still, staring at the empty space beside him.

Dragan had told the officer: *I'm Jewish.*

József does not know how long he stands there before he hears the orders to march. He stumbles on with the column, blind and deaf until he hears shooting, an endless thud thud thud of bullets. He looks over his shoulder and sees a slash of silver cross the sky: gunpowder filling the air.

*

JÓZSEF WALKS BECAUSE IT is all he remembers how to do. One hundred kilometres through Hungary with guns pointed at his head and his countrymen watching, some with smiles, some with tears. By day he can make out the Danube, gold dust scattered over black-sludge hills, and he keeps his feet parallel with it. In the dark the living dead batter him. No food. His stomach turns inside out. No water. His throat crumples into a stopper of screwed-up paper. Radnóti's notebook digs into his ribs beneath his shirt. He gropes for Dragan's hand in the dark. He cries. He calls. He realises with a jolt that he is dreaming while running and that Dragan is dead. The officers announced it, casually: we killed a thousand of you back at Cservenka, and we'll kill a thousand more. He dreams of his mother, father, food, bread, deserts, meat, water, water. He is empty. All these gestures towards survival – the saliva he swallows, his throat a dry river choking on silt; the heat building behind blurred eyes when they are ordered to lie down in a field and test fortune, and the relief when the bullet thumps into the man next to him; the reassurance when the column forms and calls out the names of the dead, and his name isn't among them – all of this is nothing, because there is nothing left of him to save.

THE COLUMN STOPS FOR two weeks to work in a tanning yard in Mohács. After Bor and Cservenka, loading and unloading boats seems an absurd joke. No one recognises József as a Jew, so he spends the nights with non-Jews on the second floor, where he finds Radnóti. He gives the poet his notebook, and Radnóti folds over it, coming slowly to squat down over the thing, rocking.

Tonight, Radnóti lies with his writing hand laid out on the floor next to him, as if the arm is some separate entity that must be saved. His face has tapered, chin and jawline thinned to knifepoints, and his eyes bulge from his skull. And yet, the poet is still writing, his shoulder shaking with the effort of moving the pen. József forces his eyes to focus on the title, 'Razglednica' – a Serbian word, he thinks, for 'picture-postcard'. The short lines would fit on the back of a card sent home; but the words may never be read by anyone but himself.

> The bullocks' mouths are drooling bloody spittle,
> all the men are pissing blood,
> our squadron stands in rough and stinking clumps,
> a foul death blows overhead.

József follows Radnóti about the yard, Radnóti's gaze so intent on the ground he is bound to find food if there is any, and maybe share it. But when the poet picks up a scrap of paper, a label for cod liver oil, he does not eat it, or even lick it. József watches the man squeeze a poem onto the damp scrap. The yellow and black label declares itself 'your medicine'.

THEY ARE MARCHING TO Győr. He might pass by Uncle's house. László is alongside him now, eight years old, racing him to the finish line. József will teach him to swim where the Danube and Rava meet, the blue and brown touching, where László will stand in one current, and József in another, and they will shake hands over the border.

He knocks into a cluster of men. Radnóti is at the centre.

'You must keep running,' one says.

'At least walk,' says another.

The poet gasps: 'I cannot go on.'

Guns fire and the men stagger forward, calling Radnóti, but the poet remains, repeating, 'I cannot go on.'

But he does, appearing in the brickyard that night, unmoving, and when the soldiers come the poet can't press into corners like the rest of them. József watches the beating that follows. He has no words in response to the poet's face, to the black void there. In the morning, a man comes up to József, whispering, 'Are you sick? Hurt?'

Hurt? Which part of him, exactly? All of him? 'My eyes . . .' he stops. Dragan told him not to tell anyone about his eyes. He told him . . . 'Željko Jokić.'

'I'm asking if you're sick. A doctor – one of us servicemen – has persuaded them to let the sick travel in carts.'

'Željko Jokić,' repeats József. The man sighs and hobbles away.

Outside, he sees the man was not lying: two carts are waiting. Twenty or so men with bandages and broken limbs are being lifted inside. József sees Radnóti amongst them.

The carts follow them to Győr, to the edge of József and Radnóti's homeland, and József suddenly wants the poet with the same need he has for food and water. He wants to hear a Magyar tongue shape his world beautifully, just once, before exile.

But when he looks back the carts are pulling away from the column. József stops walking. Shielding his eyes, he watches them lumber into the distance. He wonders how the guards will choose to kill Radnóti.

*

THE TRAIN WHEELS GRIND on iced tracks. József's world shrinks to the space occupied by his own body. The train's lumbering wheels drive him mad; shit dribbles onto his bare, frost-bitten feet; watery vomit comes up and goes down, no food, no water. He topples with the others, and cannot get up. He is lost on the bottom in a fog of his own stuttering breath. The train stops. He waits for hours, men standing on him, feet in his mouth. The doors open. Those men still living fall from the boxcar, József among them. The whiteness of the mountains blinds him, and he is jostled along with the others into a line. Orders to march, he does not know in which direction. He looks for Dragan, for Radnóti, for László, for Mama.

They run through villages as the sun goes down. They leave the snowy streets behind and are marched through the forest to a granite wall with giant doors flanked by watchtowers. A sign says MAUTHAUSEN-GUSEN. The gates open.

They march double-time past buildings that could either be kitchens or crematoriums, then endless blocks with grilled windows. If they are all filled with men, there must be tens of thousands here, but still not enough room: after being made to strip, they are herded through factories onto another forest road, mounting a hill covered with tents, where at least four thousand men push into a space meant for half that. The smell is worse than anything he's encountered yet. József collapses in the mud. Snow, clean and alpine, falls through holes in the canvas. He closes his eyes, listening to Polish tongues, German, Italian, Magyar, Yiddish, and more he doesn't understand. He listens to rumours – this place is known as the 'bone grinder', it's death by labour for the educated, for the intelligentsia; it's full of madmen. His body is seizing with cold; he is leaving it behind.

What was the labour intended for up until now, if not death; what was Radnóti, if not the educated; what was Dragan, if not another class of man. He is told that the chimneys they see are gas chambers. So it's gas they use here. He is told that women are giving birth in this field, and that a man fell into the shit-pit and drowned in it, the soldiers refusing to help. He sleeps. He dreams of labour, of blood, of mud. He wakes up to the same dream and his body refuses to give him leave of it.

He is alive. He has outlived his weeks in Mauthausen, here in the mud of the tent. But now he has to stand, to line up, to run. They are told they are going to a better place, a place with food. He has found a ragged shirt and trousers, but the material disintegrates in the snow. Five hundred men are shot on the road, this nowhere road leading nowhere. Yet there is a sign by the gate, a white placard with black letters done in a sure hand: GUNSKIRCHEN. The paint on the barracks smells fresh, just like the mountain air, and the surrounding forest has not yet withered in retreat from the hundreds of starved bodies carpeting the earth. Inside he finds the Magyar language dying. This, he realises, is an ocean signifying Europe's death by volume of blood spilt, and soon he will be just another drop.

László, it's happened. It's happened. The end is here.

machine guns and cameras

STARS AND SNOW. FROM Buchenwald to Krawinkel to Theresienstadt now nothing. The train isn't moving. If it moves, they will be gassed. If it turns back – there are officers on every corner. But the train isn't moving.

A clatter of buckles and gun snouts. Footfall, boots crunching in the snow. Shouts in German: The Russians are coming.

László is in a corner of the wagon and uses the motionless man beneath as a foot-up. He grips the wooden slats and pulls, the boys urging him up. László hauls his chin free, then his whole face. Cold air, but no relief from the smell of human waste. The wagon next to him is piled with corpses, heads and limbs, buried at each stop to make room for more. He drags his body free, waiting for gunfire, a bullet. Nothing. The snow-covered hills wink in the starlight, crossed by the swinging torches of the officers as they trip over the ridge. They are running away. The SS are running away.

A clump of men appears on the other ridge. They are armed with carbines.

'Ahoj!' the nearest man shouts. 'Je někdo naživu?'

Czech partisans. László's arms are shaking. Czech partisans. A man comes closer, raising something, not a gun, something else that glints. A camera. They came with machine guns and cameras. László hears the shutter fire and lets go, crumpling into the gold tinder flash.

ZUZKA SITS ON TOP of the Russian army blanket with her back straight against peeling plaster. It is the first time she has been given anything but straw and a three-tiered bunk bed with a four-foot berth shared between two since she was twelve. Four years ago. The cot has a steel frame and a mattress. Other children sleep on cots either side of her. They are under their blankets.

One boy, about twelve, has been crying for the past day, not responding to the passing pats of Russian soldiers or the soft words of his friends. Somebody told him his father is dead. Czech partisans brought the boy here last night for the care of the Red Cross, along with dozens more, the boys repeating when they arrived what the partisans had told them: the war is over. The war is over. In the morning, the roar of tanks woke her. Those who could stand ran out of the barracks and cheered. Zuzka did not cheer, just stood staring at the Russian tank in the middle of the square, the Reds dancing on it, one even playing an accordion, and all of them laughing as they pointed to where the inmates of Theresienstadt were hastily taking down a handmade American flag and replacing it with a hammer and sickle.

Zuzka straightens her bare, pimpled legs. She is an empty dress laid out flat to dry, the dress intended for a German woman shopping in

Berlin, no yellow star on its breast, a dress meant for a slim woman, remaining three sizes too big for Zuzka. She raided it from the ghetto workshop, and has tied it with a military belt she discovered in tooling and machinery. Zuzka's stomach is pulsing and she folds her hands across it. Pressing her knees together into two red spots of discomfort, she tries to slow her heart. The Russian soldier who drifts in and out of the barracks says she looks hübsch, his accent melting the German bullet down into alien poetry. *Pretty*. She is a body laid out to dry in the sun.

This is the measure she has learnt in Theresienstadt: to look clean and pretty enough to appeal to the mercy of Commandant Rahm, but never beautiful, Uncle telling her, *Don't give them ideas*. She learnt this lesson too late, of all the lessons in Theresienstadt. Other girls saved their mothers by pleading with Commandant Rahm, pretty girls with hair close to blonde, who begged on their knees in the dead grass by the railway siding the inmates built, dragging Auschwitz into the fortress, girls who managed to breathe in the shadow of the Central Morgue, to speak over the hammer and saw of the crematorium going up, girls who kept their mothers from going East. Zuzka tried, but her hair is brown, and she was not allowed close enough to the Commandant. The cracked sleepers stained her knees black with sunburnt sap. She couldn't get it off for days.

She has learnt the measure now, still here in Theresienstadt. She stayed silent while the Russians arranged food – bread and black coffee – and promised children under thirteen extra rations. She followed them to a house in the ghetto they designated for children, and accepted her bed with a polite smile. She knows better than to make any noise. Do not draw attention to yourself when soldiers are making decisions. Wait and see. Wait and see.

So now she is here, four days after the SS flicked the thin strip of paper at her, the stamp *Eignereiht*: in line. Transport. Uncle used to say they needed a new dictionary, because transport had no meaning now other than death. It was her turn to line up at the yellow building before the railway terminus where the sabotage crew might pull her aside as they had before, ticking her name off the list – except they'd been sent to the Small Fortress. Another word for death. She was next in line, they all were, the last alive in Theresienstadt; and then, a stay – the SS might need the living, to prove to the Allies that Theresienstadt was what they'd always said it was: a model camp.

The transport never left, but Commandant Rahm did, and now she is allowed to move freely in this model camp, this fort town isolated from the world for propaganda. She could walk into the middle of the concrete football pitch and sing the ghetto anthem: *We will pack our bundles, go home and laugh on the wreck of the camp.*

Zuzka closes her eyes against the evening sun seeping through the clogged windows. Uncle would have sung, if he were here now. She remembers him whistling the 'Theresienstadt March' with a grin whenever he passed her in the street; applauding her during the concerts; how he took an officer aside the first time she was selected, spoke with him quietly, and got her name removed from the list; his doctor's whites and yellow star in Theresienstadt's hospital, how he called it 'an antechamber to the morgue' with something like a smile. He combed his hair right to the end. She was proud to be his niece. She closes her eyes tighter, trying to contain herself in his words. *Keep playing your violin, Zuzka. It will keep you from going East. It will keep you from the stables. Do not join the mad there, Zuzka. I couldn't bear it.* The hospital staff had been put on a train East. Uncle is gone.

And now she is losing ground, unsure if she is really here, on this cot, or whether she is playing her violin on the bandstand, or learning mathematics with the other children, hidden in a closet in case the SS come looking. Maybe she is cataloguing books for the Central Museum of the Extinguished Jewish Race, or bleaching German uniforms white for the snow in Russia – maybe she is pushing through snowbanks on the march to Theresienstadt. Is she dressed in white? If not, the Russians will shoot her. Is she armed with her violin? If not, she will go East, or worse, to the stables and join the screams there, only it is not horses screaming.

They say the war is over. But she is not allowed to own valuables, even a watch, and without time such a promise means nothing, means Kurt Gerron's film for the SS could still be under completion. They will surely be sent East after it is finished, no longer required to play the living. She knows about Auschwitz, where the other children went. Lederer escaped and came back to warn the ghetto. It is only a matter of time. *You know, some of the little children cannot even tell time? We must give them an education while they are still here, before they go East. We must give them something. Zuzka, you have been with us for so long, you can help the children learn to tell time.* How to tell time without a watch? Her mother used to claim that when Zuzka was born the Prague castle cannons fired a salute – it was the midday cannonade, her father would laugh. She had learnt to skip over the Prague Meridian in the Old Town Square, singing as her mother taught her: morning, afternoon, morning, afternoon, and her older cousin would call her stupid, saying, that's not how time works. Her cousin who joined the Czechoslovak Division in France and was killed by a German sniper. There was no cannon salute for him, and she has no line to skip, no watch to read; her mother has gone East.

This is her sentence, words to keep her tethered to this ground, this time, and she holds on to it now, gripping the steel frame of the cot. They put my mother on a train to Auschwitz and I played my violin. She has said it so often to herself that the words are flattened, pulped, hammered, stretched, fired, until they are just words, no meaning really, just words she could commit to a page to communicate herself as her number did. They put my mother on a train to Auschwitz and I played my violin.

THE RUSSIANS GAVE THE children forty-eight hours to do as they wished and the Theresienstadt boys said they were going out for food. László joined them, because it beat waiting around for nothing, taking the bridge over the River Ohře – where below boys and girls laughed as they ventured out onto the iced aqueduct – and following the snow-encrusted road around the Small Fortress, László noticing how the others kept their eyes averted from its high walls. There is no birdsong, and few human voices. László shrugs the military greatcoat the partisan said was British up around his shoulders. He stamps in his boots, found discarded in a pile.

After the Russians lured them together with soup they registered the boys and girls, demanding countries, births, names. That's how László was first taken, on the way to Győr – Mama sent him to be with Uncle as the bombings and rumours of deportation worsened. She thought, with his lighter hair, he could hide amongst Gentiles on the train; that once he reached Győr he'd be safer. She said she'd call him back after she secured protective papers. It was a school friend at a small station where he changed trains who pointed at László and shouted, 'He's a Jew!' He was forced onto a different train, a box of darkness whose margins he tries to keep to in his mind; the train went to Győr, where his uncle may have been one of the men and women forced into the darkness with him. A woman told László it would be all right, we're part of a deal, blood for trucks, they're not going to hurt us. But the train didn't go to Strasshof as promised. When they reached Auschwitz, László was desperate to get out from amongst the corpses, falling onto the platform, confused by the sound of a band. The Germans were pulling women and older men out of the line. A Jew in striped clothing kicked his ankle and hissed, 'You're eighteen and you have a trade.' It seemed a mad thing to say, but he repeated it when an officer asked his age, and was forced back onto the train.

After a day of standing still under the grey sky, he was given a quarter of a loaf of bread and some sausage. A prisoner who came to clean the wagon told him he was lucky. The train shunted out, destined this time for Buchenwald. He told the communist prisoners who had the internal running of the camp that he was eighteen and had a trade. The comrade gave him a small smile and nodded him towards a tiled room where he was forced to undress. When water dribbled from the shower heads the boy next to him, a boy József's age, vomited. László's golden hair was shaved off; disinfectant seared his penis and testicles. As he arrived at his bunk a dead boy was lifted out of it.

And now he's told the Russians he's twelve, because they were giving extra rations to anyone under thirteen, and that his name is Czigány, not Zyyad. Some boys just refused, saying they were going home. László doesn't know the way home. His shoulders feel as though he is still carrying the rocks of the Buchenwald quarry, and lice have formed a second skin under his shirt. The Theresienstadt boys are joking around, climbing over dead horses, searching upturned wagons for cigarettes. One of them, Pavel, says they were filmed on this road, arriving at the ghetto.

'Filmed?' says László, in Yiddish. 'Doing what?'

'Don't you know?' says Pavel. 'We're movie stars. Kurt Gerron made a film about us.'

'What did you have to do?'

'Just walk down the street. But you know, it was a dead giveaway. They had us all in our best clothes and shined shoes walking in the mud. So much for realism.'

'What else?'

'I jumped in the Ohře,' says a boy.

'I played in the football match,' says another.

'Sounds like you've all suffered terribly.'

The group slows. Pavel looks at László. 'Don't talk about what you don't understand.'

László stops. 'Don't tell me what to do.'

Around them, bare trees creak in the wind. Pavel laughs. 'Our brave survivors, Muselmänner of the death marches. You think it makes you so tough. You Magyar crack me up.'

In his pockets, László's hands turn to fists. 'Why?'

'Always celebrating the worst luck.'

He is thinking of a response when they hear an engine. The boys turn and see a Russian UAZ coming. They step out of the way, but the car is slowing. The soldiers are looking at a couple of men who have just emerged from the field down the road. The men are wearing the jackets of German privates. László can taste blood in his mouth.

'Hey,' he shouts to the Russians. 'Lend me a rifle.'

The other boys stare at him.

The Russian driver laughs, asking in German, 'You think we have so many to spare, little boy?'

'I think if you're not going to shoot those pigs, I will.'

'Ha. Little man, I see.' The driver opens his door, planting a boot on the ground. The Germans have hesitated on the road. The Russian takes a knife from his belt and holds it out. 'Here you go.'

László shoulders past Pavel. The Russian looks just as László has always imagined Peter the Great, giant, loose-limbed, hair like winter sun. He takes the weapon: it has a black wooden handle, shaped so that the blade curls towards László's body, not away.

'You know how to say thank you in Russian?'

'No, sir.'

'You're Magyar?'

'Yes, sir.'

The man grins. 'Then you'd better learn. You're in Theresien-stadt?'

'Yes.'

'Bring the knife to the Small Fortress when you're done.'

The man slams the door shut and the engine groans back to life. The UAZ moves on towards the ghetto. The Germans are standing still. The road is a long black line drawn through dead fields, and there is nowhere else to go. László pushes through the group and marches towards them; after a few seconds, the other boys follow.

When they are close enough, one of the Germans calls, 'What do you want?' His uniform is mud-stained. A scar blots his cheek. He has no gun. Neither does the other man, whose arm is wrapped in a makeshift sling.

László stops a metre from the man. The other boys circle around them.

'Say that again,' says László, gripping the knife. The handle has warmed his hand, bringing blood to his veins.

The man licks his lips. 'What do you want?'

László smiles slowly. 'I've waited years for a man like you to ask me that. What I *want* hasn't seemed to matter to anybody. Not for a long time.'

'Look . . .' The man glances around the ring of boys. 'We didn't do anything.'

Pavel leans down and dislodges a rock from the snow. 'You didn't?'

'No,' says the man with the sling. 'It wasn't us.'

'We're just trying to find a way home.'

Pavel says, 'Let's sluice them.'

'What?'

'Sluice,' says Pavel. 'Search. We had to go through the sluice tunnel in Theresienstadt. It means steal. You took everything, didn't you?'

'It wasn't us,' says the man with the scar. 'We don't have anything.'

'Prove it,' says Pavel. 'Turn your pockets out.'

'We should make them strip,' says another boy. 'That's another thing we did for your film. You filmed us all showering. Let's see *your* beytsim, find out how big they are.'

'I bet they're looking pretty small right now.'

'We'll give you what we have, we'll give you everything . . .'

László watches the man shake his coat. Bits of bread fall out. The other man is struggling because of his sling. The knife is burning László's hand; he is sweating all over, a slick sheet under his clothes, a sudden fever, worse than the lice. The German is digging into his coat pocket. He comes out with pennies. Pavel spits on the ground. The man with the sling still hasn't got his coat off.

'Hurry up.'

The sling tears. The man is wearing a watch. It is not the watch of a private. The strap is gold. Pavel tells him to take it off. The man hesitates and someone jostles László, and suddenly he's in a circle of bodies all as hot as his own, and there's a German man crying at his feet and he is holding a knife. He turns it so the sharp edge faces outwards.

'Achtung!'

László snaps to attention. So do the other boys. No one says a word. No one moves. László stares at the German with the scar, who belted the word with such force even he looks shocked. He spreads out his fingers, the way a man might approach a starving dog.

'You don't want to do this,' he says.

László tries to speak and realises he cannot think of any words. He's lost them. Everything is red, and something is wrapping around his tongue, crawling down his throat, binding his lungs. He can breathe fire.

'That man will not get up again. You understand?' says the German. 'He will always lie on this road, because you put him there. He will not get up again. Do you understand?'

The knife tightens its grip on László's hand.

'Give us his watch,' says Pavel.

'Of course,' the German says softly. He slowly goes to his knees. He whispers something to his friend, shaking his head. He takes the watch off, and offers it up to László.

'Here. Please. Take it and go.'

László's free hand opens. The watch is heavy. Pavel takes his arm.

'Come on,' he says.

László feels the boy tug at him and looks at his face. He sees József's dark fringe, that black comma, the laughing eyes, and follows. After a while he realises dirty flecks of snow are falling on his head and dripping down his neck, melted by the steam of his body. Like ash. Like chimney smoke. He stumbles down the street, the boys falling about him like feral dogs, and as they jump and dance he sees the shaggy bodies of fighting animals. He says something, and it emerges as a snarl, a horrible parody of a talking dog. He tastes blood in his mouth and spits. The ground beneath his boots changes: they are walking across a field of stubble to a wooden fence. Pavel helps him over, and he lands at the back of a grand farmhouse. There is a wagon, piled high with packages and trunks. The Germans are fleeing. The yard stinks of shit. Nearby chickens scream at them. László follows the other boys to a sty ringed by a low fence. A piglet peers at them from the door, sniffing the cold air for food. There seems to be no mother.

'Dinner time,' someone says.

László stretches his jaw, tries to locate his language, anybody's language. 'I don't think it's kosher,' he says.

Some of the boys laugh. A few say they won't be a part of it: what would their parents say?

Pavel knocks him on the shoulder. 'Come on, boy king. You've got the knife.'

Boy king? László looks at him, trying to remember if some joke had been made on the road, after the Germans. He licks his lips. 'Didn't Herod murder the boy kings?'

'Herod *was* the king, idiot. So kill us a pig, won't you, oh King of Judea?'

László puts his boot on the bottom rung of the fence and swings his body over, landing in the sty.

'Hey, you! Stop!'

A pregnant German girl is coming out of the farmhouse.

'Make us,' says Pavel, laughing.

'You must stop!'

László looks back at the stone house. The piglet has disappeared inside. He ducks through the wooden frame into the sty. The stone-walling is compacted with mud and shit and is strangely warm. László closes the door behind him so the piglet cannot escape and is left in almost total darkness. He can hear the thing shivering in a corner, hidden in the straw and mud. He edges forward, the knife out. Another inch. He knows some of the Theresienstadt boys have been making a Nazi officer clean under their beds; that was their revenge, they said – they couldn't do any more. A ten-year-old boy has been shooting one Nazi after another. He saw his parents killed. László should have knifed that man on the road; the blade is too heavy in his hand now.

The piglet squeals, and then with a sudden dash it attempts to escape around his legs, and László kicks out, catching it in the side, which is surprisingly firm. The pig tries to scramble away, but László drops onto it, hugging its thrashing waist, caught on the chin by its skull, and he squeezes harder, and the pig jerks and bucks, and he cannot see, only smell, rancid chemical fear he knows is his own. He drives the knife in, through the pig's hide and muscle and gut until it lodges against bone. László folds his body around the dying animal, and hot blood gushes over him. He keeps his eyes shut, breathing in deeply to try and stop his tears, until finally the twitching stops. Drawing the knife out, he sits up, and more blood spills into his lap. He wipes his face, smearing blood over his eyes. He tastes vomit in his mouth.

'God,' says Pavel in the doorway, 'did you have to make it so messy?'

László can't speak. His mama would never forgive him.

'Pick it up, let's go. We'll cook it back at Theresienstadt.'

László nudges the pig head from his thigh. He works the knife into his belt. In the new light, he sees a blanket. He covers the stained thing and picks it up. It is heavy, and he can feel blood through the blanket. He comes out into the day, blinking at the diluted sun. The other boys stare at him.

László smiles. 'Dinner.'

The girl is no longer in the yard. He climbs over the fence, not relinquishing the body. The vibrant lick of red on his hands seems unreal next to the snow. He sees the girl standing at the window of the farmhouse kitchen. Her face is as red as his hands. She is crying, and she bangs on the window now, rattling the glass so hard he thinks it will smash. László shifts the body into the crook of his arm as he used to with his sleeping sister, and digs into his pocket. He tosses the German's watch onto the ground. He sees her mouth close up.

'You're *giving* that to her?' says Pavel.

'I'm not a thief.'

They walk back to Theresienstadt in silence. The pig is a solid weight. He works his hand inside the blanket and strokes the cooling coarse hair.

When they get back, nobody asks them where they've been or gives them an order. Pavel organises a fire in the square in front of the boys' barracks. László sits down on a bench and holds the pig, making sure the blanket covers its face. When enough dead wood has been found, two lads approach László, and Pavel says they're farm boys – they know how to cook it. So László lets them take the pig but doesn't stay to watch what happens next. He walks to the lower water gate and crosses the Ohře, the river where survivors say they scattered the ashes of over two thousand people, and limps the avenue of naked trees to the Small Fortress.

The entrance stands open, unguarded. The cobbled yard beyond is mapped with the shadows of trees from another century; László can see great yellow houses, like dukes' hunting lodges, and the tangle of a dead rose garden. He can hear glass smashing and drunken laughter. A Russian soldier sits outside a nearby building, smoking, a sour look on his face. László asks him where he can find a tall, blond officer, and the man stares at his clothes before pointing László to the next yard. There are administrative buildings to one side – he can smell burnt paper – and a row of dark rooms to the other, each with a table and chair and nothing else. A couple of soldiers have rigged up a hose; they point the sluggish water at the floorboards. Torture cells. László's body is slowing down, inside and out. At the end of the yard is an archway, painted black on white: ARBEIT MACHT FREI. Work Sets You Free.

'Some of my comrades think we should burn it to the ground.'

László jumps, fumbling for the knife – it's Peter the Great, standing in the door of an office. He beckons László inside. The cabinets all stand open, the floor covered in ash and paper.

'I didn't think you'd really do it.'

He is casting an impressed look over László's greatcoat. László looks down at the black stains of blood, turning red on his pale shirt. The Russian eases a drawer behind him shut with his elbow, as if wanting to spare László its contents.

'Are the bodies on the road?'

László remembers what the German said. 'They won't get up again.'

The Russian smiles, but only just. 'I didn't think you'd really do it,' he says again. 'Good man.' He puts his hand out.

László stares at it, thinking for a moment that the giant wants to shake hands, but then he realises. He pulls the knife out; it looks coated with rust. The man takes it with a snort.

'Always clean a knife afterwards,' he says, and cuffs László gently about the head.

László stumbles, holding his skull where the man's watch caught him. He thinks, just for a moment, that it is the German's watch, and without considering it he launches for the man. The Russian laughs, seizing him by the shirt and lifting him off the ground. László expects to be thrown to the floor, but the Russian only holds him there.

'You do not have the size for this,' the Russian intones carefully. 'Rest.' Kicking the door open with his boot tip, he urges László into the snow. László staggers, falls. His breath is a hard pant that crystallises above his face. It feels like his first breath in years. He stretches his arms in the snow, staring up at the purple sky. Boy king, dying, he believes, of typhus.

No. 53. What story did they tell the Jews about it and did the Jews believe it

No. 59. How did the non-Jewish members of the community behave

No. 61. How many people per wagon

No. 63. What direction did the train take

No. 64. At what point did the escort first allow ventilation or urination

No. 66. What was done with the dead

No. 67. How far did the Hungarian escort travel on the train

No. 68. What German unit took over the train and how was the transfer effected

No. 73. Where and when did the transport arrive

No. 78. Did any atrocity occur at that point

No. 80. Where was the majority of arrivals taken and how did that occur

No. 81. Where was the minority of arrivals taken

No. 83. What happened to you at the auna (the baths/showers)

Three

put him in the ground

I CLOSED THE GATE BEHIND me and dropped the latch. Home. The flowers looked tired. The upstairs bathroom window was open. I dug into my bag for keys, thinking maybe a friend had come over, but they wouldn't leave the window open. Someone could have broken in, a reporter, a thief. I put my shoulder to the swollen door and was hit by the smell of roast chicken and recently made coffee.

'Mum?' I called, easing my bag to the floor.

The kitchen door opened and I bumped into my father's shadow. 'John.'

He nodded. He wore jeans and an open-necked canvas shirt rolled to his elbows. His workman's boots were as spotless as they had been when he wore them with suits and a yellow safety jacket.

'What are you doing here?'

'The funeral.' He'd gone grey, streaks at the temples like a child's drawing of age. His ears were pierced. His face had developed sun lines.

'Right.'

'Where were you?'

'Berlin.'

'What's in Berlin?'

'Dinosaurs. Are you really doing a roast?'

'How likely do you think that is?'

I almost smiled. 'Mum's here?'

'Just getting out of the shower.'

'You're here together?'

'We're here at the same time.'

'Liset stayed behind?'

'Right.'

'John – Dad – I'm sorry. About Silk.'

He shrugged. 'One of us has to be.'

I held the doorjamb. 'Has to be what?'

'Sorry.'

The creak of the stairs made me pick my bag up and hurry past John. Mum appeared at the top and ran down, meeting me halfway. The hug was off-balance, Mum suddenly much taller than me, and I was a child again, holding her around the middle. The soft wool of her jumper was laced with the smells of home, both homes, England and Australia: sun tan lotion, sea salt, embers.

I pulled back. Her platinum blonde bob covered the white hairs I knew were there. The kohl around her eyes was as dark as ever. Lapis lazuli hung heavily from her neck. A present from Silk. 'You lit the fire?'

'I came from thirty-two degrees.'

'When did you arrive?'

'Yesterday. I've been calling you every five minutes. Where have you been?'

'Berlin.'

Mum led me down the stairs. 'I know that, I saw your note on the fridge – but why?'

I stood between John and Mum. The hall was too small. 'No reason. Just to get away.'

They followed me into the kitchen, Mum's worry scattering me, John's silent storm front forcing me back until I was in a corner and there was nowhere left for retreat. They had taken my territory. I couldn't get away.

'I'VE BEEN WORKING ON the playlist for the after-party. Some of Silk and Rosemary's favourite songs.'

I glanced at John, but he gave no reaction, so I let 'The Blue Danube' into the kitchen. Mum carved as the warmth of the oven rushed into the room and the setting sun hit the windows. I thought, furnace. We discussed funeral arrangements and Mum's current case. John sat before his plate like Silk did – I had never noticed that before: forearms splayed on the table, the pale underside showing, hands open as if asking to be held, as if asking for nails to the wrist. Silk sat like that to cool his swollen joints after painting. If we were at Silk's Saturday morning salon, he might hook one arm behind my chair, and I'd loop my arm back to hold his hand, forming a sling. Silk's table was in the window of Louis' Deli, reserved for him every week. Customers reading the *Guardian* at other tables hardly bothered to look up at the artists, these silver men and women. Sometimes the Labour Party leader would come in for a croissant and shake Silk's hand. Silk played to the table, stories and gambits, the performance in the pauses he left, inviting you into space he seemed to have created just for you.

John remained silent until he crossed his knife and fork over his plate. A hotel waited for him.

'That seems like enough suspense.' His voice was coiled wire. Suspicion. Accusation. 'Why were you in Berlin?'

'To see a boy.'

'A quick recovery.'

'*Excuse me?*'

Mum stretched her hand over the table. 'Stop.'

WHY DO I REMEMBER so little of the funeral? I told flagstones with their blank-eyed skull and crossbones about Silk's vision of the world – told them how he wrote his name on the sands when the tide was out. Silk's grave was longer than Rosemary's – their heads would not lie side by side, and the gravestone would sit on top of his chest. I imagined him bearing its weight. I recited thank yous, I hung up coats, I danced, I filled teacups, this dumb-show of gestures. Mum led, spinning me beneath her arm. What else? The coffin waited for me on the gravel outside the front door, sun warming the wood. It was huge. I pictured him inside, wearing the pyjamas he died in. I walked a wide berth to the car. What else? My voice did not shake. My friends and I stayed up until dawn, going through Silk's records. Someone said that we should fill as much of the house as possible with dance, and we raced and jumped from hall to kitchen, from stairs to living room, singing, '*We gotta get out of this place, if it's the last thing we ever do.*' What else? I put him in the ground. I put him in the ground.

'OF COURSE, WHEN ROSEMARY and Silk settled here you could practically find Regency furniture washed up on doorsteps for the seizing,' said Malika.

'And now we're to select an objet d'art and take it home,' said Harold. 'Utterly Silk: a gesture that's almost heartfelt, but can't quite bring itself to sentimentality. How British. No: *Harold, you take the ammonites and belemnites, all those hours we spent walking the Jurassic Coast to find them.* No, that would be too much to ask.'

'You know what Silk would say.' Malika laughed. 'He had his meanings when he needed them, and they can't be passed on.'

'God, he would. And wouldn't he just hate the echoes of Freud? Freud and his collection of archaeological knock-offs. You know, when Freud was approaching the end, he told a friend, *Of course the collection is now dead. Nothing will be added to it. The collector is soon dead.*'

'Oh – Eva.'

I lowered the camera. Harold and Malika, both curators and academics, friends of Silk's since the seventies. Malika was colouring, a scarlet line washing through steel hair. Harold did a two-step shuffle in his blue velvet suit.

'Eva.' He coughed. 'We were just saying – just talking about . . .'

'What's a party without Freud?'

'Well, yes. Indeed. You're filming the, er, the gathering?'

'Have you chosen something?'

It was the day after the funeral. Index cards waited in decks around the house for Silk's friends to scribble something they'd like from his many collections: a paperweight; an old postcard of a hand-coloured British beach or a nineteenth-century portrait, strangers made familial; Staffordshire pottery and Sheffield steel. I had packed the vintage cameras away, and cordoned off the Blue Room: drawn tape over the doorway like a crime scene.

'It feels wrong to take it apart,' said Malika. 'He should have a museum.'

'Oh, how he'd *hate* that,' said Harold. 'D'you know, when Freud and his family fled Vienna, he had someone photograph the rooms of his house so a museum could be reconstructed in London? Not a home. A museum he'd live in, and die in. Go there now, it's September 1939. Freud stopped time. But that's not Silk. Not left anything to a museum, has he?'

'No.' I felt Felix's hand on my shoulder in the archive. My ears burnt.

'Still,' said Malika, gesturing to my camera. 'If you should want to reconstruct it . . .'

'Of course, the Freud Museum in Vienna stands empty.' Harold looked down at his glass. It was empty too. 'Has to, I suppose.'

Malika cleared her throat. 'Harold, Eva doesn't want Freud's life history right now.'

I looked away. In the corner, on a deep windowsill, sat John. He jerked his head at Harold, rolling his eyes. I grinned, briefly. I hadn't meant to.

'He put the fossils aside for you,' I told Harold. Shock and pleasure seemed to hit him simultaneously. 'Silk wanted everyone to have whatever meant most to them.'

Loose in my hand, my camera fed on light, the image sensor chipping John into colour. I approached him side on, as if I might be going to join someone else, and I might have, but I didn't. I eased onto the sill next to him. The tall window was cold at my back. No one had closed the heavy curtain for days. This room used to be John's bedroom. If you opened the built-in cupboards, you'd find the wallpaper Rosemary put up when John was a boy: castles and knights stamped in blue blocks. John observed the room now, sitting back, one leg over the other. After he left home, aged sixteen, the room slowly accepted his negligence and offered instead a little of everything. Library, Rosemary's office, second living room. An archipelago of parts: Oriental carpets and shag-pile and Omega-workshop rugs butting up against Rosemary's daybed, thick with Mexican blankets, and Silk's Breuer tubular chair, canvases leant against the dusky green walls, the childhood wallpaper torn down, the fireplace where I had jammed flowers into pots and vases, the bookshelves crammed but not untidy, Silk would say, the stereogram, the rood screen, dusty plants, all reverberating with conversation as the seventy people I'd made a buffet lunch for laughed over Rosemary's Gallé cats and remembered, yes, the Alexander Calder mobile was a gift to Silk.

'Are you going to take anything?' I asked.

'What would I take?'

'It must mean *something* to you,' I said, trying to sound impartial, curious, and failing. 'The place. The people.'

'I haven't seen most of these people for decades. I haven't been in this room for nearly as long. If he'd wanted me to have something, he would have told you. Like old Harold's ammonites.'

I glanced at the street below: the yellow bricks, white windows, black railings. The geometry of afternoon sun. 'I made that up.'

John gave me a look. I didn't know if it was amusement or something else. He drank from his tumbler. 'You're good at that. Going to Berlin to *get away*. What a nice story.'

I took a diver's breath. 'Have you ever been? To Berlin.'

'Yes.'

'Have you been to the Jewish Museum there?'

Another sip. Several seconds passed before he swallowed. 'Why would I?'

'It doesn't mean anything to you? That part of our – our history?'

'You're stuck on that tune today, aren't you? Everything has to have a meaning.'

I let my hair hide my face. 'You sound like Silk.'

John shuddered, as if trying to throw something off, and his answer was the snap of a leather belt. '*For God's sake let us sit upon the ground and tell sad stories of the death of kings.*' He snorted over his drink. 'And while you're at it, sell the house and make a fortune from your grief.'

I edged back against the curtain. 'We have to. Death duty. It's that or the art.'

'Death duty.' John nodded. 'Isn't that funny? The dead don't have duties. Just the people they leave behind. Just you, lying to Harold about ammonites. I guess it runs in the family.'

'What does?'

John shrugged. 'All these followers, weeping over teapots Oxfam would sell for one pound fifty. Telling stories of the great man, and his great love. Osip over there, the king émigré, reciting poetry. When all Joseph Silk ever did was lie, lie, lie.'

138

I flushed. *Eighteen and already a man*. I tried to keep my voice from quivering. I could hear Mum laughing downstairs. 'You mean the affairs?'

A look.

I could hear Silk telling people he enjoyed the symmetry of being eighty-eight; that he didn't think he'd bother with eighty-nine. Silk had played make-believe with me as a child, agreeing to keep the secrets of my imaginary states, while John snarled at me to leave him alone. And now he wanted me to give up my world for his. I wouldn't. 'You had your share of affairs, too.'

John laughed. 'And how could I refuse such a good example?'

My words were scrambling. This was how it happened. John would offer a calm observation, all the crueller for its laughter. I would attempt to defend myself, or, if not myself, some sense of self. Then John would smash a phone against a table until its cogs sprang loose, as he did when I was twelve, asking, *why does everyone fucking treat me as if I'm the fucking villain?* I followed a good example, he told me now. But Silk never asked me if I wanted to be quiet or be slapped. That was when Mum stopped trying to hold the tectonic plates of our world together. When she told him to get out. And in this moment, I couldn't breathe. Was there still a hint of Rosemary's perfume in the room, or was it a remnant of Silk, using her bottles up until he died? I asked him why he wore her perfume once, during one of our last lunches as a four, before John stopped coming to Fitzroy Park. Rosemary had smiled, more arch than normal, and gone into the kitchen, saying she'd make tea.

Silk clicked his tongue and said, 'I like to have your grandmother with me always.' With that, he followed Rosemary inside.

And John had said, 'He was always good with women.'

'What?'

'He loved your mother as if she were his daughter. She read books about survivors, tried to understand him. He showed her his studio, called her his own. The divorce hurt him more than it hurt me.'

'What are you talking about?'

'He's good at getting women to like him. He wears Rosemary's perfume so she won't smell them on him. Women will always draw him, with their sympathies. He holds men at arm's length. Look at Uncle László. Family is only a use to him when it comes with compliance. And he can make women comply. Men are no use. We smell his game.'

After her first stroke Rosemary asked me, not John, to look after Silk. *He needs someone to listen.*

John nodded to my camera now. 'Why do you always retreat behind that?'

I felt as if he'd tugged it from my hand. 'I don't, always.'

'I wonder how many hours and days and weeks you could stitch together. Always recording, since Silk gave you a camera, and never seeing.'

'What am I supposed to see?'

'Sit back. Look.' John nodded to the room. 'Isn't all this a farce to you? Isn't your forgiveness a farce, another *construction*?'

Sudden tears, blinked back. 'I'm not constructing anything. This is who Silk was. A house full of friends.'

'You have no idea who he was.'

I faced him, the camera glaring up at his indolence. 'Everyone gets a story. Their story of Silk. The press gets a story. Museums get a story. You get a story. Why can't I have mine?' He said nothing. 'Go on then. Let's see you take the moral high ground. Tell me who Silk was. Tell me about lies. And while you're at it, tell me about affairs. Tell me about his son's affairs. Tell me about his son punching walls to stop himself punching his wife and expecting praise for it. Tell me about Silk's lies, lies, lies. Tell me about yours.'

John stood up. 'Not all the lies I've ever told could measure up to his.'

'If you're trying to *shock* me, then just go ahead and do it.'

John's lip curled. He swayed. He said nothing.

'I thought so.' I stood up. We were too close. 'Nothing you've ever done measures up to him.'

John shrugged. 'There it is. What chance did I ever have with you, in the face of that? What chance did I *ever* have?' He walked away before I could find words to reply, but there was no reply.

Malika found me trying to fix my mascara and hugged me there on the windowsill. 'I miss him too, darling. I miss him too.'

MUM TOPPED UP OUR wine glasses and we moved into the garden, blankets around our shoulders.

Tipping my face to the stars, I asked, 'Why did he even bother coming?'

'It's his father's funeral.'

'He didn't seem to care a few days ago.'

'You know flying here is the best he can do. For John, this is like sitting down and talking about his feelings for an hour.'

'His best isn't good enough.'

'It never has been. That's the heartbreak of his life. But you have to remember his childhood, sweetheart. You have to remember it's not your fault, or his.'

I pulled the blanket higher, thinking of the box of documents upstairs. Inside was an envelope containing a head of pollen from the Heath, plucked by a first love after a first kiss, and storyboards for films I'd never make, heirlooms of childhood I'd soon recycle. Silk called it my 'history box', telling me to keep family out of it: *Make your own history, Eva, and don't trust men with clipboards.* He said the only reason to keep the last birthday card I'd received from my father, when Mum still reminded him about my birthdays, was to cry over it. *Throw them out, and when you're old, and you sit down to write your story, the landmarks left will be your own.* As if I could edit my identity. As if, by cutting history together, I could cut it down to size, and relieve its burden on my frame. As if we choose our ghosts.

I said: 'It's not Silk's fault either.'

'Nothing is ever Silk's fault when it comes to you. Nothing has nuance,' Mum said. 'But he was the first man to admit to his own failings. He once told me, *Serenity and irony are the great human virtues – how else to face ourselves?*'

I threw my blanket off. 'How was he supposed to be a good father, after all of that?'

'All of what?'

I had put the testament in the box of documents. It lay under my bed. I didn't answer.

hole

J EEPS. THE AMERICANS ARRIVE in Jeeps. Slow crawl, people on their knees, kissing the hubcaps, grabbing American hands, *food and water, food and water.* József cannot get close enough. He is on the floor, as far as he could get from the barn where he'd been sleeping on a dead man, with a living man on top of him. He watches fights over chocolate bars, watches people eat cigarettes. Needs to get closer.

Food? Water? Inching forward, mud, boots. Americans help a man in a German uniform onto the hood of the Jeep. It is the same uniform József is wearing, taken after the SS left. The man is Magyar. Most here are. Doctors, lawyers. The ground is thick with bodies, hard to know who is alive or dead, all leached grey with sores, grey with blood. Food? Water? The Magyar on the Jeep is shouting, asking them to remain in the camp, don't clutter up the roads, let the Americans in. Food? Water? He says three thousand have already left and they died in the woods, not enough strength to get any further. Wait for food, he says. Food? Water? The Americans are bringing food and water. Cries and screams, József shouting too, throwing up nothing but bile. Food? Water?

AN AMERICAN SOLDIER HAS set up an easel in the woods. József sits, leaning against a tree a dozen paces behind the artist, water canteen pinned between his chest and his knees, the cool metal soothing the sores climbing his ribs. The sky is cut into ribbons by the knitted branches above, aquamarine ribbons, fairground ribbons. The American balances a neat box of colours on his knee. Does he have the right blue? German soldiers drag wagons into the clearing, piled with corpses. Another German detail is digging the mass grave that would have swallowed József. When the Germans see the American at his easel they wave their hands, saying, nein, nein, explaining they are nothing to do with the camp. SS, they say, it is the mess of SS. József likes how the American painter just looks at them, lips pursed, and goes on sketching.

The other Yanks – they call themselves that: it's OK buddy, the Yanks are here, just wait in line for food – watch the German detail with their hands on their guns. They want the relief of violence. József has seen the same look on a lot of Yank faces. He's seen them cry. This one here introduced himself as Sergeant Berry; he is rooting through his bag for food. József has never met a black man before.

The painter is sketching the hole where the grave will be. A boy weeps at the edge. Will he be in the painting? His brother is amongst the bodies, and he's pleading with the Germans, with the Yanks, to give his brother an individual grave. The Germans do not look at him. The Yanks try to hush him gently, but the painter gestures, leave him to it. Let the boy cry.

The Germans unload the wagons gingerly. Two days before the SS abandoned Gunskirchen they made József and those who could stand bury the dead: men who'd been shot in line for the latrine because they couldn't control their diarrhoea; men taken by starvation, disease. There were women too, though you could not recognise them as women until you were up close, even the living – except those who'd been taken and used by the SS, who had scraps of meat on their bodies, whose stomachs hung, distended, with life. But still there are corpses everywhere. Limbs and rags. Now, the Germans take off their caps and wipe the sweat from their foreheads, talking quietly, maybe complaining about how the bodies are spread out across the forest; maybe asking each other how much they knew about Gunskirchen before today, who'd seen what, who guessed what; maybe confessing: I was here.

József looks at the bodies and pictures himself among them. Twenty-four hours after liberation he had decided to die alone. He'd seen others do it, find their own private place, and thought, yes, he could at least do that. The Yanks had brought water to them in German tank wagons but it had not been enough to fill him. They raided a nearby warehouse and found noodles, potatoes, soup, meat. Some people ate too quickly and died. József tried to go slowly. Dragan had taught him that. Raw potatoes – boiling would take too long, food, he needed it now – some fruit, a tin of something. It was not enough to fill him. He lay with lice burrowing into his gunmetal sores as the sun sank, listening to the talk, to people asking the Yanks if the Soviets were nearby, what news of Hungary, was the war over? Over. A word to say slowly, find meaning in. But there is a hole in József too deep to fill. So he followed a few other men and women into the woods, on their hands and knees, no one naming what they were doing, but József thinking they were right; he did not want to die in Gunskirchen. He curled around the darkness and sank.

When he opened his eyes again a German soldier seemed to be hugging him, arms around his chest, about to lift him. The man leapt back, swearing, hand going to a weapon that was not there. József stared at him, at the stained uniform, the completely circular eyes, blue and white, wide with shock. With fear. The German did not linger. He ran. That made József blink, shift a little in the boggy mud, made soft by human shit and blood. Sun tickled his cheek, chalk-white sun. Pain swarmed in. He had lasted another night. It didn't seem to matter how many times you intended to die, or how much you hoped to live.

He followed the German detail carrying corpses to the clearing. Sergeant Berry helped him to this tree, asking if he wanted any food. József nodded. The man said he'd see what he could find, then followed József's gaze to the painter. You're in time for the art lesson, he said. That's Nichols, from Detroit. I'm Berry, from Georgia. Where you from? József tried to speak, sounded like a broken tap. The soldier cleared his own throat, passing József his water canteen. Sorry, he said. Keep it. Food, József said. The man nodded, backing away, saying he'd get food. Probably the smell, József thought, the smell of me. All the Yanks keep talking about is the smell.

The grave is almost finished. Germans stand in it, their heads popping out. József sees the silver arc of gunfire over Cservenka. Sees Dragan falling into such a pit. Or perhaps an SS officer walked Dragan down into the hole, clambering over bodies, and made him lie down in a gap left by the tangle of arms and legs in order to best use the space available. József has seen that too. He wants to tell the Yanks to shoot, let them die in the grave they dug. Shoot. *Shoot.* But they don't.

The painter has sketched in the trees and the people. He is looking at his little box now, choosing colours. Flies beat a thick cloud above the pit. The boy keeps crying. József does not try to count the number of dead. There are too many. The painter isn't counting them either. The mesh of lines is one howl. But he is sitting straight, and his concentration does not waver as he knocks the remnants of a cube of watercolour into the cup of his hand, spits, and rubs with his thumb until his hand is transformed: a fist of Prussian blue. Licking at his palm with the paintbrush, the Yank rains sky down on the canvas.

The Yanks are talking quietly. From what József understands, one man is saying he's seen Jews tearing pieces out of a dead horse and eating the meat uncooked on the edge of the forest. József wonders where the horse is, and if Berry is bringing him food. A radio crackles, and József watches Berry and the other Yanks crowd around it, voices raised. The Germans are watching too, different expressions. The painter does not look up.

Berry squelches to him, a chocolate bar in his hand.

'Sorry,' he says, 'it's all I could find.'

József reaches for it. His hand is shaking.

'Let me open it for you,' says Berry, eyes fixed on József. 'The war's over. We're hearing 'bout victories all over the radio, and my guess is we'll know pretty soon for sure. D'you understand me? The war is over?'

Berry's thumb and finger pick at the chocolate bar, the little black tab. He just has to pull and it will be open.

'I guess you don't . . . Well, second bit of good news for you, we found a German supply train, full of food, and we've pulled it up to the sidings here. Way I hear it, there was a girl Austrian at the brakes. Food, you get that?'

József puts his hand out again. Berry slices through the chocolate wrapper and gives it to him. József can't get the wrapper off. Berry squats down between József's legs, shuffling back a little – József knows Berry can see the lice moving over him like the shadow of rainclouds – and squeezes the chocolate out.

'Listen,' says Berry, 'you don't want to sit here and watch this. This is for people back home, so they'll know. But you already know, don't you? Let me give you a ride back to the camp, find you some food. We're setting up medical aid. D'you understand what I'm saying? Sorry, I don't speak no Jewish-Hungarian.'

József smiles. Who does? He stuffs melting chocolate and scabby fingers deep into his mouth.

JÓZSEF IS BILLETED IN a house in Wels. That's what the Yanks call it, billeting. He's sleeping in a young man's bedroom, the son of the house, who is with the army, the mother does not know where. The father is with the army too. Nothing to do with the camp, she said. József sleeps on the floor, his mattress three cushions. He has a pillow and a blanket. An old man took the bed. There are only two of them in the room. The walls are painted, maybe green, and there is the pale shape of a missing cross above the soldier's bed. A crucifix, perhaps removed after son and father left, in the wake of the smell coming from the forest.

József is woken by voices. A Yank, and the mother. She is assuring the Yank in stilted English that she's been feeding '*them*'. József opens his eyes. A man with dark slicked-back hair fills the doorway, an M16 hanging from one hand. The mother must be behind him.

'That true, what she's saying?' the man asks József. 'Food? You got food?'

The woman has brought food for both men, even though the man in the bed has not woken up. József has been eating his ration too, but does not nod now. Maybe the Yank will make her bring more. The woman begins to argue.

'Mother here seems to think she's bringing you the farm.'

The silence stretches until József finally nods. The woman's pace only picks up.

'You know what she's saying now?' the Yank asks.

József nods again.

'How handsome I am, right?'

The woman stops as if switched off. She turns and clatters down the stairs.

'Tough crowd,' the Yank says, glancing at the yellowed man on the bed. 'How long he been asleep?'

'I cannot tell you.'

'Good English you got. Better get a doctor out here. Not enough doctors. I'm Sorantino, from Jersey. What's your name?'

József points to his throat.

'Water? Sure.' He passes József his canteen. József tips water into his mouth as he sits up, the water sliding down his chest too, a cold relief. He leans against the wall. Sorantino sits down at the end of the bed, leaving a few inches of space between his thighs and the motionless man's feet. 'So you speak English?'

'Little.'

'And German?'

'More.'

'Any Italian?'

'Little.'

'My family is from Italy. I'm Jewish,' Sorantino says. 'My grandparents still live in Italy. And my cousins.'

József looks at the man properly, tries to pick out his eyes.

'Did you meet any Italians, in the camps?'

József drops his chin onto his chest, half a nod.

'Yeah,' Sorantino says, looking above József's head to the window. 'Yeah . . . You know, we got a sergeant from Washington DC, his parents are Jewish Poles; he found relatives in Gunskirchen, still alive. You believe that? They're billeted in one of the big town houses now. I just checked on them. Doing OK.'

'Food? Cigarettes?'

'Sure. Smoke 'em if you got 'em, as they say.' He pulls two packs from his pocket. 'One for you boys on my rounds, one for me.' He strikes a match on his thumbnail. 'To impress the girls. But I ain't seen any girls for a while. Not what you'd call girls, anyway. You haven't got any numbers on your arm. We've seen those. Were you in Mauthausen?'

'Not long.'

'I heard about what was inside.' Sorantino looks out of the window again. 'But I'm not going over there. They put me on food at Gunskirchen, now this. You should see how some of these people look at me when I ask if they're feeding you. But I guess you know already. Mostly Hungarians in the camp; I talked to some of them, said they were only just marched here in the last weeks, months. Is that what happened to you?'

'Labour service. Years.'

'I guess you've seen hell, huh?'

József sucks at the last of his cigarette, making himself dizzy.

'I sure feel like I'm in it now,' says Sorantino. 'More even than the fighting. Were you in the square yesterday, no – two days ago? VE Day, they're calling it.'

'No.'

'You hear about what happened?' Sorantino's right leg is jerking up and down, rocking the old man, who does not stir. 'We were setting up the command post in the square, establishing supply lines and communication, you know, and suddenly – like there's been some kind of signal – all the shutters on the houses open and people come flooding out, shouting to us, waving, thank God we've come, saying they're nothing to do with what's down the road. And then there's this ripple from the back, news coming through, and suddenly all the people go, kaput, like they didn't ever come out. We don't know what's happened.

'But then, down the long road leading into the square, we see shapes. People. Thousands of people. I suppose word got to Mauthausen-Gunskirchen that we were here and the inmates came, some on their knees, some walking, some with crutches, some carrying others, some looking like the effort was going to kill them but doing it anyway. Thousands. They filled the square, surrounding us. We gave out what food we had, gave out water. Everyone dressed in rags, in God knows what. And not a sound, not a question, not a thank you. Quiet right up until they began to shrink from us, as if we'd done something wrong, and I didn't get it until I heard this measured clip, boots marching. One of the German garrisons that surrendered earlier, being marched in for transportation, and the camp inmates pressing to the other side of the square.

'The Germans filed in, stopped in rank, waiting for orders. And so there we have it, Germans on one side, inmates on the other, civilians watching from their windows. And you know what? Not a word. No one said a word. You all just watched the Germans, watched us organise their transport, what prisoner camp they'd go to. Just watched. I was pretty close, looking into the inmates' eyes, for what, satisfaction I guess, justice being done, hatred, that feeling I know I had of wanting to take the nearest German soldier in his neat grey uniform and kick the shit outta him. But all those eyes looked blank to me, and no one said anything. That silence lasted for at least half an hour.' Sorantino takes a huge breath. His cigarette drips ash onto the floor, wasted. He turns to József. 'Why do you think that was, none of you said anything?'

József taps the empty canteen. 'What did you want us to say?'

'That's the thing. I don't have a damned idea.'

'When you think of it, let me know.'

'Yeah.' Sorantino smiles, eyes fixed on his cigarette. 'I guess I'm just so fuckin' angry. You didn't tell me your name. Where are you heading? I could arrange something to get you started.'

József looks at him. 'Budapest.'

the dead come to life

THE DOORS OF THERESIENSTADT are closed again, the water gates drawn, the bridges shut. Quarantine. They are not allowed out. But the ghetto has many holes, and Zuzka expects those who can walk to run away, expects to find herself alone here. But boys and girls are smuggling themselves *into* the town, and at mealtimes she hears stories of Buchenwald, Oderan, Pionki, Buna, Krawinkel, stories of return to Poland, to the Ukraine, where neighbours threw stones at them, policemen shoved them up against walls, promising to correct what must be a mistake: a Jew still alive. She hears the Czechs are the only good citizens left: that a Czech train guard held his gun to the head of an SS officer on the last day of the war and told him, 'If you hurt these children, I will shoot you where you stand.' She is told Theresienstadt is a place of refuge, a place through which to find asylum, and pride worms in her chest.

Russians urge her to go to the hospital, where Red Army doctors and local women acting as nurses will look after her, girls said to have been friendly with the SS, their heads now shaved by partisans, marks of shame hidden by scarves. Zuzka refuses. She will not go back to the hospital. She waits for typhus to reach her. She thinks she is at home turning the knob on the radio, and that is where all these languages come from, Yiddish, Russian, German, Czech, Hungarian, Polish, and yet everyone seems to understand each other, exchanging sign language and the broken ends of military phrases. She believes she is at a play watching the dead come to life. She is referred to as a 'Theresienstadter'. Permits are issued to go to Prague, where locals are giving Theresienstadters free entry to cinemas and free meals, letting them live, one girl says, wie Gott in Frankreich. That was something her grandpapa used to tell her father: *Don't be a shopkeeper,* build *shops, and don't let anyone tell you Jews can't live like God in France.* Grandpapa died of a heart attack after the Munich Agreement; Grandmama died on the march in the snow. Zuzka doesn't apply for a permit to go home.

After days, maybe weeks, she hears that the Soviets plan to take them to Russia. The girls around her debate the merits and drawbacks, but Zuzka does not join them. She slips out of the barracks, her lungs filled with the dust of punctured plaster, and follows streets she first knew by letters (Q – Queer, L – Long), and then, after beautifica-tion, by their new names, Town Hall Street, Lake Street – though there is not a lake in sight. The yellow and pink Austro-Hungarian barracks have been greyed by snow; the broken windows of the grain storage howl, every window in these last years the only light for dozens of people, their imprints left in attics, basements, sheds, casements. She passes the make-believe café they were not permitted to sit in, and the make-believe bank. She tries to remember the tune to Leopold Strauss's ghetto ditty, 'City As If'. She liked Mr Strauss.

He gave lectures on good and evil in the library. He was put on a train Fast.

The face of the bank has been smashed. Peering through the wreckage, she can see the black skeleton of stacked furniture set on fire. Papers drift through the broken window: ghetto kronen, printed for the Red Cross inspection, and now used for fuel. She flattens a singed twenty-kronen note. Zuzka was told the ghetto draughtsmen were forced to draw Moses like this, his hooked nose, his devilish beard. In revenge, the artists bent Moses' arm so that his hand obstructed the commandment Thou Shalt Not Kill. The draughtsmen were sent East, once there was no longer anything useful to draw. Some quicker than others. The SS took Bedřich Fritta to the Small Fortress, after they discovered his drawings. She heard about what they did to him there, to Leo Haas, to Otto Ungar, to all of them; heard about the broken hands, the chopped fingers.

Zuzka slips the note into her dress pocket. She has not found a coat, and her chest is pink, her feet cracked with chilblains, but she cannot feel the pain of it. She picks her way past the frost-bitten grass planted for the Red Cross team, where children fattened like geese had asked the approaching inspectors, 'Commandant Rahm, sardines again?' The girls in Zuzka's dormitory had chorused this for weeks afterwards, '*Sardines* again?' Fruit and vegetables were unloaded from rustic carts as the inspectors passed by, and white-gloved bakers sorted fresh rolls. The smell drifted to the bandstand where Zuzka waited, and she can still taste the saliva that pooled around her bleeding gums, taste the memory of birthdays at Imperial Café. Her mother had always been proud that her grandmother was the first woman to join the Jewish musicians' guild, and bought Zuzka her first violin when Zuzka was four. As the SS and Red Cross neared the gazebo, Zuzka raised her bow as she had been taught, and a goal was scored at the football match, as if by providence, and shouts of joy went up, startling no birds, for there were no birds or butterflies in Theresienstadt. There were elements of this world that Commandant Rahm could not control: that was what she told herself. But she knew that life stayed away from the camp because human beings were eating the grass threading of nests and the sustenance of insects.

Zuzka climbs the steps to the gazebo. Around her, life has gone – the tens of thousands, the swell of them, the force of them, the songs, the journals, the insistence: as long as we're creating, we're alive. The square is quiet, the hands of the clock tower still, the church empty. Her neck is stiff and her jaw locked, her head pulsing with too much blood. She is sealed into her body. They had played waltzes, and marches, and folk songs, and the Commandant told the Red Cross inspectors that the Jews enjoyed a thriving musical scene. Zuzka kept her eyes on the strings. She could not look at Rahm's face. They had cleared the ghetto of over seven thousand people before the inspection. They put her mother on a train to Auschwitz, and three days later she played her violin.

Afterwards, the girls in the dye workshop asked Zuzka if she would play her violin again in Kurt Gerron's film, and Zuzka dipped the olive shirt into the white bath, her hands slipping into the cool dye, and said nothing. The liquid inched over her skin, into the cuts, around the bones and knuckles, and her whole hand turned white, like an X-ray. Her uncle told her that the man who first invented X-rays showed his wife the inside of her hand and she went insane. Why? *Ah, to see yourself without flesh*, Uncle said, *is to see death*. Zuzka looked at her hands. What of it? She could see death in the play of her fingers, in the trembling of a knuckle. She had played her violin.

There is movement in the barracks, a door opening, and Zuzka watches hundreds of men and women shuffle out. The Danes. They used to joke that the Danes were the only wanted Jews in Europe. The story went that the Danish King shipped nearly all of his Jewish population to freedom overnight, leaving only four hundred for Hitler to scoop up and send to Theresienstadt. After they arrived, Danish Red Cross packages were the only food sustaining the black market. And now the King of Denmark has sent buses to bring them all home again. Zuzka looks up into the ivy-covered shell of the gazebo. She is home already. In all of the war, she has never been more than thirty-five miles outside of Prague. But after so many years of planning – for the potatoes sunk to the bottom of the soup, for the attic to hide in, the bricks to stand on to make her taller for inspection, the friends to close ranks around so the SS wouldn't see their open wounds – now she has achieved the survival her mother and uncle told her she *must* deliver, for their family, now she can think without fear, can *think* at all, there are no plans left. There is nowhere to go, and no one is coming to claim her.

'PAVEL IS DEAD.'

László stares at the twitchy boy. 'What?'

'He ate too much pig.'

László looks over the boy's shoulder, where other children are filing onto a bus. They are no longer going to Russia, and the British Mandate Authority has refused entry to Palestine, but the Jews of

Britain want them. Three hundred will go to Prague, then to England. László didn't think he'd make it, in and out of life in the hospital, waking with violence to protect his slice of bread. A Czech woman with soft hands taught him how to walk again. Reds and Yanks and Poles and men from the Jewish Brigade and others with PALESTINE stamped on their epaulettes gave him biscuits and cheese.

'A few others died, too,' says the boy. 'They looted a ton of chocolate from Travčice. Gorged on it. Pavel was vomiting for days in the hospital.'

'Greed doesn't pay, my mother always said. She had a funny view of economics.'

'What?'

László shrugs.

'Do you know where your family are?'

Rumours are static in the air. The communities of Eastern and Central Europe are gone. Jewish life in Europe is dead. He's heard about the labour battalions in the Ukraine and Serbia, about the last Jews of Hungary hiding in cellars and attics, about the *Nyilas* seizing whatever gold was left hidden in hollowed table legs or coat linings, these last talismans of a future, and shooting people where they stood; torturing patients, doctors and nurses in Moros Street Hospital; shooting children into the Danube; raiding the Glass House and killing Jews with protective papers. He avoids his own eyes in the reflection of the bus. 'Maybe England,' he says, and joins the queue. Everybody is talking and laughing, even the little ones, boys and girls four years old, five, six – it's impossible to tell, they're so thin. Going to England. The phrase is magical. London and the King are a better bet than the Reds, even if they did save us. The SS are scared of them, and that goes both ways. A sharp bead of pain makes László lift his shirt. A red rash crawls over his torso. He hugs his coat around his body and closes his eyes, falling asleep on his feet.

When he wakes he is almost at the bus. A Russian soldier checking them off the list snaps, 'Vy, potoropis.' László digs his heels into the dirt. A girl he hasn't noticed before is standing a few feet from the queue. An apparition bruised into being. She reminds him of Violetta Napierska in that postcard József pinned up in their bedroom, her eyes turned down in sadness, but such big eyes, and so deep she could brush gold dust over them with the length of her thumb. But this girl's eyes are blackened not burnished, and the dark curls fall in dry knots. The bones of her face have been sanded to an edge. Her body is the same. She is all corner, all shadow. But she still reminds him of József's pin-up.

'Potoropis.'

László waves, gesturing the girl to go in front of him. She looks surprised, as if seeing her requires a special skill. But she responds, climbing into the bus. László follows, giving the Red a look of what he hopes is defiance but his body isn't playing along, his legs failing on the final step – the girl catches his sleeve. Closer, her eyes are the amber bed of a cloudy stream. He closes his hand around hers. Her bones are so delicate he feels they might break under his grip. He sits down. The girl's hand remains in his. She seems not to realise. He holds on to her all the way to Prague.

#onthisday

THE CLATTERING REFRAIN OF Silk's sleepless mornings made me fumble, the bin bag sagging, the congealed potato salad sliding down the plate. Dawn touched the windows of the Blue Room, framing John's back-and-forth. I set the plate down, trying to control the trembling of my hand as I reached for the kettle.

'I wasn't expecting you until later,' I said, opening the door to the studio.

John gestured to the painting half finished on the easel. 'This is you?'

'How can you tell?'

John shrugged.

I gathered my voice. 'About yesterday. Are you OK?'

He smiled. 'Have you come to comfort me in my time of grief?'

'I don't know how to comfort you. But I would if you'd let me.'

He sat down on the ragged sofa, leaning his head back.

I placed the coffee on the side table, then backed away. 'You didn't say what you thought of the service. The eulogy.'

John shook his head. 'When are you going to stop doing that?'

'Doing what?'

'Seeking fatherly approval.'

'I wasn't aware that's what I was doing.'

'You weren't? OK. I thought your eulogy was saccharine and insipid.'

I took a deep breath. 'Do you even hear yourself sometimes?' I sat down in front of the easel in Silk's director's chair. 'I remember when I was younger, telling you about a school play or something, and you said, *What makes you think I'm interested?* I remember telling you it was normal to expect your dad to be interested. It's normal to seek fatherly approval.'

John looked at his boot tip, turning his foot this way and that. 'I don't remember saying that.'

'You never do. Which makes it worse. If what you say means so little to you, why say it at all?'

John poured himself coffee, stirring it with the end of a paintbrush. 'Rosemary once told me the reason I had so much trouble with you is because we're too similar.'

'How convenient.'

'All your questions. I used to have questions. I just didn't know how to ask them. You do. But you're asking the wrong man.'

I tried to box my rising bile, to smile. 'You're the last man standing.'

He rolled his eyes.

'What questions do you want me to be asking?'

John paused over the coffee. 'None.' He passed me a cup. 'You've got to learn to recognise when a man grandstands, Eva.'

It was like this, sometimes – ice or maudlin or fury, and then he'd become an outside observer of himself, calm, fatalist, and we would shake our heads together over his flaws, as if they were the flaws of a friend we knew well, loved, and pitied. But I knew this wasn't John grandstanding. *Lies, lies, lies.* He didn't mean affairs, and I didn't think he meant Silk's first life either, the testament, or Silk's age. He didn't want to know about that: hated Silk's silence, but wanted it filled with something other than his father's pain. Wanted a space for his own pain. *Lies, lies, lies.*

'Silk would have told me whatever it is you think you know,' I said.

I wasn't convincing myself, and the thought tipped me with vertigo. He had lied to me. I told Silk everything: my fears, my loves, my pains. He told me his dreams. I thought he trusted me. Silk was the only man who'd ever made me feel special just by looking at me. It was something I'd guarded, this tie. This knot of pride, love, vanity. Burden.

John plucked at the throw draped over the sofa, working his finger into a hole. 'The muse's couch,' he said. 'I remember this French actress posing for Silk when I was thirteen or so. I had a poster of her in my school locker. Silk got tickets to a play she was in and took me backstage to meet her. I only wanted her autograph, but he asked her if she'd model for him. He did it so casually, as if there was nothing more normal in the world than asking every man's fantasy to take her clothes off for him. And she said yes. Immediately. So, one day I come home and I see from the kitchen that he has company in the Blue Room. And it's her. She's sitting on the couch, completely naked, and he's sketching. As if there's nothing more normal in the world. I sat down outside the door and listened. They were talking about parenting. Silk suddenly had opinions on parenting. She was telling him that her son cries when he sees her on set. He doesn't like her looking different. And Silk said, *Why should he, when you're so beautiful as you are?* I remember the way she looked at him, how she said: *Mr Silk, is this the part where you try to seduce me?*

As a child, I curled up on that sofa and read aloud to Silk while he painted, and he'd turn and smile when I managed difficult words. 'Do you remember what happened next?'

John closed his eyes. He looked exhausted. 'Something about Robert Graves. He told her . . . he told her that Robert Graves said a beautiful muse could put an end to total wars, machines of destruction and unregulated finance systems. She said, *Is that what I'm doing for you?* And he put down his brush and told her, *Well, you're doing something.* He'd never seemed cooler. And I'd never hated him more.'

'Where was Rosemary?'

'I don't know.'

'Did they . . . I mean, did you see . . . ?'

John opened his eyes. 'Would you be less righteous and pissed off at me if I did *see*? Would that help explain it all to you?'

'John. Dad.'

'Is it because what I did was less glamorous? When I had affairs it was with women who were depressed and lonely? Because your mother had to take my *mistress* to the hospital after she arrived at the house having cut her wrists, while Silk slept with breakfast television intellectuals?'

I swallowed. I felt faint. 'Is *what* because?'

'Forgiveness for him is unconditional, and for me it's . . . unforthcoming.'

'It's because you frightened me, and he never did.' It came out as a whisper. I couldn't complete the rest of it. *It's because he loved me, and you never did.*

John drummed the paintbrush against the sofa. 'I suppose I did frighten you. It's not a nice thought, but I suppose I did.'

'You once took me to a building site you were developing, but you'd forgotten the key, so you lost it and tried to kick the door in. And you *suppose* you frightened me?'

'I do remember that. I remember I wanted to show you my work. But I fucked it up. Of course I remember the things I say. I remember telling you to call me John, telling you I didn't want to be a father. I don't. OK? I never did. But you still got a father, in him. I didn't get one. I just got a self-pitying narcissist. And I'm not allowed to feel aggrieved?'

'Well.' I put my cup down, and stood up. 'While you're busy feeling aggrieved, the rest of us are grieving. So go do it somewhere else, will you?'

I left him in the Blue Room, the acid taste of relief at finally having walked away turning to poison as I looked over my shoulder, and saw him slowly fold at the waist, his hands interlinked, his head dropping, as if he had been forced to submit before the temple of Silk's blue.

JOHN LEFT. I NODDED to him, a gap of six feet between us.

I took Mum to Heathrow, where we stood entwined at Departures. I felt like I was six years old and would have a tantrum just to keep her here.

The house went on the market soon after, and I gave tours to hoteliers and bankers. I liked the man best who asked what my grandfather had done for a living. 'Ah,' he said, 'that explains the walls.'

I followed @yadvashem on Twitter, the Holocaust Memorial Centre in Jerusalem, who produced litanies: *#onthisday a transport to a murder site was held with no food & water for 3 days so the SS could go on holiday #onthisday Tova Mendel, Salomon Findling & their children were deported from #Stropkov, #Slovakia*. The void was open, and I filled it with numbers, though it failed to fill. The European elections passed. The *Guardian* called the UKIP gains a storm to victory. In France, Le Front National gained 25 per cent of the vote. Greece's Golden Dawn received 9 per cent. In Germany, the National Democratic Party, modelled after the Nazis, gained its first seat in the European Parliament. My phone kept chiming, telling me that #onthisday an unidentified Jew from Hungary arrived @ Auschwitz, telling me that on this day in the twenty-first century four people were shot and killed outside the Jewish Museum in Brussels.

I ignored interview requests from the *Guardian* and *Camden New Journal*. I arranged removal vans and filled two skips. I burrowed into Google, ordering books – Primo Levi and Imre Kertész, Martin Gilbert and Randolph L. Braham. I discovered that Braham, Hungary's foremost historian of the Holocaust, had recently given his medals of honour back to the government, because of what he described as the 'history-cleansing campaign of the past few years calculated to whitewash the historical record' in order to 'absolve Hungary from the active role it had played in the destruction of close to 600,000 of its citizens of the Jewish faith'. I found photos on Twitter of protestors tearing tarpaulin from a statue the Hungarian government were erecting to commemorate their national suffering. Braham said it was an attempt to 'homogenise the Holocaust with the "suffering" of the Hungarians – a German occupation, as the record clearly shows, that was not only unopposed but generally applauded'.

Braham's words made me realise how little I knew about Hungary, then and now. I pored over his chapter on 'Labor Serviceman at Bor, Yugoslavia': Braham told me that, after the march, after the camps, 'only a handful survived'. I felt Silk's hand on mine, urging me to close the book. I pushed him away. I longed for him to come back. He wouldn't.

I HAD NOT TOUCHED the Blue Room. Winston said we should use bubble wrap on the rocks of amethyst and bottles of Evian: Robert Graves's children had turned his home into a museum, let people lie on the muse's couch. I said I'd deal with it alone.

I had asked John, what are you not telling me? If John wouldn't answer, if Silk would exhort me to pack this history away, if both men were determined to leave me alone with their ghosts, I would do it by myself.

I searched through envelopes filled with tiny squares of oceans snipped from atlases, and comics from the 1970s, Batman's blue-black cowl. I crawled under Silk's desk, hauling out a bucket of broken blue china, and a small pine trunk with blue letters stamped onto the lid:

AGRICULTURAL EXPORT CO LTD

TEL-AVIV

KCS PACKER

EGGS

PRODUCE OF ISRAEL

To my knowledge, Silk had never received or kept a package from Israel. I almost used my toe to urge the trunk back under the desk, but then I remembered John's laughter. I forced the stiff lid open, and held my breath. Inside, a lump of lapis lazuli the size of a human heart glittered weakly. It was bound with string, a small tag: *Sar-E-Sang, Afghanistan*, a place of blue seasons, the veins of lapis lazuli only accessible once the snows on the mountain pass had melted. Silk had tried to go there over the years, stopped by wars. Next to the stone was a bundle of airmail envelopes. The return address belonged to László Zyyad. I thumbed through the bunch. Most of the stamps were Israeli, decorated with Hebrew letters and faded pomegranate. Some showed the Queen: Silk's replies. Why would Silk have letters he'd sent to László?

The envelope that seemed most thumbed was date-stamped weeks before László died, and I knew why Silk had his letters back. László's friends must have sent Silk's few replies to him after the funeral.

József –

Have you seen the footage of Muhammad al-Durrah's death? No one knows – or isn't saying – who loaded the bullet, who pulled the trigger. Barak and Arafat keep saying we must have peace for the children. For how many decades have we children needed peace.

I must tell you – I think something is wrong inside me, inside all of us. I must tell you a daydream I keep having, one that feels so real I am ready to follow its instructions. Or perhaps it's a nightmare. I give my telephone and radio to charity. I drop my car keys down a storm drain. I do not travel anywhere, do not swim in public baths, avoid pastry shops and espresso stands. I consider giving away my gold watch and Star of David to a non-religious Jew but remember that Christians who agreed to safeguard such treasures were tortured; that others reported the transaction to the police. I see Arrow Cross officers in the streets of Tel Aviv – Magyar Nazis, let's call them – forcing old men to strip and beating their bare backsides with rubber truncheons until the skin is sloughed off, flayed until bones break, liquids shoot out. I see hunchbacks forced to perform gymnastics. It isn't until I tear the house apart in search of my car keys that I realise exactly what I am doing, and why. I want to gas myself in the garage, but can't, because I've dropped my keys down a storm drain, as per the orders of the Magyar government.

Instead, I give my television away, so I can avoid watching Muhammad's death another time.

I must tell you that I do not know how our mother died. She might have been put on a list of leading journalists and artists the same day the SS arrived. She might have been called up for labour service on 2nd November 1944 because she knew how to sew. She might have marched what became known as the highway of death, or the Arrow Cross might have taken her from our yellow-star home to a train station. I saw a train full of women when I was taken, naked, dead, so starved they were just bone. She might have been one of them.

I must tell you that the ease with which a human being can disappear haunts me. I must tell you that sometimes I imagine our father surviving, imagine him returning to Budapest in 1947 from a POW camp in the Soviet Union. I imagine his pain at discovering we did not wait for him. I must tell you that when I see children die I think, always, first, of Alma. I must tell you, and the fact that I must tell *you*, shows me that my life here is exactly the same fantasy, the same daydream, that has me searching now for my car keys.

I scrabbled for Silk's reply, needing his reassurance, but found nothing. I opened another letter from László, decades earlier, postmarked 1967.

József,

I am told your exhibition was a great success. My congratulations. I did not hear back from you after my last letter. I journey to Auschwitz and that doesn't get your attention. Now we know Father died there, isn't it the only grave we can visit? Maybe you disagree, maybe you don't, but I can only know if you write back.

I finally have news about Alma, and I'll confess to considering not giving it to you, or even holding the information hostage, forcing you to ask for it, or to say no to it. But I am not as cruel as you; or perhaps I am. You do not wish to know, you've made that clear, but I cannot be the only one sitting shiva, and I will put cloth over your mirrors even if it is selfish – and it is. So do stop reading here, big brother, if you would rather ~~stay in the dark~~ not know.

I found Alma's name on a list of 'Christian' children living in a protected house. As far as I understand it, the Arrow Cross learnt these children were Jews and removed them from the home. They were made to walk barefoot in the snow down to the bank of the Danube, and then the Arrow Cross men started shooting. They shot four children into the river, and the rest began to cry and scream, and the men let them go. I think Alma was one of the four.

A boy who survived had five toes cut off because of the frostbite. I sent him a description of Alma, and he says he thinks he remembers a girl matching it, though of course it's only my memory of our sister, with nothing else left. But Alma Zyyad is an unusual name, and I've found it nowhere else.

Do you think it was Alma? Do you think Mother put Alma in the protected house, or was that someone else's work? I'd like to think she thought Alma was safe. God knows what she thought of you and me, or Father. At least she thought she had saved Alma.

Write back, József. Did I lose all my family in the Shoah?

László

I slipped Silk's reply free, my shaking hand threatening to tear the paper.

My disinclination to engage with this history of yours does not constitute a crime against you. It simply means that I have chosen a different history. As for the rest — the crimes we can count, the crimes I am accountable for — let's say I was blind in more ways than one. I didn't see how deep your feelings ran. I couldn't see you, then. You remember jumping in that lake? I should have been keeping an eye on you, but I couldn't bear to look at your pain. And so I missed things. Important things. And for that I am sorry. But that's all you get from me, and you're lucky to get it, after what you did to me in return. You wish to tell me so much now – you should have told me what mattered, then. Maybe I could have stopped it. I should at least have been allowed to try. Please, leave me be now, László.

I didn't know what Silk was talking about. What had Great-Uncle László done to him? And in return for what? *Lies, lies, lies.*

László's answer was heavy with ink, as if stamped by the weight of his need to be understood.

József – or Silk, as it seems the world calls you now – I don't know how you can talk about crime, when you refuse to acknowledge the great crime – the greatest crime – that you and I were victim of, witness to. Don't you see that what happened to us, what happened between us, was the result of the Shoah? We kept warring. Don't you see that? We might have stopped scheming for bread and water, but we were both still afraid of air running out. We were muscling each other for space, for the space to self-define. Don't you see that forgiveness is the only answer? You were so rigid with me. And so deceiving of Z. If I can forgive you that, can't you see that I was only doing my best by her, my best to survive? I was a young man, ageing fast. I feel too old for the revolutionary spirit of this decade. I was old at fourteen. England is no place for you. I read about the graffiti in east London, the swastika and those words: WE

ARE BACK. I suppose you'll tell me that the scrawled 'sod off' beneath the swastika is good enough for you. But you must see England isn't your home. We can only age together. Israel is our clock now. I wish you'd come and see me. I'll only know how old I am when I see my big brother. Come and kick me in person. Isn't that the man's way? I am teaching history now. I am seeing a woman from the school. Life in the White City is beautiful. But the happier I become, the worse my nightmares are. One day, they'll take over. Come and save me, come and kick me, whichever, just come.

Your öcs

I replaced the letter carefully. *So deceiving of Z* – I didn't know who Great-Uncle László meant. Of the women Silk had deceived, I couldn't name one whose name began with a Z. Perhaps Rosemary could have. Perhaps John could. What personal crime took place between them – between all of them?

I pulled a blanket around my shoulders, retreating to the couch. These letters were a breach that scared me, and I wished now that I'd obeyed their unwritten FOR YOUR EYES ONLY, that I had obeyed Silk's limited vision, kept within his eye line, as he used to tell me on the beach: *Stay where I can see you.* I didn't understand this new vision of him, and didn't want to. I wanted the blue around me. I wanted the man I knew. I wanted his lies.

I was just what John had accused me of: a little girl, hiding behind my camera, asking to be deceived. Asking to grieve, not to be aggrieved. Asking for a good father. I wriggled out of the blanket, stubbing my toe on the coffee table, and pressed CALL as pain throbbed through my body.

'Ja?'

'It's me. Eva Butler.'

'Oh.' Felix cleared his throat. 'Hello. It is most good to hear from you.'

'I'm sorry to call you.'

'You are?'

'I meant, I don't want to bother you.'

'You are not bothering,' he said. 'How are you?'

I turned my back on the Blue Room, walking through to the empty living room. The imprint of removed furniture left its dye-pattern on the walls. 'We had the funeral,' I said.

'I heard. How was the eulogy?'

'OK.'

'Did your father attend?'

'Yes.'

'Ah. How was this?'

'Not as bad as it could have been. Not good. We're selling the house.'

'Do you have a buyer?'

'Yes. But there are still small things to decide, whether to keep his cufflinks, things like that. The clean-up. Listen, the reason I'm calling . . . can I ask you something?'

'Certainly.'

'Do you know of anybody – a woman – in Silk's history whose name began with a Z?'

174

'No . . . why?'

'It's nothing. At least, I think it's nothing. What was your reaction, when you heard Silk was dead?'

A long silence. 'I cried.'

I sat down on the edge of the remaining chair. 'I thought you might be interested in seeing the Blue Room.'

'Pardon me?'

'I haven't sorted out the Blue Room yet. I just thought you might like to see it.'

There was no breathing at the other end. 'Why would you show it to me?'

'Because you are a safe person. And if you're going to be writing about him in the future, I mean, maybe you'd like to see it.'

'I would. Very much.'

'OK then.'

'Would you — is this an invitation to me as a representative of the museum, or me as . . . me?'

'If it's the museum?'

'I'd like to take photographs for the exhibition.'

'So he's still going to be in the show?'

'Yes.'

I skirted my feet through floorboard dust.

'I could just take them and we could agree later on whether they are used?'

'Maybe this isn't a good idea.'

'I will come as only myself. If you would like me to.'

I looked at the champagne oval where a mirror had once hung. My shadow vibrated against the wall. 'I would like you to.'

'I will let you know when I am to arrive?'

'Thanks, I mean, fine. Goodbye.'

'Auf wiedersehen.'

I hung up as my phone chimed that #onthisday the BBC had reported an estimated 700,000 Jews had been murdered in Poland.

a painted egg on his tongue

JÓZSEF IS DRIVEN TO Vienna in the back of a truck with four American war correspondents, friends of Sorantino, who ask him questions and frame his answers in telegramese. WHEN WE UPCATCH FINAL NAZI WE'LL FIND THE LAST JEW SKELETON IN HIS TEETH LIKE TRACKED TIGER CARRYING LAST KILL STOP. He wants to tell them, *Make a note that those are your words, not mine.*

THE RUSSIAN DOCTOR IN Vienna holds the cutters to his rotten toe and tells him to take a deep breath, about to snap the blade shut while asking, 'You're from Budapest?'

József nods.

The doctor smiles. 'You're welcome.'

Budapest has been liberated. His heart kicks into life as the blades close.

*

THE BROWN RABA SURGING into the blue Danube. Dragun tells him, look, Bus, you can still see the world.

A CONVOY OF RUSSIAN vehicles. He had passed Soviet soldiers rounding Magyars and Germans into boxcars at Sopron's railway station. A Roma on the road, still wearing the striped shirt of his camp, had told József the Red Army were taking soldiers back to Russia as forced labour. They have lists, the man said, not names but numbers: how many to take back, it doesn't matter who you are. Make sure you're not wearing any military insignia and tell them you are a Jew. József had asked: Will that stop them taking me? It might. Now, the first and second trucks in the convoy pass, showering him in dust, but the third jerks to a halt. József puts his hands up, saying, 'Zsidó, Juden,' his heart thumping. It is like giving away a hiding place, a crypt where you have kept yourself, before the interrogator has even asked.

The driver closes one eye against the sun and says, 'Budapest?'

'Yes, sir, comrade.'

The man nods him onto the back of the truck. József looks at the people inside. They are reflections of himself. He does as he is told.

Settling on a wooden bench, he squeezes between a shirtless man and a girl whose hair is growing back in patches.

She smiles at him so he says: 'Time to learn Russian for *Jew*.'

'I don't think they care,' she says. 'Isn't it a relief not to be someone's biggest problem?'

*

WOMEN WATCH THEM FROM doorsteps with sour expressions, as if this convoy is a sight they've had to chew over for too long. He was dreaming, before a crater in the road woke him. Dreaming of their apartment on Falk Miksa Utca: a family dinner. They are approaching Herceghalom, and the mountains glint bone-white through dense trees. The houses and stations have been splintered by bombing. József swallows, a gruesome crackling, no spittle to soothe his throat. He has to get home.

Next to him, the girl, who is called Margit, says, 'Will they throw us a grand parade, do you think? Hail the returning Jews, how sad we were to see you go.'

He manages a half-smile. 'I'll settle for a street named after me.'

'You think small.'

'Most of my wit resided in my big toe.'

'A great tragedy then.'

'Yes,' he says, looking at the line of trucks behind them, men and women and children crowded awkwardly around munitions and food crates, which they break into with quick hands and nervous, shrewd eyes. 'A great tragedy. Are your family with you?' he asks, looking around at the others. He will not tell her his name, he has decided – he realised on the road how many months he'd gone without telling anyone, and feels it now like a painted egg on his tongue, taking up space in his mouth. Useless to swallow it, unwilling to spit it out.

'Not anymore,' says Margit. 'My mother and sister, we were put onto the trains together last year. But – not anymore. My father was in labour service in Ukraine.'

'So was mine. Have you heard from him?'

'No. Some American soldiers told me most of the Magyar units were wiped out. Some were taken prisoner by the Red Army.'

József's throat closes. 'Jews too?'

'Yes.'

'What will you do?'

The girl shakes her head. 'What about you?'

'I'm sure everyone will be there when I get back,' he says. 'I'm sure you will find your father waiting for you, too.'

THE HILLS ARE SPECKED with grey roofs that were once sunburnt red to him and Budapest is near: first the outer towns, all crumbled, and then the workers' suburbs, the apartment blocks punched, squashed. He does not look at Margit. The Reds drive them through City Park, where trees are torn down, to Heroes' Square, as if they really will have the parade Margit wanted. Most of the Magyar chieftains are intact.

'Ruins,' says Margit, drawing József's attention forward.

They are driving down Andrássy út, and at the far end he can see the Buda Hills, the green line trembling, and he knows the Danube is waiting for him. The river cannot be destroyed – but Andrássy út has been stamped to the ground. This street he knew for its grand shops, the New York Kávéház where his father would smoke and drink coffee with writers and thinkers, the Parisian shops, the gilded crenellations and balconies, they are all ruins dripping with blue: facades peeling and punctured, girders on the floor, signs upside down, crevices filled with collapsed rubble. He sees a chandelier hanging in a half-bombed apartment where nothing else has survived. People on the street stop to watch the convoy. A tram rumbles by in the opposite direction, and the boys hanging out the back stare with open curiosity. A little girl in a blue silk tattered dress waves at him and he lifts his hand in return. Her mother nods so familiarly he wonders if they know him. No. Only Mama will recognise his face now. The interrogation building has fared a little better, propped up by wooden stilts. Russian and American soldiers pass through the ruined doorway.

He says, 'They can never rebuild all of this.'

Margit shakes her head. 'Who wants it? I'm not staying here. How could we, after this?'

'Where would you go?'

'America. Anywhere. Look,' she says, gesturing to the Opera House, which has sagged to its knees. 'Give them the shops and apartments left standing, the spoils, give it all to the Magyars, to the Reds, to the Allies. Let them keep it. *We* are not the ruins they want. My father won't be there, your father won't be there. We're what's left. And they don't want us.'

József says nothing. He has thought it all before, a terrible kaddish with each step over another dead man, another dead woman. As he left Dragan behind. As he left Radnóti behind. Father will not be there. László will have been taken to the camps. László, gone. Mama, Alma – the Soviets in Vienna told him Jews were still alive in the Budapest ghetto. József dries his eyes. His mother will be there, with Alma, their home restored, as the Russians and Americans and British reset the board; his mother will be waiting for him. He has to get off the truck; he has to get to her now.

'If you need anything,' he says to Margit, 'come to 6 Falk Miksa út and ask for Emmuska.'

'Is that your mother?'

'Yes.'

She gives him a pitying smile but he does not bother to argue: he is clambering over legs, over a woman with flies in the open wound of her cheek, climbing to the back and jumping out. Skipping over the tramline and onto the pavement, scattering the crowd there. His foot seizes and he is left to limp and hop the length of Andrássy út, past the shops that are still open, past a wave of coffee, and into the side streets, snow-slides of rubble as the August sun tracks him. When he reaches Szent István krt he steps onto a tram and the passengers shrink. He says nothing to soothe their anxiety, just stares. The woman nearest is wearing a mink coat. She has her hand to her mouth, and he can see that the cuff is matted, a cat in a storm. He smiles at her, showing his canines. Ahead, Margit Bridge looks jagged, but he cannot spare a step further to see if it is damaged, because Falk Miksa út is on his left. Home.

There are bullet holes in the walls and he hurries, dragging his bad foot, darting between people with their shopping, past the open door of an antique shop – a flash of radios and telephones that do not look antique – and on, until he arrives almost on his knees at number four.

He has no key.

He prepares to shout, but the iron door opens. A soldier, half his face bandaged. He slips around the man and into the courtyard.

'Mama! Alma!'

A crooked lady emerges from number two.

'Tell them I'm coming!' he shouts, dragging himself up the stairs. The old lady slips inside. He doesn't care. He's home.

The green door, the basket empty of flowers. The lock is blasted and twisted: shot open. Bile surges up his throat. He hammers on the wood, sudden strength in him.

He is ready to kill any soldier he finds inside, any man he does not recognise. He is ready, now, to kill.

The door opens. A woman his mother's age, but not his mother. Blue eyes.

'Go away,' she says.

'Where's my mother?'

'Go away. This isn't your house.'

'Isn't my . . .' She is small and he looks over her shoulder, sees the tall window of the dining room, sees the carpet from his father's dye workshop, and pushes his way in. The woman backs up rapidly, more scared of him than he can warrant. Blood rushes to his head, a buzzing crowding his vision. He shuts the door behind him, locking it.

'Go away!'

'No,' he says, looking around. 'Where is my mother?'

'This isn't your house. We were given it. The government gave it to us. We deserved it.'

'Why? Did a Jewish grocer put you out of business?'

She glances from him to the locked door. 'My husband's here.'

'Then he's a pretty poor husband.'

He looks through the open doors into the living room. There is the marble-topped sideboard, his father's decanters. Bullet holes stud the patterned wallpaper, which dances in his vision, as if pouring with rain.

'He's coming home soon.'

'This isn't your home. Where is my mother?'

'I don't know. Please, I don't know.'

'She hasn't come back?'

'No.'

József moves further into the apartment. She backs away from him. He bends to the fireplace and picks up a long-handled brush. He remembers the girl from the plains sweeping out the grate of their old home; remembers his mother bending over this one.

'I'll scream. I'll shout for help.'

He takes a few paces around the dining room, looking at the pictures on the walls. None of them belong to his family but they are in the same positions, using the same nails.

'I tried that once,' he tells her. 'Shouting for help. You know what good it did?' He lifts one of the paintings off the nail by an inch, peering underneath. 'They left me hanging another hour.'

'Get out.'

He lifts another painting, replaces it.

'It must be nice. Knowing you can scream for help and someone will answer. But maybe not. You haven't shouted yet. Maybe you don't think your neighbours will come running. Maybe some of them are *my* neighbours.'

Another painting.

'I'm telling you to leave. This isn't your house. I'll have you arrested.'

The last painting. And there it is: László's initials scratched into the wallpaper. 'Not my house?' József drops the picture. Glass sprays the floor. He knocks on the wall with the end of the brush. 'My brother did that with his penknife. Our nanny hit him so hard he almost blacked out.' He faces the woman. Grips the brush. 'I could hit you harder.'

184

The woman holds her cardigan around her body, her expression faltering between fear and stubborn pride that won't let her back down, as if backing down means losing the argument, as if losing the argument means losing everything. He strides past her to the main bedroom, his parents' bedroom. He doesn't cross the threshold. It's the same bed, and he wants to drop to his knees and bury his face there, but it's not the same smell. The bristles of the brush sliver his palm but he does not loosen his hold. He has nothing else to hold on to. He sways in the door, looking at the bedhead, the blue dye of the material. He moves down the hallway, peering into László and Alma's room, then his own, empty of their belongings. The shell of it.

'There was nothing here when we moved in.' Her voice is smaller now. 'Just — just these few things.'

He turns, seeing the woman at the far end of the hall. He leans against the doorframe, finding that he suddenly cannot move at all.

'Where is my mother?'

'The ghetto,' she breathes. 'Try the ghetto.'

'Where?'

'The Jewish Quarter.'

'Thank you.'

He moves towards her and she flinches against the wall. He replaces the brush, carefully, and takes a final look around. Then walks out, closing the door behind him. He points his body towards the Danube, and when he finally looks up he finds that the bridges are down. Chain Bridge is sunken into the river, its girders shuddering and confused.

*

'I AM LOOKING FOR my mother.'

The Russian soldier shrugs and steps out of his way.

'Thank you.'

József staggers on.

The ghetto is in ruins like everywhere else, but he thinks there is a different smell here, and there are more British and Russian soldiers. He doesn't want to know what the smell is. The Great Synagogue has survived. The bronze and golden domes, the red-brick, the white of the Heroes' Temple, all a ghostly pale to him but standing, standing. He limps to the open arches of the Meditation Garden – and stops.

The ground is uneven, broken by mounds he knows with one look, covered in haphazard headstones, the markers leaning against each other. *Sándor. Langer. Goldberger. 1945. 1945. 1945.*

'They're only guesses.'

József jumps, scrambling away from the hand coming down on his shoulder. The woman looks at him with a curious smile.

'The stones. They were left by people who think their family might be down there. You've just come back?'

'I'm looking for my family.'

'The old Zionist institute on Bethlen Gábor tér is helping people. You should go there.'

'Will they know where my mother is?'

'They might.'

He looks back at the markers.

'We were lucky,' the woman says, 'in the ghetto. We're the only ones left, apart from you boys and girls returning. And there are so few of you.'

'Lucky?'

She smiles. He thinks he sees tears in her eyes. 'We need new words, you think?'

He looks at her. Only if we wish to speak.

do not deny the truth to anyone

ZUZKA HURTLES DOWN THE winding staircase, past open rooms where she sees the angel of death playing cards. She had followed him onto the bus because of the black blood spattered on his coat, blood that must have belonged to somebody else, for surely so much loss would have killed him. That seemed like good luck to her. She followed because of his dirty golden hair, and his soft eyes. She followed because he was short but stocky and young but somehow very old. She followed because she followed, and now she runs, the question on his face staying with her as she bursts through a group of women to the door. She had closed her eyes when they arrived, the angel guiding her into the hostel, and kept them closed, unable to stay, unable to leave, until the pips of a piccolo flute from somewhere above thrust her from the bed, downstairs, and out –

Belgická Street.

Where she is stopped with the force of a cello swung wide against a brick wall. By the palace-grey apartments next door, by the building next to it and the one after that, mint blue and red wine that deepen to teal and clay in the rain, by the cobbles beneath her feet, by a sky whose avenues are bisected by cream piping and hooded windows like dreaming eyes.

Vinohrady. Her childhood. They have brought her back to her childhood. Back to Prague.

She swings towards the park – no, she can't – and veers back, scrambling up Záhřebská. One side of the street has been bombed. Notes chase her. She can't breathe. She is racing up to the square, its cellars loud with talk and more music, across Americká, beneath balconies where children play. The two towers of the synagogue climb up behind the apartments – the onion domes and stars that coordinated her world. She hurries out in front of a tram, its horn puncturing her ears, zigzag zigzag, like there's a sniper at her back, and trips in front of the temple.

The doors are nailed shut. She holds on to the brick and pulls herself up. Blood oozes like jam from cake, like sap, over her knee. She presses her face to the window. It is filmed with dust. Inside, there is nothing but rubble. She steps back into the street. The front of the synagogue is standing, the columns, the stained glass, but the roof is gone, the building is gone, the synagogue where the Nazis brought in confiscated furniture and her mother and their neighbours catalogued it, telling Zuzka to stack the vases in order of size, to fold the clothes carefully, the synagogue where the rabbi would wink at her and sometimes give her a sweet, the synagogue where everybody she'd ever – anybody she'd –

A horn, a car swerving, hands like blacksmith's gloves at her waist – Zuzka yells as she is lifted onto the pavement – the hands go back in surrender, a man who looks like a hungry bear saying

189

whoa, whoa, a man with yellow burns on his face and blond hair turning prematurely white – a man who was a boy she knew. Those fists grab her as she jerks back: the oversized hands of the son of the violin maker.

'Hey!' he says. 'Are you all right?'

Aleš, who she's alternatively loathed and imagined might kiss her one day since she was eight years old. Aleš who joined the Resistance. The son of the violin maker whose workshop her mother took her to, Zuzka sitting in the master's chair, sinking into the groove left by his backside, afraid of hammers and blades that made the ribs and saddles look vulnerable, the violin maker a giant drawing out strings of tail gut and telling her, if you are to be a true musician, you must—

'Miss? Are you all right?'

Blood drains from her head. Miss? He used to call her Zuzana, because he knew she hated it. Aleš doesn't know who she is. Aleš doesn't recognise her. She goes limp in his hands, which fall away.

'I'm fine.' A whisper.

'Are you looking for someone?' he says, glancing at the synagogue.

'No. No.'

She turns, head down as he calls after her, marching towards Náměstí Míru, towards the Royal cinema and the Pavilion, into the shadow of the church, pigeons scattering, and then a voice calls: 'Wait!'

She spins – it's not Aleš.

It's the angel of death, watching her from across the road, waiting for a tram to go, the impatience of his body a spring released as he races to her, saying: 'You're hurt.'

Zuzka puts a hand to her ear. He hovers in front of her, seemingly undecided, and then takes her arm and urges her to a bench. He kneels down, taking a handkerchief from his jacket and pressing it to the drip of blood. She is stung back into her body, and there is nowhere left to run.

'You used to live here?' He speaks a combination of German and Yiddish.

She nods.

'I'm sorry.'

She opens her mouth. No sounds come.

'I think we should go.'

Go? Go where? To Havlíčkovy sady, to knock at her apartment building and be taken in by neighbours: fed cake, fed grief, fed pity. They would wash her knees. They would say they understand how she feels. They might let her into her home. She could stand out on the balcony where her father taught her to play chess, telling her that if he lost on purpose it would be an insult to her intelligence, so she never won; she could look down over the grotto, Neptune bearing the weight of his ocean at the fountain; could breathe in the dense wall of fir, and beyond it the hill of vines Mama's family had money in. Vines as tall as men: she used to slip amongst them, stealing grapes, young enough to tell herself that they belonged to her, old enough to know it was make-believe, and it's time to grow up, Zuzka: pretend will only get you so far. You can pretend you do not have enough rage in you to destroy yourself, that the synagogue still has four walls and a roof, that the rabbi will have a special word for you after your recital, and that Mother will check your hands for the purple stain of grapes and tell you, Darling, pretend will only get you so far.

'It's not your fault.'

She is jolted back. The angel on one knee in front of her. The kindness of his eyes.

'One of the boys – he told me there were over ten thousand children in Theresienstadt. That there's only a few hundred of you now. He said that he feels . . .' He chews on his words. 'It's not your fault. That you're here.' The handkerchief rasps with blood and grit. 'It's what your family would want.'

She is ready to bite him.

'Come with me. You can't stay here.'

Can't stay here, can't stray too far. You might not come back. Her father had been consulting on the construction of a factory in Przemyśl when the Germans took southern Poland for two weeks before handing it over to the Soviet Union. His colleague, a luckier man, told them what happened. Papa had been executed amongst forty of the town's leading Jewish citizens. His death is a scar she can ignore until given a mirror. But this boy wants her to endure the rain as it starts to fall, slicking the streets, wants her to walk past patisserie windows, to withstand silver plating.

He opens his hand. 'I'll look after you.'

She breathes. Clears her throat. Says, 'Köszönöm.'

It's the first word she's spoken to him and he asks with astonished eyes, 'You speak Magyar?'

'I speak Theresienstadter.'

He gives a snort – of appreciation. Smiles. 'You're welcome.' He points to his heart. 'I'm from Budapest.'

She nods, seeing how his finger indents his coat.

Her mother tells her: Stay in your body.

'Will you come for the photograph? So people can identify us.'

She grips the bench. 'I don't . . .'

'Didn't they put your name down for England?'

'Yes.'

'Which is?'

She tightens her grip, keeping herself tethered. 'Zuzka.'

'I'm László. Come with me, Zuzka.'

She follows him back to the hostel, where the others are piling out onto Belgická Street, and no one asks about the tears on her face; they don't ask because they don't see her next to László, so she follows him to the tram, the driver shaking his head at their money, drawing into the city, into the earshot of the castle cannonade, if it still sounds. László talks loudly beside her. He is only fourteen but the other boys call him Boy King. When she asks why, he gestures to his ill-fitting suit and says, 'Don't I look the part?' Jumping from the tram, he marvels at the twists of Old Town, the intimacy of shutters leaning towards each other over the lanes, telling her, my mama would love this. She slows down – she knows what comes next – but László says they mustn't hold up the photographer. They are passing beneath the Astronomical Clock and death is ready to ring his bell. The boys push her forward, past the clock, into the square, onto the line where time falls.

'My mother would *really* love this. Zuzka?'

The newspapermen call for them to gather in front of the Jan Hus Memorial. The echo of three hundred boots in the square, bouncing between the precision of Austro-Hungarian windows and Moorish curves and art nouveau corners, and the blackened Gothic church rising up emblazoned with gold. A dream. A dream that's real.

'What does it mean?' asks László.

He's nodding to the words around the memorial. Some of the boys are climbing it, using the feet of the exiles for help. Others mill around, comparing heights.

She tells him, in what escapes as a whisper: 'Live, nation sacred to God, do not die. Love one another, do not deny the truth to anyone.'

Jan Hus watches her, standing above the stake. The words continue around the base: *I believe that after the storm of rage passes . . .* Mama held her in her arms as she laid flowers at the memorial – Zuzka can't remember what they were celebrating or mourning, just the swing of her mother's body, and the smell of stone and bronze and roses.

László tugs her to the front row.

'Don't be scared,' he says, squeezing the shoulder of a little boy beside him. 'Give your family a smile.'

László's own smile is that of a man who has reached the end of a long, bloody fight, and is daring his assailant to get back up. Zuzka drags up the same colourless good manners she gave the Russian soldier. She wants to tell László: *Never invite your observer to take a closer look. They might cut you from the picture.* She laughs – that's just the kind of joke Uncle would make – and the flash burns bright.

THEY ARE TAKEN TO Prague airport, where British officers in neatly pressed uniforms check their small suitcases and packages and ask for proof of age. Most have no papers but all say they are under sixteen, even the ones who aren't. They have been warned anyone over sixteen will not be taken, and the airmen listen to the clustered dates of birth with small smiles. A line of planes waits for them. They all have bullseyes painted on the side, and no doors, just holes cut into their bellies with hinged flaps. A British soldier carrying a girl's suitcase pats László on the back.

'They're Lancaster bombers. We've emptied them out for you. You get it?'

László doesn't know what the words mean, but the man looks soft, so he nods. Half a dozen Russian soldiers have accompanied them, one Red telling a Pole: 'Look, my boy, you are going to England. When you join the army or the air force, and you are asked to bomb Moscow, I hope you will refuse. Don't forget we saved you.'

The British airman asks László what the soldier is saying. László shrugs, climbing the wooden ramp into the black belly of the plane, where he loses Europe's sun on his neck. It is his first time on an aeroplane. There are no seats, only straps and riggings hanging loose like guts, and empty clips for bombs. He follows two girls holding hands and sits at the edge of the Plexiglass bubble of the gun turret, wrapping a leather strap about his wrist. Zuzka sits opposite, her eyes closed. The plane has waited for hours and it is hot inside. His stomach sloshes.

'Are you all right?' asks the older boy. 'We've got some bread for you.'

László nods, swallowing bile. Other boys and girls duck inside, the plane growing humid with breath and sweat. One boy is wearing an American military uniform; he says a US tank picked him up after liberation and he joined the front. You kill Germans? You bet. When the engines jolt into life some of them shriek. Zuzka makes no move. László grips the strap. He wants József's steady arm around him.

An officer climbs out from the cockpit and stands at the head of the plane, telling them something in comforting tones. There's a lurch and the man sways with it, a grace that reminds László of József turning somersaults at Palatinus Strand. They are nosing forward, lining up, and now they are speeding down the runway, impossibly fast, and László ducks his head, thinking, this is it, they will surely crash, but instead his stomach bottoms out as the wheels rise and the plane is no longer vibrating with the earth but the air. He is being airlifted out of Europe. How many times did they talk about this, in Buchenwald, in Krawinkel? József, they came for me. I'm free.

The RAF officer sits down on the floor, telling them it's a long journey, so we'll have some songs. László only understands a few of the words, but still joins in with the others, singing, '*Show me the way to go home, I'm tired and I want to go to bed. Show me the way to go home.*'

other methods

'GO TO BETHLEN GÁBOR tér.'

He goes: the world becoming dark, a walking dream, Dragan holding his hand, until he has crossed into the Eighth District, into the small square, and there is the old conservative synagogue, and next to it the ash-grey redbrick Zionist building, built as a school for the disabled, he remembers, but used for other things. They could send you to Palestine, although why you'd want to move from Budapest to some desert was a mystery to him and his father. Maybe his mother would have pursued the idea if they hadn't been so scornful.

He opens the gate, mounts the steps, passing through an arch painted in Hebrew letters. Bombs have not touched the building and he trails plaster and mud onto the marble inside. Stained glass touches his face. Dust floats in the blue beams. Doors open and there is an explosion of shouts and answers, people hurrying past him wearing rag-tag suits, wearing his uniform of nothing, nobody paying him any mind, except a woman dressed like an Orthodox Jew – nothing to hide – who points him upstairs.

'Office 209.'

He bows, not trusting his voice, and climbs the stairs. Laughter rings around the polished walls. He flinches when someone takes his arm. It is the same woman. He lets her help him to the door, where she leaves him. The hallway is lined with benches, on which men and women sleep, curled into each other like type in its box. Inside is a large office, solid desks, people waiting on more benches. A little girl looks up at him – his heart swells – it's Alma – it's not Alma.

A young woman wearing a tight skirt and blouse takes his elbow. 'Just returned?'

'I'm looking for my family.'

'Why don't you give me their names, and I'll look through our lists. They might well be here.'

'Zyyad. Emmuska, János, László, Alma. Zyyad. D'you know those names?'

She strokes his arm. 'We have a lot of Lászlós and Emmuskas. How about you let me look, and in the meantime, answer some questions? That desk is free.'

'Questions?'

'We are the Hungarian Committee for Attending Deportees, and we can help you find your family, and give you medical attention, food, money, a bed. In return, you just answer a few questions about your experiences.'

'What for?'

'Witness reports.'

'Witness?'

'Yes. Courts are being convened. It's important we know what happened.'

'I just want to find my family.'

'I'm going to look right now. Here, come with me. This desk is free. Why don't you sit here? They'll look after you.'

She leaves him to a man and a woman, both with clipboards, a covered typewriter waiting at the woman's elbow. They smile at him. Her blue polka-dot dress throbs. The man has thick glasses and wears a shirt and tie. He wonders if they were hiding under Christian papers. They look too well.

'Hello,' says the woman. 'I'm Sándor Magda, and this is Béla Benjámin. Can you tell us if you're injured?'

'Just my toe. They cut it off.'

Benjámin: 'They?'

'The Reds.'

Magda lifts a hand. 'A nurse will take a quick look.'

'I just want my family.'

'No harm in the nurse looking while you're sitting here.'

Benjámin: 'When was the last time you ate?'

'I didn't come here for food. I just—'

Magda: 'How about some pastry and coffee?'

József gives her a slow smile. 'While I'm sitting here?'

'Exactly.'

A woman in a makeshift uniform appears and kneels at his feet, attacking the stiff laces. He brushes her hands away.

Benjámin: 'Ani doesn't mind a bit of mud.'

József doesn't tell them it's not just mud, but whatever blood and shit has lasted. That it's his own blood. He undoes both boots and tidies them under the desk. His cheeks prick at the smell of his feet. The nurse touches the edge of the gauze.

'Gangrene?' she asks.

'Frostbite.'

Benjámin: 'It was a long walk home then?'

József looks at him. 'I stopped in Vienna, took in a few shows.'

Magda: 'Here's the coffee.'

Another woman appears, a girl so thin she is wires, a sight so familiar it only strikes him as sickening now with the soft hands of the nurse on his body. The girl gives him a cracked ceramic mug with flowers on it. The plate almost matches. The pastry is an imperial crumb, dusted with icing sugar, intricate as lace. Mama used to keep her icing sugar in a jar with vanilla sticks. He can't bear the smell. He thinks he might cry, in front of these people.

'Thank you.'

The nurse is tickling him and he smiles despite himself, which relaxes everybody until his wound is uncovered. The nurse opens a box, getting out clean cotton buds. 'I'm going to sanitise it and then we'll give it some air before putting new bandages on. Is that all right, sir?'

He can't find words for that so just nods. She gives him a look and his body tightens with something unfamiliar and uncomfortable. Want.

Magda: 'We're going to ask you a few questions, and once we're done I'm sure they will have checked for your family.'

'How many?'

'We usually ask about seventy, depending on your answers.'

He breathes in through his nose, holds it. 'Fine.'

They pick up sharpened pencils.

Benjámin: 'The number of your labour company, or your tattoo?'

József stares. For the first time since he began harbouring it, he is furious somebody doesn't want his name. 'I don't have a tattoo.'

Benjámin: 'You weren't in Auschwitz?'

'No.'

'You're fortunate.'

From the look on Benjámin's face, József wonders if his family has not returned, so he resists saying: *That's what they keep telling me*.

Magda puts her hand on Benjámin's arm. 'This isn't the place to talk about luck.'

József looks around at the two dozen other men and women in chairs like him. Then where is?

Magda: 'Let's carry on. Name?'

József pauses halfway through swallowing his coffee. The hot sugary liquid masses in his throat. Unswallowed, unspent. The nurse moves away, finally. He gulps the coffee down. 'Zyyad József.'

Benjámin: 'Not a Magyar surname.'

'D'you think that would have saved me, if we'd Magyarised our name?'

'I just meant I don't know how to spell it.'

He reaches for the pen, marking it down. 'It's Yiddish. Silk merchants.'

Magda: 'Your father was in textiles then?'

'He still is.'

Magda: 'Of course.'

'Date of birth?'

'Second of May 1925.'

'Place?'

'Budapest.'

'Occupation?'

'I didn't   I was a student, then a postman, a heaver, a clerk, whatever I could find. I was going to be a swimmer.'

'That's fine. Last home address?'

He chews his lower lip. '6 Falk Miksa út.'

'Location of ghetto?'

'They took me into labour service before the ghetto.'

'The first stop en route your deportation?'

József frowned. 'Which deportation? To labour service or from it?'

'To labour service.'

József rubs his face. 'I don't think we stopped until we got to Bor.'

'That's fine. In what camps were you interned, from and to?'

'Bor, Mauthausen, Gunskirchen.'

'That's fine,' she says again.

József does not ask her if she's holidayed in Austria much, how fine it seemed to her.

'We're going to ask you now about the situation from which you were deported,' says the man, 'here in Budapest. All right?'

József answers as best he can, each question requiring the careful dismantling of his own walls, until he is reduced to a hoarse voice box, reduced to some burning point of himself, from which he tells them about Dragan, tells them Dragan was only *on* the march because he was trying to protect József from Fleischer, tells them Dragan drew attention to himself to keep an SS officer from noticing József, tells them he did nothing to stop any of it, Magda passing him a handkerchief, its dampness letting him know he is crying, that his shoulders are shaking, his stomach is turning over, because he is crying. He tells them he wasn't taken into any showers, arrived into Mauthausen too late for any of that, and tries to find a way into their understanding, into their language which seems so different from his, as if they have become different races, as he is asked if the sick died of natural causes or something else? In pauses, he can hear other men and women giving slow answers, 'Then began the time of my sufferings . . .', people counting out sacred numbers, walking between twenty-five and fifty-two kilometres a day, half a kilogram of bread, freight cars with a hundred and twenty-two to a hundred and sixty men, inmates dying at the rate of a hundred daily, fourteen cases of spotted fever, one latrine for seventeen thousand people, five to six hundred deaths daily. József cannot think of numbers, giving them instead the faces of men he knew, the mud that reached his knees on the march from Mauthausen to Gunskirchen, the man who was made to dig a grave, and then, standing inside it, was beaten to death by the SS, beaten so that the insides of his skull showed, the rain and the trees of Gunskirchen, the snails and nettles he ate, the smell of frying human flesh, cuts of the dead sold to the starving by fellow inmates, the huddles of men with typhus who could not admit to it for the certain fear of being shot. 'Did you eat any human flesh?' Benjámin asks him. József looks up into the blue-stained light. 'I didn't have anything to trade. But I would have.'

The nurse comes back, bandaging him, and while he explains that he didn't return to Budapest by train she takes away his infested boots and replaces them with worn leather shoes.

'When did you arrive in Hungary?'

'Today.'

'Do you have any first impressions?'

József shrugs. 'The Allies should have finished them.'

'Finished who?'

'The Magyars.'

'You don't see yourself as Magyar anymore?'

'No.'

'What arrangements have been made to provide you with food and accommodation?'

'This coffee was something.'

'Have you received any financial or other help?'

'I don't need financial help. I just need to find my family.'

'Are you just passing through Budapest or do you intend on staying here?'

'What?'

'Are you just passing through Budapest or do you intend on staying here?'

Under the table, József nudges the new shoes into place, thinking they look like boats ready to cast off. 'I'm going to take my family away from here.'

'Have you brought any documents or photographs of your German camps?'

'Photographs? No, I don't – there are photographs by prisoners? I thought, just the Yanks . . .'

'Some people managed to take a few, yes. Others brought back mementoes.'

'Like what?'

'Bits of German guns, that sort of thing.'

'What for?'

'I don't know,' says Magda. 'Evidence.'

'Why would we need evidence? The camps are there, right there, the buildings, those chimneys, just go and look at them, go and smell the air.'

'József, it's all right, lower your voice. Take a breath. Just a few more questions, OK?'

'Fine.'

'How do you picture your future and have you any concrete plans?'

József sags in his chair. 'I don't know. Find my family. I don't know. Is that it?'

Benjámin: 'Where are you looking to fulfill those ambitions?'

'Excuse me?'

'That's the last question,' says the man. 'Where are you looking to fulfill those ambitions.'

József pushes into the shoes. 'Have they looked up my name yet?'

'Someone will take you to a place where you can wait, and we'll get you some more food,' says Magda. 'And József, there are always options, places to go.'

József sees her fingering a stamp: THE JEWISH AGENCY FOR PALESTINE. 'What's Palestine got to do with me?'

'That's up to you.'

'No it isn't.'

He is led to a bench in the hallway, a bench where a woman sleeps, a tattoo on her arm. He sits next to her. She is not disturbed by his presence, seems even to move towards him. József does not retreat when her leg presses against his. His eyes are closing but he tries to stay awake, watching more people shuffle up the stairs, watching officials squeeze through the mass of expectant and sleeping bodies, gathering and filing those waiting here, the hundreds, each with their own answers to those questions, each going somewhere to fulfill those ambitions, some of them with pieces of guns, some of them with silver brushes, some of them with God. America, Britain, Palestine, Australia, or perhaps only a dreamland, József sinking there now, sinking down towards the dinner table, towards Dragan, towards Mama and Alma, towards János, towards László, where they ask him, what other methods besides gas were used to kill people?

No. 104. What do you know about the camp leadership

No. 105. Was it the SS itself in direct charge of procedure or did they leave that to prisoner functionaries (kapo)

No. 106. Who were the kapo (German political prisoners, criminals, Poles)

No. 109. Were you tattooed?

No. 111. What was a day in the camp like

No. 113. Were you given soap, towels

No. 115. What kind of food did you receive. Was it enough

No. 120. Did the sick die a natural death or as a result of something else

No. 121. What happened to those who died

No. 124. Did people know the reason for their selection and could they argue against it

No. 126. What do you know of the fate of those selected

No. 127. Is this through your own direct experience or through hearsay

No. 128. What other methods besides gas were used to kill people

Four

end of its tether

I PRETENDED I WASN'T PUTTING any extra effort into my clothes
that morning, but the pretence fell down on the fourth outfit. Now,
waiting on the doorstep for Felix, I made sure my black vest was
tucked into the skirt. I saw him three doors down, glancing between
house numbers and his phone. He wore a blue shirt rolled to his
forearms, and I wondered if he'd put thought into it. I stood up.

'You made it.'

He looked up at the house, seeming to trace its outline. 'Ja.'

'Do you want to come inside?'

'Ja.'

'OK flight?'

'Ja. Yes.'

I let him in ahead of me. 'Tea? Coffee?'

'Yes.'

I smiled. 'Which one?'

'Coffee, please.' The fingers gripping his rucksack were white
at the knuckle.

'You can put your bag down.'

'Thank you. I should take my shoes off?'

'If you want to.'

He relinquished neither, just stood looking at the kitchen walls, nickel yellow, turquoise green, cerulean blue.

'It was more, you know, like a home. But I've been packing.'

He didn't respond.

I lit the stove and leant one hip against the Aga, watching him as he edged back onto his heels to peer out into the hallway. 'Phthalocyanine and cinereous blue,' I said.

A giddy grin flashed over his face. 'Yes.'

'How do you like your coffee?'

Sun scattering the stained glass across the lime table. The curator fidgeted with his cup, big hands moving in and out of the gumdrop light. He said, 'Thank you for inviting me.' He was looking at the crisp copy of Miklós Radnóti's poetry that I'd left on the table, the spine showing little sign of wear.

'I've been looking into the march,' I said. 'Radnóti, he was there. I've been reading his poetry. Do you think there's a chance Silk knew him, there, on the march?'

'It is possible.'

'In 1937, he wrote a poem predicting how he'd die, predicting it almost exactly.'

'I have held the original notebook in my hand. For the exhibition. You bought his poetry?'

'I found it on Silk's shelves. I didn't think he read any Hungarian writers.'

'And this is why you are wondering if perhaps they met on the march?'

'Yes.'

'It's possible,' he said again. 'What did Joseph Silk read?'

Meaning Death, meaning Death, meaning Death. 'A lot of T.S. Eliot.'

Felix raised his eyebrows. 'Really?'

'Yes – why?'

Felix hesitated. 'There was a – a stir, yes? You know the Anglo-Jewish poet Emanuel Litvinoff? After Eliot republished anti-Semitic poems he'd written before the Holocaust, Litvinoff – he was invited to read before a crowded hall of writers, and stood up with a new poem. It was called "To T.S. Eliot", and just as he announced the title, Eliot walked in, unexpected. Litvinoff said later that God must have a marvellous stage manager. He read the poem anyway. He blasts Eliot's eminence, his cold snigger, imagining what sort of poem Eliot might have made of Treblinka, had he the pity. He finishes:

> Let your words
> Tread lightly on this earth of Europe
> Lest my people's bones protest.

Felix glanced around, as if Silk could hear him.

'How did Eliot react?'

'The hall was chaos. Eliot had his head down on the back of the chair in front. But he was heard muttering to himself about what he'd just heard: *It's a good poem, it's a very good poem.*'

'When was this?'

'1952.'

Silk's early paintings dated to 1952. He was finding a way to see the world, with Eliot's help. *Living to live, to resign my life for this life.*

'The artist R.B. Kitaj,' said Felix, 'in his manifesto, he puts it this way: *Paint the opposite of anti-Semitism.* And he quotes T.S. Eliot: *The rats are underneath the piles, the Jew is beneath the lot.* He says, *Hi, Tom. Fuck you in my art each day.*'

'Unlike Silk.'

Felix shuffled in his chair. 'I think your grandfather would point out that with Abstract Expressionism – never writing a manifesto – we don't know what he was saying. It might have been *fuck you* to history. It might have been an embrace of the future. He left himself open to – to interpretation.'

He left himself vulnerable. I drained the last of my coffee and stood up. 'This way.'

Felix followed me through the French windows and across the garden. I put the key in the door and tugged. Spiders scuttled from the doorframe.

'Come in.'

Felix bowed at the door and took off his shoes. Drawing his palm over his mouth, he said, 'Gott,' as if the passage of his hand had uncorked the word. He turned in a tight circle, his still form reflected in glass bottles. He studied the open *Draper's Dictionary*, muttering, 'Bologna crepe, bombazine . . .' He peered at the framed print of the world's first colour wheel, not yet a wheel but a Star of David, the tips labelled, *y, o, r, v, b, g*. Next to it was a framed wheel, the colours distorted, wrong.

'This is his?'

'Yes. He did it in his twenties.'

'*Gott* . . .'

He stared at the corkboard of clippings and swatches, so close I saw the ribbons shivering beneath his breath. He studied the magnesia bottles and Silk's blue Penguin paperbacks. I remembered looking through H.G. Wells's *A Short History of the World* when I was younger. The final chapter was titled 'From 1940 to 1944: Mind at the End of its Tether', and I asked Silk what happened to a mind beyond its tether. Where did it go?

Fifteen minutes passed in silence, twenty, twenty-five. He had stopped by the half-finished canvas, studying the grey swathe of my hair.

'Thank you,' he whispered, so quietly I almost didn't hear it.

I nodded, and left him. I couldn't speak.

FELIX STAYED IN THE Blue Room for two hours. When he emerged, I asked to see his notes, and he handed over his journal with a light smile.

'German,' I said.

'That is the language Germans tend to write in.'

I gave him a baleful look. Flicked the pages. 'What does "Rittersporn" mean?'

'I don't know it in English. It is a flower.'

When I suggested he stay the night he said he'd cancel the friend who was expecting him.

'Do you like Indian food?' I asked.

'Ja.'

'Do you like Ealing comedies?'

'I don't know what this is,' he said, hugging the journal.

'Then you're in for a treat.'

We got a takeaway and watched *The Lavender Hill Mob* in my flat. We began on opposite ends of the sofa, but after the tin foil boxes were thrown away I brought out a bottle of wine and soon my toes were tucked under his legs, his hand resting on my ankle.

'A couple of glasses of champagne,' I said, 'and two strangers suddenly have a rich and happy past.'

'Champagne?' he asked, tilting the glass.

'Well, no. But you're no Ingrid Bergman either.'

'I hate to disappoint.'

'That's OK. I'm no Leslie Howard.'

'For which I am grateful. You are much prettier than Leslie Howard, whoever he is.'

I looked at him over the glass. 'I'd have to disagree.'

He bowed his head. 'What will you do with the Blue Room?'

'I take it you have something in mind?'

'The director asked me to try and persuade you to gift it to the museum as a permanent exhibition – an exact re-creation of his studio.'

'You can tell her a geometer from the Tate Modern has already mapped out the precise angle at which Silk last set down his glasses.'

'You have said yes to them?'

'Not yet. I've spent my life in the Blue Room. I don't know if I want strangers psychoanalysing his cornflower fetish.'

216

'Then you are safe with the Jewish Museum. Our bust of Freud is simply there for decorative purposes.'

I showed him photos from the wake, the laptop balanced over our knees. Ivor and Osip red-faced in a corner, Winston and me dancing, French windows thrown open despite the rain, the carpet a waterlogged stain. I showed him photos I'd taken of Silk on a trip to Devon, his easel set up next to the RNLI lookout on Bigbury beach. Felix tapped the zoom key, saying, 'I do not know this painting.'

'He didn't finish any of the paintings on that trip.'

'Was this usual?'

'Granny Rosemary had just died.'

He brushed the back of my neck with his thumb.

We shared my bed. The sofa was not discussed. I wasn't drunk enough to not know what I was doing, so I didn't do anything. We just lay with our bodies curving away from each other, two inverted speech marks.

'Felix?'

'Ja?'

'Were any other testaments missing from the Jewish Museum in Budapest?'

'Not that I know of.'

'I'd like to find out how it ended up in Berlin.'

'I am looking into it.'

'You know I asked you about the women Silk . . . if there was a woman in his life whose name began with a Z?'

'Ja?'

'Well, what about Silk's family – my family?'

'I don't think . . . Emmuska, János, Alma, László. Emmuska's parents were called Eszter and Sender, János's were Hanna and Lazar. I can't think of a Z.'

I couldn't name Silk's grandparents. 'What happened to them, Emmuska and János's families?'

'They died in the ghetto. Why do you want to know?'

'It's – it's nothing.'

He stayed quiet. From my brief glimpse before he got into bed he had nice legs. I could reach out now and brush his shin with my foot, touch his arm, smile, recover our ellipses. I could urge his hands over my body, dragging up feeling from somewhere. I could let him sink into me.

'You are not tired?'

He was looking at me in the half-dark. I shrugged, the duvet whispering. He shifted slightly, lifting his arm. I edged into the dip between his shoulder and chest, rested my head. His arm closed around me. He made no further movement. I wanted to tell him that I hadn't been sleeping properly, and that when I did I had strange dreams: that Silk was on an index of souls ready to be uploaded to heaven, but lay in a camp bunk waiting because they hadn't got to his name yet. No points for Freud on that one. I wanted to tell him: I was losing Silk twice: first to death, and now to you, the gatekeeper of Silk's lies, lies, lies. I wanted to tell him that between gusts of black humour and frenzied packing I locked myself in the bathroom to cry. I wanted to cry, there, in bed with him, but didn't, just listened to his breathing. To give my grief away to his archive, to offer up pain I found unendurable to reason that said otherwise, to hear again what an extraordinary life Silk led, that I was lucky to have had such a close relationship with him, that time heals all wounds, as if time could now be my friend – no. My grief is a private grief.

HE DIDN'T MENTION THE exhibition or the testament over breakfast. He didn't mention our entangled legs. When he said goodbye at the door, he wished me luck with the house.

'Danke,' he said, 'thank you.'

I bowed my head, echoing, 'Danke,' aware I wasn't saying it quite right.

He said, 'Well, if you're ever in Berlin . . .'

'I've got to be somewhere.'

The smile stayed on his face beyond the garden fence.

That afternoon I thought the knock on the door was him, come back, but it was a delivery man wearing a zip-up fleece despite the heat. He was hugging a mad bunch of flowers, four delphinium Fausts falling under their own weight.

The note was just one word: 'Rittersporn.'

I SAT ON A bench on Kite Hill. London was a dusky pink. The safe clump of the trees at Highgate was at my back. Ahead, I could just trace where the Thames invited us in and out.

I've got to be somewhere. I turned László's letters over in my hand.

'Are we not to have a homeland? Are we not to have a home?'

Silk, looking calmly about the kitchen: 'What do you call this?'

Lies, lies, lies.

I had suggested to Silk that we go to Budapest, film some of the documentary there. He said Budapest had nothing to do with him or me. Don't I get a say about who I am?

MY LAST NIGHT AT Fitzroy Park. I stood in the empty Blue Room. Silk stood with me, telling me they were somebody else's walls now, plain white and spotless. I told him, sometimes saying goodbye to a place is just as hard as saying goodbye to a person. I'll live with this home inside me for the rest of my life, know its corridors and where the cups hung in the kitchen and how the garden glinted after rain. It will be the stage of my dreams. But for now, the post had been stopped, the phone number transferred, and no one would need me here anymore. I had booked a flight to Budapest. I was going to finish the documentary. I'm the one left tending the family tree. It's mine now.

leave thy fatherless children

A PLACE CALLED CARLISLE. NIGHT. 'Children, children, hot cocoa, hot cocoa.' A tall, thin man with silver hair advances towards them and is vomited on. A woman puts a towel around László. A camera goes off.

HEADLIGHTS PAINT TUNNELS OF wet trees and sudden bodies of water so quickly swallowed up they may not be real. Billboards promise Wills Cigarettes and ask her to 'Keep Cheerful! Don't let yourself become weary and depressed. Buy Doan's Backache Kidney Pills'. Zuzka watches all this with her forehead pressed against the window, leaving a clammy half-moon. Her heart is rabbiting. She might be sick again. On the plane, the pilots had invited her and another girl into the cockpit. After a while the man at the controls – a handsome man, his cap gleaming – had jabbed a finger at the window. Zuzka peered down at the scrubbed fields.

'Boom!' he said, making her jump. He shook his head, smiling, 'Boom, boom, Dresden. You got it.'

She could see a city, or what used to be a city. Now it is precarious chimney stacks with no buildings beneath. 'Deutschland?'

The man grinned. 'Kaput. Here, have a bite of this.'

He passed her a chocolate bar, and because he was still watching her she bit into it. Sugary saliva dribbled from her mouth. She quickly swallowed, and was quickly sick. He leant over and ran a warm hand over the knobs of her spine – such frightening tenderness.

The engine coughs and the bus shudders to a halt. Zuzka bolts upright. Across the aisle, László looks just as panicked, but when he catches her eye he smiles reassuringly. The driver and the women in charge rattle at each other until the driver clambers out onto the lane. The women apologise, red in the face. There's no need to panic, they say. No need to panic.

A boy near the front stands up. 'It is an honour to break down on a British road.'

The two women laugh into open hands, seemingly at a loss in the face of such courtesy. Outside, the engine bucks. One of the women tries the ignition. The headlights return, revealing a cyclist coming around the lane, wearing some kind of uniform. The woman leans out of the door and waves to him. The man slows, leaning closer.

'Japan has surrendered!' he calls. 'It's over. The war is over.'

Zuzka watches the cyclist disappear. How many times can a war end before it's really over? The women are both talking at once, calling the news to the driver. The war is over. The war is over. Wasn't it over months ago? asks one of the boys. One of the girls says she likes England already. Zuzka stares at her grey reflection. It's over.

A PLACE CALLED CALGARTH Estate. These syllables sound flat and hopeless to László, and the buildings are clearly army, RAF they say. He does not want to be on another military base. A barrier swings down behind them. He wants József. A doctor listens to his heart and declares him fit. He is led with soothing tones down a corridor. A door opens. The man says something. He turns on a lamp. It is a small bedroom. The man nods and smiles until László is on the bed. Yours, he is saying. Yours. The man closes the door behind him but does not lock it. László turns in a tight circle that slowly expands, touching the iron bed frame, opening the wardrobe, which he finds empty for his things. Things. He sits down on the bed. A stuffed mattress. Cotton pyjamas are folded on the pillow. He has a towel, a toothbrush, a bar of soap wrapped in paper. It smells of his mother's perfume. There is a shelf next to the bed, on hinges, he realises, and he flips it up and down, up and down.

THERE IS A SHAVING mirror. Her father's jaw reversed in age under his steady hand, tired white to shy pink. Zuzka turns the disc to the wall.

A PLACE CALLED LAKE Windermere, a sound like a ticking engine, where secret planes were designed, they are told, that helped beat the

Germans. Dinner in a huge hall. These strangely smiling men and women cut up bread, more bread than he has ever imagined. It is unbelievable. Trifle so sweet it is dizzy, rich tea, which is served with cold milk, and cheese, and fruit. László sees other boys stuff sandwiches into their trousers and pocket the apples. The women say there's no need, if you want more food, you'll be given it. The plates are passed along the table, and László pinches a bit from each one, as the others do, all laughing at the hungry tenth boy who whines and cries. Zuzka is not eating. László folds the stiff bread around the jam and puts it down his shorts, not caring that the crease between thigh and dark hairs will become sticky and lined with crumbs like the seam of an over-used bed. Food keeps coming, and everybody laughs, because this is it, they survived and this is it, for life, they are certain. *The Lake District.* Three unknown words. Paradise, cracked open to harbour them. Some of the boys say they are only here in preparation for Palestine, that the British aren't accepting Jews and will send them off soon, but László doesn't believe that. Not when they have been given so much. It won't be taken away, he tells the younger boy next to him. He shoves bread into his pockets, where it crumbles. *It will be taken away.*

ZUZKA LIES ON TOP of the blanket, boots still on her feet, trying to keep her eyes open, because in the blinks she is in a concert hall where all the chairs are broken and there is nowhere left to sit.

THE NURSE COVERS HIM in a blanket and asks if she can get him anything. When she leaves, he thinks he might be sick. I've gorged myself to death, he thinks. I've had too much food. I'm going to cry. There is a knock on the door. László calls out, mixing German and Hungarian without meaning to. A man with a long grey beard appears in the doorway, the rabbi who sat with them at dinner, a rabbi without a hat, he realises, and he grins a little. The man pats his head knowingly, pretending he has forgotten it.

'I am Rabbi Asch,' he says in Yiddish. 'May I come in?'

László says nothing. The rabbi ventures forward, sitting on the chair. He puts both hands on his chest, as if owning himself. 'I am Polish,' he says. 'I came to Britain before the war. I am here to help. Where are you from?'

'Budapest.'

The rabbi gives a slow nod. 'We are going to help you. Whatever you need. There will be religious services.'

'Do you know how I can find my family?'

'We're going to look. For all of you. Is there anything I can get you now?'

László shakes his head. The rabbi stands. He does not touch László as the nurses did, just bows his head. László stares at the closed door. He tries to breathe, but he can't. When he said *Budapest* the rabbi seemed to flinch, as if László had cursed. László's eyes are stinging. He is crying. He has not been alone for days, months, years. But he is alone now. He is full, and there is nothing to plot for, and nothing else to think.

You do not know if you will ever see your family again.

He cries himself to sleep.

*

225

THE LIGHT LEAKING AROUND the blind is first gold, then lilac. Day is breaking. Zuzka rolls the blind up, then sits on the edge of the bed, watching light fill the tree outside her window. A butterfly drifts by – it takes her a moment to realise it is not a leaf or a scrap of wasted material. She stands up, watching it go. She wishes she knew what kind of butterfly it was. Zuzka looks down at her wasted body. Something unfamiliar is making her clench inside. Not hunger. Not pain. Not need, not want. Desire.

FROM THE BED, THE blackout blind gives him no indication of time. László touches the blind with his fingertips: the paper is hot. Day. No one has woken him. He grips the paper and tugs – it goes shooting up like a comic tie. Below, a lake stretches out beneath the early sun, and for a second he is standing with Mama on the warm shore of Lake Balaton. He tugs open the window and leans out, spotting other shaved and thin heads doing the same. They all laugh. Zuzka is not among them.

A DOCTOR ARRIVES WITH a white coat like Uncle's. Zuzka says she doesn't need to see a doctor, she is fine. The nurse spends a long moment looking at her and then says she'll carry out the examination herself. They go behind a curtain, and the nurse asks her to take off her clothes, miming buttons being popped.

'We have new clothes for you,' she says. 'Clean clothes. Look.'

There is a pile on the chair; a pair of stockings still in their pack, a white brassière.

'It's all right,' says the nurse. 'You're perfectly safe.'

Zuzka turns her back on the woman. She holds her breath and picks a spot on the corner of the wall to study while she undoes the buttons down the front of her dress. Her nipples harden. The dress collapses to the floor, no hips to stop it. She turns around, keeping her eyes over the woman's head. The touch of the stethoscope on her chest makes her gasp and look down. Dirt like a leopard's skin spots her body. Her ribs punch outward.

'Breathe,' the nurse says.

Zuzka squeezes back tears and breathes.

'You sound fine, just need more food and a good warm wash, hmm?'

Zuzka stands dumb while the woman drapes a thin towel over her, warm puffy hands dabbing her back.

'Can I look inside your mouth? Your mouth. Go *ahhh*.'

Zuzka obeys.

'Mmm. You'll need to see the dentist.'

Zuzka smiles with her mouth closed.

'Can you tell me if you've already begun your menstrual period? Your . . .' The woman pats her own stomach. 'Bleeding. Monthly bleeding.'

Zuzka picks over the English words she knows. 'Years not, no.'

'But you did, once?'

'Before years.'

'Years? Not months?'

Zuzka says nothing.

'Is there any way – we have to ask, you see, whether there's any way you could be pregnant.' She describes an arc over her abdomen with her hand. 'With child. A baby.'

'I was never . . . No.'

'Good. Good. Now, you carry these clothes and I'll show you where the showers are.'

Zuzka stares at her.

'You don't want to wash?'

Zuzka wants to tell the nurse what Lederer said about the showers, but she has no words for it, so just follows, clutching the nylons and brassière to her chest.

THE NURSES MUTTER OVER not just László's rashes and badly healed bones, but his ribs and stomach. He thinks the blonde one is local, and the darker girl from a city – she says she works at the Manchester Jewish Hospital. László keeps his eyes on a small pair of scissors that could be used as a knife. The doctor looks sick. László tries to force his stomach out, to look fit for work, and the local nurse laughs. She doesn't understand, he realises. She doesn't understand because it's different here. She says she was sure the bomb would do it. The Jewish nurse murmurs yes, fingers creeping over László's badly reset arm. As he listens he feels like his ears are being probed by piano wire, and then, pop, he remembers the Scottish nurse they had when Alma was born, an old red-faced woman who told stories about the bridges her father helped build. He hasn't thought about her for years.

'You see who they had up in court? The mother what abandoned that child at the railway,' says the blonde. 'Seems she did it for desperation. Left a note on the child, the police said, asking, *Will someone please take pity on this baby? His father is dead, and his mother has no pension*. She sold all her clothes to try and keep him.'

'Where did they find the mother?'

'Glasgow. And get this – the father's not dead at all, he's a Canadian soldier in Lancaster Hospital, gone and lost his memory.'

'I'll bet he did.'

The doctor presses his pen harder into his notebook.

László clears his throat and says in his best English, 'Leave thy fatherless children, I will preserve them alive, and let thy widows trust in me.'

The local girl stares at him, her mouth a perfect O. The Jewish nurse is suddenly crying, and just as suddenly not. The doctor stands up. He says László is suffering, but László doesn't understand the list that follows. He is given medicine and the nurse takes careful notes.

'Did someone take pity on the poor child?' the Jewish nurse asks, passing László a towel.

László wants to say, *Yes, you did*. The local girl says the baby has been adopted, smiling at László as if he brought such mercy with him. He wraps the towel around a sudden and unexpected erection.

ZUZKA SHOWERS ALONE. IT is a big room, with many shower heads, but she is given privacy. The water is hot and turns her feet the colour of raw meat. She scrubs and scratches and collects black dirt under her fingernails and fills her mouth with water until she's choking.

*

THE BOYS WASH TOGETHER. The water is safe, and they splash and chase each other around the tiled room. Afterwards, a man pops his head through the door and says there aren't enough new clothes. The delivery is late. So they hang around by the lockers, the beginning patter of a storm on the roof like the hollow pop of jar lids. They open the doors. This unknown country is rain electrified by brittle sun and a mud track and fir trees and bicycles leaning against a fence. Jan is drumming on a bench with the back of his heels, and Eryk suddenly breaks into song, a national anthem or a nursery song, and grabs a younger boy and whisks him out into the rain. Eryk spins the child round and round, and the boy breaks out laughing, shouting, faster, faster. László follows the others out into the warm rain, and everybody dances, all of them in their underwear, all to different music, all barefoot in the mud. László stamps and spins and waltzes. A couple of men appear from another building but do nothing, just watch, and all around great hills draped in cloud watch them too, and there is nothing to stop them, no fence no guard no tower, so they get on the bicycles, László seizing a red one – remembering hurling József's postman bicycle into the Danube after using it, against regulations, to help take their boxes and bags to their yellow-star home – and still the men just smile, so László wobbles his bicycle out into the lane, the seat hard on his testicles and thighs but he doesn't care. He races and slides and bumps down the hill, sure to crash, sure to fall, and the others follow, and everybody breaks out laughing, everybody breaks out, everybody breaks.

THE SUN SETS ON their first day in England. They walk around the lake shore, a big group of them, cobbling Yiddish together with

Polish, Czech, Hungarian, German, some wearing new clothes, others still in pyjamas. The day's rain drips from the trees. Zuzka walks next to László. The skin under his left eye is broken, but he is laughing, joking with the others. He got in a fight over the clothes. One boy smashed two plates and a chair. Another boy punched his friend in the face, trying to steal his jumper, but when his own clothes were supplied he offered his vest to his friend freely. The women looked so distressed Zuzka wanted to tell them, *We are well versed in madness. Teach us some new verses. Show me the way to go home, I am tired and I want to go to bed.*

'We rode the bicycles for over an hour,' László tells her now, 'and we passed a gang of local boys who shouted that the bicycles belonged to them, but we didn't stop, and they chased us on foot for nearly a mile.'

'Boy king and bicycle thief,' says Jan.

László grins. He is a few inches shorter than Zuzka, but he wears his shirtsleeves rolled to his elbows and chews on the end of a cigarette. 'In Theresienstadt, we used to put on plays, cabarets, things like that.' Zuzka listens to herself. 'There was a man called Karel Švenk, he wrote a play called *The Last Cyclist*. It was an allegory. Two men break out from a mental asylum and terrorise a city, killing all of the cyclists and anyone who's ever had anything to do with a cyclist, because they blame them for what's gone wrong in their lives.'

A labrador bolts through the group, wagging its tail. The older boys stroke it. Two Englishmen come by, dressed like pictures of Englishmen, flat caps and boots. One nods and says, 'It's a lovely day today.'

Eryk nods after a pause. The Englishman whistles the labrador back to his side, walking on.

'Did they mean what I thought?' László asks.

Eryk shrugs. 'They think it is a good day.'

'Why tell us?'

They walk on. László helps Zuzka over a fallen tree, and as she brushes the soil from her dress she can feel him watching. She glances up – his eyes are on her chest. He flushes. 'You were telling me something,' he says, 'about the production.'

She shrugs. 'The Jewish Council banned it before the first performance. They were worried the SS would see the satire.'

'So it was never performed?'

Zuzka looks out at the water. A duck bullets across the surface, destroying the calm. She remembers waiting in the wings with her violin, watching Švenk, who played the last cyclist, fire up a rocket the madmen had built as a final solution. He stuffed the lunatics inside and sent them all the way to the moon. He called to the empty hall, waiting for an audience that would never come, 'Go home! You are free!' but his girlfriend – Zuzka can't remember who played the girlfriend, only that she blushed whenever they kissed – told him: 'Only on the stage is there a happy ending. Out there, where you are, our troubles continue.'

'Zuzka?' says László. 'You never saw it?'

'It was based on an old joke. We all told each other the joke instead.'

'What joke?'

'You know – a man cries, "The Jews and the cyclists are responsible for all of our misfortunes!" Another man asks, "Why the cyclists?" The first shrugs. "Why the Jews?"'

Jan grins over his shoulder. 'I love that one.'

They are snaking around an enclosure, and there is a white cottage on the corner, with a thatched roof. A woman digging in the garden stands to greet them.

'Lovely day today,' she says. 'You children need any water?'

'No,' says Eryk. 'Thank you.'

They hurry on, giggling.

'If this counts as a day *so* lovely two strangers think it worth mentioning, then we are in trouble,' Eryk says. 'It rained for two hours straight! Hey, Boy King – can you skip stones?'

'Better than you, anyway,' says László.

'Come on then.'

Zuzka hangs back while László slides down the bank. A few other boys join him. Her stomach is tight – because she wants his stone to skip the most, she realises. As if it matters. He reels his elbow in, snaps the stone free. It bounces three times. Everybody shouts.

'Who taught you to throw?' says Eryk.

'My brother,' says László, cheeks spotting red.

'Yeah?' says Eryk. He whips his stone, managing six.

Zuzka leans against a tree, her hands in her pockets. The undergrowth cracks, and she turns to see two women with sheepdogs, watching. They smile at her.

'Lovely day today,' says Zuzka.

233

welcome back to the Zyyad family

T HE DANUBE FLASHED BROWN-BLUE. Bridges threw their hooks across the water, tethering land to land, Buda and Pest. The castle sprawled across the Buda Hills, its blue dome and polished windows like something from a fairy tale. Love at first sight flickered into my body, forming an epicentre I hadn't known I was missing. I skirted a group of Japanese tourists, the Széchenyi Chain Bridge behind them. Nasturtium and tangerine houses occupied the opposing bank, narrow old timekeepers; to my right were hotels and cafés where my family would have sat and had coffee. I walked with the sun coating my body and my camera spooling, until I saw an armed soldier in a brown uniform with knee-high leather boots and mirrored sunglasses watching me from the shadows of parliament, and my love trembled under unreasoned dread.

Bronze shoes lined the river, rust-red high-heels, sandals, boots. A plaque said they commemorated Hungarian Jews shot into the Danube by the Arrow Cross in 1944. People had left tea lights and rose petals inside the shoes, crushed ribbon and rain-blotched photographs curled by the wind. The phones and cameras of tourists around me were too hungry, devouring my sandals near these petrified boots, my feet on Silk's feet, dancing as a child, Alma's feet on József's, dancing as a child. I hurried to a set of steps hacked into the side of the bank, and sat down at the bottom. Here, caught in rocks, the Danube gave back what people threw away: the smashed remnants of a wine bottle already turning to sand, beer cans, wire, cloth, a McDonald's cup. It returned what it could, all our unwanted things.

I raised my camera. A ferry pulled around Margit Island, and the Danube touched my toes, cold and electric. My sudden love felt contraband, my homecoming nothing more than tourism, a pilgrimage to the site of a home now missing.

THE HOLOCAUST DOCUMENTATION CENTRE was down a side street. A limestone wall branched out off-kilter, at once a shield and an arm inviting me inside. A police car sat at an angle to the security doors. The engine was off. I could see the officer's elbow pressed into the open window.

In the courtyard, columns jutted from the ground, supporting nothing, as if they had been holding up a house whose roof was sacrificed to a storm. The courtyard wrapped around a white synagogue. The memorial wall shimmered black and grey. It was endless. Looking up at the columns of names gave me a sudden feeling of vertigo. They weren't alphabetised; I couldn't find any order. The entrance to the centre was underground, and the door was set into a tower marked 'Lost Communities'. The names of towns and cities built on each other. The curl of a crawling plant had been plucked away, leaving behind the bony impression of a long-buried fossil.

I walked into the cool air-conditioning clutching my camera to my chest. At the desk, a woman asked if she could help me.

'I'd like . . . I'd like to see if any of my family are on the wall.'

She directed me upstairs, where a display cabinet in the blank corridor contained objects relating to labour service. I hovered near it, eventually leaning close enough to see the word 'Bor'.

Creeping forward, my reflection stretched over the glass. There was an A4 watercolour painting of Bor, the mountain steppes, mineshafts like a nerve system sliced from the body. Silk, did you paint this? The colours were normal, the blue sky a weak scud. It was unsigned. Did you have a name, then, there, to sign?

'Hello?'

A man waited in the doorway to the office. The curls of his hair were turning silver; he was close to John's age. 'I am Károly Farkas. Karl Wolf, to you.'

'Károly? I need to practise my Hungarian.'

'How long are you here for?'

'I don't know. A few weeks.'

'A few years, you can practise your Hungarian. In the meantime, I am Karl. You have an appointment?'

'They sent me up here. I'm Eva Butler.'

He stood back against the open door. The office was made up of pine furniture, maps, books. I sat down on one side of the desk, Karl on the other.

'It is my job to look for names,' he said. 'Butler does not sound Hungarian to me.'

'I'm looking for anybody under the name Zyyad.'

'Zyyad is not Hungarian either, it is Yiddish – most families Magyarised their names, but not all . . .' He opened a database on his computer. 'This should make our search simpler. Do you have the first names also?'

I passed him a piece of paper: EMMUŚKA ZYYAD, JÁNOS ZYYAD, ALMA ZYYAD.

'Do you have any dates?'

'I know they lived in Budapest.'

'OK. Let's try the women first . . . these were your family?'

'My great-grandmother and great-aunt.'

He nodded. I tried to clamp down on my elevator stomach as he drew a hand over his light grey stubble.

'No results for either, I'm afraid.'

'None? I thought – there are so many names . . .'

'We can try János Zyyad.'

'Thank you.'

He typed quickly, hit enter. I could see the database loading, reflected in the framed map behind him. He glanced up at me, then back down at the paper.

'Are you related to the artist Joseph Silk?'

My passport stuck to my thigh through my pocket. 'He was my grandfather.'

He nodded, saying gently, 'It's my job to look for names.'

I waited for him to ask me about the testament. The computer churned.

'Is this your first time in Budapest?'

'Yes.'

'Then I can say welcome back to the Zyyad family.'

My throat was suddenly dry, and my voice creaked when I said thank you.

'There's a memorial day being organised by the Open Society Archives for the twenty-first of June, marking seventy years since Jews were forced into yellow-star houses. You should come.' The computer clunked. Karl hunched closer. 'Ah – yes. János Zyyad is here.'

'Here?'

'I will print it out for you.' Karl took a booklet from a drawer as the printer spat out a yellow page. Slotted together, they looked just like Silk's funeral programme, without the blue. Karl opened it for me, moving his finger as if teaching me how to read. 'This is the information we have.'

Név: Zyyad János
Születési hely: Budapest
Születési idő: 1903. december 10.
Lakcím: Budapest, 5. ker
Halál ideje: 1945. február 24.
Halál helye: Sopronbánfalva
Az áldozat neve a 9. sor 68. oszlopának alján található.

'This means he was born in 1903, and died in 1945, in Sopron-bánfalva, northern Hungary. This means the victim's name can be found in the bottom row, column sixty-eight. It says here that he was in Labour Company 101/601, and died of . . . végelgyengülés . . . there isn't a clear English translation, but I suppose you would say senile decay.'

'Senile decay? He wasn't that old, was he?'

'It means being exhausted out of life. It means that somebody died of starvation, fatigue, sometimes torture. It was a term used for many labour servicemen and -women, many of whom were not yet twenty.'

I stared down at the sheet of paper. 'Is Sopronbánfalva near Sopron?'

'Yes, just outside it.'

I tried to picture Felix's reaction. His grandparents had lived there. 'Where do you get your information?'

'In this case, the labour company officers of the time wrote it down.'

'I'd been told – people say he died in Auschwitz.'

'There is a lot of misinformation. It is only recently that details such as this were put together. If you like, I can look into your family further for you.'

'Is that part of your job?'

He lifted his shoulders. 'Sometimes.'

'Then, yes, please. That would . . . help.'

He pushed a pad my way. 'If you just give me your email address.'

I wrote it down, my letters jerky. I dropped the pencil as quickly as possible. 'Do you know why he's on the wall? Did somebody request it?'

'The first sixty thousand names were registered labour servicemen. Let me show you the way to the wall.'

Karl walked me down the corridor slowly, and though inches remained between us I felt as if he were holding me upright.

The exit led out into bright sun. I blinked up at the columns, the surrounding houses, the roof garden shaking in the wind. The memorial wall stretched around me. I tried to guess the font size of the names: fourteen? Less? The columns were numbered at the bottom, and I walked from 408 – where the wall was blank, waiting – to 68, my eyes on the shelf running along the bottom, where people had left more candles, photographs, poems. I wished for the heart of lapis lazuli from the Blue Room. Reaching 68, I knelt down, growing panicked that he wouldn't actually be here.

LANGER GYULA
FOHN NÁNDOR
ÖZV. WALD IZRAELNÉ
RÓZSA ELEK
STERN LAJOS
FLESCH IMRE
ZYYAD JÁNOS

A quick rush of tears took me by surprise and lasted a few seconds. I sat down. The arms of that double Y looked like branches, splicing into my own family tree. I knew János owned a textile factory. Did responsibility lie with him for Silk's love of colour? János, were you a loving husband? I squeezed my eyes shut – I sounded like someone drafting another gravestone, this time for a stranger. Loving husband and father. I knew nothing about this man, except that he was married to a woman named Emmuska, and together they had three children, one of whom died, two of whom lived, one longer than the other, one of whom had a son, who had a daughter.

I took my camera out. In the footage, my face is tired, reflected in the gleaming wall, and my body is small.

I WAS WRAPPING MY camera in my scarf when the side door to the courtyard opened.

'Oh good,' said Karl, 'you are still here.'

I stood up, shielding my eyes. 'Did you find something already?'

'No. I just wondered if you know anybody here?'

I glanced at the sixty-eighth column. 'No.'

'Do you have plans for this afternoon?'

'No . . .'

'Would you like to go to a protest?'

'A protest?'

'Yes.'

'Aren't you working?'

'Not anymore.'

I looked up at the synagogue. 'Yes. I'd like to protest.'

On the way out, Karl nodded to the policeman, who frowned back. Karl grinned at me. We turned into the busy road. Builders working on a derelict house stopped and stared.

'This is the only district where you must be careful,' said Karl. 'Crime is high here. Since the end of the communist era the Roma community has come under the worst attacks from the government. Before at least there were unnecessary factories to hire them, now they are unemployed, and forced to give up travelling, forced to settle. There is a lot of anger, a lot of poverty. The government tacitly encourages violence against them – it has stretched to marches, suggestions of camps. That's what led me to the Centre. My parents were Roma. They gave me to Gentiles before they were deported.'

'I'm sorry.'

'Thank you.'

'Are they on the wall?'

'Yes. Two-euro donation for inscription and upkeep.'

'So you're a historian?'

Karl smiled. 'I'm a writer. Bad poetry, derivative plays, and moderately readable prose.'

'You really know how to sell yourself.'

We reached the Metro. 'The trouble is,' said Karl, 'that Primo Levi did it all in five words. *If This is a Man.*'

'Why keep writing then?'

'Because I have to.'

On the Metro, a group crowded in wearing combat trousers and leather coats stitched with AUSTRIAN NIGHT DEMONS. Karl and I sat down and the men ringed us, talking loudly. I kept my eyes down, studied their shoes: trainers, open-toed sandals, biker boots.

Karl leant closer, murmuring, 'Do you want to know what we are protesting against?'

'Whaddya got?'

'Pardon?'

'Marlon Brando. Most people think it's James Dean.'

He told me about the memorial depicting Hungary as the Archangel Gabriel under siege from a Nazi eagle. I remembered seeing it on Twitter, the statue the Hungarian government was erecting, the statue Braham argued forgave the Hungarian regime. Karl said, 'Holocaust survivors who have protested have been arrested, dragged off by police. It's a PR nightmare for the government, and now the thing is just sitting there, half complete. They say we might be able to stop it being finished.'

His eyes fixed on me with an intensity I found discomforting because I could not match its certainty.

We got off the Metro, leaving the Night Demons behind, and walked to Szabadság tér – Freedom Square, Karl said. The buildings around us belonged to another era, once important, now soot-stained and asleep. There was a green patch in the middle, with a TV screen, and two ringed-off memorials at either end, with a few people gathered already, and a stall selling beer. Here, a column supported a golden communist star. At the other end, an empty plinth awaited an angel. Police cars sat dormant. An officer leant against the door, holding a video camera. He wore the same uniform as the man I'd taken for a soldier outside parliament. The road running before the memorial was littered with offerings: a photograph of Hitler and the Hungarian Regent Admiral Horthy shaking hands, shoes, an EU flag.

There was no one here to protest.

I almost jumped when the officer spoke, exchanging words with Karl.

'What's he saying?'

Karl glanced at me. 'No protestors today.'

I looked at the snout of the policeman's camera. The red light blinked at me. I got my own camera out, raised it to my eye. In the footage, the policeman remains inert as I turn and track over the broken memorial and the square filling with football fans. When I shut it off Karl asked if he could buy me a beer. We sat on the dry grass, watched the screen come to life, and I waited for kick-off so I could scream about something else.

ALL I HAD WERE fragments. Why, in so many years of living together, had I not pressed Silk for more information, ignored his truculence, his wincing, and pushed? What did I have of that life, the life of József Zyyad? It didn't seem so important then – why, in his absence, did it feel so vital now? I only had what Silk had given me. Hungarian pastries, a few paintings recalling, he said, the Danube, a neglected volume of Miklós Radnóti's poetry. What else? Silk finding me in the living room watching *Of Human Bondage*, the way he paused in the doorway, squinting at the TV.

'Who's the cripple?'

'Disabled. Leslie Howard,' I said. 'Ashley in *Gone With the Wind*.'

'Ashley in *Gone With the Wind*. Of course.'

'He was actually British, Leslie Howard.'

Silk watched for a minute, his head tilted. 'I suppose he was. His father was Hungarian Jewish.'

I turned around on the sofa. 'I didn't know that.'

'Mmm.' Silk stayed where he was, eyes on the screen. 'A fine actor.'

'You want to watch with me?'

'No. You enjoy it.'

I don't think we said any more than that.

Lying in my hostel bed, I switched my phone on. Midnight. Emails popped up: friends telling me that *Ham & High* had reproduced one of my blog entries without my permission – did I want to call them? Winston telling me they'd had several proposals for tea towels and mugs reproducing Silk's work, and though Silk had dismissed such things, maybe now . . . I swiped them away. Felix's number was saved under Curator. I pressed call. The ringing cast out into space.

'Eva? Are you all right? I have been trying to contact you.'

'I'm in Budapest.'

'Ah. You are meeting with the Jewish Museum there?'

'No. No, I'm . . . I don't know. I can't sleep. When I do, I . . .'

'Might I – can I – help? Can the museum help?'

'Help?'

'I could come to Budapest.'

I laughed.

'I'm serious. I can get a flight, a train. I can help you.'

'I want to know why the testament was removed from the archives here but I don't want to tell them who I am. Silk wouldn't want me to be here.'

'I've been looking into it, I have people there I can talk to. I can come tomorrow. OK?'

I looked out at the electric blue of near dark. A plane scrawled nothing of importance. 'OK.'

The Scarlet Pimpernel

A BLUE AND WHITE FLAG flaps, the star at its centre hidden and rediscovered by the wind. Behind, the desert is a peeled orange. The boys around Zuzka cheer, deep-throated and immediate. Rabbi Asch explains that the buildings just visible to the right are Jerusalem. He seems like he would say more, but the soldier with missing thumbs is changing the reel. The new reel clunks into place. A black-and-white Big Ben chimes, and the clapping is renewed, the boys talking about when they'll go to London. Strings take over and the screen tells them they are watching Charles Laughton in *The Private Life of Henry VIII*, directed by Alexander Korda. One of the pre-war refugees gets up, ready to deliver a live translation in rapid Yiddish that will collapse the boys in laughter.

László grips her sleeve, whispering, '*Korda Sandór!* He's a big Magyar filmmaker, you know him? He made *A vörös Pimpernel*, you know, *The Scarlet Pimpernel*! Leslie Howard!' The others hush László, but he just leans closer, whispering so that his breath warms Zuzka's neck: 'My brother used to read me *The Scarlet Pimpernel*. Baroness

Orczy is Magyar, you know, and so is Leslie Howard.' *Shhh*. 'Leslie means László, you know. My grandparents lived near Orczy House. I used to think – I thought my brother would save me, disguised like the Scarlet Pimpernel.' Zuzka turns away from the sudden open wound in László's eyes. *Shhh*.

'WHAT DOES IT MEAN?' asks László.

'Fuck?' says Eryk. 'It means to make with a girl, but they also use it as a way to say they are angry. Or they say fuck off, which is like get away.'

'Who told you?'

'A local boy. I was talking to his girl.'

László grins. 'No you weren't.'

'Oh yeah?'

'So prove it.'

'What she gave me can't be proved.'

'Fuck off.'

'There you go.'

László shakes his head. They are in the eating hall, but it isn't lunchtime. They have been here for a week, and this is the first time they have been called in from running wild without food in exchange. He leans back on the bench and swings his legs. Zuzka is sitting in the corner with the other girls, but she isn't talking. It's strange: when someone engages her she turns on like a bulb, but as soon as they stop looking at her the light goes out. He wants to tell her, *You're beautiful, you know?* Just go right up and say it. József told him once about a boy in Budapest, a printer's apprentice, who loved a girl so much he set her name in type and swallowed it. He wants to tell Zuzka, *Just give me the letters.*

Rabbi Asch comes in with three of the youth workers, Jewish refugees from before the war, and a sandy-haired man they haven't seen before. He explains that this is Dr Posner, a psychiatrist, a Jew from Germany. He says the doctor has come to help with – his Yiddish becomes awkward, vague – with what is happening now.

'This is it,' says Eryk.

'What?'

'Palestine. We're going to Palestine.'

The rabbi moves into the centre of the room, smiling calmly. He has thick envelopes stuffed under his arm.

'We're going to show you some lists we have received from the Red Cross. Does everybody understand so far?' There are a few murmurs. 'If the person next to you doesn't speak Yiddish but speaks another language you know, please translate. The Red Cross has sent us the names of survivors. Just some names. If your family isn't here, it doesn't mean – it might just mean they haven't been found yet.'

László's throat is dry. Eryk is explaining to the table. In the corner, Zuzka gets up. She is leaving. No one follows her out. László tries to breathe. The rabbi unfolds sheets as big as newspapers, calling out letters. László pushes through to the last table, Z. Z for *Zsidó*, he thinks, Z for *Zyyad*. He muscles to the front, gets his elbows on the table, reads down the list, S and T and X, a boy next to him slumping down on the bench and putting his face in his hands, past Zs and Zr and Zv. There is no Zy.

They're not there.

László wriggles free from the table, knocking through people, scrambling for the door.

They're not there.

The doctor tries to stop him but László pushes past him, staggering out into the air. The sun hits him, too high, too bright. He can't breathe.

They're not there.

Buildings and trees and a road and the lake. He slides down the bank, scraping his knee, and into the water, which is so cold he is forced to breathe, *whoosh*, and he wades forward, the water rising above his knees, soaking through his trousers to his testicles, around his ribs, his heart, and he kicks out and starts to swim as strong and as fast as he can, but it's been years since József taught him to swim at the Danube Bend and he is slow and ungainly and water is getting in his mouth and he can't find the bottom, can't stay up – hands grab him around the waist, József in Palatinus Strand keeping him afloat – he turns – it's Zuzka.

'Come back,' she says, tugging at his shirt under the water. She pulls him to the shallows until his toes scrape the soil. They stand, waist-deep in the stirring blue. 'Come back.'

He says, 'I can't live without them.'

'You have for years.'

László coughs up lake water, tears coming on suddenly. 'It wasn't living.'

'Neither is this.'

'What do you mean?'

She gives him a little smile, and kisses him on the lips. László stumbles closer, and the sharp points of her hips dig into his stomach.

He holds on, silt swallowing his toes, his feet, his ankles. She wipes his cheeks, and he thinks he hears her whisper again, *neither is this.* He holds on.

László feels the need to remain landlocked to her, the insecurity of new geography, but she shifts from him as Calgarth Estate raids its improvised field bag, trying to address the wounds of separation, and he is left alone with Doctor Posner, tangling and untangling his hands in his lap. The desk is olive green, the window perfect in its dimensions. The psychiatrist looks out of place here, wilfully dishevelled, inviting the defective and the compromised, his hair unbrushed, his moustache European, his beard disguising a jaw knocked askew by a Brownshirt, his stomach British, his eyes guilty, his accent confused. He is talking, he says, to those boys who cannot yet find family members. Most of you, he adds. We want you to know that there are other channels, other methods – nothing is known, yet. Nothing is known.

'If you know nothing,' László says in German, 'what qualifies you to speak to me?'

The man tugs his moustache. 'Only good intentions,' he says. 'Do you understand?'

László sits forward. 'I speak German. I speak Czech. I speak Polish, and Yiddish, and Russian. I speak Magyar. And here they are teaching us English with such care, a lesson every day, and they are patient, and some of us are slow to learn, because it won't kill us not to learn, and some of us are quick, because we want to be human beings like you. Do *you* understand?'

'Yes.'

'If I told you the things I've seen, the things that were done to me, you wouldn't sleep again. Do you believe me?' The edge of the seat is cutting into his thighs.

'Yes.'

'I've heard some of the officials here say we are exaggerating our *adventures*. Do you believe we are exaggerating?'

'I wish I did.'

'Do you want to hear my adventures?'

'If you want to tell me.'

László stares, fierce, ready to fight. Posner's expression does not change: peaceable, cultured, the look of his father's friends in Budapest, remembered as the smell of cigar smoke, the way thought expressed itself as a sound at the back of their throats. He sits back. 'My family are dead.'

'They may be, yes.'

'I saw a newspaper listing the casualties of the British Empire and the United States of America. Did you see that?'

'Yes. 945,122.'

'Do you know how many Jews died?'

'No.'

He kicks the desk, a hollow thud as his voice rises. 'Because they can't be counted. I was there at the end, and I saw it. Do you understand? You can't count them. There are too many. But not me. Not me. Do you understand?'

'Yes.'

'I had a chance to . . .'

'A chance to what?'

László looks down at his bunched fists.

'Some of the boys here have been talking to me about revenge,' the doctor says carefully. 'They say Russian soldiers gave them permission to assault Nazi soldiers, but they refused. American soldiers, too.'

'Are they proud of that?'

'Yes, they are.'

'Because it means we are human beings, not like the monsters who did this to us.'

'They're proud of the way they were raised. Proud to have followed their parents' teaching.'

'Are *you* proud of them for that?'

The doctor tugs at his moustache. 'Yes.'

László snorts. 'If a man kills your mother, and your father, and your brother, and your little sister, and your grandparents, and your aunts and uncles and cousins, and you do not kill him when the chance arrives, *what are you?*'

'Vengeance is not Jewish.'

'Neither am I.'

'Do you mean that?'

László feels himself burn scarlet. 'I don't know.'

'Do you attend services here?'

'Yes. But I do not know what I attend them for. How could God do this to us, to my family? Who chooses a people for this?'

'Keep believing. You can be angry with God. There is no one else to castigate here. No Nazis to kill. We will leave that to the Americans, to the courts.'

'You all say Nazis, you refugees. It was the Germans.'

'I am German.'

'Are you Jewish?'

'Yes.'

'Then how can you stand yourself?'

Doctor Posner smiles softly. 'You are an intelligent boy. Think.'

László stands up, the chair juddering back on its legs. '*I don't want to think*. They killed my family, they murdered my family.' His hands land with a slap on the desktop. 'I want to smash every windowpane. I want to break every stick of wood. I want to burn the building down.'

'I can't let you do that,' says the doctor. 'But you could hit something.'

'What?'

The doctor stands up. László veers back.

'Follow me.'

Posner leads him outside, taking the slope towards the treeline. Beyond, the lake glints, silent, waiting. László can hear other children laughing in the kitchen as they help peel potatoes; he keeps his whole body bent away from the doctor, who picks something up from the shade of the building: a bat. László raises his hands, then sees the ball.

'Have you played cricket before?' Posner asks.

'Football,' says László.

'Good team, Hungary. In football. I doubt you have a cricket team.'

'Better than Germany.'

'I'm sure,' the doctor says with a polite smile. 'Good swimmers, too, the Hungarians.'

László's throat swells, as if still choked with lake water. 'My brother was going to be an Olympic swimmer.'

'Did he teach you how to swim?'

'Yes.'

'Here, you take the bat. Stand here. That's it. Now I bowl to you.'

'You what?'

'I throw the ball, you hit it. As far as you can.'

'If I hit it as far as I can, it's going in the lake.'

'Show me then.'

Doctor Posner throws underhand, his rangy arm suggesting László is eight years old. László swings, a dizzy circle. The ball drops to the grass. He kicks it at the doctor, tells him he can't throw for szar. Posner says, OK, and backs up a little, this time putting more into it, and László gets the ball with the tip of the bat. It ricochets off, rolling down the slope. The doctor chases it, bowls again, harder now, and László spins like a released cog and the ball meets the bat with a thud and flies over Posner's head, who whoops, chasing it with a sudden turn on the slick grass that makes him stumble. László swipes the air with the bat. Laugh all you want, the doctor says. I bet you can't hit it from here. József used to say that. László whacks as hard as he can and gets the ball straight on, harder than he's ever hit anything, and it flies straight at the doctor, who with a harsh smack accepts it into his hands.

'Are you all right?' pants László. 'I didn't mean – did that hurt?'

'Not a bit.'

'Are you sure?'

'Quite sure. Go again?'

'If it's OK.'

'You might be a new regional champion.'

László grins, bounces, the bat ready. He swings and the ball flies into the trees, showering Posner in leaves. The doctor claps, shouting, champion, champion, just like József. Just like József.

IT IS CALLED AFTERNOON tea, the woman says. Zuzka nods and smiles. They are in a village called Ambleside. So few of you girls, the women had said. You deserve all the pampering there is. The woman beside her demonstrates the proper ordering of milk and tea, and Zuzka smiles, not lifting the cup. Milk means you're sick, that they don't expect you to last many days. She wants to ask whether they're being so kind because they think the girls won't last long. The Polish girl opposite is showing signs of tuberculosis. The doctors must have noticed. So it must be pity.

Everyone is looking at them. The short double stare, like when they first had to wear the star. Her father said it would be a badge of honour one day, pointing to the yellow felt hat he'd been told by his grandpapa had been in the family for generations, the first badge of shame Jews were forced to wear in Czechoslovakia, the hat they went on wearing even after it was replaced by yellow ruffs and yellow veils, the elders eventually stitching its image into the emblem of the Jewish Town. As he said all this Mama tugged Zuzka's scarf so it would cover the yellow star before letting her go outside to play – except the playground was now *verboten*.

Through the windows, this English street is dark slabs, forest encroaching. The nurse asks her something, concerned but hopeful. Zuzka nods and lifts her scone, closing her eyes against the clink and scrape, the echoes and strings of the barrack hall where she joined Verdi's 'Requiem'. The chorus took one hundred and fifty people. Zuzka had replaced her mother, after the train East. Maestro Rafael Schächter used to conduct them as if moving chess pieces. The woman is touching her elbow gently. Holding László up in the lake, Zuzka had considered leaving him on the shore to walk into the depths, disrupting its lace of leaves. She would have needed to weigh herself down first. Like Ophelia. But her mother abhorred a cliché. Zuzka had laughed at that, startling László and herself, the sound continuing even after she closed her mouth. No. It was birdsong, which she can hear now trapped in the chimney of the café – the *teashop*. How long has it been since she sat and listened to birds calling to each other? She can't remember. She tries to picture her bedroom in Prague, how close her bed was to the window. She tries again, measuring steps, this way, that. She can't remember that either. It's gone.

Zuzka ducks – a German army song is on the air. The English girls in the teashop stir too.

'Just those field workers,' says the woman, lathering cream on another scone for Zuzka.

When she first saw the tents, Zuzka thought they belonged to the Women's Land Army, but the soldier with no thumbs who sits awkwardly at the table – everything about him awkward, his presence here amongst women, his discomfort in his tweed jacket, the way he holds the miniscule cup – told her on the drive that the tents are for Germans and Italians. Men imprisoned by war. László told her the soldier was taken prisoner in North Africa, that he can be trusted: he has seen the inside of our walls and fences. The soldier said there's nothing to be afraid of, the POWs know better than to run. Eight men tried it. The local police rounded seven of them up. The eighth man was last seen up to his chin trying to cross the Tyne.

Their marching tune is an off-note that the birds can't fix. She covers her ears, trying to recall where her rocking horse sat, but she cannot.

'Are you all right, dear?'

She could draw all the cellars and attics and locked doors of Theresienstadt. If anyone asked, she could tell them that Gideon Klein dragged a legless piano into an attic and locked himself in there to play. She could give them the attic, if anyone asked.

Gideon was sent East.

Move me, Maestro. Move me.

FOR THE FIRST FEW weeks László could hear other boys crying, even a couple sleepwalking into doors and walls, but they are storm-bruised and quiet now. At night, he is alone with mathematics and present participle verbs. He tries to hold off sleep, to cordon off his nightmares, summoning instead the warmth of his mother's stomach against his forehead when she gave him a sudden hug in the hallway, interrupting his play. His father's laughter and József diving for pennies. The whirl of music at his cousin's wedding, the heart-thump of hide-and-seek with József and Alma on Margit Island, finding József underneath the water tower. He wakes with his pyjamas soaked and the sheet a pool of sweat. Breathes. Forces his way into the moment Zuzka clapped and cheered when he scored at football, the spots of happiness high on her cheeks, and the one kiss she gave him in the lake. He breathes. He imagines her kissing him again, feels his penis stir, and reaches down.

In the morning, he picks at the stiff spots on the sheet and hopes the Jewesses, as the rabbi calls them, won't change his linen.

LÁSZLÓ REACHES TWENTY-ONE KEEP-IT-UPS before the football bounces off into the browned leaves.

'Next match, you'll see, I'm going to beat Eryk.'

'I have no doubt,' says Zuzka. Calgarth Estate is still; a third of the children have been moved to hostels in Manchester or elsewhere. Eryk is one of the few older boys remaining and she isn't sure he'll be here for the next match. Their visas described them as visitors, but the road to Palestine is closed and the cities of England open, temporarily. She has not asked László where he intends to go, and he has not told her.

'Twenty-*three* . . .'

Zuzka laughs as László rushes after the ball again. She looks up the hill, her eyes following the path to Troutbeck Bridge. A ridge of houses makes up the village, with one pub, from whose door she has occasionally heard the quick strings of a fiddle. She has not stepped inside. Beyond, mist clings to the mountainside.

László is counting again – one, two, three, oops, four, that counts – and Zuzka does not tell him to stop and look when she sees a figure emerge from the wet onto the black road of the hill. A tall man, but not, she realises as he gets closer, one of the men from the village, or any of the men in charge here. He doesn't have the sloping walk of the villagers, the quick shuffle of Rabbi Asch, the tired tread of the doctor. The man looks around as if everything he sees is new. He is wearing an open mackintosh coat, and boots, with dark trousers and a fisherman's jumper.

The stranger comes to a stop at the bottom of the lane, and she sees that his hair is slicked back with a messy fringe. He is staring at László, and without knowing why she is reminded of kronen put on the eyes of the dead – perhaps because this man looks like his maker has just let him see again. Zuzka stands up. She knows who it is.

'László,' she breathes.

'What?'

'Turn around.'

László lets the ball roll away, doing as she says. His whole body goes slack, and for a second she thinks he might fall down. But he doesn't, he is scrambling, running, shouting, 'József! József!'

The man remains still, his face turning white. He does not even move when László runs right into him, only buffeted an inch. László throws his arms around the man, and it looks like he's head-butting him in the chest. Zuzka takes a few steps towards them. The man brings his arms up, closing them around László's back as if László has been burnt and he's afraid to touch his skin. Zuzka watches the colour return to the man's cheeks, watches a half-smile dent his face, watches him look down at his brother, tears gathering in his eyes. His look is one of inspection, verification. He gently takes László's arm, and lifts the sleeve by a few inches, and then clamps his hand on László's neck and pulls him into his body.

After a few minutes, the man eases László back, and lifts his eyes to Zuzka. He tilts his head. Then, in German:

'You're the girl from the picture.'

'You're the Scarlet Pimpernel.'

The man laughs, and Zuzka's insides shift. He offers his hand. 'József.'

'This is my brother,' says László, clinging onto József's arm. 'This is my brother József. This is József.'

'It is a pleasure to meet you,' she says. 'I'm Zuzka.'

József shakes her hand. 'A pleasure to meet you also.'

He looks at László again, and she thinks the movement of his gaze could be measured in microfractures: first László's dirty hair, then his broad forehead, then his wide eyes, his chapped lips, his thickening body. He nods, and says something in Magyar, something soft, passing it down from his mouth to László's like a mother bird.

No. 139. Were you aware of any political groupings (communist, Zionist)

No. 142. What were the aims of such groups

No. 151. What major towns or rivers were in the vicinity of the work camp

No. 153. Were you disinfected

No. 163. Were prisoners allowed to talk to each other while working

No. 168. Did you help each other

No. 170. How were you treated while working

No. 172. Was it possible to sleep

No. 176. Were you aware of any acts of sabotage committed by German and non-Jewish workers

No. 207. Could you get any information about the state of the war

Five

the memorial tour of Europe

I MET FELIX AT CENTRÁL Kávéház, a café that looked like the Budapest of my imagination, wood panelling and chandeliers and dark corners where hungover intellectuals could discuss the day's events, the corners a little dimmed now, a little sore-eyed from years under the dust sheets, years waiting for the communists to leave and decadence and debate to return, now a little over-priced, if it wasn't back then, tourists queuing in search of lemon macaroons and authenticity, tourists like me.

I couldn't really believe Felix had got time off work, bought a plane ticket and would be arriving for breakfast. Maybe the museum was paying for it. Maybe there were funds for vested interests. It took me a moment to recognise him in the mirror above the art nouveau bar, which seemed ridiculous after studying the pale freckles dotting his collarbone for long sleepless hours. But this was a more assured Felix, a man surer of his ground than he had been in London. I stood up, and he turned and walked towards me with a smile. He wore a white T-shirt with THIS IS A GENUINE REMNANT OF THE BERLIN

WALL clustered around his heart. We shook hands, preposterously, with the corner of the table jamming into my thigh.

'May I sit?'

'Of course. Thank you for coming all this way.'

'You have ordered?'

'No – but don't run off for a dozen helpings just yet.'

He gave me a lopsided grin. 'I told you I would learn to ask what you like.'

I twined my hands in my lap. 'You did. I was waiting for you.'

'I came as quickly as I could.'

'No, I mean – I was waiting to order.'

'Not waiting for me in a cosmic sense, then?'

'Not that I'm aware of.'

'Then I will learn to understand you better.'

'These are big intentions.'

'I didn't buy a return ticket.'

We ordered eggs and coffee and Felix laughed at my request for a jug of cold milk with tea. Savage, he said, and it was so like Silk it hurt. He asked why I'd come to Budapest, and I watched myself lie in his glasses, not mentioning László's letters or Silk's failures, telling him I simply wanted to see the Danube. I told him about the museums, the omissions I'd discovered in locked display cases, with no room for five hundred thousand dead Hungarian Jews. I told him that one museum said Hungary had no choice before occupation but to restrict the rights of Jews *without violence*, although labour service was already underway. Only the Documentation Centre told the whole story, from Hungary's first anti-Semitic law in 1920 – the first in Europe after World War One. I told him that attempts by

266

Magyars to rescue Jews increased after the Arrow Cross came to power, a flicker of hope; about finding János Zyyad's name on the memorial wall; about my sense that the grief I felt was somehow deferred, displaced, unreal, and yet the tears were as real as they could have been. He resisted – I realised later – talking to me about the psychology of second and third generation survivors. I told him about Karl Wolf and my plans to go with him to the yellow-star houses memorial day, showed him the list of events at apartments and basements where Jews had been forced to squeeze in alongside dozens of others, leaving their homes behind.

'What kind of name is that? Wolf?'

'I don't know how to say it in Hungarian, which seems fair given he insisted on calling me Éva.'

'You spent time together?'

I raised my eyebrows. 'A little.'

'He is from the Holocaust Documentation Centre?'

'Yes.'

'Does he know about the testament?'

'You tell me.'

Felix wiped his forehead. 'What does he want with you?'

I put my knife and fork together. 'How's the exhibition coming along?'

Felix pushed his glasses up his nose. 'We are sorting through photographs. We have a policy: we do not blow up pictures of men or women about to be shot into the pits. They are often naked, and try to cover up their bodies. It was not their choice to be photographed like that. It is evidence now, but we will honour their attempts to hide themselves.'

'Doesn't the same thing apply to Silk's testament?'

'That is up to you. The testament is signed by two people, Sándor Magda and Benjámin Károly. I spoke to a researcher in Israel who wrote a piece on DEGOB in the eighties; she gave me the contact details of a woman who worked as an interviewer then and still lives in Budapest. She might be able to help me get in touch with either Sándor or Béla, if they're still alive; the Israeli researcher said that the interviewers all took their own approach to the testaments, they were very invested, they felt responsible. They might still feel that way.'

'You think if a testament went missing they might know why?'

'I hope so.' He paused. 'There is something else. The painting at your house, in the bathroom, the lake and sky melting together – *Coniston Blue II*?'

'Yes?'

'It seemed very unfinished to me, very early perhaps in Joseph Silk's career, and it wasn't signed JS, which is very unusual. It got me thinking about the title.'

'So?'

'Did your great-uncle ever mention the Lake District to you?'

'László emigrated from Hungary to Israel. He was never in the Lake District.'

Felix looked around at the empty tables. 'I began to wonder what contact Joseph Silk might have had with the Lake District so early, and I remembered something I'd read once. The Windermere Boys – over three hundred Jewish refugees taken from concentration camps to the Lakes in 1945. I got in touch with an archivist at Manchester Jewish Museum, and he gave me the number of a survivor who was in Windermere—'

'Why are you telling me this?'

'This man, a Czech survivor settled in Manchester, he remembers your great-uncle.'

'That's not possible.'

'He also remembers László's big brother arriving one day.'

'You're wrong. Silk arrived to London Airport in 1945 on a mail and cargo carrier. It was raining. His only contact with the Lake District was a Northern girlfriend in the late forties. He talks about it on *This is Your Life*.'

'He was lying, I am afraid.'

'Excuse me?'

'The Czech in Manchester said it was very exciting, this big brother arriving, proof that families still existed somewhere. And he struck quite a romantic figure, seemingly.'

My throat was suddenly completely dry. 'Did he remember the brother's name?'

'No.'

'Then maybe he's thinking of someone else.'

'He does remember that this man seemed to have something wrong with his eyes. Bleeding around the iris.'

I sat back. 'Why wouldn't Silk tell me that he and László were in the Lake District together?'

'I do not know. But a friend found this for me at the British Library.'

Felix drew a photocopy from his pocket, unfolding it on the table between us. A newspaper. **JEWISH REFUGEES IN LAKELAND: County Council Concern.** My eyes skipped down the column – the arrival of children from Prague to Troutbeck Bridge had raised fears of tuberculosis, but the Ministry of Health found there was no longer need for such alarm, as the number of children 'was being greatly reduced' due to rehousing. The date read 17th November 1945.

Felix persisted: 'In an interview once, Joseph Silk said that when he arrived in London, the first thing he did was go to an exhibition on American art at Whitechapel Gallery. He said he was lucky to catch it in the last week, because it introduced him to Abstract Expressionism.'

'So?'

'So the exhibition ended on the thirtieth of November 1945. Just after the Windermere Boys left the Lake District.'

'You're really earning that internship, aren't you?'

'You know it is more to me than an internship.'

'Sure. You're a regular gumshoe, hunting down the facts. I guess I'm your best find. A live source.'

'*You* are more to me than an internship.'

'Am I?' I pushed the paper away. 'I don't understand this. I don't understand any of this.'

A small pause. 'There are other . . . irregularities?'

In the mirror above the bar, I looked scooped out. 'You tell me. You're the one digging up history he wanted to stay buried.'

'That's not what I mean to do,' said Felix. 'There are at least two unauthorised biographies currently in the works, and a documentary. Art in today's world isn't sexy. But secrets are. I read that piece in the British paper about his affairs with different actresses. People will make quick money, and they won't care how.'

'Then all you're doing is leaving breadcrumbs, all these phone calls, these friends, these favours.'

'But I *care*. And I know you care, too, about his life. Why else are you here?'

I knuckled my forehead. 'I'm here because I miss him. Because I – I want more. But I won't do this to him.'

'The world will give attention to a terrible atrocity because your grandfather is standing in the middle of it. What are you afraid of?'

I looked away, at the black-and-white photographs on the wall, poets and writers and artists who used to talk over breakfast here. Miklós Radnóti was there. I kept my eyes averted as I said, 'I'm afraid it was all a lie. That I was just his audience. His cameraman.'

Felix touched the edge of my sleeve. 'There are other irregularities?'

WE WALKED ALONG THE Danube while I told Felix about Silk and László's letters, what happened to Alma – a glance to the bruise-blue water – and the display cabinet at the Budapest History Museum which asked, *Which of these items do you think were found at the bottom of the river?* I told him about the furious lines exchanged between the brothers. About an argument over Z. We walked past the bronze shoes, stuck in their place, past the soldiers, past the White House where Russian secret services used to listen to wiretaps, and onto Margit Bridge, talking over the rumble of trams. We crossed onto Margit Island where people our age lay in the sun, stomachs bared to a cloudless sky, listening to music, passing beer around their circles. I imagined I was here on holiday and that Felix and I were sightseeing together. I imagined holding his hand. We picked our way down the bank towards the river. I tugged my shoes off, rubbing the red impression of the metal eyelets on my toes. Felix sat beside me, elbows on his thighs, body tight. After long minutes, I leant closer and said, 'Thanks for coming.'

'You already thanked me.'

'You deserve to be thanked twice. I know I'm kind of mean to you.'

He smiled a little. 'I know it too. And I know why.'

'Learning to understand me quickly, aren't you?'

He rested his head on his forearm, squinting at me. 'You are mean to me because I won't be mean back, and you need someone to bite.'

'And why's that?'

'Because you feel lost, and betrayed, and horrified with all you are learning.'

I looked out at Buda. 'I remember when I was seven or eight being told at school to ask my grandparents about their memories of the war. I asked Silk if he ever saw Hitler. I think he said yes. I think he said he saw him in a march, a parade – that there were tanks . . . But I was so surprised by the answer I didn't ask anything else. Scared by the answer. Around the same time, I asked Great-Uncle László what languages he spoke, and when he said German I told him I didn't do German at school. He said he'd learnt it in Buchenwald. Silk snapped at him to be quiet. I thought he was shouting at me and I cried. That's the only time Silk didn't come to make me feel better. It's just – I wish I'd stayed away. I read that in Mauthausen women were made to shave off all their body hair in icy water, and afterwards inspectors would tell them they hadn't done a good enough job, and make them – make them shave pubic hair that wasn't there, opening cuts that would freeze . . . or else they'd hose them down until their bodies iced over, and leave them like that to die. I keep thinking about that.'

Felix cleared his throat. 'They prefaced the first audio guide to Mauthausen with a warning. This will not be the whole truth. If we told you the whole truth, you would go mad.'

I rubbed my eyes. 'I don't know what I'm doing here.'

Felix sat forward, opening my bag. He untangled my camera and offered it to me. 'So do something.'

I took the black thing, wiping grime from its screen. Opened the lens, and switched to REC. Pointed it at him.

'Felix Gerschel, we are here in search of some kind of truth about Joseph Silk. Can you tell me what that truth might be?'

Felix ran a hand through his hair. 'No.' He put his hand out. 'But maybe we're here in search of some kind of truth about Eva Butler. Can you tell me why?'

I gave him the camera slowly, taking off my sunglasses. I felt microscopic in its unforgiving eye. In the background the Danube is vertiginous, threatening to swallow me. 'We are here because history doesn't happen in the past tense.'

FELIX WAS STILL ASLEEP when I slipped back into the twin hostel room. He had taken the other bed. I stood with my clothes clinging to my skin, still damp from the shower, looking at him. Felix opened his eyes. I didn't look away.

'Guten Morgen.'

'Did you sleep well?'

'Yes,' he said. 'You had nightmares.'

I dropped my stuff onto my bed. 'I hope I didn't disturb you.'

Felix stood up in his boxers. 'You were crying. In your sleep.'

'Sorry.'

'Do you dream badly often?'

His face was soft with concern, with care. I imagined telling him that last night I dreamt a man was trying to beat the door down, and my father looked on, unmoved, as I fumbled with a gun I could not load. How to say I also dreamt of you, and I don't think it was a nightmare – but it still scared me.

I ran a hand through my hair. We were inches from each other. Kiss me.

If you kiss me, I'll forget what today is.

Felix shifted towards me.

Don't touch me.

If you touch me, I'll fracture.

Felix put his glasses on. His look travelled. I remained still.

'We will meet your Wolf after the first event at the American embassy?'

'Yes.'

'You say his family was Roma?'

'He was raised as Gentile. But yes.'

'We are sure to get on.'

Felix left for his shower. I dried my hair, chose a face to wear. I checked the testament: it said that the Zyyad family moved to 18 Károly krt on the twenty-first of June 1944. Their yellow-star house.

Felix came back in wearing a Jüdisches Museum Berlin staff T-shirt.

'Are you sure you want to wear that today?'

'Today? Yes, I am sure.'

WE WAITED FOR KARL outside 18 Károly krt. My camera strap seared my shoulder. The apartment blocks around me were blank faces. I fiddled with the programme, a map of Budapest with yellow stars dropped like Google pins. Around us, the same crowd we had followed from home to home, star to star. The couple wearing T-shirts that read D-DAY NORMANDY 2014, on the memorial tour of Europe. The white-haired woman who kept doing up her coat and then undoing it, her hands nervous creatures.

'Want to hear a joke?' said Felix.

'What?'

'A joke.'

I smiled at him. 'OK.'

At that moment, Karl crossed into our sunlight, his voice carrying too loudly: 'A Jew, a Gypsy and a German walk into a bar?'

Felix turned into the sun. 'I was going for the one about the Russian space dog. You must be Karl.'

'Such is my fate. Didn't that dog die?'

'You don't find dead dogs in space funny?' said Felix, his face passive.

Karl bent to kiss me on both cheeks. The two men shook hands.

Karl nodded to Felix's T-shirt. 'A fellow researcher, blinking like me in all this sun. Éva says you are researching Joseph Silk. I have been looking into what happened to János Zyyad.'

Felix was flushing, asking how far Karl had got. I looked at the black door above us. A yellow star was stuck to its rusted postbox. At its centre, black words asked, Tudta-e Ön, hogy ez az épület 1944-ben csiggalos ház volt? Karl had told me it meant, 'Did you know that this building was a starred house in 1944?' But children of survivors coming from overseas had found that online translations jumbled and joined the words, asking if they knew that in 1944 this had been a house of chaos, a wandering house. In one of László's final letters, he said he'd heard – but not where – that János Zyyad had been nailed naked to a post in the snow and left to die. I felt outside of my body. Karl was fixed on Felix, a look of cold intensity, as if he had known Felix for more years than Felix had been alive, and they had been pacing a cage together for all of that time.

'Shall we?' said Karl.

We walked up the stairs, and I switched the camera to REC, capturing the climb of my scuffed shoes, Felix's worn boots, Karl's Converse, and, around the courtyard, closed doors, any of which might have once housed Emmuska and her children.

A door on the top floor was open. We stepped into a stranger's living room. Peach sofas, an elaborate fish tank, chairs laid out like a theatre. In the corner, sharing the space with a TV, a poet silently mouthed her lines. Karl accepted coffee on our behalf. We sat near the back. Musicians were checking their strings. Other people joined us, the slow walk of trespassers. In the kitchen, an old woman sat bent at a table. The light coming through the window scattered her sparse hair. I studied the unseasonal wool of her jumper. Silk had been cold, too, near the end.

'Shall I translate?' said Karl.

'I'd be happy to,' added Felix.

'He speaks Hungarian,' said Karl. 'Wise for one so young.'

I blinked, drew myself back to their ugly looks. 'I think I'll go and help with coffee.'

The old woman's daughter said they were fine, smiling at me. Her gaze lingered on my camera. I hovered by the table, saying, 'Excuse me? I'm sorry, do you speak English?'

The old woman raised red eyes to me. 'Some.'

'Do you mind if I ask you a question?'

Her daughter paused, the coffee pot off-kilter in her grip.

'I think my great-grandmother lived here in 1944.'

The old woman held my gaze, the pressure of keeping her head up making her nod in stutters. 'Name?'

'Zyyad. Zyyad Emmuska.'

The woman sat back. 'Yes.'

A tremble of china as her daughter almost spilt the coffee. She shuffled the objects on the tray into geometrical order. 'Why don't I close the door?'

She left us alone.

I sat down. My camera counted out the seconds. 'You remember them?'

Her head sank slowly. 'Yes.'

'Do you mind if I record this?'

The woman gestured around. 'That is what today is.'

I put the camera on the table, set it to run.

'What do you remember about the Zyyad family?'

'They moved into the flat below us.'

My feet twitched.

'Along with three other families. I remember Emmuska.'

'Why? What about her?'

The woman smiled a little. 'She used to sew for my mother. She was nice to me. I called her Emmuska Néni.'

I was aware of my heart beating, returning to my body. Emmuska, suddenly, was real.

'She looked like a princess. And she acted like one too. For her the curfew, this was nothing. For her, she would go out when she had to. She was always . . .' The woman scratched frantically at the plastic tablecloth, an animal burrowing. 'For her children. She was trying always for her children.'

'Do you know what happened to her?'

The old woman cupped nothing in her hand. 'I was never told. Do you know?'

'No. I was never told either.'

I slipped out, Karl and Felix half rising from their seats, the poet at the front fumbling her line. But I just waved my camera and left, clattering downstairs to the flat below. I raised my fist to knock, and stopped. The door was black, the window meshed with wire. Flowers hung in a basket rattling in the wind. Towels hung over the balcony. The number was done in lustrous brass, polished carefully. I stepped back, lifting my camera, and filmed Emmuska hauling her boxes to the door, and behind her József and László coming up the stairs with the last of their possessions, because there was not very much to carry now, at this stage – the same volume as the old woman's cupped hand. The footage shows a blank staircase, silent in the face of my imagining.

fit back together

'**W**HAT'S WRONG WITH YOUR EYES?'
   József uses his thumbs to pull the lids down over his eyes, gently, and then opens them wide, saying cheerfully, 'Nothing at all.'

They are in the dining hall. Zuzka ran to fetch the rabbi, fetch the doctor, fetch Eryk, ran as if there was a fire to put out.

'The colour of your irises, it's bleeding out. What happened?'

'What happened to your fang?'

László snorts, mirroring József by pressing his thumb to the gap of his missing canine. 'Rifle butt.'

József's whole body seems to contract. 'Did they – are you . . . ?'

László has never seen József unable to speak. 'I'm fine. I'm fine. Where have you been? I looked on the lists, the Red Cross lists, you weren't there.'

'I was in Budapest, trying to find you. Then Germany, then Switzerland. That's where I found this.'

László laughs, and tears come too, as József puts the Czech

newspaper on the table. There he is, smiling for his brother in the front row.

'I knew you'd see it. I knew. Where's everybody else? Are they with you?'

'László . . .'

'Mama, Alma, Papa – you found them too? Didn't you?'

József looks down at the paper. His hand lands on it as if the muscles in his arm have given up. 'Just you. Just us.'

László tries to speak but something is stuck in his throat, and then the doors swing open. The doctor and Rabbi Asch stand side by side on the threshold, but are knocked aside by Eryk and Jan and a dozen others, who pile in, then stop abruptly, staring at József.

József puts the newspaper in his pocket, standing up.

László brushes away his tears. 'My brother! This is my brother!'

Rabbi Asch and Doctor Posner come forward and shake József's hand, both talking at once, József answering their questions. 'József, this is Eryk, József.' József shakes Eryk's hand too. 'And Jan. And Meyer, and Harry, this is József – I know them from – we were – we met in Theresienstadt.'

József clears his throat. 'You are all very difficult to find.'

'That's the idea,' says Eryk, laughing. 'I hear you're a champion stone-skimmer.'

József slides his hands into his pockets. László waits, head suddenly blazing. 'None better,' says József. 'None better.'

*

ZUZKA WATCHES THEM WALK down to the lake from the kitchen window, holding her breath.

'IT'S NO LAKE BALATON, but it's beautiful, isn't it?' asks László.

József looks out with wrinkled eyes. 'Balaton is no Balaton.'

'What do you mean? Was it shelled?'

'I mean nothing at all.'

The sun has been wiped grey by clouds. He wants heat; he wants to show József a running jump into the water. He wants József to say something, not just walk next to him with a pinched frown.

'Where were you?' he asks again.

'Serbia. Hungary. Austria.'

'But *where* were you? The camps?'

'There's no point talking about it.'

'What do you mean?'

'It's over. We lived.'

László watches a duck glide in circles. 'Doctor Posner says it's important to talk.'

'What is he, a doctor of words?'

'Psychology.'

'Jewish?'

'Ultra-Orthodox.'

'Just what you need. Freud and God, both believing they are qualified to be the other.'

László hesitates. 'He's a good man. He hasn't done anything to you.'

József breathes out through his nose. He looks so much older.

He gives László another half-smile, and now László thinks about it, he's never seen that smile on his brother's face before.

'I'm not angry,' he says. 'I am . . . you are alive. I am made again. That's enough. Why pick over the bones?'

'Or count them?'

József raises an eyebrow at him. 'This is no time for poetry.'

'If not now, when?'

'Ha. They treat you well here?'

'I told you, they're good people, kind people.'

'Jews who got out before the war?'

'And Englishmen. The English are stranger than you can imagine.'

'Strange how?'

'Everything is nice. Nice day, nice hat, nice tea, nice weather, nice boy. No other words are needed.'

'They let you come for free?'

'Yes. They said it was temporary, that we would go to Palestine, but something called the White Paper means we cannot. At least not yet.'

'Palestine.'

'Yes. The British Jews heard about us, in Theresienstadt. I mean, I wasn't *in* Theresienstadt, I was on a train. I was in Buchenwald. Were you ever – were you ever there?'

'Buchenwald?'

'Yes. I used to sometimes imagine – I used to think we might find each other.'

'No. I was not in Buchenwald.'

'Do you know what happened there?' László is struggling to get words out.

'Yes.'

'You do?'

'Yes. Don't – you don't have to speak of it.'

László doesn't want to speak: he wants to show his brother the scars on his shoulder where he was forced to carry wet sacks of concrete up and down the quarry of Buchenwald to no purpose, the tooth marks in his calf from the attack dogs the SS and the Hungarian guards set on him at Krawinkel, the grooves of his ribs saved from starvation by the Hungarian Jewish doctor who got him onto kitchen detail so he could eat potato peel, the burns on his forearm from a detonation he couldn't limp clear of in the Thuringian Mountains, the thinning of his hair, the gradual retreat of jaundice. He wants József to kiss his bruises better – as he used to.

'Where were they taking you, on this train?'

'Auschwitz.' László tries to catch József's expression, but they are walking under the black bower of a tree. 'The Reds were advancing, and the SS stopped the train. Partisans freed us.'

'Serbs?'

'Czechs. They took us back to Theresienstadt, and the Reds looked after us, and then the British came to fetch us.'

József nods, a single stroke down. He does not lift his chin, but asks, vocal cords pressed together, 'Do you know where Mama was sent? And Alma?'

László breaks a brown leaf from a bush. He rolls it between his fingers as if preparing a cigarette. His hand is shaking. 'No. They were in the yellow-star house when I was taken. You had no sign of them? Or Father?'

'No. Magyars are living in our home.'

'You mean others Jews?'

'I mean Magyars.'

László throws the leaf away. 'Then we'll take it back, József. We'll take it back.'

'László . . .' József stops, looking him over. 'There is no going back.'

'What?'

'We're not wanted there.'

'But it's our home.'

'It never was. There is no Budapest.'

'No Budapest? That's mad. That's a mad thing to say.'

'Budapest is destroyed. The Chain Bridge is in the Danube. Buda Castle is in pieces. The British Mission is known as the Sleepy Hollow, and pengös drift in the street, not worth the mud they are stuck in. I wrote to dozens of organisations searching for you, and you know what I used? Ten million pengö stamps. Everything is the dollar now.'

'That doesn't matter. We were born there. Papa always said they can't stop us being Budapesti.'

'Can't they? Winter is setting in, and famine with it. When the wind blows you hear the sound of flapping paper, because that's the only thing left to block up whole *sides* of buildings. Allied officers live in villas in the Buda Hills, paid for by the government – the villas our family and friends used to own, and haven't come back for. The Park Club is now the Allied Officers' Club, and any officer you meet in a bar will tell you jokes about the Russians. *Stalin made two mistakes – showing Europe to the Russians, and the Russians to Europe.* Or, *The atomic bomb dropped on Hiroshima, and exploded in Moscow.* Budapest is a training ground for petty

284

differences. They don't mention that it was the Hungarian army who invaded Russia, and the Reds who saved the Jews of Budapest – those alive to be saved.'

'Then let's be Russians in Budapest! God, József, what does it matter what we call ourselves? If the Reds want to give us our home back, take it from them!'

József's eyes are wet. 'The Russians have blown it,' he says. 'When they first arrived, people laughed at how they enjoyed going round and round in revolving doors, and stole bicycles from street corners. Wasn't that their fair reward? But they kept on taking, and not just diamonds or radios. They took women too, and not only Jews – that our fellow Magyars might understand. There is outrage, from every side. Taking a car from a banker, that's understandable; but taking a coat from a starving man, taking the rings a Jew buried in his garden, that is not. The Russians aren't our friends. They won't save us twice.'

'Then the Americans—'

'You aren't listening! No one walks in Budapest at night. Drunken soldiers rule the streets, along with criminals the Nazis freed from jail on their way out, as if Hungary didn't have enough criminals. You want to know the first two words I learnt in Russian? Spasibo, and davai. Thank you, and give it up. You think the Americans care? You think our countrymen care? But it's well enough because I have nothing to say to our neighbours, and they have nothing to say to me. You want to know another new joke? If you rush into the streets of Budapest and punch the first man you see right in the face, you probably won't be wrong. For the Russians, Americans, British, for all of *them* the Magyars will turn on the charm. They are desperate for everyone to forget whose side they were on. But they won't turn on any charm for us. There is no Jewish Budapest anymore. Do you hear me? There is no culture, no peace, no poetry, no hope. Budapest is gone.'

'We can take it back.'

'Look at the two of us, and say that again.'

László tastes bile at the back of his mouth. 'Then where will we go?'

'I don't know. All I know is that, for the first time in years, there is a *we*. There is an *us*. That's all that counts. Not what happened. Forget all that. Look at where you are. This lake. The mountains. Wouldn't you rather be born again, here today, and forget all that came before?'

László looks into the sheen of József's face, the knifepoint conviction. He is making his big brother cry. He will never speak of any of this again – only to the Windermere Boys. Grief strangles his throat. He tries to smile, holding himself back from shaking József with all the violence in his body, shaking into him: *Listen to me. I can't be silent. You have to listen to me.*

ZUZKA LINGERS AT THE end of the corridor, fingernails digging into the flaking paint of the wall. Watching the boys crowd around József's new bedroom, all talking at once, and amongst them all László explaining: this is your cupboard, this is your shelf, this is your towel. He is talking even louder than normal, and she wonders if the others can hear what he is really saying: you are mine, you are mine, you are mine – a desperation that cuts.

*

LÁSZLÓ HAS NEVER BEEN to The Crooked Duck before, put off by the Troutbeck locals who talk a version of English even more private than the nurses from Manchester. One of them keeps a horse tied up by the front door, and if it is sunny, he lets the horse lap from a bucket filled with the same black stuff as his pint glass. Once László saw the horse fart, tail flapping like laundry in the hands of impatient women. But after dinner József said they should celebrate and asked if there was a town nearby, a coffee shop, a bar. They explained that Ambleside was a two-hour walk away, and József glanced around the dinner hall as if it were a trap. László felt his gut clamp, but before he could offer anything, Zuzka – who never suggests doing anything with the group – said, what about The Crooked Duck?

The locals welcome them noisily, saying they'd been waiting for the boys to join them for a pint.

'Just don't give me what they give the horse,' László whispers to Eryk, who laughs. László hopes József is watching. They sit in a corner and the nurse Rebecca – who invited herself – says she'll order. József offers his help, and László watches him stoop under the low ceiling beams to the bar.

'Are you all right?'

László turns to Zuzka. 'Of course. Why wouldn't I be?'

'It's a big shock.'

'I'm fine. I'm great. He seems fine, doesn't he? I mean, does he seem all right to you?'

'I don't know him.'

'No, I know, but . . . Zuzka?' She is no longer looking at him. László turns to the door. Three men carrying music cases have squeezed inside. They exchange greetings with the barman and go to the corner. They are big men, and remind László of barrel-rollers on the banks of the Danube. When one gets out a fiddle the sight of his paws twisting the slender neck makes László laugh. He turns to Zuzka, expecting her to join in, but she is staring at the floor.

Eryk spreads his elbows on the back of the seat. 'Get ready for your new national music.'

'Not so new,' says József, in English, setting a tray of drinks on the table. 'They are like our . . . what is the word for Roma? Gypsy?'

'I wouldn't say that any louder,' says Rebecca.

'I mean it as the highest compliment.'

'Of course you do,' she says. 'You're probably a Marxist.'

'Probably,' József agrees. It makes Rebecca giggle. 'No coffee,' says József to the table, 'so I got those *underage*, as the barman put it, root beer – root of what I do not know.'

József sits on the other side of the table, sandwiched between Zuzka and Rebecca. He lifts his glass, which is filled with something the colour of dehydrated piss.

'A toast,' he says, 'Britannia, and all who sail in her.'

'To all who sail in her!'

'I don't think you said that quite right,' says Rebecca.

Eryk laughs. 'I think he did. You play football, József?'

'You have matches here?'

'We've got a competition going, but we keep losing players. You should join us.'

László is light-headed. He wonders if just a few sips can have made him drunk, if there really is beer in this, if he is shocked, as Zuzka says. Suffering from a shock. He saw a man thrown into the air once after touching the electric fence, a long-jumper in reverse. He breathes, and feels like he is not taking in air but drawing acid up from his stomach instead. The musicians have started up – the fiddles are quick, argumentative – and József is wrong, it doesn't sound anything like Magyar gypsies. László turns and looks at the window over his shoulder, which is blue and golden, reflecting the lamps of the pub. He watches József's black reflection merge with Zuzka's and glances back to see József whisper something to her, and Zuzka shake her head. He thinks he sees József pass her something white under the table – tissue? A handkerchief? – but then everybody claps, and József leans over and clamps him on the arm, dislodging the tears waiting in his throat.

József pushes his glass across the scarred table to László. 'Try some,' he says in English. László clasps the warm glass. 'Öcs.' László pauses with his lips on the rim. József continues in Magyar: 'Ne sírj.'

Don't cry. László swallows. The taste burns his throat. Don't cry. József used to say that to him when he scraped his shin or when father shouted at him – *Don't cry, little brother, don't cry* – and it would seal the indignation building in his chest because it was delivered so gently, so kindly, that it also meant I love you. Don't cry, I love you. But now he looks at the broken smile on József's face and sees only a rigid requirement. Don't cry.

In Buchenwald, he would rehearse the sensation of slotting his smaller hand into József's, fingers interlinking, knuckles making room for each other. Keeping his eyes low, he studies his hand clutching the drink, his forearm tensed on the table, muscles knotted. Across the table, József is drumming on the wood with a misshapen index finger, sending an urgent one-word telegram. László pushes the drink back. József closes his hand around it and retreats. No. It won't work. They won't fit back together.

the dimensions of a man

K ARL ASKED IF WE'D like to join him and some others for
dinner. Felix stayed quiet, so I accepted for the both of us. We
headed back towards the Danube, to the tip of the Fifth District.
The apartment blocks with their heavy iron doors looked different
to me now. Dinner was at the home of one of Karl's friends, a poetry
translator and campaigner who ran their circle.

'Do you have club cards and a password?' asked Felix.

Karl grinned a little. 'No point. Tibor's apartment is bugged.'

We were buzzed into an apartment block. Karl led the way to the
top floor, where a red door was propped open with a fern.

'I hope I'm dressed OK,' I said.

'You?' Karl laughed. 'I am bringing József Zyyad's granddaughter
to dinner, and she worries about how she is dressed.'

'You get points for that, bringing József Zyyad's granddaughter?'
asked Felix.

Karl nodded to Felix's museum T-shirt. 'Don't you?'

The apartment was built on books, dark and crowded with them.

I followed the pale stripe of Karl's shirt into the kitchen, where a group of young men and women sat around a long table that looked for a moment like the lime table from Fitzroy Park, now in storage. They all called out hello, shaking Karl's hand. Through the open double doors, I could see a silver-haired man I took to be Tibor, and with him a woman in her thirties, both standing by the stove. The air smelt of paprika, cigar smoke and stale sweat.

'This is Éva,' Karl said, taking my arm lightly, 'the girl I told you of, and this is her guardian, it would seem, Felix Gerschel of Berlin.'

'I'd be flattered, if you meant that as a compliment,' said Felix.

'I'm sure I did. Everybody here is something thoroughly beloved to the government. Writers, poets, painters – and Éva herself is a filmmaker.'

I sank into a leather sofa, Felix next to me. I looked around for likely places to hide bugs. Karl slipped into the kitchen, put his hand on Tibor's shoulder, and whispered something into the man's ear that made his spine quiver into a straight line. Then the girl sitting on the arm of the sofa moved and the curtain of her hair blocked my view.

'What kind of films do you make?' she asked.

'Documentaries. Or, at least, I want to. So far, my record is a twenty-two-minute film about Hampstead Heath. What do you do?'

'I'm a translator, too. Tibor was my supervisor at the university until – I suppose Károly told you, Tibor was forced to quit.'

I looked again at the man in the kitchen. 'What kind of things do you translate?'

'At the moment, instructions for a dishwasher company. But I am working on a poetry collection that will make all dishwasher instructions seem prosaic.'

I joined her laughter, and felt the taut strings of my body relax. Karl reappeared, two boat-size glasses of red wine in his hands.

'For you both,' he said, sitting on a footstool. 'Tell me, Felix, why do you work at the Jewish Museum? You are not Jewish, Éva tells me. So: you feel guilty?'

My breath caught in my throat. The girl on the arm of the sofa punched Karl in the shoulder.

'I'm an art historian,' said Felix. 'That's all.'

Karl balanced his own glass on his knees. 'No guilt to be relieved of, then?'

'I'm twenty-nine years old. What am I guilty of? Unless you believe in guilt by blood. You wouldn't be the first to have that idea.'

The hollows of Karl's cheeks pooled red.

The girl leant forward. 'Do you understand any Hungarian, Éva?'

'It's all Greek to me. As is Greek, I suppose.' A weak joke to equally weak laughter. Next to me, Felix remained rigid. I turned with an over-bright smile. 'D'you know that one? Felix and I have been trading idioms.'

Karl looked at Felix with a sneer. 'I can give you the German version. Ich verstehe nur Bahnhof – I can only understand "train station". But then, that's the only word Germans needed in the mid-part of the twentieth century.'

Felix sat very still. 'I don't think the Hungarian government had any trouble understanding Bahnhof, either. So don't blame me.'

'I don't. I blame your museum for thinking it has ownership over our pasts. For taking evidence that belongs to us.'

'We will have no theatrics just yet.' It was Tibor, standing in the doorway. He was in his sixties, wearing faded purple corduroy trousers and a yellow shirt. A grey beard clung to his thin face; his rimless glasses made the look of mild consideration seem sterner. 'Dinner is ready, and this is not the floor of parliament.'

The meal began with soup, and I'd only had one mouthful when Tibor leant on an elbow towards me and said: 'So, you are interested in the bloody Jews?'

I lowered my spoon. 'You could put it that way.'

Tibor smiled at Felix. 'And you too, young man, from your T-shirt. You are both very welcome here.'

The sentence, 'Thank-you-for-having-us,' tripped off my tongue, pre-programmed, the way it would when Silk took me to one of his friend's houses for dinner.

'Not at all, not at all. I am delighted. We will talk about the Jewish question . . . of course, there has always been a Jewish question, and there always will be, but in most of the world it lies dormant, or has been until recently. In Hungary, the situation is unique because this is the *old* Jewry. Young men and women who survived the camps came back to this apartment building and lived here for another fifty years with the people who denounced them. Sometimes, when I give a talk, I come home and find a yellow star spray-painted on the door, and it does not peel off like those well-meaning stickers. It's growing worse under this government. Now we are hearing things we have not heard since the 1930s. Now people are frightened, Jews and Roma.'

'Why do you stay?'

He answered almost before I'd finished the question, the flat of his hand coming down on the table: 'Duty.'

I looked at the stiff cartilage of his fingers and, for a brief moment, imagined his knuckles daubed with paint. He was a grand performer, giving me his whole life, telling me how people on the bus tap him on the chest, 'Their way of saying . . .' He clenched his fist. 'But they are too scared to acknowledge me out loud.' I suspected I would get the same gust of charisma from him in the deserted wreckage of a bombed building or on an empty stage. This was not a man who needed props, or supporting acts, just words to carry the show. He reminded me of Silk so much I had to stop eating for fear of the pit of acid in my stomach.

'You are related to the Zyyad family?' Tibor asked.

I wanted to shrink behind my camera. 'Yes,' I said. 'My grandfather was Joseph Silk. The artist.'

'A great merchant family, the Zyyads.'

'You knew them?'

'My parents did. Don't look so surprised. It's a small country. I can tell you a story about your grandfather's uncle. He made a lot of money with paper factories, I think it was. Anyway, he owned a villa in the Buda Hills. He was the first man to invest in racecar driving in Hungary, and he had the track built so that it would pass by his villa gardens. His daughters used to stand out there on the balcony and wave the racers on.'

'Do you know what villa?'

'No. Only that it was taken by an Arrow Cross officer, who answered the door to a Soviet soldier and was shot in the head. It was a completely different world then – racecars in the living room. The communist era took a funny turn. I remember being dressed in knee-high Victorian socks. I used to kiss a framed picture of Stalin goodnight. Everything became ironic: when you talked with a friend, you always knew you were joking, everything said with a wink in the eye. But you didn't know who was listening – the spy network was everywhere. Decades spent in an absurdist joke without being able to laugh. You learnt to self-censor. Translation was a way out of the prison-house you built inside yourself – poetry, a gate to the West.'

'Tibor was one of the first to translate Miklós Radnóti,' said Karl.

I tried to remember if I had told Karl that Silk and Radnóti were on the same death march, but I had drunk too much too quickly and couldn't recall.

Conversation turned to Hungarian literature. Tibor watched me with his head tilted. He crooked a finger, and we went into the living room. I sat in an armchair while he paced up and down his bookshelves, pulling out spines, dismissing them, until finally he took down a stiff paper journal.

'A gift for you. *Kúpa*. The last issue. Owned by your great-grand-father, and edited unofficially, I understand, by your great-grandmother.'

The cover showed a Gyula Derkovits woodcut. The language resisted me. The pages were thick and soft, like furred cotton. Tibor slowly dropped to one knee. His arms moved around mine, and, in the dim light, Silk was next to me, turning the pages to a centre-fold, where a painting by his mother waited, a watercolour of the Danube, the colours made uncertain by time, the river doubting it was ever real.

'Emmuska Zyyad painted this.'

I looked into Tibor's lined face. 'Were your parents survivors?'

'My mother.'

'Did she talk to you about what happened to her?'

'Eventually.'

'Did talking help?'

Tibor covered my hand. 'It's the only thing that does.' The door opened, and Karl hovered on the threshold. Tibor dusted his knees as he stood up. 'I will leave you both.'

Karl pulled up another chair. 'I'm sorry about earlier, with Felix.'

'Isn't Felix doing what you'd *want* Germans to do?'

'Surely he makes you uncomfortable, Éva? Makes you pause, even for a moment, makes you wonder if you are safe?'

His question twisted in my chest.

'Maybe it's my age,' said Karl. 'Blue eyes, a German accent. Maybe the second generation remembers better than the third.' He sighed. 'We know about Joseph Silk's testament. We know the German curator found it in his basements. We know you are considering giving it to him.'

'You've known this whole time?'

'Éva, we want you to give it to the Holocaust Documentation Centre and the Budapest Jewish Museum for joint ownership.'

I spread my fingertips over the cover of *Küpa*. 'What would you do with it?'

'People will have to listen to what we are saying when it is Joseph Silk talking.'

'I think you're drastically overestimating the importance of an English painter in the twenty-first century.'

'And I think you're drastically underestimating the importance of a Hungarian Jewish survivor with a voice in the twenty-first century.'

'The man's dead,' I said, swallowing a sudden unexpected surge of tears. 'What voice do you think he has?'

'Éva, you don't have to be alone. There are people – we are people who are equipped to deal with this as it should be dealt with. You can trust us with his words, his voice. You can trust me.'

'I can't leave Silk here. Or give him to Felix. That was his vigil. To stay away.'

'Then how will things get better?'

'I don't know.'

Karl sat back. 'They won't. The answer is they won't get better. My life is a matter of shouting in the street while people walk by pretending not to hear.'

I could feel the thrumming fervency of his dedication from across the room, a heat shimmer burning him to exhaustion. 'I'm sorry.'

'Sorrow is not enough. It is never enough.'

'It's all I have to give.'

Karl considered me from beneath greying eyebrows. 'We all have to be braver.'

I felt Silk duck his head, try to locate some deflection or diversion, a way out.

Karl sighed. 'I can tell you that your great-grandfather is most likely buried in an unmarked mass grave in the hills of Sopronbán-falva. The SS and Arrow Cross slaughtered three hundred and fifty labour servicemen on a march there. The ground has never been exhumed. I am sorry I can't offer you more. But at least you know what happened to your grandfather. I do not know where my parents died, or how.'

'WHAT WAS YOUR JOKE about the Russian space dog?'

Felix put his drink down. 'What?'

'Your joke, earlier. What was it?'

'Why did nobody hear Laika bark in the night-time?'

'I don't know. Why?'

'Because in space, no one can hear you bark.'

'That's really terrible.'

'Spasibo.'

Around us, the bar appeared and disappeared in strobes: dancing bodies, a roof made of strung netting, crates forming a bar, communist cars turned into tables, a Heidelberg press whose arm seemed to move in time to the beat. We were in a romkocsma – a ruin bar slotted into a bombed-out space between two buildings – in the Jewish Quarter. Locals still called it the ghetto. On the way here we'd passed the Great Synagogue, its red tessellations soft in the lamplight, its gift shops closed, as well as smaller synagogues propped up by crooked beams and punctured with bullet holes.

'What shall we drink to now?'

'Convenient nostalgia,' said Felix, 'and selective memories.'

'You mean Karl? Don't listen to anything he said. It was bullshit.'

'I meant the ancient TVs behind you.'

'Oh.'

'This place gives kitsch a new meaning.'

I looked at the bank of old monitors playing black-and-white footage, what looked like home videos from the 1920s and 30s: Christmases, boat trips, a wife undressing for her husband in the dark. 'I like it.'

'Then we shall drink to hipsters.'

'Don't tell me you're complaining. They serve gluten-free unleavened bread at two in the morning.'

Felix leant in. 'You do know the way to my heart.'

I cleared my throat, glanced at the screens again. 'Kind of reminds me of Tacita Dean.'

'What does?'

'The films. The angles. She's a video artist. Have you seen *Fernsehturm*, the film she made of the Berlin TV tower?'

'Your German accent is terrible. And yes, I have. She uses "By the Beautiful Danube", or "The Blue Danube", as you call it.'

'We played that at the party.'

'What party?'

I felt my face go red. 'I mean the wake. Silk loved parties.'

'Do you?'

'I used to. Not to sound utterly ancient. I just . . .' I watched the dance floor. 'Since Silk's been ill, I've felt uncomfortable in crowds. Tired.'

Felix brushed my arm, his fingers folding around my camera. 'Does this make you feel yourself? Filming?'

'John says I do it to hide.'

'Do you?'

I shrugged.

'You are making your film about Joseph Silk still?'

'It's just fragments. Clips. I don't know what I'm making. Tacita Dean, she says that making a film is always connected to loss and disappearance. You're trying to work out how to film something that isn't there. But it is there, too. Loss is tangible. So is silence. It forces absences onto your life, absences that are physical, felt in the gaps. Does that make sense?'

'Yes.'

'Why are you smiling?'

'Because you make me smile.'

I played with the cuff of his shirt. 'Can I ask you a personal question?'

He laughed. 'How can I refuse you?'

I looked at him: the sweat-sheen of his hair in the neon light, the patience of his grin. I felt that if I leant in to kiss him, it would feel right. But I couldn't. I raised my voice over the music. 'If you met me, and I was just Eva Butler, not Joseph Silk's granddaughter – if I was just me – could you refuse me then?'

'I'm not refusing anything. In fact, I'm readily agreeing.'

'But are you agreeing to me, or the Blue Room?'

Felix frowned. 'You think I'm, what, trying to collect you?'

'I don't know.'

His hand slipped from the back of my neck. 'So not everything Karl said was bullshit to you.'

'No. That's not it. Look – you can't blame me for asking.'

'I can't? OK.'

'I'm sorry.' I scrubbed my face. 'I didn't mean to say it that way.'

He pushed air from his body. 'We never drank to anything.'

The glass was slick against my fingers. 'So what should we drink to?'

'Dead space dogs.'

We drank. Felix fixed me a look across the table. 'Can I ask *you* a personal question?'

I sat up straight. 'Yes.'

'What's the strangest job you've ever had?'

I laughed, queasy relief. 'Goat wrangler. A summer at Kentish Town City Farm. You?'

'This one.' He was staring directly at me.

I felt my smile drain away. 'So this *is* a job to you?'

'Yes.'

'Oh.'

His jaw shifted, and then he seemed to come loose, shoulders falling. 'It was. But it hasn't been for a while now. Whether we would have anything in common if it weren't for this, I don't know. But I don't think it matters. At least, it doesn't matter to me. It might to you.' He let go of my hand. I hadn't realised I'd reached for him over the table; hadn't realised he'd accepted my hand before I'd held it out. 'So why don't we keep from burning the house down until you know.'

My head was colourful fog. 'Burning it down?'

A small smile. 'An English idiom.'

'I think you mean, we get on like a house on fire.'

'If you say so.'

They'd turned smoke machines on. After a moment's silence, Felix said, '*The scent and smoke and sweat of a casino are nauseating at three in the morning.* That's my favourite opening line of a book.'

I laughed. 'Bond, James Bond.'

'At your service.'

We danced. I remember his hands on my hips. I remember leaning my head into his chest, finding a small dip at his breastbone. As we left, men and women wearing civilian layers and headscarves tight against the cold walked across the black-and-white monitors, a man in a military coat and a fur hat filling the screen. The yellow star on his chest was rumpled. If it were possible to be illiterate in the signs of the time, it could be an autumn leaf. A poster said the exhibition was part of Yellow Star Memorial Day. It said that the building that housed the archives was once the headquarters of Leo Goldberger's textile business; that Mr Goldberger had died of starvation the day Mauthausen was liberated. I followed Felix out onto the street. My fingers weren't working and Felix helped me into my coat. We stood under a mural of a Rubik's cube unfolding across the side of a building.

'Is that really your favourite opening line?'

'Maybe I just wanted to dance with you.' He shrugged. 'I remember how you like your imperialist symbol.'

'Smooth.'

'You're not the easiest girl to be smooth around. I am in danger of being pricked.'

We stood a few inches from each other. I wanted to reach for his hand again. I wanted to dig my hands into my pockets. 'Do you have a real favourite first line?'

'Beloved imagination, what I most like in you is your unsparing quality.'

'What's that?'

'André Breton, *Manifesto of Surrealism*. I am, what would you say, a manifesto enthusiast.'

We fell into step down the small street, past dark coffee shops and print studios. I thought: I could move here. Live here. Love here. The words jogged about with each bump of his arm. This here could be mine, beloved, and in it I could love, and be loved.

'Do you know if Joseph Silk ever considered writing a manifesto?' asked Felix.

I didn't answer. Talking would mean telling him what I wished my imagination would spare me. I'd read that the Nazis took Admiral Horthy's son to Mauthausen to ensure Horthy cooperated when it looked like the old man was having an eleventh-hour change of conscience. Horthy's son said afterwards that he was kept in a dark room with a small mound of ashes. The ashes instructed him on the dimensions of a disintegrated man. I kept picturing that heap of ashes, moon-silver.

I didn't want to talk. But I couldn't reach for his hand either.

Here I am, there you are, and between us – between us this battle over the dimensions of a man.

'The Jewish Museum here has found one of the DEGOB volunteers who interviewed Joseph Silk,' said Felix. 'He's in a care home in Győr. He's agreed to talk to you. To us. If you want me to come.'

I kept my gaze on the canopy of murals growing over us. 'I'd like you to come. If you want to.'

'I do.'

'Where is Győr?'

'Northern Hungary.'

'Near Sopron?' I asked.

I felt Felix's body move away. 'Where my grandparents lived? Yes. But I don't – they're not family I was close to.'

'Silk's father is buried outside of Sopron.'

Felix stopped walking. I stopped too. I wanted light. I wanted to see his face.

'I'm going to get the train there,' I said. 'To the forest, where he's buried. If you – if you want to come, I'd like you to.'

He released a breath. The blare of a bar as a door opened in another street. 'OK,' he said. 'OK.'

you will find no horizon

'**W**E'VE GOT TO GET good seats.'

József turns to Zuzka, pretending to whisper. 'He's been mad for Leslie Howard since he was seven and I snuck him into the cinema to see the first Scarlet Pimpernel. Love at first sight.'

It is Troutbeck Bridge Mart today, the annual grading of fat sheep, and Zuzka suggested they escape the smell and blare, catching a bus to Appleby, where The Cosy Cinema is showing *Pimpernel Smith*. She'd found it in the paper, bringing the *Coming Shortly!* to László with the care of a clerk delivering a peace treaty. She's wearing a dress one of the nurses gave her: when she stands a certain way, he can see the small curves of her breasts. 'Leslie Howard's father was Hungarian Jewish, did I tell you that?' he says. 'And his mother was German Jewish and English. He was born in London, though. He was a hero in the Great War, you know. We look alike, Leslie Howard and me.'

'Of course you do,' laughs József.

'When I was younger, I thought our mother, Emmuska, was

secretly writing the Pimpernel books. That's Baroness Orczy's first name.'

They sit in the second row of folding chairs, László and József either side of Zuzka. The room fills slowly. People are looking at them: have they heard, all the way over here, of the Windermere Boys? The projectionist's beam is hot and clattering, and the advertisements and cartoons flicker with the shadow of people's cigarettes. During the newsreel, László tries to catch the line of Zuzka's knee, the curve of her thigh. Finally, the certificate spools over the screen. *Pimpernel Smith* – directed *and* produced by Leslie Howard! In 1941 – it's three years old and he didn't even know it existed. Gothic script appears on the screen: *Berlin in Spring, 1939.*

László leans over to József. 'What is this?'

'It seems the Scarlet Pimpernel has a remarkable life span.'

'*What?*'

'It's a retelling, László.'

'About us?'

On the screen, two SS officers fix their eyes on him.

'Do you want to leave?' asks József.

László says nothing. The Scarlet Pimpernel had been planning to save him. He is now Horatio Smith, a professor of archaeology and antiquities disguised as a journalist to infiltrate Camp Grosseberg. László hasn't heard of it. The gate to Grosseberg is the kind you might find on a farm to stop cattle from straying. It has been strung with barbed wire. The scene could have been filmed here in the Lake District.

'Let me show you our little camp,' says the Commandant. 'You will see how happy everybody is.'

László jumps when something skirts his hand — it is Zuzka, her fingers twining in his. Laszló clenches her small hand in his own.

As the Commandant and Smith walk through the camp, men pass by with crates of vegetables, bread, butter, jam, fruit, presumably orchestrated in time for this visit. But the blocks the Commandant calls houses cannot have been manufactured just for the inspection: they have the solidity of permanency. This is how Leslie Howard believed it to be, with only five men sharing a block, and all of them dressed properly, with a table running down the middle for civilised conversation, and a bunk per man. Leslie Howard has no understanding of where László has been.

'Is everybody happy?' the Commandant asks the prisoners.

'Yes.'

'Were there eggs for breakfast?'

'Yes, Herr Commandant.'

Zuzka is slotting her nails above and beneath László's own, fitting them together, digging in.

László is very cold, suddenly. He wants to bury his face in József's chest. When he opens his eyes again Smith has been caught. The SS officer takes Smith into a tiled room, where they are to wait for a special train.

He is going to be killed. The Scarlet Pimpernel is going to be shot by the SS.

'I have a pistol,' says the officer. 'It has eight bullets. Eight lives.'

'And I have twenty-eight.'

'Oh?'

'Scientists, men of letters, artists, doctors. Twenty-eight saved from your pagan pistol. And all you've got is my humble self. Not a very profitable transaction.'

'We can afford to make a loss. Our profits will be tremendous.' *Mama, Papa, Alma.* 'Tonight, we march against Poland, and tomorrow will see the dawn of a new order. We shall make a German empire of the world!' The man sighs. 'Why do I talk to you? You are a dead man.'

'May a dead man say a few words to you, General, for your enlightenment?' The camera moves closer to Leslie Howard's face, stern and unafraid. 'Tonight you will take the first step along a dark road, from which there is no turning back. You will have to go on and on, from one madness to another, leaving behind you an illness of misery and hatred, and still you will have to go on. You will find no horizon, and see no dawn, till at last you are lost, and destroyed. You are *doomed*, captain of murderers. And one day, sooner or later, you will remember my words.'

A train whistle, the champ of wheels.

László is going to be sick.

They are going to shoot him.

László shuts his eyes.

'László, look,' whispers Zuzka, 'look.'

On the screen, there is a puff of smoke, and no Scarlet Pimpernel.

'Don't worry, I shall be back. We shall all be back.'

'He escaped,' says Zuzka. 'He escaped.'

László sinks in his chair. He laughs, covering his face. Around him people are gathering their coats, finding hats under seats. Behind, a large woman arranging her scarf gives a huge sigh.

'Such a pity about Leslie Howard.'

'Oh, isn't it. So young.'

László twists in his chair. 'Mit mondtál? What did you say, please?'

The woman peers down at him. 'Leslie Howard, love. He was shot down in 1943.'

'Shot down?'

'Yes, *shot down*, by the Germans,' she echoes, as if he doesn't understand English. 'Over the Bay of Biscay.'

Her companion nods. 'Only fifty. And he only came back to Europe from Hollywood because he so believed in the war effort.'

'He's dead?' repeats László. Something is gripping his arm, hard. 'Dead?' The thing at his arm pulls him. Dead? The women hurry away.

ZUZKA WAITS AT THE door to the hall. A few boys are queuing for the next showing. They look like farmers. One grins at her. He is about her age. She doesn't want to leave the auditorium; she'd have to walk past him, and maybe he'd say something to her. She twists her feet into the deep carpet, into the small crunch of corn kernels and paper confetti, torn slips from Housey-Housey, a numbers game the nurses play, always initiated by a girl standing at the kitchen door and calling, 'Housey-housey! Housey-housey!' And if József is around, one might wink at him and ask, 'Want to play house?' and all the girls would fall into giggles. The auditorium is dark, but she can make out József and László at the front, captured in the yellow haze; can see József crouching over his brother, talking to him urgently, and László sitting slackly, as he has been for the past fifteen minutes. They look like father and child, one with shoulders tensed, ready for burden, the other unable to stand for himself. Want to play house?

She wonders if László has considered József's coat: the worn rubber and chewed-up cloth, the discolouration. It belongs to a beggar, a traveller, a no-land's-man, each stain another stamp in his passport, searching for László.

She hadn't noticed until József gave her his handkerchief last night. It happened quickly: the fiddlers started up, and the bite of the wooden bench beneath her thighs was no longer a seventeenth-century plank in the Lake District but a chair in the Theresienstadt auditorium, and the music is not fiddles but violins, and she is playing to Mother and Uncle and her music has the power to keep the SS from the door. At least, that's what she tells herself, although she knows it's fear of disease that keeps them away – still, she keeps playing. It will save her life, and her mother's life, and her uncle's life – until it doesn't.

Then József leant over, and she was back in The Crooked Duck, anchored by the gentle curve of his fingers on her arm.

'Do you play?'

She stared at him. 'No.'

József considered her, suddenly, frighteningly, intent. He tugged a handkerchief from his pocket and gave it to her, and then removed his arm. She found her cheeks were wet. In bed that night, she examined the scrap of material. It was made of something similar to bandage or canvas, and had pale red spots in the corner. Watching him in the hall now, she thinks his coat and the handkerchief are both scraps of the same thing. He is a shedding bird, feathers dropped over the sea-miles of his determination, and now he comes to them with his bones exposed.

László cannot see this depletion, or perhaps it grieves him too much. He cannot reconcile himself to this bedraggled Pimpernel who so desperately tells him, Do Not Cry, seeming to think their language is impenetrable. But she knows his code. So she will bridge the silence between them; if she is nothing herself, then she can be bricks and mortar. She can play house, too; she can ease their burden; and maybe, she can be eased.

'SAJNÁLOM. SAJNÁLOM.'

József's voice is a radio in a storm.

'*László.*'

József is trying to pull him up. The metal chair scrapes on the boards.

'It will be all right, László. We'll be all right. The Thames – would you like to see the Thames?'

'I want the Danube.'

József breathing through his nose. 'I would give you the Danube from Black Sea to Black Forest if I could. But it isn't mine to give anymore.'

'What are we supposed to do here?'

'*Live.*' József puts his arm around László's neck. '*Live*, László. You can do that for me, can't you?'

László clings to the chair, locking himself to it, to the floor. He wants to throw József off, throw him to the ground, pick the chair up, and bring it down on his brother.

HAND-PAINTED BANNERS FLAP WELCOME HOME. The local football pitch has been taken over in celebration of the telegrams this week. HAPPY NEWS: Our Prisoners Released in the Far Eastend. The Cadet Band is fumbling its notes. The Peace and Victory Dance takes place in a floodlit marquee with a boarded floor that makes people's shoes squeak. Zuzka sits in the corner with the two brothers – László's jaw has turned the colour of an overripe plum after going eight rounds in a boxing match. Zuzka watches József's foot stir on the boards, keeping irregular time. *Do you play?* he had asked her.

He slaps his knee and stands up. 'Would you like to dance?'

'Dance?'

'Yes.'

Zuzka glances at László. He is watching Eryk and his local girl. The napkin of ice pressed to his cheek drips pink. She says his name, but there's no response, so she puts her glass down on the pressed tablecloth and stands up. József's grip is certain as he leads her to the centre of the floor. Her heart is a rigged metronome, and she is worried he'll feel it through his shirt if he pulls her any closer. But he keeps an inch between them. She asked him before the match if László knew how to box. He told her: 'Of course. Intellectual Jews are famous for teaching their sons how to brawl.' He turns her in a gentle three-step now. So this is what Budapest Jews taught their sons. Zuzka's father taught her how to dance. She's never been held like this before.

'How old are you?'

She catches his eye, looks away. 'Sixteen.'

'You're all sixteen. But Eryk must be my age, at least.'

'Eryk's eighteen.'

'Just like me, then.'

Zuzka bites her lip. 'László says you're twenty.'

He stops turning, just for a second, and then finds the next step. 'It's easier to get a visa this way.'

She can feel the muscles of his arms tense, so she doesn't say, *No it's not. You need to be sixteen or under. Eighteen, twenty: neither will move an official with a stamp to mercy.* Zuzka knows that just as well as József does. But she thinks it's fear that has him ready to fight or flee, and what is time, if not made up?

'I'm sixteen,' she says. 'But you're right about Eryk.'

He relaxes, a half-smile. 'I thought you were older. Or younger. There's something about you. My father once told me there's nothing in the world so enjoyable as not understanding a beautiful woman.'

Her cheeks blaze.

'How long were you in Theresienstadt?' He asks this quietly, as if trying to let the question go unnoticed – as if he himself is trying not to notice it.

Zuzka looks down. 'Four years.' His shirt is tucked into his trousers, but the final button is loose, and she can see a line of hair.

Silence. And then: 'You should come with us.'

'Where?'

His fingers are searching out the keys of her spine. 'London.'

She glances up at him, startled to find herself so close, to see the stubble on his cheeks. 'Why?'

'I can take care of you.'

'Why?'

He looks uncomfortable. 'Everybody needs family.'

Zuzka ducks her head again. The throb of blood in his stomach is heating her body. She wants to tell him this is impossible; she wants to kiss the depression at his throat; but the song ends, and his hands drop, and when she looks for him again his attention has strayed. László is coming towards them, and Rebecca has arrived, wearing a forget-me-not dress. József's eyes fix on her. The band keeps playing, and Zuzka dances with László, who tells her he will be a boxing champion. József is whispering into Rebecca's ear, and when the couples turn Zuzka sees the shell of Rebecca's ear turn sunset red.

kaddish

MR BÉLA SAT IN a cluster of armchairs at the far end of the care home's dining room. A chessboard had been left on the coffee table with its pieces packed away in Tupperware. The curtains had not been drawn on the tall windows, and outside Győr was black and orange. When we'd arrived that afternoon, we'd seen the Bishop's Tower and the gold star of the synagogue facing each other over the conjoined rivers. The nurse and Felix were speaking soft words to Mr Béla that I did not understand, but he raised a shaking hand, cutting them both off. His yellowed eyes landed on me.

'You are really the boy's grandchild?'

'Yes.'

Silence.

I sat down. Felix took the other chair. The nurse stood a little way off.

'Do you mind if I record this?'

Mr Béla looked at my camera as if it were an alien artefact. 'It is important we keep records. Yes. Keep records. Keep records.'

I switched to REC. 'Thank you. Did you used to work for DEGOB?'

'I volunteer. Yes. Volunteered.'

My voice was shaking. 'Do you – do you remember interviewing a man called Zyyad József? He was eighteen then. He'd just come back from Mauthausen–Gunskirchen.'

Behind me, I heard the nurse's shoe scuff the carpet. Earlier, Felix and I had gone to the restored synagogue. The woman at the desk had flipped up a laminated sign: THIS SYNAGOGUE IS NO LONGER FUNCTIONING AS A SYNAGOGUE.

'I remember.'

I sat forward. 'You do?'

'I remember all of it. Don't let these people – do not believe them about my memory. I remember it all. I remember that boy, because of his eyes. Zyyad József. He became a painter. Joseph Silk. I would see him sometimes in the newspaper.'

'Mr Béla, a testament has gone missing from DEGOB. The testament belonging to Zyyad József. It's important that we know how it went missing.' I tried to keep my voice level. 'You're not in any trouble.'

He gave me a long hard look. 'It doesn't matter now. She's dead. Can't matter now.'

'Who's dead?'

'Do you mean Sándor Magda?' asked Felix. 'Your interview partner?'

'Yes, of course. Yes. Dead for years. Moved to Germany, died. Ha.'

'She moved to Germany?' Felix said, almost standing up.

'Yes. What of it? Died.'

'Did she – d'you know if she ever went by Magdelena, or Alena, in Germany?'

'Alena?'

'Do you know if she married a man called Rosenzweig Max?'

'She died,' the man said again. 'What can it matter?'

'Max and Alena Rosenzweig gave Joseph Silk's testament to the Jewish Museum in Berlin.'

I sat forward. 'It doesn't matter. Do you know why József – why that boy's testament went missing?'

'She took it.'

'Do you know why?'

'He paid her.'

'What?'

'The boy. József. Paid her to, to . . . elpusztít, yes? After the interview.'

His voice hoarse, Felix said, 'Destroy it?' He had the look of a jockey sensing the home stretch, heedless to the pain of his horse.

'Yes. Destroy.'

'But she didn't?' I asked.

'Couldn't. Took it.' Mr Béla sniffed. 'How did he do?'

'Pardon me?'

'How is he, the boy? Worrying one. I remember the worrying ones.'

'He – he's just fine, Mr Béla. A painter, like you said.'

'Hmm? Oh yes. He find his family?'

I swallowed. 'He found his brother.'

Mr Béla looked around the empty hall. 'Lucky.'

316

'Yes,' I said. 'He was very lucky.'

Afterwards, the nurse closed the door on us firmly. An aeroplane dropping mosquito poison droned invisible overhead. We stood on the street, shivering a little. Silk had been marched past this city. Radnóti had been shot and buried, naked bone and fathom-deep.

THE TRAIN TO SOPRON was full of festivalgoers, teenagers with green hair, twenty-something guys already drunk. Amongst them middle-aged couples guarded sensible campfire cook sets. We played thumb wars and Felix let me pin him twice in a row. We played a game of eye spy that lasted an hour because Felix was spying abstract nouns. Regret. Hope. Luftschloss. Love. We arrived into Sopron at 10.30 p.m. We threw our bags onto the platform and jumped down after them. The air trembled with bass so loud it was like weapons fire.

Our taxi nosed through late-night traffic and skirted the edge of the town. The hostels and campsites were full so we had checked into a monastery – now a hotel I would pay for with Silk's money – in the Sopronbánfalva hills. Felix kept his face turned away from me; in the car window, his glasses were two blank squares.

'Do you want to try and find your grandparents' old house tomorrow?' I asked. 'Do you have the address?'

'I have it.'

'Shall we go and look?'

He shrugged, keeping his face turned away. 'I'm not interested.'

Rounding the last slope of the dirt road, our headlights spilt over a pale chapel. I paid the taxi driver, who said 'Hello, goodbye', and then the car lurched away, leaving us facing the huge wooden door.

The building still felt sacred, and I knocked hesitantly. No answer. I gave a push. The door swung open into a hall lit by candles. A man behind a glass screen sat up.

'You are Mrs Butler?'

'Ah – yes. We're here to check in.'

'Welcome, please. To sign here.'

The receptionist handed Felix a key with a heavy wooden fob. Felix gave it to me. After paying we followed the man down cool cloisters to a lift. A double room had been cheaper than two singles, but as the man opened our former monks' cell that wisdom wore off. Polished dark floors, lacquered furniture, gold and silver bedsheets. The attendant turned on the soft lamps, told us breakfast was at 8 a.m., and left.

'What a shame we have to suffer like this,' said Felix.

I smiled, putting my bag down in the corner.

Felix opened the French windows onto the balcony. I followed. He gripped the railings and lowered his chin to the cushion of his arms. His silence grew up between us. I peered out at the black hills and sugared stars before turning my back on them. Felix glanced at me. Our eyes remained locked.

I asked, 'What does Luftschloss mean?'

'A castle in the air. An unrealistic dream.'

I took my hands from my pockets. I touched my cold fingers to his bared nape, tracing the bump of his spine, dipping down beneath his T-shirt. I was shaking. 'It doesn't have to be unrealistic.'

After a minute, Felix straightened, standing in front of me. I could only see the curve of his shoulders, the edges of his smile. He stepped closer, and I stopped breathing when his hands brushed my ribs, my stomach, settling around my waist.

His beard tickled my chin, and then I found his lips, and we kissed slowly, hesitantly. After long minutes I tugged at his T-shirt. His belt buckle pressed against my stomach. Urging him back a few inches, I pulled my shirt and vest off. Felix's fingers bit into my hips as he lifted me onto the balcony ledge, one arm wrapping around my back.

Running my hands over his warm body, I found an invisible bump.

'What is this?'

'A tattoo.'

'What of?' I said, raising his shirt.

'Longitude and latitude of Sar-e Sang in Afghanistan.'

'Really?'

Felix caught my hand, guiding me to the numbers. I traced the directions to Silk's most sacred blue as Felix gathered my skirt up in folds.

I TRIED TO SLEEP against the thump of synthpop and the growing rumble of Felix snoring, my body holding on to an ache I could not name. The ache of knowing him, of being known. I jerked awake at 6 a.m.

Felix remained asleep as I slipped out from his arm and scooted to the end of the bed, tugging on a jumper. Outside, the hills were draped in mist, which separated here and there to show bottle-green forest and brick-red earth. Light rain bounced in the trees. Somewhere in that earth lay the body of my great-grandfather.

I gathered my camera bag. Felix woke up as I laced my shoes.

'You do not want company?'

His eyes were swollen with sleep, and he knuckled them open, sitting up. He wasn't wearing a shirt, and I looked to the deltoid muscle joining shoulder to chest. Small alternating figures: 36-16N 70-49E.

'I'd like your company.'

We walked out of the monastery grounds into the hills. The wood around us was silent. The soil was damp and pulled at my shoes. I tried to picture János Zyyad stumbling down this path, but could only see Silk as an old man, leaning heavily on his stick. The unmarked ground fed on unredeemed bodies, one of them my blood, and it would offer me no reclamation of my dead today. I raised my camera. Sun shafted through the leaves, flaring in the lens. A cemetery reared to our left, but the gravestones climbing the hill were white crosses and Soviet stars. We followed the road in silence to the top. Above the trees, I saw something I thought might be a monument and my heart leapt, desperate, I realised, for this kind of miracle. It was an electricity pylon. All I had were hills and forest and soil, and their silence. All I had was Felix and myself, on this ground together. I wished I knew how to sing kaddish for the dead. We stood at the crossroads and peered up into the rain-veiled crests.

Felix's phone chimed.

'Sorry . . .' he said, taking it out, and in the footage my camera catches his shock, his look of savaged uncertainty.

'What's wrong?'

'I – it's . . . it's Silk's grave.'

'What about it?'

'It's been defaced.'

Numb, I heard Silk telling me that deface came from Middle

English for blot out, destroy the reputation of, efface their writing or painting.

'What do you mean?'

'They found it this morning. Somebody's painted a swastika on it.'

The camera lurches a little as I lose ground. Then, remotely: 'What colour?'

'What?'

'Painted in what colour?'

'Red.'

The camera swings away, blurring the trees. 'He wouldn't be able to see it anyway.'

FELIX SAID MAYBE I shouldn't comment while I was so upset. I told him, waiting for the phone call in the hotel's meditation garden, that there was unlikely to be a time when I was not upset. Winston wrote down my one-line statement without interjection:

If Silk were here, he'd be the first to say you don't get any points for fucking originality.

My words appeared on BBC online less than an hour later, scaffolded with neutrality:

In a statement released on behalf of Joseph Silk's estate, this morning's vandalism was called a reprehensible act. The family asks for privacy at this time.

Winston called back. The red paint had been removed. Several news pieces would run tomorrow about the rise of anti-Semitism in Britain. Felix sat listening with his chin pressed to his chest. I squeezed the pinecone I'd picked up from the forest floor.

'A last thing,' said Winston. 'We had a message come through on Silk's website, the information request box.'

'Yes?'

'It was a little weird, that's the only reason I mention it.'

'If it's something anti-Semitic, I don't want to hear it.'

'It's nothing like that. It's a request for you to get in touch with a man claiming to be an old friend of Silk's in Serbia.'

'Serbia?' I turned to Felix. 'What's this man's name?'

'Dragan Ivanovic.'

I repeated the syllables, forcing them together. Felix's face bled colour. He said something, but I couldn't hear him. I squeezed the pinecone, but its ridges did not bite into my hand – it lay between my feet on the perfectly manicured lawn. I remembered Silk's testimony – *sometimes there are pains that make your heart sink so low you cannot lift it again. My friend, the man who saved me, he died.*

Silk, it is possible, sometimes. It is possible to reclaim the dead.

miscellaneous wants

*T*HE LINE OF THIS *jacket-waistcoat is trim and tailored and shows a great saving of material. It takes merely two yards of thirty-six-inch cloth for a thirty-four-inch bust measurement* – Zuzka pauses, reaching for her pencil. A knock makes her jump, crumpling the newspapers on the bed. She crosses to the door. József is waiting, hands behind his back.

'Good afternoon,' he says. 'I am hoping you can help me.'

'Where's László?'

'Playing cricket. But it's not his help I need. Rebecca told me she gives you the weekly papers.'

'To help with my English.'

'Do they list any jobs?'

'Yes. Are you – are you leaving?'

'We all are, once I've saved enough for a hostel in London.'

'I haven't said yes yet.'

'You haven't invited me in either. But I have a good feeling about it.'

Zuzka retreats to a chair in the corner. He sits down on the edge of her mattress, picking up the papers.

'The Situations Vacant are listed at the back, near Miscellaneous Wants.'

'Near what, please?'

She says it again, sounding each vowel.

'What are they?'

Zuzka hesitates, but his smile pulls it from her: 'High pre-war pram wanted, in good condition. One or two pairs of baby shoes wanted, in good condition. Second-hand eighteen- or twenty-two-carat wedding ring wanted. Modern piano wanted. Small safe wanted, in good condition.'

József's eyebrows are rising. 'Who would be selling a wedding ring?'

She shrugs. 'Not all of the telegrams were happy.'

'No.' He looks down at the open paper in his hands. 'They weren't. Dare I hope you know the . . . vacant situations by heart, too?'

She laughs.

'Did I say something wrong?'

'No. There are many vacant situations. Girl for domestic help. Van girl required for confectioner's town round. Domestic companionship for genteel lady.'

'Is there no use for men?'

She chooses a wry smile. 'How would you like me to answer that?'

'Ha. Delicately – that is the word, yes?'

'It's *a* word. If you are a handyman and gardener who can also provide a wife for the cottage kitchen, you are much sought after.'

He leans forward, elbows on his knees. The backs of his knuckles hover near the folds of her skirt, almost touching. 'I'll look for a wife, then.'

She holds his gaze, not breathing, and he does not look away. When she finds her voice, it is deeper than she remembers. She sounds like a woman. 'There's a girl in Grasmere who requires a German tutor, two or three lessons weekly.' His fingertip brushes her knee. 'They're also looking for farmhands. Britain needs more milk.'

A half-smile. 'And the girl's knitting group tells me liberated countries need warm socks. All these miscellaneous wants . . . what do you want, Zuzka?'

She swallows. 'What do *you* want?'

'I want very much for you to say yes.'

'Why?'

'I like the rhythm of your voice.'

He frees the latest sheets of Situations Vacant and leaves her, still sitting without a response on the bed. She walks her smile to the mirror to measure its authenticity.

LÁSZLÓ TIES UP THE sack and carries it to the far end of the garden. He can see Mrs Farnhill through the smeared window; she sits in the same chair every day, her head tilted towards their conversation, though she cannot understand a word. Perhaps the rhythmic thud of József taking apart the overgrown damson reminds her of the now-silent foundry next door. Her husband died over the summer, he heard, and she has just received a telegram saying her son will not be returning from the Far East. He heard she hit the messenger with a loaf of bread.

'Öcs – she'll catch you staring. Come hold the bottom of the ladder.'

László re-treads the path they have freed of thorns and grips the wood, looking up at the underside of József's mud-clogged boots. A yellow leaf is curved in the tracks.

He wants József to look down at him, to smile. When they were younger, before, László would cover his eyes and pretend to be invisible, and József would turn over cushions and peer behind bookshelves, crying, where is my öcs, has anyone seen my öcs? Now, József twists the papery sinews of the limb until it is wrenched clean off, and does not turn to check whether, in his silence, László has disappeared.

ZUZKA EASES THE HALLWAY door shut behind her and pauses, listening for any sounds from the doctor's rooms ahead. Her tooth is pounding so hard she feels dizzy. She needs a pair of pliers, painkillers, anything, but she cannot bear to have someone open her mouth and squeeze their fingers inside. The last person to do that was Uncle, sparing her the dentist. She can hear nothing, so creeps forward in her stockings, keeping to the edges of the corridor where the boards are least worn. She has reached the first doctor's room when she is brought short by the creak of leather furniture, and József's voice.

'What am I supposed to do?' he is saying.

'Just tell me what you see.'

Zuzka stiffens. Through the narrow slit, she can see József sitting on an examination table, and Rebecca arranging a set of placards.

'Where did you even find these? Is this a new art project for the boys?'

'Stop being so mean. Here, what do you see in this?' Rebecca holds something up – she is standing side on to Zuzka, who can just make out coloured dots: green, blue, red, making a number.

'What do I see? It's just a blue circle.' Silence. 'Isn't it?'

'That would be cheating, Mr Zyyad. This one?'

'I see . . . a grey circle, with a faint blue three in the middle.'

'This one?'

'I don't know – just black and grey.'

'Any numbers?'

'I think you're prompting your student.'

'Fine – this one?'

'Art.'

'*József.*'

'I see different greys, with – it's like a rainy day.'

Rebecca shuffles the cards on the sideboard, and once she no longer has anything to organise she tucks her hair behind each ear, straightening and smoothing. The cards are splashes of colour, like someone has split open paint tubes and stamped on the open bodies.

'I'll pass your answers on to Doctor Royle.'

'You don't know what they mean?'

'There are different kinds of colour blindness—'

'So we're talking blindness?'

Rebecca is blushing. 'There's dichromatism, difficulty seeing one of the three primary colours, and there's anomalous trichromatism, reduced sensitivity to certain colours. I can't tell which you have. But you're not blind.'

'Who came up with this test, anyway?'

'A Japanese doctor, I think.'

'I thought they were all cruel, mindless devils who tortured your husbands.'

Rebecca faces József, turning her back on Zuzka, who watches as the nurse puts her hands on her hips.

'You have a strange way of asking how I am.'

József looks up at the ceiling. 'I heard your fiancé is alive.'

'Yes. I got a telegram from Delhi. He's flying home.'

'Where's he been all these years?'

'Siam. The Japanese picked him and three others out of the water.'

'So: how are you?'

Zuzka holds her breath. What is this strange new intimacy?

Eventually Rebecca says, 'I think *I'm* supposed to be shining the light in *your* eyes . . .'

'Nothing's stopping you.'

Rebecca takes a pencil torch from her kit and crosses the room. Her hips sway from side to side like a cheap dancer. She does not stop until she is standing directly between József's open legs. There, she fiddles with the torch at her side, but doesn't switch it on.

'I haven't seen him since I was seventeen. My mother's over the moon. She keeps saying I can give up medicine now.'

'He has a job already then, the future Mr Rebecca?'

'That's not the point. The point is . . . You know I work weekends at the pharmacy in Ambleside – well, we've just got these new adverts for milk of magnesia. *I'm clocking in – at home! I've said goodbye to that war job, and now I'm going to enjoy the simple home life I've been so eagerly planning . . .*'

József circles her waist with his arms, fingers plucking delicately at her shirt. Zuzka feels a sudden pulse between her legs.

'And are you going to enjoy it?'

'You're not listening –' Zuzka watches Rebecca tap József on the knee with the torch, as if testing his reflexes – 'I love Robert. I mean, I loved him then. But training as a nurse, and now this . . . I remember Mr Churchill saying once, *We are fighting by ourselves alone, but we are not fighting for ourselves alone.* When I worked in Manchester Hospital I sort of knew what he meant, but not *really* – not until I met you Windermere Boys. I understand now. I don't want to give this feeling up.'

József gives a tug, and the tails of Rebecca's shirt come loose from the woollen skirt. The material is wrinkled from the curve of her body. Zuzka waits for some sound of protest, but of course none comes, because of course this is not the first time this has happened. Zuzka's body is slick with sweat. Rebecca lifts the torch and switches it on, shining the beam directly into József's eyes.

'What do you see?' he asks.

'What do *you* see?'

'You.'

Rebecca puts the torch down on the table, where it pendulums, rolling this way and that. József's hands are moving over Rebecca's body. The shirt is pushed off her shoulders to the floor. She wears a peach silk slip beneath – what colour does he see? – and she arches her spine when József kisses her neck and undoes the clasp at the back of her skirt – how many times has he taken her apart like this? – and soon the skirt is pushed to Rebecca's shoes, and she steps smoothly free of the material as József urges her back a little, saying something soft in Hungarian, then English:

'I think we should change places.'

He lifts her onto the table, pushing her knees open with his body, and Zuzka can hear the sound of his rough hands moving under Rebecca's stockinged knee, and then his hands disappear from view, and Rebecca's knickers – white – join her skirt on the floor. Soon Rebecca is making noises like a cat complaining for its supper, and József is yanking her body towards him, wrapping her legs around his back, forcefully, almost violently – she still wears shoes, they'll trail mud over his shirt – and he is undoing his belt. There is a sudden movement. Rebecca gasps, hurt. He sounds . . . satisfied. He begins to move, thrusting into her, and the table judders. Rebecca presses one palm flat to the table top and moves with him, whispering, yes yes yes, and he is grunting something in Magyar again, and the blood is pounding around Zuzka's tooth, until József finally sags, slumping over Rebecca's body, his shoulders relaxed, his Magyar gentle now, József giving his language away.

In her room that evening, Zuzka inserts the wire cutters into her mouth. She wants to close her eyes but she's got to look in the mirror, which steams up. She can just see the tooth at the back, swallowed by puffed gums.

'What are you doing?'

Zuzka jumps, dropping the mirror. It smacks between her feet and breaks into three neat pieces. In the doorway, József is staring as if he's just found her knotting a noose.

'My tooth is infected.'

'Ask the dentist!'

Zuzka looks away. Her reflection is pulled in different directions by the shards at her feet.

'I can help.'

She wraps her fist around the wire cutters.

'Let me do it.'

She is shaking her head, backing up on the bed. József closes the door behind him. He is wearing the same belt he unbuckled before drawing such vehement agreement from Rebecca. Zuzka wants to swipe and scratch at him. He leans over her, and she can feel the buckle pressing against her pelvis, can feel the muscles of his thighs against hers, can smell his skin. His fingers wrap around the pliers.

'Let me help,' he says, softer this time. She lets go, and he takes the weight and heat of his body away, bending down to gather up the broken mirror, laying the pieces on her dressing table. 'This can be fixed.' He sets the wire cutters on the dressing table.

She moves to the edge of the bed. József pulls the chair up, so they sit knee-to-knee.

'How about we just do this the traditional way?'

'I won't let you tie me to anything.'

'I should think not. Tilt your head back. That's it.'

He is cupping her jaw, and Zuzka is sure he will feel the hammer of her jugular. If he does, he doesn't say anything – he is gently opening her mouth, like a man wary of a dog's bite. The ceiling is speckled brown. His fingers dip inside her, fingers that dipped inside Rebecca. He is making soothing noises, telling her it looks sore, she's been brave to bear it . . .

'I'm going to pull now.'

331

Her whole body seizes when he grips the tip, she wants to jerk and thrash against him but all of her is tethered to his gentle fingertips.

'One, two – *out*.'

Zuzka tastes the blood as she sees it, dark and stagnant like her menstrual periods, now returned to her. She buries her face in his neck. He is stroking her back.

'Don't cry,' he says. 'Don't cry. Look at me. Who could hide such beauty?'

Zuzka jerks back, staring at him. His neck and collar are stained with her blood. She thinks of the vampire stories they used to tell in Prague. We could feed off each other. We could feed off each other until there is nothing left.

'There.'

He opens his hand, showing her the tooth, the pink roots. They are inches apart. He is looking at her lips. He might kiss her.

'Do you want to keep it?'

'They put my mother's gold tooth in a barrel, filled with gold.'

Did she say that out loud? He sits back, and wipes the blood from his neck.

Learn a new song, little bird.

LÁSZLÓ WEARS HIS RED poppy on his lapel. The flower flaps in the wind, and he keeps his hand over his heart, as if swearing an oath. József said he wasn't interested in attending the wreath ceremony. Zuzka has packed a picnic, blankets, the day's newspaper. László brought his swimming towel. József told him not to be mad, but don't the old men play chess at the Széchenyi Baths in winter? They

332

have driven to England's tallest mountain, which guards its deepest lake. Eryk left this morning, and Jan. All the girls are gone. Rabbi Asch and Dr Posner thought Zuzka would leave with the others; he heard them whispering that she's their last real cause for concern, that she's not recovering. But she doesn't seem sick to László. Scafell Pike is wrapped in white clouds. At its feet, Wasdale is darker than any body of water László has ever seen. Black, on a bright day.

Zuzka says, 'It was nice of Mrs Farnhill to bake you this cake.'

'I think she's lonely,' says László. 'She enjoyed having us there.'

'A woman would have to be lonely to enjoy that.'

László pulls up some grass and throws it at her. She laughs, red in the cheeks. József leans over and plucks a leaf from her lap. He stays on one arm, as if he might rest his head on her thigh.

'Aren't you going to swim, László?'

'I thought you said it was mad.'

'I do. I think you are going to put one toe in that water and scream yourself blue.'

'I'll take that bet. A half-crown.'

'You're on.'

László walks around a rock to the water edge. There, he takes off his shirt and shoes and trousers. He spreads his towel out in the sun so it will be warm for his return, like Mama used to. The trick is not to hesitate. Run. Run and don't stop.

'Are you ready?' he calls.

'With my first aid kit!' József responds, but he is not looking. This will make him look. László dashes for it. Go go go – he throws himself forward, his whole body breaking the ink surface. He is instantly numb – no, he is itching with uncontainable excitement. He kicks out, swimming a loop, reaching for his toes. Then something reaches inside him, and he can t stand it anymore, he's got to get out, he's got to get – he throws himself onto the land.

On the bank, József is whispering something to Zuzka. She is blushing. Their fingers are linked.

József glances up, and drops Zuzka's hand. 'Are you *insane*, you'll catch flu!'

'It's not so bad,' pants László.

'Get out now! Get your clothes on!'

'Where's my half-crown?'

The panic drains from József's face. 'You'll get your money, you terror. Come here.'

László sits with the towel around his neck, catching the icy water running from his hair. He wants some intimation of what they were saying when he was beneath the water, some thread to pull on. But Zuzka is asking József, 'How is the Grasmere girl's German?'

'Einfallslos. Not like your English. Go on, show off. Read us the news.'

Zuzka laughs. She looks so pleased with herself, and with him. The thought makes László lose balance.

'Poppy Day,' she reads. 'Please give more generously than ever before this year. Most of you who read this article would have . . . would have been in the gas chamber long ago but for the lads and lassies who defended Britain when Hitler looked like winning the war.'

From beneath his arm: 'Read something else.'

'A cow hit by a car turned a somersault and landed on the driver.'

József leans over to look at the paper. 'You're making that up.'

334

'How dare you?' She turns the pages. When she stops it is with a rigid expression, as if she has seen a face in a window at night.

'What?'

Nothing.

József touches her arm. 'What is it?'

Zuzka purses and releases her lips. 'The circumstances of Adolf Hitler's death under conditions of sordid melodrama grim enough to be revolting have now been revealed.'

László feels as if he's listening from behind a screen, and behind the screen with him is the Hungarian SS guard who whispered, 'Hitler is dead. You'll soon be free,' and the boy who shouted, 'I have outlived Hitler, what more do I want?' Another officer shot the boy as he danced, a man who hardly bothered to watch the boy die.

He is jerked back by József's imperious 'Give me that.' József folds the paper up, into quarters, eighths, forcing the fat bundle into his pocket. 'It's time to go,' he says. 'It's time to go to London.'

No. 212. How did the Germans try to cover up signs of their crimes and did they have the time (destruction of gas chambers, crematoria, mass graves, disposal of corpses)

No. 219. When did they order the evacuation and how was it carried out? Was it orderly or done in a panic

No. 238. What was the mood among the local population

No. 239. Did they still believe in German victory

No. 242. What was the most likely fate of those left behind on the march

No. 305. Is there any evidence that the German command wanted to liquidate the camp and its inhabitants

No. 311. How did the prisoners (Häftlinge) behave at the moment of liberation (describe everything you saw)

No. 313. How many prisoners were still alive on the day of liberation

No. 319. How did local people behave towards you, and how far did they help liberated prisoners

No. 325. How many prisoners in the camp had cultural interests (film, concerts, literature and other things like sociological or political presentations)

No. 328. Did prisoners concern themselves at all with the future

Six

a Serbian thief

W E GOT IN THE back of a taxi outside Belgrade train station. Three old Nokia phones jostled in the gap between the two front seats. The guy grinned at us over his shoulder.

'I am a businessman,' he said, pointing to them. 'You English?'

'I am, yes.'

'And you?'

'Berlin.'

The car swung around the corner and out onto the motorway. 'Cool, man, cool. I give you the tour. My name is Radovan. I can tell you all about the Dunav – the Danube. I have PhD in impact of EU regulations on Danube salmon at Iron Gate.'

'Are you doing this to pay for your PhD?' Felix asked.

'I tried to find job but everything here is corruption now. Taxi driver pays better. No visas to work abroad. UK and US think we're all terrorists. But who needs a visa? I've been to six countries – Serbia, Croatia, Slovenia, Bosnia and Herzegovina, Macedonia, Montenegro.' Radovan laughed. 'My brothers and me, we've been telling that joke for years.'

I looked out the window, watching the trees shake their fists on the hilltops as the ribbon of road pulled us deeper into the capital. In the testament, which waited in the rucksack between my feet, Silk described Dragan as a Serbian partisan, a hero, the man who kept him alive. *He protected me, after I lost/damaged [transl?] my eyesight. He called me little brother. He saved me. You want to think — when you are in the worst of it, you want to think that you will be the best man you can be. I have seen strangers die holding hands. I have seen a son leap on his father for a crust of bread. Dragan was the best man he could be. I wasn't. When the time came, every time, I let him die to save myself.*

'This palace is where Alexander the first was thrown from balcony, and that is where Djokovic lifts his trophies, you know?'

Felix touched my arm.

'These skyscrapers are New Belgrade.'

He raised his eyebrows: are you OK?

'There is Statue of the Victor, you see?'

I nodded, and reached for my wallet. Radovan gave Felix the number of one of his phones in case we needed anything.

We stood in the constrained shadow of a pastel yellow tower block. Overhead, telephone wires gleamed black with recent rain. We had written Dragan Ivanovic's address on the back of the Sopron hotel menu. The door was sheet metal, with a narrow window laced with wire. Felix pressed the bell. I thought I heard a man clearing his throat on the intercom, but no words followed. There was a small click, and the door relented an inch. The lift was out of service. On the stairs, we passed a woman carrying a tired dog, and two children firing cap guns, sulphur whispers filling the air. Silk had described a silver arc across the sky. *The men told me it was red. The red line of gunpowder.* I tried to order my words: Mr Ivanovic, I'm sorry I didn't get in touch with you earlier. I didn't know you were alive. I didn't know you existed. Exist. Mr Ivanovic, I'm Joseph Silk's granddaughter. József Zyyad's granddaughter.

'Are you ready?' whispered Felix.

We were at his door. A flaking cardinal red.

'Am I pronouncing it correctly?'

'What?'

'His name. Dragan Ivanovic.'

'It's Drag*an*, I think, not Drag*on*. But I'm sure he won't mind.'

'Silk would.'

Felix leant closer. He hadn't heard me.

I forced my voice. 'What about József Zyyad?'

'What about him?'

'Am I pronouncing it correctly?'

There was movement on the other side. I shook my head, and knocked.

The door opened cautiously, and then a man appeared around it, a man with swept-back white hair, and rock-salt eyes.

'Dragan Ivanovic?'

'Eva Silk?'

'Yes.'

The door opened. Dragan put his hand out. The left side of his face was scarred. It looked like his cheek had been chewed open and stitched back together using wire, staples that had fused with his skin, burnt brittle and glinting.

'It's a pleasure to meet you,' said somebody. Me.

Dragan took my hand, which had frozen half raised. He squeezed.

'The pleasure is all mine. And who is this?'

'Felix Gerschel. I'm a curator at the Jewish Museum in Berlin.'

Dragan tilted his head back, peering at Felix. 'If you insist. But you look far too young to me. Come in. I must thank you for meeting me.'

'Thank you for getting in touch,' Felix said, when I said nothing. I couldn't. There was something wrong – I felt like I was moving too slowly. It was time. It was Dragan's purple and red face, his clawed hand gripping the back of a chair, his breathing coming hard, painfully hard. The result of saving my grandfather's life; of ensuring mine. Time had resisted its telling. He was here, he was alive, he was real. It was true, these essential facts: what people could do to each other, what people had done, what people do. It couldn't end in a fairy tale. Silk telling me: *An ugly truth, like all my truths.* Even miracles hurt.

'Oh dear,' said Dragan. 'I have given you a shock.'

'No,' I said, trying to wipe the tears from my eyes quickly. 'No – not at all.'

He smiled, a broad grin that made his eyes spark, and I saw, suddenly, the man Silk had been attempting to inhabit his whole life.

'Never mind,' he said. 'It is perhaps impossible not to be shocked by an old man who manages to remain so irresistibly handsome. Even for a young woman such as yourself. You have something of your grandfather's face about you. The cheekbones. But you are far prettier. You will excuse the familiarity. I feel, somehow, as if I already know you.'

'You do,' I said. I cleared my throat. 'In a way. Thank you for having us.'

'Please, come out to the balcony. I have made coffee.'

I looked around the flat. It had the regularity and neatness of a single life: one armchair, one side table, a small bed visible around the corner, its sheets taut.

'I'm afraid I can't stay inside,' said Dragan, leading us towards the French windows. 'It's my cousin's daughter. She means well. Works for IKEA in Italy. Insists on filling my home with these things.' He kicked a cabinet, before pausing, half in, half out. Felix hadn't moved. He was staring at the walls. I hadn't noticed the collage of colour. It seemed natural to me. The frames hung in close proximity to each other, jostling for inches. Paintings, mosaics, charcoal drawings. Amongst it all, near the centre, maybe where it all began, was a small, framed certificate, with the words GOLI OTOK, and a date, 1956. Felix was peering at one painting in particular, but I couldn't see past his shoulder.

'You know these artists?' asked Dragan.

Felix seemed to flinch. 'Yes. At least, I think so.'

'I am surprised.'

'I'm an art historian.'

Dragan's chin jutted out. 'If you insist.'

I brushed Felix's sleeve. We followed Dragan out.

We could see all the way to Kalemegdan Fortress, where the Danube and the Sava met. Bruised clouds clamped the sky, and the rivers were laced with lightning.

Dragan pointed with a shaking hand. 'You can see the Victor. The pillar, at the castle, you see? As if he's offering boxing gloves to the Fruska Gora Mountains on one side and the Austro-Hungarian Empire on the other. I used to be like that.'

We sat down. The coffee set was lido blue with white spots. Silk had a mug almost exactly like it.

'Young man,' said Dragan, 'you may pour.'

Felix jerked forward. 'Of course, sir.'

'Ha. No need for that. It is not *me* you are here to charm, or so I imagine. You said, in your message, that you are arranging an exhibition in Berlin, with the cooperation of the Silk family.'

'Yes.'

Dragan raised an eyebrow at me. 'And you approve of this?'

'I don't know. I don't think Silk would have approved.'

Dragan narrowed his eyes on Felix. It felt suddenly like I was introducing Felix to a father as my boyfriend. Then Dragan chuckled, and folded his hands around his cup. It stopped him shaking. 'I read about Jószef's funeral. I have told my family I wish to have my ninetieth birthday at the cemetery, so they know where to visit me. I was accused of being . . . like a ghoul, yes? There we are.'

'I'm sorry we couldn't invite you. I didn't know – not until I read Silk's testament. It says – it says you died. You were killed.'

Dragan raised an eyebrow. 'I thought he had it destroyed?'

'So did he.' I pushed my coffee aside. 'I'm surprised you know about it.'

'He told me.'

'He – he knew you were alive?'

'You look surprised. Jószef never mentioned me at all, I see. We met in Italy in 1958. I have not seen him since.'

I was back at Fitzroy Park and John was standing over me. *Lies, lies, lies.*

'He had a happy life?' Dragan asked.

My attention became stuck on his scarred cheek.

Dragan waved. 'Don't let that bother you. It looks worse than it is. I am in it, this testament?'

I breathed: 'Yes.'

'It says I died?'

'Yes. It says – it says it was Silk's fault. József's fault.'

'He was wrong. He did not have any power; he cannot have any blame. I told him that, but I could see he didn't – or perhaps couldn't – believe me. It was as if, for him, I was still dead.'

I fingered the camera hanging at my waist. 'Do you mind if I ask about your labour service?'

Dragan followed my motions. 'You are documenting your, ah, discoveries?'

'Yes.'

Dragan set his cup down. A slosh of coffee hit the table. The shaking of his hand had been released, his fingers seeming to pick at the air. He touched his collar, the white stubble at his Adam's apple, a froth of spit on his lip. I was leaning forward to apologise, to tell him to forget my questions, when he caught his breath and turned to Felix. 'You are historian or *art* historian?'

'I'm both,' said Felix, sitting utterly straight.

'Do you know what those words mean, on that certificate in there?'

'Yes. I do. They're release papers.'

'Yes. I like to have them out, where authorities can see them. Should they choose to stop in again. My idea of a joke. One that makes only me laugh, because they don't stop in. Goli Otok . . .' His attention moved back to my camera. 'You know what Goli Otok was, historian?'

'A prison island.'

'But –' I felt like a child again – 'I thought you were a partisan, a hero?'

Dragan's fist shook and again I thought of Silk. Dragan did not possess Silk's armour, his beloved stage set and cast; the grey flannel jacket he wore was frayed at the edges and the red handkerchief poking from his pocket looked crusted with salt. Between his shirt buttons, I could see the wire of silver hair and thin bones.

'I was a partisan. A captain at twenty-three. And afterwards, when I crawled my way back to Tito, I was a hero, for a time. But then we were asked to swear allegiance to Tito, and renounce Russia. Stalin had given us weapons. Stalin saved us. So I said no. I was sent to a prison island on the Dalmatian Coast for eight years. Then one day, Khrushchev and Tito made up. I was released.

'Goli Otok was a place . . . a place where you were made to tell stories. And tell them. And tell them. Until you believed those stories. You wrote down every *bad* thought you'd ever had, every wrong desire, every betrayal of the state, from birth to manhood. You told your stories aloud, into the faces of screaming friends, your fellow prisoners, friends made to produce such anger they seemed capable of killing. Until you believed they *should* kill you. If only they'd kill you. That was Goli Otok.' Dragan shrugged one shoulder. 'And so, I am not so comfortable telling stories, now. But I will, for you. Press record. And afterwards, well – afterwards, we can decide to show the film the light, or not.'

I pressed the button, leaving the camera on the table, Dragan's hands the only things in shot. I couldn't trust my hands to lift it.

'In his testament, Silk says you took care of him. On the march.'

Dragan took a deep breath. 'I tried. But really he took care of me.'

'What do you mean?'

'I was arrested for blowing up German train lines. I didn't have much hope left. But of this we will talk later, perhaps. He was a sweet young fool, and braver than he knew. A boy who could still laugh in all of that . . . Well.' Dragan reached over and tapped Felix's arm. 'I suppose, Mr Museum Professor, you would like to know how he came to that extraordinary vision of his?'

'Yes. Yes.'

Dragan laughed. 'A rifle to the back of the head and eleven hours in darkness and you will also paint masterpieces.'

I fingered the edge of the table. 'In the testament, it says you were shot. The massacre at Cservenka.'

'I was.' Dragan pursed his lips, making the scar twitch. 'Four of us survived. It was a *pokolj*. A bath of blood. The SS made us line up, twenty facing each side of a pit, with four German officers behind us.' Dragan rapped his finger on the table. 'They fire.' His fingers crooked at the knuckles. 'We fall. One man was shot in the neck and still lived. Two others found a trick of jumping just before the bullet. Me, I had a strange fortune. When it came to my turn I tried to pray but I could not remember any words. So I looked around at the officer. I do not know why. He told me seeing my face was no problem to him –' another *tap* on the table – 'and fired. The bullet went through my cheek. I fell into the pit. I thought I was dead. When I realised what had happened, I hid amongst the bodies. I stayed there until the sun rose, under those men. Some died slowly. I comforted them. That was the longest night of my life. When I felt the sunlight, I didn't care if there were still soldiers up there, I had to get out. I climbed to the top. There were a few SS men standing by the pit. They saw me. I waited for them to shoot, and then one said *run*. I did **not** hesitate. I heard later that they let the other three men run as well. Four, from a thousand.'

'I'm sorry.'

Dragan shrugged. 'Again, you are sorry, but it was not your fault. I survived. József thought that, after I had cared for him, he shouldn't have let the SS take me. He thought he should have stopped me joining the march with him at Bor in the first place rather than staying behind – a notion László only made worse later, with his research. Many who stayed behind were saved by partisans. László told József that. I wish he hadn't. *Fault*. What a notion. But shame came back to us when we were men again. I wouldn't have let him save me, even if it had been possible.' Dragan looked at Felix. 'You will know, at your museum, that people have been surprised by how few suicides there were in the camps. We were too busy surviving. But that night, in Cservenka, it suddenly came to me. Here was a decision I could make. When the SS officer questioned us, I told him I was Jewish. I lied. I chose myself for the pit. Because, in truth, József had saved my life up until that moment, and I no longer wanted it.'

Silence. I was robbed of words, knew that anything I did say would be ludicrously empty, polite, unfit and unwanted.

Felix: 'You said you met in Italy? How?'

'József was staying in a villa just outside Venice with his wife Rosemary and your father. Painting the Adriatic. I had written to him when I was released from Goli Otok. He sent me a postcard, saying to come and see him. I sailed over from Piran.' Dragan drew his thumb over thin, pale lips. 'To reach this villa, you had to climb a steep coastal path, the sea to one side of you, so blue it was blinding, and dry fields stretching away the other. When I got to the top, I was out of breath, and didn't recognise this man at first, leaning on a polished walking stick at the villa gate, wearing an ironed shirt, leather shoes. He put out his hand, smiled as if this were the happiest moment of his life, and said, *My name is Željko Jokić, and I am a Serbian thief.'*

Felix shuffled next to me. 'I don't understand.'

Dragan focused on him. 'That was the cover story I gave him. At Cservenka. To keep him hidden from the SS. They wanted the Jews. And he remembered it. After thirteen years he remembered. He had been living in hiding all that time. But not as a Serbian thief. As Joseph Silk, English as the English Queen.'

I twisted my cup around. 'I hear she's German.'

'Ha. Aren't they all? We had dinner, I met his wife, Rosemary, and his son, John. We traded war stories in the dark, the two of us and the sea. I had dreamt of that moment, and he gave it to me. I believe, young man, that you were not only taken by the art of my fellow prisoners on Goli Otok who later made me gifts of their work, but also that of József. He gave me a painting, when we met. *Laguna Veneta I.* I am told it is worth a lot.'

Felix nodded dumbly.

'Why didn't you remain in touch?' I asked.

Dragan tugged absently at the pucker of his stitches. 'I suppose it was weakness on both sides. Guilt. Pride. I couldn't bear to let him see through it, to see through me, really. To tell him how broken I had become, first by the Nazis, then by my own country, which I still love to this day. How to explain that? When he looked up to me so? Absurd, I know. But it meant a lot to me. Means a lot. How he looked up to me.'

He tugged again at his cheek.

'As for him – well. I couldn't persuade him that *this* was not his fault. He couldn't bear to look at me. His smile disappeared as soon as I turned my head, and never truly returned. Terrible how many nights a man can spend examining his guilt, when all the world would rush to sanctify him if he could only speak his fears. After I left, I missed him. And then I forgot him.'

Dragan looked out at the rivers meeting. 'That is not true. We need a different word. There is a kind of forgetting . . . You remember the name of every man who died, and you remember the names of men you helped, and the men you did not help. You feel shame for having lived, as if you took the chance of others. You feel shame for what happened to you. *Or*. You put on a new suit of clothes, you work in a tired office, you fall in love aggressively. Those nights examining your survival, those nights will never let you rest. So you forget, and live an ordinary life. And you never forget.' Dragan pushed his coffee away. 'Come, I wish to show you something.'

He stood up slowly, glancing about the way Silk used to when he couldn't see his stick. I slipped to his side, offering my arm. He clasped my hand.

'Where are we going?'

'For a drive in a Yugoslav car. This will be an experience of historical interest and so should please our museum friend.'

We moved through the flat, urged slowly by the insistence of Silk's brushstrokes hanging on the wall, by their regretful certainty.

foreign birds

THEY'VE ARRIVED AT THE bridge of goodbyes.

József is about to tell László and Zuzka that the RAF pilot he shared a smoke with around Birmingham told him there's a platform at Euston station known as the bridge of goodbyes – goodbyes shared between soldiers and girlfriends, between parents and children – but the clamour and shriek of the train is too much, so he just puts his hat on and picks up Zuzka's case.

The step down is against the muscle memory of returning from summer months with his uncle, the leap from train to platform in Budapest, and he is righting his bearings when pillars of steam shot with white light hit him, gritting his eyeballs. Black drops on him. He can feel László tugging at his shadow, but he is suffering signal failure. A porter in a hat like a naval captain almost knocks him down, and he is apologising in Magyar and the man flinches as steam folds him in waves and he can't find a kijárat sign – what is it in English: exit? Escape? – and Zuzka is telling him, with the soft incantation of prayer: Look up.

The crosshatch of wrought iron.

Blue

Cuts of blue.

He forces his eyes open, closed. Rolls his eyelids over the bump of coal. The sting and well of tears.

'We'll use the station hotel,' he manages.

'Rabbi Asch gave us an address,' László objects, his voice taut. 'They're expecting us.'

Zuzka says, 'There's a policeman. I can show him the address.'

Her face will be one of careful blankness. He keeps his words just as measured: 'We'll try the hotel.'

The edifice reminds him of the American embassy on Szabadság tér, and he tries to hold on to that, let it ground this vertigo, let the sea-sky above calm his waters. Inside, the velvet curtains suck all sound from the foyer, leaving him with just his heartbeat. He approaches the lustre of the brass counter. The clerk is a grey scream that says good evening, sir, the sir a question. József tries to assume his father's smile, but his mouth is not doing what he wants, all because of the train, the smoke in stacks – 'Excuse me, please, do you have rooms?' – and this man flinches too, and he can't ignore it this time.

'No, we do not. Sir.'

His fist tightens on Zuzka's case. 'One room would be suitable.'

'I really don't think it would.'

'LECHA DODI LIKRAT KALA, p'nei Shabbat n'kabelah!'

The press of body to song leaves József's body with nowhere to retreat. He is struggling not to drown in this house, in Princelet

Street, in the houses on either side, these walls membranes for gagging drains, barrels of pickled fish soured by sun, for garlic, for men arguing in Yiddish on the corner, for the rag-and-bone man's cry, for the stamp and rattle of sewing machines, for mothers screaming at children to come and eat, for laughter, laughter everywhere. And more, here in the parlour, books packed into boxes, too many bodies, and challah bread being broken. The table seats twelve, just, and there is a dresser with cut glass that winks in the candlelight and crowded pictures on the wall and the smell of beeswax on empty shelves.

His hosts are moving from Whitechapel to Golders Green. Those colours pop at him, colours that could drag him out of the grey net cast around him if only there was blue enough to fuel them, if only there was real colour in this room. It is dark outside, and there had been no way to say, No, no thank you, I am going for a walk, as Mrs Rivkin urged him towards the table, telling him they are having baked herrings stuffed with forcemeats and a side dish of boiled kohlrabi root, that she hopes it's their kind of nosherye; it's egg powder and lemon substitute but what can you do? So here he is, with four Rivkin children, and three other guests, with no escape, and the look of gratitude on László's face across from him. Dr Posner had told him: 'Your brother has forgiven God.' Just as you'd speak of a boy forgiving a father who belted him.

Mr Rivkin is the son of Russian refugees who fled from the pogroms of Tsar Alexander III. His father was an itinerant glasscutter, and now Mr Rivkin owns a glass factory. Mr Rivkin told József this almost as soon as József took his boots off, showing him the house but talking about the past with a backed-up stammer that Mrs Rivkin whispers developed during the war, you just have to be patient. Rivkin speaks as if attempting several sentences at once, telling József that during the Great War his father had been declared an alien and sent back to Russia where he was forced to join the Tsar's army, the son of the Tsar who had let his village burn. He tells József that fire seemed to follow their family: his father trapped in a garrison set ablaze by excited revolutionaries in 1917, his mother never found after a night of bombing in 1941; one son in the aliens' Pioneer Corps fighting forest fires in West Africa, not trusted on the front lines even though he volunteered, even though he changed his name to MacRifkin, as if we're a Scottish clan; and one in the Jewish Brigade rounding up Germans, seeing first-hand those ovens, God preserve him, handing out food to – to the blessed, like you. Nazi fire took you across the land, it took us from the sky. Hard to believe they can't reach us now.

The blessed. József swallows that word with the pickled cucumber and grated onion and baked potatoes Mrs Rivkin heaped on his plate, László and Zuzka's too, their portions bigger than anyone else's. The children's stares are ugly, one of them a brilliantine boy with a black eye who Mrs Rivkin calls an anarchist with a snort, which makes the boy blush fiercely. It's too much. József longs to say, *Stop giving me your food, stop giving me your family, stop giving me your fortunes*, as the Rivkins' other guests rattle politics like dynamos that can't cease whirring for fear of falling apart.

József is surprised they're even friends, Mr Rivkin and Mr Greenberg, who, if József passed in the street, he would take for an Englishman through and through, from his bush moustache to his pinstriped trousers, and his wife too, with her pearls and pastel. Mr Rivkin wears a yarmulke, like József's grandfather did, one that never left his head. Mr Greenberg wears a paper cap Mr Rivkin has leant him. He is a banker, and hundreds of years ago his name would have been Grünberg. Then there is the man on József's right, Mr Lipchitz, who has brought his own yarmulke and no wife and smells of ink and anger, who bangs his fist on the table, insisting there *must* be a Jewish homeland, and that homeland is Palestine. What brings these three men and their wives together is something called the Board, and something else called the Anglo-Jewish Association, which is raising money to help boys and girls abroad; boys and girls just like you.

László clears his throat, wrestling with the top button of his shirt. 'We will always be grateful to you – to Mr Montefiore and Miss Hahn-Warburg, to Miss Blond. Everyone at the Central British Fund.'

Lipchitz laughs. 'I would have loved to see you throw up on Monte's tie.'

László chokes on his mouthful.

'Ignore him,' says Greenberg. 'It's our duty, my boy, to guard Jews from these backward lands.'

'You and the Cousinhood and your *backward lands*,' snaps Lipchitz. 'You would call Lithuania a backward land, I suppose.'

This is a new language. Greenberg is a Cousin: settled Jews, publishers, lawyers, Members of Parliament. The Cousinhood negotiated emancipation in the nineteenth century. Greenberg shrugs. He has had this argument before, it seems, and asks Lipchitz without heat: 'What do you call the country that drove your mother out?'

'All right,' says Lipchitz, 'so once we've saved Europe's Jews from these tribal places, these backward lands that were once Berlin and Paris, where then do these *foreign birds of passage* go? And you can say it wasn't you who put those words in the editor of *The Jewish Chronicle*'s mouth till you're blue in the face for all I care, 'cause I know different. I know it was you who said the Board represents permanents, as if me and mine aren't permanent, as if me and mine aren't taking over the Board. But tell me this, where else can these birds fly, if *you* don't want 'em, and the government is slamming the door on 'em, what else can we do but kick the door of Palestine down?' Lipchitz jerks his chin at József. 'If this anti-alienism sounds barbaric to you, you can ask our camouflage Jew to explain it.'

'You say that like it's an insult,' says Mr Greenberg with a diplomat's smile.

Next to him, Zuzka is wide-eyed, as if a doctor had just announced her diagnosis to a roomful of strangers. József knows she is camouflaged, but he doesn't know as what.

Mrs Rivkin leans across the table, into the light. József is reassured by the deep lines of her face, the folds of her thick arms, the bruised meat of her hands. She could hold a ship breaking apart at the timbers. 'This is no proper welcome.'

But Mr Rivkin does not want her tact and says, 'No, no, no,' pinning his chin to his chest, trapping the consonants. 'I wa-wa-want the answer.'

Mr Greenberg takes a huge breath, threatening the candles when he finally lets go, and in the wobble of the flame József is blind. 'It's just this, you see. Anti-Semitism in this country . . . well, it's a medieval problem, do you understand? Our society is essentially the product of Enlightenment, essentially liberal, yes? But in times of . . . well, in days such as these, in times of economic *pressure*, certain members of the uneducated *masses* will turn on us as scapegoats, and there will be a return of anti-Semitism. So what we mustn't do – we must never appear as we do in stereotype. That's why we've set up the Trades Advisory Council, to put a stop to Jews in the black market – and we've got to *educate*. Educate the masses on what Jews have contributed as patriotic members of British society. Persuade people we belong here, that we're just as British as they are. And if the World Jewish Congress and our friend Lipchitz here start saying there's a global Jewish race with one agenda and one country – well, what's to stop the British government saying to us, off you go then, enjoy farming in forty-degree heat?' He turns to Mr Rivkin. 'What's to stop Hoxton boys telling your lad here to go back to Palestine, giving him a black eye?'

Silence. László's breathing is short. Zuzka is fiddling with her napkin. József feels that he's supposed to step in, that even the boy with the black eye is looking to him to complete some kind of circuit, as perhaps refugees who've stayed here before have done, as his father or mother would have done, with urbanity, with wit, but he can't find any words, except: *So now I have to sell myself to you, too?*

Mr Rivkin taps his finger on the table. 'Ob-ob-*obfuscation*. You didn't *want* us Eastern European Jews, and you don't want these Central European Jews now.'

Mrs Greenberg – who has red hair that looks grey to József, a young face aged – lays her hand on her husband's arm. 'The heart of this is factionalism,' she says. 'You're pretending your community is any less wary than ours. None of this is part of the contract. Emancipation is a gift.'

'Yes,' seizes her husband, 'that's it, a gift, and it can be taken back. In return for the government accepting refugees, we agree to foot the bill. In return for our seats in the chambers, we keep our religion in our homes. We are held to our promises. The reason our fathers were wary of your fathers is because you settled here, in Whitechapel, in visible groups, provoking existing communities. You are Orthodox. Now I'm not saying – we all know we're coreligionists –'

Lipchitz, red in the face: 'How can there be coreligionists but no world Jewish race?'

József doesn't want László listening to this. If being Magyar is a losing bet, joining a world Jewish race has about as much chance as sinking your fortune on a horse starting from the slaughterhouse.

Again, Greenberg's wife intervenes. 'It's quite clear there isn't a world Jewish race; after all, you're unsure of our new friends because they're by and large not Orthodox, and won't contribute to your society, just as they won't ours.' She looks at József. 'Are you? Orthodox?'

He grips the frayed tablecloth. 'No, ma'am.'

'You're progressives?' She sounds like a schoolteacher.

'My mother was.'

A small pause. The candles seem to bow. 'And you?'

László is holding his breath. Zuzka is hiding beneath the fall of her hair. 'I'm – I'm secular.'

Mrs Greenberg throws her hands in the air. 'There we have it. Intellectuals – painters and psychoanalysts.'

Lipchitz pounds the table, and László nods with him as Lipchitz shouts: '*None of this is the point.*'

József's head is throbbing. Zuzka's little finger brushes his hand under the table. Static fires up his arm.

Mrs Greenberg: 'What *is* the point, then?'

'Hampstead!' explodes Lipchitz. 'Nearly three thousand people signed that petition. That's three thousand people calling for German and Austrian Jews to go back where they came from, and if they can't be repatriated, you know what they wanted? Internment.'

László leans in. Zuzka's hand disappears.

What about Hungarians? What about Czechs?

But Greenberg is rolling his eyes and saying, 'Which only goes to prove my point.'

'Prove *your* point – you honestly think the refugees in Hampstead were taking up so much room it drove people to this?' Lipchitz's neck is engorged, his sweat filling József's nostrils. 'Or do you think the Mayor of Hampstead and the Women's Guild of the blasted Empire decided to exploit a housing crisis brought on by Tory slums and years of bombs in order to turn indifferent neighbours into Jew-baiters?'

'Look here, old man,' says Greenberg. 'You're only telling half the story. Hampstead Council condemned that petition, councillors on both sides. And there *is* a terrible squeeze on houses.'

'You and your *apologias*! So ready to *understand*, to help put the problem back in its box, to raise money for European orphans, but God forbid we interrogate what happened in Germany, that other post-Enlightenment country with its classical music and banking systems, or call out those apes that turned up to the Left Book Club protest. You weren't there, you didn't hear it.'

As Lipchitz tells the story József feels the anger radiating from him, sees it lighting in László's eyes. The Left Book Group had met in a church to protest the petition. The rabbi began the meeting by saying that fascism in all its beastliness is not the prerogative of any one country. He'd said its first beginnings are often hard to detect, but that this petition, in his opinion, was such a beginning. And one of the petitioners who'd crowded in – a crowd that amassed to hundreds outside of the church – shouted, 'You're talking rot! This ain't nothing to do with fascism, it's to do with who's taking what's ours!' A woman MP tried to reason with the crowd. She asked if they realised that a great many refugees were Jews, but the crowd yelled that they were Germans, spies most likely. Miss Rathbone warned them that something cruel, like this petition, could end in something bestial – that word again, as if the three thousand names on the petition were the names of beasts, let off the hook of humanity – that it could in fact lead to deportations. And the crowd shouted back to her: yes. Yes, we realise that. Do you want the refugees to go back to Germany? Yes. Yes, we want that. Do you realise what happened in Germany? Yes. Yes, we realise what happened.

Lipchitz says now, 'And don't think it's just the uneducated. The British Medical Association wants to send refugee doctors, people who helped our soldiers, back to their countries. The Vice-President said we can't be stepfathers to the whole of Europe.'

Mrs Rivkin is setting a baked date pudding in front of József. He leans into its steam to cover his face.

He can hear his father's last words to him as János shrugged into the navy wool coat József had tried on from boyhood, hear the catch in his father's throat, as if he knew this was the last time he'd ever see his children or his wife. *My boy, remember what the Talmud says. In a place where there is no man, try to be a man.*

I have a father. I don't need a stepfather. And László doesn't either. I can be his father.

He looks across at László. He can't read his brother's expression. There is no reflection there.

'This looks delicious,' says Mrs Greenberg.

Mr Greenberg is toying with his spoon. 'Hundreds of people went to that protest.'

A groan from Mrs Rivkin.

'Yes,' says Lipchitz, 'and that Jew-baiter who beat Mark Rose in Stepney, broke his glasses, and told him to go back to Palestine, that was the behaviour of a savage, the judge said, not someone in an alleged civilised country. It's a big word, *alleged*. That's an Englishman, not some island native we like to call savage, an *Englishman* – and he isn't alone.'

László's right hand has curled into a fist. Zuzka is eating too fast.

'That's why we have to be educators,' says Mrs Greenberg. 'He was just a labourer, that vile man.'

'Educators!' Lipchitz jabs his finger at József. 'If you want educating, give this kid a microphone. Let's see where treating vile men as small problems gets us.'

József seizes.

Don't ask me to talk.

Don't ask me to tolerate the looks of incomprehension on your faces; don't ask me to make room for your disbelief.

The anarchist son scrapes his chair back, and József sags in thanks for the tidal pull of the table in his direction.

Mrs Rivkin: 'Sit down, young man.'

The boy is trembling. 'Ain't the Archbishop of Canterbury an educated man? He gave a talk last month, me and my mates snuck in. First he said that this country would never truck with anti-Semitism, then he said there were *some* reasons for anti-Semitism that weren't wholly unreasonable. There's hedging your bets on stocks and shares, and then there's hedging your bets on the chances a people got of living. I

363

don't call that fucking enlightened. And I don't call it compromise, or conciliation. It's collaboration, and there's no two fucking ways about it.'

In the hysterical back-and-forth that follows, József pushes his plate away. Whitechapel is a map he does not recognise: no Andrássy út giving him its east–west line of sight, no Danube north–south; a map that closes ever inward, burrowing to Kiev and Berlin and Russian bog-land and the Jews' exile from England seven hundred years ago, a map the people at this table have locked themselves inside, subsisting on sites of prayer and sites of grievance, requiring a key he cannot read, and does not want to learn. He will keep his mouth shut.

visit the living

Dragan's car was mustard yellow with an engine that coughed all the way down the hill and over the slender Sava. We crossed behind Great War Island, following Bulevar Nikola Tesla along the Danube. Dragan drove in silence, peering at the road in front as if it were miles away. Next to me, Felix was looking around with growing concern. I wanted to ask what was wrong, but the silence in the car had poured over us and set with cracks enough only to breathe. My camera continued to record.

We parked at the base of a bridge. A manicured green struck out into the river. At its edge, a monument rose black and solid. It looked like two broken hands unable to contain an amorphous star. I expected Dragan to lead us towards it, but he didn't, walking slowly instead towards a collection of shacks now serving as houses surrounding a pavilion. A tower rose from the middle, its windows clogged with ivy. I stopped.

'Is this Sajmište?'

Dragan nodded. His head didn't come back up again. He kept

walking. I followed, Felix's shadow touching mine. The buildings of the old camp looked like peeling flesh. The trees had taken over. People lived in the fairground buildings, in lean-tos constructed from a long, low building the Nazis had used as a mortuary. Wire lines spun the trees, heavy with washing. A blue car gleamed like a sucked sweet. We paused at a cross-section. A man watched us from the square metre of his garden, a kind of stubborn curiosity on his face. *They kept us in Sajmište for Yom Kippur. Hundreds were taken to be tortured. We were lucky.*

These people were living on graves.

A gentle tug at my sleeve. Felix. He gestured the other way: Dragan was striking in the direction of the monument. We followed. Felix looked carefully blank. I felt like I was losing my balance. At the monument, Dragan was straightening a tired bunch of flowers, a pile of stones, these keepsakes that nobody kept. Over the bank, terracotta homes and steeples waited for the wash of rain.

'I never told him.'

I drew closer, watching the shudder of Dragan's bent spine. 'Pardon?'

'I never told József what they did to her. I couldn't. It would have frightened him. But I should have, afterwards. To let him know it wasn't his fault, me giving up. Do you know, my museum friend, what the SS did to people here?'

Felix said nothing. I could tell the answer was yes.

'Then I'll tell you. The fairground was built in 1937 to celebrate a new future. The tower was white then. When the Germans occupied Belgrade, they chose this last post of the Austro-Hungarian Empire as their concentration camp. Before the war, seventy-five thousand

Jews lived in Serbia, fifteen thousand in Belgrade. One of them was my wife. Jelena. There were restrictions, where they could live, and so on. But we married. Her family forgave us because they considered themselves Serbs first. Her father loved Serbia. He trusted to good times. I remember him telling me once, *Well, they cannot kill us all, son*. He was wrong. At first this place was only used for labour service, and her father told me again, *They will not kill us because they need us*. He became famous for being wrong.

'I joined the partisans. I thought I could help. I thought I could win the war single-handed. I was wrong too. For every German soldier we wounded, they would kill fifty civilians. For every German soldier killed, they would murder one hundred civilians. By civilians, they meant Jews – at least, whilst there were still Jews to shoot. Almost every Jewish man was killed by firing squad. Jelena was going to come with me into the hills, but it was too late. When the orders came I was miles away and could do nothing. Jewish and gypsy women in Belgrade were told: pack food for three days, lock up your home, and turn the keys over to the police, tagged with your name and address. Five thousand women, children, a few surviving old men were moved into Sajmište, each with the living space of a square metre. It was a cold winter. Many women committed suicide by jumping from the upper floors. My wife was pregnant. She did not kill herself. That is my belief. Only a belief.

'The Nazis first used a gas truck in 1941, in Ukraine. Then in Leningrad, Sebastopol, Berlin, Majdanek, Lvov, Pyatigorsk, Danzig, Vienna, Belgrade. The SS officers who arrived here with their hermetically sealed Saurer truck were named Wilhelm Götz and Erwin Meyer. One would drive, the other would feed the gas pipe into a hole in the underside of the truck. It was known as Soul Slaughter. The Jewish Council was told the women would be taken to a camp in Poland with more space and more food. People climbed into the back of the Saurer truck peacefully, gratefully. On each short drive between the fairground and Jajinci, at the foot of the Avala Mountain, eighty people died. Then five Serbian prisoners opened the doors of the truck, and the suffocated bodies tumbled out. The prisoners dug the graves. They were told they'd be transferred to a nicer camp in Norway. They were shot afterwards.

'The inmates staying behind soon asked those being taken to leave a piece of paper in the luggage truck as a sign of safety. No paper appeared, and the inmates stopped getting into the Saurer so peacefully, but by then it didn't matter. I don't know whether Jelena was on one of those first trucks, when she still thought she was being taken to a better place, or after, after there was no paper. The truck came every day except Sundays. The guards grew kinder and the food got better. Later, the Nazis decided to burn the corpses buried at Jajinci. Jelena's body, after two years of rotting in the ground, was robbed of gold teeth, wedding ring, watch, and then burnt. The ashes were sifted in search of any overlooked valuables. Her wedding ring was sent to Berlin, and maybe lives now in your museum. Her ashes were given to the Sava, and afterwards people found belt buckles and buttons on the tide.'

Dragan's knee shook. I caught him under the elbow and lowered him to the marble base of the monument. We sat there together, facing the decrepit buildings. Felix kneaded a hand over his heart.

'This is where it happened, Eva. Soul slaughter. They got mine too. When they brought József and me here, it was too much. I knew what had happened, I'd been told. I couldn't bear to drag my soul on. I have come here every Sunday for almost fifty years with flowers. I have considered walking into the river and drowning myself many times. To be just another body floating along the Danube. But such dramatics mean nothing.' He tapped my camera. 'There is no narrative for you to tell, no suspense, no closure. There is just this ground. I am not a true witness. The true witnesses – well, *you* know.' He was looking at Felix.

Felix shoved his hands deeper into his pockets. 'They didn't come out of the pit.'

'Yes,' said Dragan. 'Yes. That's it. The rest is just beginning, middle, and then beginning again. Only they know the ending.' He smiled at me. 'But you, you make me feel a little better.'

I wiped my tears with my sleeve. 'I am very glad to have met you. Thank you, for everything you did. If it weren't for you, I wouldn't exist.'

Dragan grinned at that, seeming to consider it as an idea. 'Yes. The pleasure is entirely mine. You can go to Silk's grave and tell him he was always too hard on himself, about this, about László, about everything.'

'I will.'

'And you might tell your father for me too.'

'Why?'

'Because he is not in his grave yet. It is important to visit the living, before we are stone.'

I didn't want to let go of his hand.

transmigration

THE JEWS' TEMPORARY SHELTER waits, a hostel with other boys and girls from Windermere, but no one is sure what to do about József, so tonight they sleep in the Princelet Street attic, borrowing MacRifkin and the hero of the Jewish Brigade's beds. Another stoplight.

Zuzka is downstairs with the children. She escaped after dinner, agreeing to look at the youngest boy's collection of toy flags. László's dreams are making him frown, curled tight. Packing up his room in Windermere, he had told József about his nightmares, keeping his gaze on books and clothes as he described the German soldier who hacked a woman to death with a spade on the railroad, and now chases László nightly down the track. József hadn't intended to sound so strict when he told him: 'It's over now. We're safe.' He'd meant it as a promise. But he saw the disappointment on László's face, knew the grief and exhaustion of never being comforted, tiredness he sees now even as László rests. His little brother has been filled with age, not László's own age, but theirs, all of them; this age they are living in. And József doesn't know what to do about it. His comfort isn't comforting; his promises are demands; his love is not equal to the equation at hand, neither balancing László's loss, or his own.

Downstairs, Mrs Rivkin is crying, the anarchist slamming the door, Mr Rivkin trudging to the outhouse, shouting as he beats his way through laundry that at least his good-for-nothing boy has expanded his vo-vo-vocabulary: compromise, conciliation, collab-ab-aboration, *oi vey*.

They have been given a candle. In its guttering light, József throws the blanket off and pulls a box towards him. There are dozens of boxes in here, probably filled with more books. But when he opens the first it's not books but newspapers. He opens another. Pamphlets. Advice books. Apologias. The boxes are like Mr Rivkin's stammer, how the man has to tuck in his chin to pin the words down; he's fixing the whole world in these soggy boxes that boast the best glass in London.

József dumps the damp *Jewish Chronicles* on the bed, opening one to the centrefold.

ANTI-JEWISH RIOTS IN SLOVAKIA

NAZI AFTERMATH IN SWEDEN

CZECHS RESTORE SOME JEWISH PROPERTY

US IMMIGRATION QUOTA

JEWS IN MANILA DESTITUTE

ECUADOR DOES NOT WANT JEWS

VIENNA'S JEWISH REMNANT

The editorial asks where Jews can go but Palestine, so harried about, so hunted, so despised, what country can they call home but their own, so the British *must* turn Palestine over to them. For every other plan has fallen through: Texas, British Guiana, the Kimberleys, Cyrenaica and Tripolitania. And what justification is there, the British Military Administration in Tripolitania had asked, for Jews to come here, what historical connection? Where then, but Palestine?

László is talking in his sleep, the nonsense words of a baby. József wants to hold his hand, smooth back his hair, tell him: *I have a historical connection to you, and I won't let it break*. But he is too afraid of waking him – of continuing the argument begun at dinner.

The newspapers go all the way back through the year. József quickly passes Nuremberg – SICKENING REVELATIONS IN INDICTMENT – and the Belsen trial with its hangings. His shoulders are burning but he keeps going, leaning over the tight words, eyes watering, not knowing quite what he is looking for until he's found it.

BUDAPEST JEWS' FATE SEALED

A Jew who succeeded in escaping from Budapest last week – this was February – said that the ghetto was fired by the Germans on Jan. 16.

Where had he been on the sixteenth of January – what road, what factory, what field, what hole? He can't remember.

Although many Jews died in the flames some succeeded in escaping, in spite of German shots at the fugitives. The Germans, according to this man, dragged out those Jews still in the capital who had protective passports from neutral states and, after butchering them, threw their bodies in the Danube.

He sees his mother backing away from flames as the floor around her buckles.

He sees his mother being dragged in the street, a fist at her skirts, sees her trying to wheel away from the man's grip.

He sees a butcher's knife.

He sees the Danube, sees its light, sees its depths.

He feels her fear in the last moment.

László kicks out. József buries Budapest in the box, buries it with another headline he must keep from László if he wants to keep László.

THE 'SCARLET PIMPERNEL' OF ZIONISM

His heart is beating too fast, as if harried itself. They say he won't be allowed to stay, won't be allowed to work, that he and László and Zuzka and all the Windermere Boys are here with permission to visit only, held to the promise of transmigration. But he's made it this far, and there is no stamp of disapproval that will stop him trying to live again. He shakes the advice pamphlets out on the bed – pamphlets asking for money to feed children like László, pamphlets asking for sponsors to come forward with homes. He chucks them aside.

DO'S AND DON'TS FOR REFUGEES.

DO Talk English as much as you possibly can. Bad English is preferable to German.

He remembers the porter and the clerk flinching at his accent. Had they thought he was German? Had they thought he was Hungarian Gentile?

DO be as quiet and modest as possible. If you do not make yourself noticeable, other people will not bother about you.

DO be as cheerful as possible. Everyone sympathises with you in your difficult position. A smiling face makes them still more your friends.

His smile had failed, at Euston Station Hotel. He had no mask to pick up.

DON'T talk German in the streets, in public places or any places where others may hear you. You will learn English more quickly by talking it constantly. And there is nothing to show the man in the street that you are a refugee and not a Nazi.

József's mouth is lined with cinders.

There is nothing about him, here in this body, in this accent, in these clothes, to say he is a camouflage Jew, not a camouflage Nazi.

He is shaking when he picks up *Mistress and Maid: General Information for use of Domestic Refugees and their Employers*, and the words hurtle about the page. It says permission must be obtained by the Home Office to work. It says they're entitled to medical care under National Health Insurance. It says it is good manners in this country to speak and walk quietly, and he thinks of how his father talked with his hands. It says English houses are often colder than Continental ones, and you must expect to guard against the cold by wearing thick underclothes and woollen indoor coats. No kidding. He can see László's breath shivering on the air. It says maids should read English books and learn English history and if they are lonely, they should go to the library. It says if you are in trouble, the police here are always kind. It says a maid must carry a yellow domestic registration card. Yellow.

'You can't sleep either?'

He looks up. Zuzka is at the top of the ladder with a woollen shawl hanging from her shoulders. She is looking at the pamphlet in his hands.

'Mrs Rivkin said she'd take me to the Labour Exchange on Monday.'

József tosses the book back in the box. 'You're not being some Englishman's charwoman.'

She laughs, climbing into the attic. 'Why not?'

Because you're not carrying yellow identification papers. 'Because it's a waste. I see your face every time music is played.'

She is struck blank now. Then: 'We'd better not wake László.'

'So come closer.'

Hesitation, and then she sits on the end of the bed.

'So? What do you play?'

She shakes her head. 'You're imagining things.'

He finds a half-smile. 'I have better things to do with my imagination.'

Zuzka glances at László, then back at him. She is beginning to smile too. 'Such as?'

He moves closer. 'Variations on a theme.'

She looks at him, right in the eye. There's something in her face he's not used to, a glimmer. 'What's the theme?'

'You.' The *Mistress and Maid* pamphlet had warned employers: many of the girls dread loneliness. He asks her now: 'Are you lonely, Zuzka?'

Her finger brushes his knuckle. She doesn't answer.

'I could keep you from being lonely,' he says.

There is excitement at the edge of her mouth; in the heat coming off her; in the way she sits with one leg folded under the other, her bare toes poking out; in the promise of her eyes. He wants her, with his whole body he wants her. He could show her what Rebecca showed him, and a couple of other nurses too, introducing him to what their husbands did or didn't do. He could open the top button of her cardigan, just that.

Finally, she speaks: 'Are *you* lonely?' His hand stills over hers. Her voice has dropped. 'I could keep you from being lonely.'

This is a trick of Zuzka's, he's realised. She deflects questions, but in that deflection seems to have an insight into the heart of things, as if the void left by her refusal to divulge herself leaves space for others to pour themselves into her. But he has no desire to pour out his pain, to tell her about his mother being dragged through the street, about the butcher's knife. Sometimes he hears Zuzka talking when there's no one but her in the room. Does she want him to be the other half of the conversation? He won't. The paper said a number of refugees were confined to mental hospitals when they first arrived, refugees who, having recovered, are now relapsing because they have nowhere to go but the hospital, and the hospital walls are infected with madness. They need homes, and it's up to Jews and Jewesses to educate their neighbours, so that doors now closed from understandable misgivings would open to these helpless victims. All these people talk about is doors: doors slammed shut, doors kicked open. The paper said the world today is suffering from more barriers than ever before, barriers that prevent people from crossing borders and class boundaries, prevent free intercourse between human beings. He does not want her to cross his border. Greenberg and Lipchitz and Rivkin and the papers and pamphlets, they don't understand that there is a wound at the heart of him, a wound Zuzka has exposed with her soft words; they don't understand the number of people pressing on it, fighting to name it, pouring ink into it; they don't understand the number of ghosts. He doesn't want her to cross his border. But he wants something else. He wants to kiss her, to find out how the smallness of her mouth would respond, if his stubble would tickle her and if she'd laugh, if she'd cry with relief at the end, as he had the first time with Rebecca. If her body moving with his would close the door on the world outside.

But László lies across from them.

László who wants Zuzka.

What does the boy think, that at fourteen he can take care of a girl like this? László doesn't need a girl; he needs a father, and a mother.

József whispers: 'Do you want to spend the night?'

Zuzka bites her lip. 'Spend it how?'

'Recklessly.'

She hesitates. He makes room for her, offering his hand, offering to fold her into his body. She's cold to touch. She fits next to him, her head tucked into his shoulder, and he doesn't ask if he can open the top button of her cardigan, he just puts his arms around her.

He almost doesn't catch it when she breathes, 'You make me feel like I'm inside my body.'

He looks down, his lips brushing her hair. 'Why would you go anywhere else?'

He knows it's not a question she'll answer. That's why he asked it.

If being Jewish means no home or one home or home with yellow papers, means Yiddish or English or Hungarian but not all three, means God or queer intellectualism, means apologising to the man in the street, means a long story, means hyphens, means searching for a new way to be a chosen people, a new way to be European in exile, a new way to *be* – then wouldn't it be easier – hail smacks against the window, Zuzka is asleep, László is dreaming unhappily – wouldn't it be easier to simply not be Jewish? To be simply British. To be a man without a story. To be a man whose story is of his own making. He remembers his mother reading him *The Pendragon Legend* before he really understood it, remembers the Hungarian scholar looking back at his adventures in England and reflecting, *All my stories begin with my being born in Budapest*. What if he could be reborn?

Zuzka stirs, her thigh pressing against his groin, her breath warm on his neck, her hand twitching, as if threading a needle, or gripping a bow, drawing a language from a cello or a violin, a language she will not speak during the day.

Let us be born of a new language. Let me find the language of my dreams.

JÓZSEF SAYS HE WON'T join them at temple. He says he'd appreciate being given directions to the nearest library. He wants to get out an English dictionary. Mr Rivkin pulls at his beard.

'The University of the Ghetto. I suppose books are for wor-wor-worship too.'

'The university of what?'

Mrs Rivkin says he'll understand when he gets there and gives him directions. He asks Zuzka if she'd like to join him. After glancing in László's direction, she says yes. László is bent in hushed conversation with the anarchist. He hasn't been speaking to them all morning, since finding József and Zuzka in bed together, Zuzka asleep in József's arms.

When they step out into the weak sun, Zuzka reminds him to thank the Rivkins for their kindness later.

'Keeping my soul clean?'

She shrugs. She seems more solid than she did in Windermere. She has borrowed a blue polka-dot dress that's too small for Mrs Rivkin. She looks like she belongs in the modern world.

'Do you remember the last time anyone thanked us for anything?' he asks. 'People used to thank me for little things, like holding doors for them, or delivering parcels. All we do now is give thanks. I'm tired of giving thanks.' She raises an eyebrow at him. 'For *some* things, anyway.' She takes his arm.

Brick Lane is bombed-out rubble shored up in banks, posters about dances and public lectures, the garlic and ginger of kosher delis, Russian and Latvian and the English accent of the anarchist, it's a grocer with a blackboard that shouts *We Sell Bananas!*, it's a man in a white vest tightening chains over his assistant and yelling: Place your bets, ladies and gentlemen, this man is going to escape what binds him. Blue breaks up the clouds, a salty ache in his eyes, filling Brick Lane with the taste of it as a Hassid walks by him without any air of shame or fear at all.

When they turn onto Whitechapel High Street he can already hear it, the insistence of Yiddish arguments. The pamphlets had said Englishmen talked and walked quietly, but here, on this street that stinks of incendiaries and horseshit, here the doors of The Passmore Edwards Library stand open, and inside the University of the Ghetto is training East End intellectuals. The force of their conversation is the confidence of his mother and father and their friends. Jewish poets, Jewish painters, Jewish revolutionaries.

'Don't you want to go inside?' asks Zuzka.

He looks around. Latches on to a sign. 'No. No. Let's go in here.'

Next door is a building unlike anything he's seen so far in London.

Its stone glows against the sky, bleeding with blue. Its doorway stands beneath a grand arch. Its façade twists with leaves, as if bombs have scattered trees against the body of the building. Gold lettering reads: *Whitechapel Art Gallery*.

His eyes fail to adjust at first and it's Zuzka who talks to the girl at the desk, leaving him amidst the cloy of cheap paint and dust. Zuzka takes his arm again, putting something in his hand. A pamphlet: *American Art*.

'It's free,' says Zuzka.

The windows coax him back. He is standing in the middle of the exhibition space: four walls, European ceilings, the hush of concentration.

His palm itches.

The Yank had rubbed blue into his palm.

Zuzka says, 'Look at this,' gesturing towards a painting of skyscrapers, but József's attention has gone to the end of the room, is pulled there, this undertow. Zuzka follows him.

She says, 'Lyonel Feininger, *Old Stone Bridge*.'

József blinks away the tears suddenly in his eyes. Zuzka is squeezing his hand. Yes, an indigo bridge with four glowing vaulted archways, a bridge over a river and beneath a sky, a river and sky he knows, the water the blue of dirty puddles and sapphires and steel and the slow melt of stained-glass windows, glassy and translucent and throbbing with a dimensionality he could walk into, the sky fractured and heavy and willing to give, the watercolour diffusion of early night, the coarse rush of pastel, the passion of ground smalt and spilt lapis lazuli.

There is a world, a language, in which he can live.

my father's house

M Y FATHER'S HOUSE WAS a great stone thing set amongst arid vineyards, too far inland for the Tyrrhenian Sea to cleanse unforgiving soil. In the evening dusk his windows shone Van Gogh yellow. A vast timber shed, open to the elements and choking on a tangle of broken machinery, blocked access to the front door. John had become a handyman. A churn of gravel told me the taxi was pulling out. I picked my way through pyramids of tyres and faded tubs of paint labelled 'washer rings' and 'roofing bolts' in scrawled Sharpie. The strip lighting flickering to life overhead revealed banana crates, covered in yellowed newspaper and electrical tape, labelled 'Books – living room' and 'Records – study'. He packed those boxes in London a decade ago. I was brought up short by a restored Citroen ID 19 that gleamed blue-black. My father had become an artist.

I climbed iron steps to a veranda. The door was oak, thick and squat, resistant to weather and invading armies. I raised the knocker.

John opened the door holding a glass of wine, and the liquid wobbled when he saw me.

'I thought you were Liset.'

'She's not here.'

'She's dramatic.'

I looked past him. 'Can I come in?'

A beat. John moved his shoulder, letting me slip into the kitchen. The fridge hummed and rattled. The walls were gloss white. The lights were off, and John did not touch them.

'What are you doing here?'

'I wanted to talk to you.'

'So you came all the way here?'

I sat down at the table. Pine planks unevenly joined together. I wondered if John had made it in his shed, just like Silk made the lime table at Fitzroy Park. He passed me a too-full glass and sat down, his feet coming to rest on the bar under the table. I felt the jigging of his foot in vibrations up my leg. I realised, for the first time in my life, that he might be more scared of me than I am of him.

'I've been in Hungary,' I said.

'What for?'

'I've learnt some things about the family. What happened to Silk's father. What happened to Silk in labour service.'

'How?'

'Silk testified after the war. I'm going to give permission to the Jewish Museum in Berlin to include what happened to him in a new exhibit.'

'He'd love that.'

'No kidding.'

'Did you consider asking me about this?'

I looked at him. 'Not really. You forfeited that right a long time ago, don't you think?'

'Because you gave Silk sponge baths and kept him company in his loneliness?'

'As good a way of putting it as any.'

John drained his glass. 'You know, at some point you have to stop hating me.'

'I already have.'

John had raised his eyebrows, and they remained stuck now high on his forehead. 'Is that right? What's it been replaced by?'

'Nothing.'

John got up, opened and closed the fridge. The noise stopped. He stayed in the corner. 'Did it occur to you that this is where you and I meet?'

'What?'

'You're only the third generation because I'm the second. Because I'm the child of two survivors.'

'You mean one.'

John shrugged. 'You're right. I forfeited the both of you a long time ago. And Joseph didn't want to talk about it – the past, any of it. He left you his estate and an urge to remember. He gave it to you. So I may as well give you the rest of it. Rosemary was not my mother.'

My glass landed too hard, a heavy smack. Dragan's words, which I had been refusing to decode, broke apart. *His wife, Rosemary. His son, John.*

'*My* mother was a Czech woman called Zuzka. She was in a camp with Uncle László, and after the war she came with them to England, where she married Joseph. She left before I was one.

László followed her to Paris, where they had an affair. I'm told that suicide after liberation was fairly common. She gassed herself in a Paris flat in 1951. László had thought he could save her. He didn't tell Joseph until after Zuzka was dead where they were; that she was seeing things, hearing voices. And after she was dead, Joseph didn't want to know.'

I gripped the edge of the table, searched ridiculously for the knots of Silk's lime. 'She was a Windermere Boy?'

'If that's what it's called. László told me on my sixteenth birthday. You're a man now: welcome to the truth of your home. Welcome to your world.'

Around us the house was silent.

'He told me Zuzka had been murdered twice. First by the Nazis, and then by Joseph's refusal to remember her. He told me we had to make up for Silk's failures.' John sniffed, stuck his chin out. 'But I am my father's son. I just repeated them. He told me later he never should have given me her picture, if I wouldn't sit shiva with him.'

I could only parrot, 'There are pictures?'

'One.'

John left the room, and I listened to his slow step on the stairs, so much like Silk willing his legs on.

Lies, lies, lies.

When he came back he dropped an envelope on the table and retreated to the corner. I freed a newspaper clipping. It was too dim to see anything, and I reached for the light switch, seeing John flinch in the moment of exposure. I leant over the black-and-white picture. Children lined up in a square, a statue behind them.

'László is in the middle, front row. She's the girl next to him.'

A sum of fractured dots, a wavering smile, a rigid back.

When I finally spoke, my voice came out rasping and small: 'Why didn't you tell me?'

'Why didn't Silk tell you? Why didn't he tell *me*?'

My hand flew up and knocked against the table. The jug of flowers wavered. The gesture ended there.

'You're not going to defend him?' asked John.

'How can I defend what I don't know?'

John snorted. 'There's your answer. Joseph lied to me, and he lied to you, because it meant he didn't have to defend himself against the truth. The evening László told me, I went to Rosemary. I asked her if she was my mother. And she cried. The kind of crying that comes after someone has been ill for a long time and dies. A relief. Joseph found us like that, and you know what he told me? What he said? Absolutely nothing. *Absolutely nothing.*'

He was shaking.

I was too.

'You think it was so *special*,' said John. 'You and him. He lied to you just like he lied to everyone else.'

I stood up, backed to the doorway. 'That doesn't mean it wasn't – wasn't what it was.'

'Doesn't it?'

I held on to the doorframe. I would have fallen if I didn't.

Silk's home, Silk's love. It was the points on a compass. Without it, I'd be nothing.

I could hear Silk telling me, *Make your own maps. Don't trust mine.*

I could hear John asking me, *Why do you always hide behind that camera?*

385

I could hear John slamming doors closed.

I could hear the crawl of fear that had been encroaching across the surface of my mind all my life. Silk told me once about a lost explorer who radioed the wrong coordinates and was eventually given up for dead. They found him, years later, in a flooded cave. That terrified me, as a child. That if I strayed from the script, from scheduled silences, accepted cues, desired responses, they'd give me up. To hold back that tide, it was better to lie, lie, lie. Granny Rosemary had lied. Silk had lied. John had lied.

'Does Mum know?'

John shook his head. 'If she had – well. It doesn't matter now.'

'What?'

'I would have called you Zuzka.'

My grip on the doorframe came free, a knuckle at a time. 'Why didn't you tell her?'

'I've never told anyone.'

I took a step into the room. The floorboard sank beneath me. 'You haven't?'

He shook his head again.

'What was she like? Zuzka?'

'You think I remember snatches of Czech from the cradle?'

I remained still. 'What did László tell you?'

'She was beautiful. Mysterious. He thought she might have been involved in propaganda filming in Theresienstadt, but he couldn't find the footage. Maybe it's there now. I'm sure you could ferret it out if you wanted to.'

I searched for his eyes, but he had retreated to the hallway door.

'Do you want me to?'

'It doesn't matter to me.'

I stepped closer. 'John, I don't hate you. I just don't know if you love me.'

'Maybe I don't. Maybe I'm not capable of it. You had Silk, at least.'

'That's it?'

'You didn't come here for a reconciliation, did you?'

I had no answer for him.

No. 330. When did you first receive news from home, and what kind of news

No. 349. How long was your journey

No. 350. What main line stations did you pass through

No. 352. When did you arrive in Hungary, what was your reception and what were your first impressions

No. 354. What arrangements have been made to provide you with food and accommodation

No. 355. Have you received any financial or any other help

No. 356. Are you just passing through Budapest or do you intend on staying here

No. 357. Have you brought any documents or photographs of your German camps

No. 358. If yes, are you willing to surrender those documents so that a record might be kept

No. 359. How do you picture your future and have you any concrete plans

No. 360. Where are you looking to fulfill those ambitions

Seven

tinder to oil

LÁSZLÓ COMBS HIS HAIR one last time and knocks. Sounds from inside the flat: János crying, Zuzka's light step along the corridor. He straightens his shoulders as the door opens.

'Good evening.'

Zuzka laughs. 'Good evening? Are we on such formalities now?'

She kisses him on the cheek, enveloping him in the honeysuckle perfume József buys, an expense he bats away with the justification that Floris perfumed King George IV, and only the best will do for Susie Silk. That Zuzka earns most of their money seems to be lost on his brother.

'I'm just cooking before they get back – will you join me in the kitchen? Maybe you can stop John wailing . . .'

József and Zuzka moved to Camden Town after the hostels were disbanded; József hadn't wanted the Committee for Care of Children from the Concentration Camps to put one of those advertisements in the *Jewish Chronicle* for them – **seeking kosher but not Orthodox family home for married couple and younger boy, Hungarians and**

Czech – or help pay his board. He didn't want a Jewish Refugee Committee counsellor to make a tour of landlords and employers and try to introduce them to the concept of trauma, to explain why babies crying or being cheated of a lunchbreak is tinder to oil. He'd found Lissenden Gardens instead, cheap because bombing had destroyed ten apartments and weakened the essential structure of the mansion block. László had followed the couple home from the ceremony at Hampstead Synagogue, and his brother insisted he must love the wrought-iron bannisters, so like Budapest, and the carved redbrick and the decorative tiles and the stained glass, which, he says, remind Zuzka of home. But Zuzka's home sent her running: doesn't József know that – that he's simply caught her in flight, as László had? He insisted László must love dawn swims in the Lido, too, the rectangle of unheated blue the balcony overlooked, where no men play chess because once you're in the Lido you're too cold to think, let alone strategise. And beyond all these demands was another, stretched to breaking: love Zuzka as your sister-in-law.

He trails her now into the kitchen. The flat has changed since he left. The indoor plants are gone, filling the windows with Parliament Hill turning violet, and the dark furniture has been brightened with cluttered blue lamps and the Bristol blue glasses László sells on the stall and a blue tablecloth, but not the blue dye of Szentendre. Lipchitz often tells László: 'I could smell that I'll-do-it-myself streak on your brother the moment I met him. No sense of the collective.'

'Did you manage to get any smoked salmon?'

László tries to present the bag with a flourish. The crib in the corner is blaring. 'I also come bearing the latest newspapers from Prague and Budapest,' he says. 'Did you know you could get papers weekly from the Oxford Street Bookshop? They're open till two a.m. *and* they serve coffee. We should make a night of it.'

Zuzka's smile stays fixed. 'How much do we owe you?'

The newspapers crunch under László's sudden fist. He lets go too quickly. They thump onto the table. 'Nothing.'

In the hostels, talk had been about staying together. The Home Office had agreed one thousand child survivors could be given temporary visas to Britain. A thousand couldn't be found, but the seven hundred and thirty-two who eventually came together formed the Primrose Club after the hostels were closed, so they could remain a family. When Israel declared independence, László's closest friends in the Club went without permission to defend the new state against Egypt, Jordan, Lebanon, Syria, Iraq. The holy land was on fire, and József and László argued about it for ten days before József finally slammed László against the games room wall, his words coming through gritted teeth: 'Do I have to lose you too?' So László stayed, going to the Oxford Street Bookshop with Lipchitz because Susie and Joseph are too English for coffee over newspapers after midnight, and if József hasn't lost László, László has certainly lost himself, and József too.

He stands over the crib while Zuzka describes the menu. János is red-faced and furious with the world at only two months old. The letter in László's pocket digs into his hipbone. *We regret to inform you* . . .

'Do you want to hold him?' Zuzka bends over the crib. 'Look, John, it's your Uncle László . . . here we go . . .'

László works his arm under János's head. The crying softens to a whimper.

'How have we managed without you?'

She is wearing something that looks like the advertisements he's seen on hoardings, but he knows she will have put it together herself, maybe at work. The black skirt is wide over her hips but hugs her corseted waist, unless she's lost the weight from carrying this quickly, and her grey silk blouse clings to her breasts, which are much larger now. Flour streaks her apron.

'Sorry I haven't been around,' he says. *We regret to inform you that we have been unable to locate the whereabouts . . .* 'The markets have been busy. I picked something up for József from Petticoat Lane yesterday – a pair of binoculars for his river painting.'

'Oh, he'll love that. But, László – you will call him Joseph tonight, won't you?'

'And you Susie.'

She sighs. 'Please don't start that again. It makes him happy, and I'm in the middle of cooking a three-course meal.'

'Sorry.' László sits down, arranging János in his lap. 'You didn't spend his birthday together?'

'He went to the Royal Academy Summer Exhibition with Ivor and Rosemary.'

'Rosemary is Ivor's cousin, right?'

'Yes, you met her at Christmas.'

László makes a face at János. The less said about *Christmas* the better. 'You didn't want to go to the Academy?'

'John was fussing. And besides, I had to go to the Selfridges in Orchard Street – it's the only place that sells peppers hot enough.'

'You took János with you?'

'And caused quite the scene in the cheese aisle.' She is facing away from him, chopping something, her elbow busy. 'How have you been?'

'All right.' Her elbow jerks up and down faster. She doesn't approve of his working at the markets, wants him to at least attend the ORT school with the other boys and learn a trade. As if what József is doing is a trade. 'Glad it's summer,' he says, for something to say. 'My room is finally warm.'

'I keep telling you we have the spare room.'

László watches her feet turn in her black suede heels.

'László? Your bed is still up in John's room.'

'I know.'

'Will you stay with us tonight? Make an early start together for the Festival?'

The Festival of Britain opens tomorrow. László's journey on the Tube was nothing but red, white and blue posters promising a Britain of the future. 'If you'd like me to.'

'You couldn't give Joseph a better present.'

'Are you back at work?'

'Not yet – but Mr Creed has been so kind about it all. It's very unusual, I'm told.'

'You're very unusual.'

She lifts one shoulder in a shrug. 'I don't suppose you'd be interested in a position as a nanny?'

'Haven't you found anyone?'

'Rosemary offered. She wants to move up to London.'

'You won't take her up on it?'

Zuzka's knife pauses and she tilts her head. It reminds László of

397

a dog hearing its master's step. 'That's Joseph coming up the stairs. Will you go and greet him!'

'And spoil the surprise?'

László can hear his brother's loud voice now – still tainted with a Magyar accent, but fading. *We regret to inform you that we have been unable to locate the whereabouts or final resting place . . .* Behind his chatter is the laughter of two or three others. The door is pushed open, and he can hear umbrellas being shaken to their last drop and hats and coats hung up.

'Susie?' calls József.

Zuzka gives László the same secretive smile she first gave him in Prague. 'In the kitchen!'

László listens to József telling the others to sit and wait, he'll be back in a moment, and then the door opens.

'László! I thought you couldn't make it! Put John down and let me kiss you.'

László does as he's told and folds into his brother's embrace. József is still so much taller. He is wearing what looks like a suit belonging to an Edwardian, from tapered trousers to velvet collar. József wears honeysuckle, too – *to carry Susie with me always.*

'How are you?' József clamps him by the arm.

'Fine, fine. And you? A good birthday so far?'

'The best. God, smell that, László – what are you cooking, Susie?'

József passes to Zuzka, plucking up her hand and spinning her around – always the last couple to leave a dance floor – before circling her waist with his arms. He sways with her like that, chest to back, as he peers into the pots over her shoulder. They are fitted so closely together that Zuzka's skirt spills out between József's legs.

He must be able to feel every inch of her hidden body against his pelvis. Burning red, László waves his fingers at János. He hears József giving Zuzka an exaggerated kiss on the cheek.

'What did I ever do to deserve you?'

László feels a snarl on his lips.

'Isn't she just the most fabulous creature you've ever laid eyes on?'

László drags his head up. 'You're in a good mood, József.'

A beat.

'And I'd like to continue to be in one.'

'Oh – sorry. I forget you are English now, with an English name, and an English wife.'

'Six years is a long time to forget something. Maybe it's because we hardly ever see you. You don't visit, you don't call. I'm surprised your nephew knows you.'

Zuzka slips out of József's hold. 'You know, I've never seen a better impression of a Jewess and her son than the pair of you. If you will keep rowing, at least go and entertain the guests with your show.'

József laughs, rubbing his chin. 'Right as ever. Come and say hello, László.'

'You don't need any help cooking?'

'I only need peace.'

József takes László's arm. 'Come and help me make drinks.' They go into the hall, but József pulls him short with a jerk, whispering: 'Don't you know better than to upset her?'

'I didn't—'

'She's fragile, since the baby.'

'Is that why she didn't come to the exhibition? She's *fragile*?'

József tries to laugh, but it's him who looks like he's snarling

399

now. 'You're a walking accusation, you know that? Anything you can lay at my feet you will.'

It's the same fight every time, and László climbs into the ring with his heart already pounding. 'You've got the whole world at your feet. A beautiful apartment, a beautiful wife, a beautiful child, waiting for you to return after whatever has taken your fancy loses its shine. This cheap imitation of Mama and Father.'

A catch in József's voice. 'It didn't come cheap.' He shakes his head. 'When are you going to get it: what a man does for his family, what a man is?'

'I suppose that's what you'd tell Father, if he was here?'

'You want to know what Father would think? He'd tell me well fucking done, young man.'

'I won't let you slight his—'

'He'd tell me well done for what I do every day for her and for John and for *you*.'

László hisses, 'This isn't about me.'

'Of course not. It's about me. It always is. It doesn't matter I came and saw you three times in your *Jewish King Lear* with its happy ending of a business empire divided. It doesn't matter I got you a new bicycle to take on the Club trip to the Isle of Wight. It doesn't matter I came to the Club debate on the future of Palestine, and watched you make fools of yourselves in your Arab dress, your English top hats, your bloody Zionist overalls. None of that matters, because I won't carry a banner alongside you in Trafalgar Square for Israel proclaiming us the boys from the camps, and I won't let you die in a desert despite your clear desire to make me mourn you.'

There are tears in József's eyes.

The conversation in the living room has dimmed.

'That's not what I want,' László breathes. 'You know it's not. And it's not why I moved out. You know that too.'

József drags air into his body. 'I didn't mean . . . I'm sorry.' He holds László's gaze. 'I really am sorry.' László can't tell if they're talking about the same thing. 'You know what the Talmud says?'

László snorts, not able to help his grin. 'You're going to quote scripture at me?'

József laughs. '*Quote* might be generous. It's been a long time. But I do remember one line. *If there aren't any men left, you have to be a man.*'

Their shared relief turns to stone.

'Every time,' says László. '*Grow up.* Don't you think I already did my growing up?'

József steps back, knocking a picture. 'I'm trying to – I'm trying to tell you. It's not easy.'

'What isn't?'

József opens both hands, closing them on nothing.

László fingers the letter in his pocket. 'I know. I know it's not. But József, there are things we have to—'

József ducks away. 'Not tonight. I can't.'

mourning nights

I SLEPT DOWNSTAIRS IN AN apartment John rented to tourists on Airbnb, the rooms infused with alien life: framed paintings of Provence, the kind you might buy at a local market, stubbornly realist. A bookshelf with children's DVDs and wrinkled books. *Lonely Planet France* and a French–English dictionary. Penguin Classics in pink and green. And a slim orange book with black glossy writing on its spine: *Braham, The Hungarian Labor Service System 1939–1945*. I sat on the edge of the bed staring at that spine until the thrum of moths battering the lamp drew me to my feet. I closed the shutters, undressed, pulled the cold sheets over me. I stared at the black-and-white newspaper, repeating to myself, Zuzka. Zuzka. My grandmother. I thought about those first mourning nights, how I kept to Silk's sleepless patterns, the rhythm of the lost, how I imitated Rosemary's comforting tones, now only administered to myself. The displacement between Silk and Rosemary, filled with Silk's wanderings and Rosemary's threats to leave, the love between them, palpable and painful, the cord of agreement they never came to snap. Zuzka. Granny Zuzka.

At midnight, I heard a door slam above me and a sudden, shrill shout followed by a snarl. Liset was back. I sat up, drawing the cover higher. I heard John thump something, the rebound of whatever it was against the wall. Maybe the fridge. God. I should never have come here. She was screaming at him now. I picked up my phone. I had to go. But who could I call? A taxi. My phone had no data, and I had no number and no French. I was slick with sweat. I was six years old and my father had just swung a chair against a wall. He'd later try and fix it and the bar between its legs would pop out every time I'd tuck my feet beneath me. I scrambled out of bed, pulled my jeans on, forced my jumper over my head. Upstairs Liset's voice was unstoppable, a broken dam that only gained in strength with every bark of John's. I should go up there. Get in the middle. I should leave.

I swiped to my homepage, hit favourites, and called Mum. It rang just once before she answered.

'Eva?'

'I'm at Dad's, he's – Liset is here and they're – they're fighting and I don't know what to do.'

'OK. Take a breath. A deep breath. That's good. Can you leave?'

'I'm in the middle of nowhere, I came by cab, I didn't take their card.'

'OK. Keep breathing. You're safe, sweetheart. It's their fight, not yours. There's nothing you can do about it. They fight all the time, it's not new.'

'How do you know?'

'John told me. Where are you?'

I sat on the bed. 'I'm downstairs. I don't know why I came.'

Upstairs I heard John shout, for fuck's sake, Liset, for *fuck's sake*. I remembered him shouting that at Mum.

Panic like barbed wire curled in my throat. I tried to breathe. 'I want to come home. To visit you.'

Shouting at Mum: *For fuck's sake, you're the only person I've ever loved in my life.* And he hadn't told her about Zuzka. He'd told me. I glanced back at the slim volume of Braham. *Has it ever occurred to you that this is where you and I meet?*

'Darling – I'd love that. I wanted to tell you, at the funeral – you shouldn't be there alone.'

Another breath. 'I'm going to buy an open-jaw ticket. I'm going back to Budapest, and then I'll come and see you.' *Who will be on the next boat? Maybe you, Eva Butler, chasing the world.* 'I can't keep standing still.'

'What about Silk's estate, the new exhibitions?'

'I'll come back for them. Silk can afford it.'

'OK, darling.' I could hear her smiling. 'What's happening there now?'

I looked up at the ceiling. Dust drifted down from the light fixture. A door slammed. I heard John shout something out into the night. A car started.

'He might be going. Or it might be Liset.'

'First thing in the morning, get onto John's wifi and book yourself a cab to the airport. Call me to let me know you're all right.'

'I will. I love you.'

I sat back, picked up the clipping. My hand was shaking. I looked at Zuzka's surprised smile. I tried to find similarities between our features. The envelope John had tossed onto the table before me was soft with age. Its lip had already sealed again, unused to being opened. I forced it, finding two more pieces of paper inside. The first was a square black-and-white photograph of John as a baby in a pram. He was wrapped tightly in what looked like a woollen shawl. I listened for sounds upstairs. Nothing. I knew I should go and see if whoever was up there was OK, but my heart was beating too fast. Earlier I had imagined John was more frightened of me than I was of him, and maybe that was true, when the sea was calm. In peacetime, I could even tell myself that my anger at him, my fear of him, was affection, the continuation of an act because I had no new lines. But I couldn't pretend, with the bile of fear clogging my throat; I couldn't pretend I was OK.

I drew the other piece of paper from the envelope. It was a letter dated from last year. The address in the corner read Cimetière Saint-Vincent, 6 Rue Lucien Gaulard, Paris 75018. I got the French–English dictionary from the shelf. It took me ten minutes to piece together the five lines.

Monsieur,

We are writing in regard to the grave of ZUZKA WES-SELY, division fourteen of the Cemetery of Saint-Vincent in Montmartre, Paris. The grave has been left untended and is in a state of dishevelment. We attempted to contact Monsieur Zyyad László, who previously took responsibility for the site, and were given your address by his friends. If the grave remains untended, we will remove the remains to the ossuary in Père Lachaise so that the grave may be reused. Please contact us if you wish to maintain the site.

Great-Uncle László must have travelled from Tel Aviv to Paris to bring flowers to her grave until his death.

From the dark, Silk reminded me that an ossuary was a vault for the bones of the dead, carcasses left after carnage, unnamed and uncatalogued. I looked back at the newspaper, at Zuzka's frail body, at the small letters underneath: THERESIENSTADT.

EARLY LIGHT PICKED OUT the fissures of the house and the exhaustion of the vines climbing its side. I found John sitting on a slate bench on the veranda with an empty plunger of coffee by his side. He looked like he hadn't slept. I sat down next to him. He moved his leg away from me.

'Are you all right?' I asked.

'Wedding's off.'

I looked up at the sky, wet powder blue, its depth the burden of night not yet thrown off. *I don't know how to comfort you. But I would if you'd let me.* 'That might be a good thing,' I said. 'I don't know how many guests will view having *Babe: Pig in the City* on DVD as recompense for being kept awake by you shouting.'

John closed one eye against the sun. 'No one likes a sequel.'

I smiled. I suddenly wanted to tell him: *You do make me laugh.* '*Are* you all right?'

'I'm fabulous.'

I leant back. 'OK. I'm going to go to Paris. I've booked a flight from there to Budapest.'

'Why not fly from Nice?'

I held up the envelope. 'Did you answer this letter?'

John stood up, leant against the balustrade. 'No.'

'I'm going to go to the cemetery. I'm going to see if it's too late.' I waited for him to ask me why it mattered where she was buried, if she had words on a headstone, if her bones were lost.

John looked away. 'How are you going to get there?'

'Train.'

He stroked his chin, thumb resting over his lips. Then his hand fell. 'I'll drive you.'

his brother's shadow

LÁSZLÓ FOLLOWS HIS BROTHER'S shadow to the living room. He knows three out of five of the guests. Simon and Ivor are *that way*, and he feels uncomfortable when Ivor kisses his cheek. Rosemary is wearing a corn blue summer dress that matches her eyes, and her straw hair is tied up in a twist. She looks like a painting of a country girl, not the real thing.

'And this is Comrade Roger and his wife Lizzie. The Comrade is a playwright.'

'You can call me Roger. Your brother is roasting me.'

'Are you a member?' asks László.

'Aren't you?'

'Don't start, Comrade,' says József. 'Who wants what to drink? May as well make a start while we wait for the others.'

The others are Osip and Ruth, both artists too. Osip is the oldest guest, a Russian émigré to London before the war. He nominated József and Zuzka for membership to the Allies Club. It is a non-political sanctuary for refugees from Hitler, but László declined their offer, just as József declined the offer to join the Primrose Club. He declined on Zuzka's behalf too. What the difference is, László doesn't know, except that the Allies Club seems filled with artists who only encourage József's aimlessness.

László chooses a spot on the deep sofa with Rosemary, the only other person not in a couple.

'Are you enjoying your time in London?' he asks.

'Oh yes, wonderfully. Do you think Susie needs some help in the kitchen?'

'She says she's better alone,' says László, expecting more argument, expecting Rosemary to gather up Ruth and Lizzie and take them into the kitchen with her. But she stays put.

'Your brother says you work on the markets. You must meet some fascinating people.'

'My boss is a card. Always on the deal. He can get anything you want. What they call a proper Aldgate Jew.' She doesn't look put off by the word, like some English do. 'Speaks almost entirely in Jewish Cockney.'

'Really? Like what?'

'He'd call you a flour-mixer.'

'Why? What does it mean?'

'You know what a shiksa is?'

'László?' It's József, fixing him from across the room. 'Go and see if Susie wants help serving.'

At dinner, László sits to Zuzka's left, at the bottom end of the table. Ivor and Rosemary have already flanked József, and a boy–girl pattern is attempted, with Simon seeming to play the part of a woman. Before the lid can be taken off the fish soup, József clears his throat, tapping his spoon against his glass. Everybody else follows, and the room is filled with ringing.

'A toast to my beautiful wife Susie, and this wonderful meal.'

Glasses clink, everyone chorusing happy twenty-fifth birthday. Zuzka looks pink with happiness. The back of her stockinged leg, twined around her chair leg as if to tether her, is smudged white with flour.

Roger slurps the soup open-mouthed, talking without pause. 'You have to admit, Joseph, you have to admit that it's *ideology* that makes *A Sleep of Prisoners* the best play in town. It's the only serious thing written for the Festival.'

'*Seriousness* is not what I look for in an evening's entertainment. And prisoners of war dreaming themselves into the Old Testament isn't my idea of seriousness, anyway. It's my idea of the absurd.'

Osip presses his elbow on the table. 'You're both wrong. Fry's play *is* the only thing of account in town, but it's not because of ideology; it's because his writing *sings*.'

Roger spits globules of fish. 'Not the ideology that counts? Bevan and Wilson resign, we lose our first men in Korea – what else *can* count at a time like this?'

Ivor wags his finger. 'I don't see you complaining about the frivolity of the Festival, *at a time like this*.'

'The Festival is the iconography of the masses! It's a new urban environment for the people!'

József bursts out laughing. 'How do you know? It hasn't opened yet!'

'How the two of you,' says Roger, pointing his finger at Osip and József, 'of *all* people, can scoff at the clearly *imperative* need—'

József spreads his arms. 'We are *Jewish*, Roger. The world already thinks we are socialists. Why bother paying for Party membership?'

It seems to László that József is only Jewish when he can get a laugh out of it. Over the chicken paprika, József tells stories of the hospital where he is carrying out his national service as a conscientious objector, scrubbing down frail veterans who ask him where his stomach's at, why he isn't fighting. László stares at him down the table. Why aren't you fighting, now you're a flag-waving Englishman? All talk and no balls. You tell me it's hard to be a man while I'm getting into fistfights with the last of Mosley's fascists and you're sitting here conducting mock intellectualism for a mock twenty-fifth birthday.

The letter waits in his pocket. He knows he shouldn't give it to József on his birthday, but he needs them to come together now – if not yesterday, if not tomorrow, if never at all after the wedding day, God, he needs his brother just this one day.

'What about you, László?' Osip asks, turning on him. 'You've been here five years, you can apply for citizenship now, but Joseph tells me you don't want it? Are you thinking of going back to Hungary?'

We regret to inform you that we have been unable to locate the whereabouts or final resting place of your mother, father and younger sister. We realise this is very distressing news, and assure you we will continue to search records as they become available . . .

'No, not Hungary. Not anymore.'

'Good,' says Osip. 'You don't want to become that old joke about the two refugees immortalised at Madame Tussaud's because they hadn't applied for naturalisation.'

László says nothing.

József clears his throat. 'It doesn't get more natural than washing down the masses at the Baths.' He works nights at the Imperial Hotel Turkish Baths. Buried in a basement amidst flaking oriental decor, it still draws the best of London society, whom he ruthlessly rubs down for tips. 'The glamour of being an artist. But I am ever grateful to Ivor for my new position as weekend cleaner at the British Colour Council. We can only presume this was meant as a cruel hoax.'

Osip waves a hand. 'Don't worry, Susie. We'll make him a rich painter yet.'

'A rich painter?' says Ivor. 'Is that a newly discovered species?'

'Ha!' József leans back. 'Susie, tell them what we saw at the zoo with John.'

Like a puppet, she smiles, opens her mouth, her necklace glittering in the candlelight. 'The chimpanzees there drink afternoon tea.'

'What have I been telling you all these years about that foul substance? I stand vindicated.'

They give presents in the gap before dessert. József opens the binoculars first, and gives László a kiss on both cheeks, before shaking his hand. He looks thrilled, and László feels eight again, bathing in his brother's approval. He is not the only one who has taken the cue of József's long walks – Roger and Elizabeth give him a trunk with brass clasps to carry his brushes and paints. When József tells them it's too fine a gift, Ivor says they bought it from a shop selling lost railway items. Rosemary tells him not to be mean, and insists that József open her present next. It is wrapped in blue paper with turquoise ribbon.

A box of paintbrushes from the King's Road. They must have cost Rosemary the price of a train ticket home. László glances at Zuzka, but cannot tell anything from her expression. József opens Zuzka's present last, pulling a copper coffee pot from the paper.

'Where did you find such treasure? Look at this . . .'

Zuzka smiles at him down the table. It's a look László knows well: she has always been a secret keeper, gracing the person on the other side of her fortifications with this look of soft amusement. As if to say, do not breach me. You would go mad behind my walls. But this time he knows her secret, because he went with her to the restaurant supply shop on Greek Street, and watched her talk the manager into a deal. Not that the man needed much more persuasion than her smile.

'Shall I make the first pot?' asks József.

'I'll do it,' says Zuzka. 'I have to prepare dessert. Show them your latest piece.'

József takes them into John's room. It might have been a generous cupboard in somebody else's flat, but here John's baby things and László's old camp bed take up half the space. The rest is occupied by József's obsession. Canvases are stacked against the walls, which have been ruined by József testing blue swatches. Paint and paper and pencils litter every surface. The women perch on the bed. László slots himself into the corner, where a walking stick rests.

'I won't bother to ask what it is,' says Osip, peering over his glasses at the easel.

'Don't you know the Thames by its white and grey sails? White and red to you, I suppose.'

'And these are the foreshoremen forcing mud back onto the banks?'

József grins. 'They call themselves mudlarks.'

'Do they now?'

'From what point on the river?' asks Simon, looking closer.

'All of them.'

'What do you mean?'

'I mean all of them.'

'So it's . . . the whole Thames?'

'Tell them where you paint,' says Rosemary.

József laughs. 'This girl finds it thrilling.'

'As you mean her to,' says Ivor.

László looks at the canvas. It is a storm of blues, mad and busy and persuasive. It is gibberish. And it is the Thames.

'There are brilliant painting spots along the water,' says József. 'The top of Adelaide House.'

'Isn't that private?' asks Ruth.

'There are public gardens up there. Haven't you been? You must. There's even a miniature golf course. No one pays any attention to me. Sometimes I go to the Tower and play at Kipling's *Kim*, sitting in defiance of municipal orders astride the gun. I like to paint amongst people eating their lunch.'

Roger nods. 'Turner would have approved.'

'Of such rude behaviour, or the painting? Don't answer that.'

'Tell them where you walked last week,' prompts Rosemary – as if József needs prompting.

'I followed the river from Tower Gardens to Kew. Fine Wren out in Blackheath Village, you know.'

'That's miles!'

'It's not so long,' says József softly, and László wishes he'd glance this way, that they could briefly share the miles they both walked. But he is studying the painting, one eye closed. He's no longer breathing.

Osip claps him on the back. 'I think Joseph has forgotten we're here. Let's go and entertain Susie.'

The others leave. László clears his throat. The letter from the Bureau for Displaced Central Europeans is slick in his hand. József does not look around. László waits. József picks up a brush, licks it, beats it against his palm.

'József?'

His brother leans closer to the easel. The hairs shiver against the canvas. László shoves the letter deeper into his pocket and bangs out to the living room. The women have gone to the kitchen, except Rosemary, so László asks, knowing his voice is all accusation, as József had said: 'Do you go on these walks with him?'

She looks surprised. 'Oh, no. He shouldn't walk so far anyway.'

That checks him. 'Why not?'

'The arthritis in his feet.'

László frowns. 'The what?'

'Oh goodness, I thought he would have told you. It's not too bad.'

'Arthritis? You mean köszvény? Our parents didn't have that. Did they say – was it labour? Marching?'

'I really don't know, I'm sorry.'

'I'll ask Zuzka.'

She looks like he's pricked her. 'Oh yes. Susie will know, I'm sure.' And then, as if to cover for the red spots in her cheeks: 'Don't you admire Susie? Her work at the tailor's is so exquisite. To be honest, I'm a little in awe of her.'

'You spend a lot of time with them, don't you?'

'You should come on one of our expeditions, The ones we're allowed to join Joseph on, anyway! We went up to Kenwood House the other day – did you hear? Joseph paid what must have been a duke to show us around. The most incredible library I've ever seen. And the paintings this man owns – Rembrandt, Gainsborough, Reynolds. Joseph raved over Landseer's lake landscapes. But the best bit – or at least for me, but don't tell anyone because they'll think I'm terribly unsophisticated – was the hour-long conversation Joseph got into with the tinker who keeps a caravan in the park.'

'What did they talk about?'

'Stained glass, mostly. This man had a stained-glass window, completely intact in its frame. Joseph has started visiting stained-glass workshops – he says you can pay *them* to show you around too. I think that man could talk his way into anything.'

'Let's hope he can talk his way out of it, too,' says László.

'What do you mean?'

He is spared replying by the appearance of coffee and strudel.

When József's friends finally leave, the flat smells of cherry wine and smoke. János cried twice during the party, Zuzka slipping from the room to tend to him. Now he hardly wakes as Zuzka carries him to the small room, László following with the towel she has given him wrung around both fists. He drops it onto the bed, closing the door with his heel. It is midnight.

'You'll sleep with your Uncle László,' whispers Zuzka, laying János down. 'If he cries, I'll come out.'

'I can look after him.'

She smiles, wiping her hands on her dress. 'Did you enjoy the evening?'

'Yes. Rosemary's nice.'

'Isn't she?'

'Yes. Odd, though – she smells of honeysuckle too.'

In the small room, Zuzka's halting breath is like glass cracking. 'Why is that odd?'

László grasps her by the wrist before she can move away. 'You're not *fragile*. I can feel you. You were never *fragile*. You're unhappy. Aren't you?'

'*Keep your voice down*. You'll wake John.'

'He's made you unhappy.'

'You don't know what you are talking about.'

'Don't tell me that. Don't tell me I don't know what I'm talking about when I am talking about *you*.'

'László . . .' She looks away, to József's paintings. 'Things are . . . complicated. That's all.'

'That's all? While you smile and dance and cook and laugh to keep him happy and every bit of it is a lie? It's *complicated*?'

'Not every bit,' she whispers. 'Only . . .'

'Only what?'

'I haven't been myself since . . . Having a baby is difficult, László. But the doctor says I'll feel better soon. Cooking and laughing – that's the cure. So don't tax me for it.'

'Doctor?'

'You're still so young.'

'*Don't*. I wasn't young when I helped you onto that bus and I'm not young now. That's József talking. And yes, I'll call him *József* as much as I please, and I'll call you Zuzka, because *it's your name*.'

Somehow, without realising it, he has pushed her up against the wall. The letter crunches. József's canvases slide and clatter. She tells him to be quiet but doesn't tell him to move. He can feel her body, feel her bones and flesh like József had earlier. He has wanted this for years, and it takes a moment to push past his imaginings. Her waist is thin beneath his hands, and he thinks he can feel warmth between her legs. He pushes harder.

'It's your *name*, Zuzka. When did you give that up? Why do we have to give it all up so he can be happy?'

His hands are running up her body now, across her breasts. He feels close to orgasm, close to violence.

'When was the last time he gave anything up for you?'

Her eyes are closing. 'He gave me Hampstead Synagogue. He gave us independence.'

'*Gave you* – a man worthy of you would give you the *world*, and you took stamping on a cheap glass!'

'I thought it would make me happy.'

'That's not true.'

'It is, László. He was all I wanted. But it's only pretend. I'm not really here.'

'Yes you are. I can feel you.' He strokes the side of her face, hovering over her lips. He wants to kiss her – needs to kiss her – but feels she'll resist that if nothing else. 'You deserve better than him. You need someone to take care of you.' His pelvis is moving, making her skirt whisper. He murmurs into her ear as he's seen József do a thousand times: 'Let me take care of you. Let me take you away from here.'

'I'm going away by myself.'

'Going away?' He grips her harder, pushing himself into the creases of her skirt. 'Are you taking John?' Nothing. 'Where?'

'I don't know – I just have to get away. I should never have been here at all.'

'Let me take you and John to Israel. Israel, Zuzka. We'll go to Israel. We'll go to . . .' He can't speak, his body is bursting, soiling the inside of his trousers.

'Step back,' says Zuzka calmly. 'You'll wet my dress.'

László looks down, flushing scarlet. 'God, Zuzka, I'm sorry. I didn't – I'm sorry. Forgive me.'

'It doesn't matter.'

'Let me give you Israel. Let me look after you, and John. What else have we got in the world?'

She smiles at him, patiently. He hates that smile. 'Goodnight, László. I'll see you in the morning.'

city as if

SUSIE HANGS UP HER dress. She can see Joseph watching her in the mirror on the inside of the wardrobe door and smiles at him. He is sitting on the bed in his trousers and shirtsleeves, lips pursed, and doesn't catch her smile: his eyes are on her midnight blue shift, revealed from under the grey of her clothes, and his gaze remains fixed as she walks around the narrow space to her dressing table. Sitting on the stool, she drops the lapis lazuli earrings he bought her on their honeymoon into one of the boxes László sells. His attention has remained on her, and he watches now in the small table mirror as she unhooks the matching necklace.

'Have I ever told you that you're the most beautiful wife a man could have?'

Susie unpins her hair, shaking it out. 'You may have, once or twice.'

Joseph shuffles across the bed, swinging his legs over so that he is sitting directly behind her stool. He moves her hair aside, kissing her neck. She watches him in the mirror. 'And did you believe me?'

'In the moment of utterance, always.'

He pauses. 'Not after?'

'You are surrounded by beautiful women,' she says. 'Everywhere you look, it seems.'

Joseph's hands urge her to turn and face him, her knees to bend, her legs to move onto the bed, around his waist. He pulls the stool closer with his feet, and now she can feel him where she felt László minutes ago.

'How can you think I would look anywhere but you?' he asks, pushing her shift upwards, revealing more of her pale thighs. He circles her waist, bringing her closer still, so that she is almost in his lap. 'You are my miscellaneous want.'

Susie laughs. 'And you are mine.'

His eyebrows raise a little. 'You want to . . . ?'

How with any grace can she demur now, already pressed to him like this, already entangled? Whenever he asks, do you want to, it is too late for her to say no. But she never has said no, though at times it has been like renting her body out in exchange for a half-smile, in exchange for a reminder that she lives in the world, his semen dripping from her twenty-four hours later, she holds herself that tightly, forgetting to breathe. As he lowers his lips to her breasts, she doesn't want to say no. László's thrusting has left her wet and empty. She wonders if she and József will both be working off the frustration of another, or whether this will be what it ought to be. Two alone in a bed, for the last time.

Susie reaches down for his belt buckle, tugging his shirt free and his zip down. He moves to slip the trousers off.

'No,' she whispers, gripping his arm. 'There's no time.'

'No time?' A baffled smile. 'Where are we going at one in the morning?'

'There's no time,' she repeats, slipping her hands into his trousers. 'This is our first night together, and you want me with so much urgency you cannot wait.'

'What's got into you?'

'It's your birthday.'

That seems enough. 'I can't wait,' he agrees. 'I've got to see your body, Susie. I'll die if I don't.'

'Zuzka. Call me Zuzka.'

He is silent. She grips his penis through his shorts and he jerks into her hand. She hasn't felt power like this since before falling pregnant.

'Zuzka,' he whispers, pulling her shift up over her hips, over her breasts, throwing it to the floor. Her brassière is midnight blue too, as are her knickers, and the garter belt holding up her stockings. Let Rosemary have her summer dress and the smell of honeysuckle. Zuzka stands up, slipping out of his grabbing embrace. She circles, unhooking the knickers, dropping them to the floor. Does she look like the dancing girls Osip takes him to see in the nightclubs? She looks better, she decides, by the twitch of his penis. But he isn't moving, and she is suddenly unsure.

'Don't you know what to do with me?'

He smiles. 'I know exactly what to do with you. I always have.' He stands up, commanding: 'Come here.'

She obeys, taking his hand. He gently spins her under his arm, laughing. Then kisses her, softly, insistently, pushing her towards the mattress. She lies down on the pale blue sheets, expecting him to follow her, but he just stands there. His hands move to her knees,

422

and he gently spreads her legs, looking at her. She manages not to blush as he touches her, manages not to think that to him the folds of her vagina are grey, asking instead, 'What do you see?'

'You.'

The echo of Rebecca sounds in Zuzka's mind, but she pushes the nurse back, that and any other girl Joseph may have given this compliment too, as those hands that hold a paintbrush so delicately draw her out, until she is only feeling.

His fingers hook into her hips.

'Like our first time?'

'Yes. Yes.'

'I believe we weren't married then; a great shock to us both when we realised our oversight.'

'Yes.'

He pulls her towards him, ruining the neat sheets.

'I believe we kissed, you on a bed, me standing like this. The law of Hollywood.'

'Yes.'

His fingers run over her, and Zuzka moans loudly enough for László to hear her.

'Do you want me?'

'Yes,' she hisses, closing her eyes.

'I want you, Zuzka,' he says. 'I'll never want anything more.'

She feels the tip of his penis against her, but doesn't look. He pushes inside, and she is anchored, unable to move. He keeps her that way, hands pressing down on her hips as he begins to thrust in and out.

'Make that sound again,' he says.

She moans. He speeds up, moving into her hard enough to hurt but she does not complain, saying instead, 'Touch me, József. Touch me everywhere, like you did then.'

He squeezes her breasts, still sore from feeding John, but she only groans. He grasps her thighs, his grip stinging. He covers her hands with his own, pinning her to the bed. She can't move. She doesn't want to. Wants only to be contained by him, wants only the expression on his face, eyes screwed shut, whole being ready to pour into her. Give me your language one last time.

He does, and she bucks and keens under him, József József József, set free.

'Don't you like calling me Joseph?'

His face is buried in her neck. She strokes his back, slick with sweat. 'I'll call you whatever you like, darling.'

'What about Silk? Would you prefer that?'

'Whatever you want.'

He lifts his head, grinning at her. 'I want to do that again.'

He sleeps on the far side of the bed, his back turned to her. Zuzka listens to him snoring. Street lamps leak through the curtains, orange and watching. She breathes in sex and coffee. Honeysuckle, too. József, these are my miscellaneous wants. I want you to confess so that I can forgive you and stay. I want you to tell me to leave. I want you to know that when all this began I could bear it because my father had affairs and so did yours. What I cannot bear is your love for two women. I want you to know that when I realised I was pregnant I went to a back-alley doctor and would have gone through with it if I hadn't thought, suddenly, that I had never left Theresienstadt, and that this doctor with his curved instruments was my uncle. I want you to know that I have loved you and your brother with all the love I could scrape from the bottom of a dried heart, but I have nothing for John. I want you to take me with you on your walks along the Thames; I want you to paint me. Paint every cell I have blue, paint me so that you throb with me. I want you to know that you have broken my heart but it is not such a terrible thing, because there was very little left to break. I want you to know that if it weren't for your brother I would have killed myself in Theresienstadt, and if it weren't for you I would have sunk to the bottom of Lake Windermere. I want you to know that I tried. I want you to know that I was never here. You imagined me, and when I am gone you will forget me.

'THE ARCHBISHOP OF CANTERBURY speaking now at the Festival of Britain . . .'

Zuzka sits up. The bedroom door is open by an inch, and she can hear the wireless in the kitchen. The bed is empty. John is crying, József soothing him. Silk? Did she imagine that? László is asking if Susie will want eggs, and the Archbishop of Canterbury is speaking of a new era.

'The chief and governing purpose of the Festival is to declare our belief in the British way of life, not with any boastful self-confidence nor with any aggressive self-advertisement, but with sober and humble trust that by holding fast to that which is good and rejecting from our midst that which is evil we may continue to be a nation at unity in itself and of service to the world. It is good at a time like the present so to strengthen, and in part to recover our hold on all that is best in our national life . . .'

The door opens. József gives her a half-smile 'Good morning. Would you like eggs?'

'I'll wash first.'

'John is hungry.'

She sweeps her hair back. 'Bring him to me.'

They take John on the Tube and he cries. József says the boy can sense the inferiority of any mode of travel without a view. László is silent. Ivor and Simon are waiting with Rosemary at Charing Cross station, and when Ivor sees them coming he shouts, 'Hurry up, Joseph! It's so beautiful I'm weeping!' József runs ahead, and László follows, unable to look Zuzka in the eye. Zuzka negotiates the stairs with the pram, coming upon the view across the Thames last, Ivor telling her, 'Those colours! When did you last see such *colours*?'

He is right. The wet air doesn't matter a thing. It has been years, living in this grey, penny-clutching city, brow-beaten by the drab cost of victory, since she saw pink and red flags, let alone whole buildings painted red and white. Years since she saw buildings sing. To József, it would still be the same grey, but the Festival designers have saved him from that by letting blue stream forth from every tower, every pole, every window.

Joining the crowds, they cross the river to enter by the Chicheley Street Gate. The world has lost its compass. There is no main walkway or triumphal arch – instead there is a warren stretching between the Dome of Discovery at one end and the Royal Festival Hall at the other. They weave through yesterday and today – there a view of the Houses of Parliament, here a building that looks like it has landed from another planet. The Thames seems to have shrunk, bringing Whitehall Court into the Festival grounds, overcoming what József calls the tyranny of the vanishing point. He looks thunderstruck. His hand has fallen away from her back. He is wrapped up in the future: fly-over bridges, glass buildings, radar dishes, the ground rupturing and collapsing.

It is a sea change, she thinks, as here the Sea and Ships Pavilion takes up the riverfront, propellers and marine engines leaning on one another so that they have to thread between them, becoming the only current on which such a ship could float. László is laughing, racing about, the little boy who thought the Lake District was his private kingdom, his reward. St Paul's appears over the top of colour-rinsed concrete and aluminium lattices. But they cannot stop and consider for too long because televisions swallow them in colour footage and distorted naked figures embrace in polished metal sculptures and helicopters and planes tremble on chains. Zuzka wants to retreat from the Royal Festival Hall, its walls the tremble of strings, but Shot Tower bars her way, transformed into light and radar. József implores her, the views are supposed to be the best in Britain, but when she asks how they will get the pram up he has no answer, and he is soon called away by Ivor and Rosemary. Around her, fountains breathe fire and moon clocks glow and bridges reach for the sky. City as if.

Zuzka pushes John – his crying drowned out by the cry of the people – to the Countryside Pavilion. Inside, birdsong erupts around her, the building fluttering with trapped and beating wings – no. She stops in front of a bone-white plaster tree, whose colossal branches are weighted down by bottle-eyed stuffed birds. The signs tell her that these birds represent every kind native to the British Isles. A blackbird pips out its automated tune, shaking leaves of tin ivy. Zuzka stares. She knows this petrified song, this beautiful mimicry.

Somebody bumps into her and she jolts, looking around. Her hands are empty. The pram is gone. Her eyes are glassed with tears. She pushes between bespectacled twitchers and fussing architects, bursting out onto the South Bank – where Silk and Rosemary are standing by the water's edge. Zuzka approaches slowly, moving through people now as if they are oil. Rosemary is rocking John's pram. Silk's hand is on the small of her back. Beyond them, the water runs away, pulling at the moored boats, one of them the *Dijonnaise*, which goes to and from France fortnightly. She will leave. She will leave here, leave the silkworm to spin its colours around someone for whom they will be enough. Above, the clouds are only stage lighting. Below, the Thames picks up the sheen of a summer storm and burns blue.

rivers I have imagined

THE CONSERVATOR PEERED OVER her glasses at the letter in John's hand, her condemnation climbing to his face.

'Are we too late?' I asked.

'Peut-être, possibly not. One moment.' She turned her computer back on. She had just been packing up for the day.

'Merci.'

She sighed, then pushed her glasses up her nose. 'It is not a problem. Sometimes we wait three, four years for a reply. Then the deceased is removed. You may be in time.'

Next to me, John's attention moved to the window, the crosses and angels steepled by Montmartre.

'Where do we go to visit the remains if they have been removed?' I asked.

'Visit?' The conservator shook her head. 'They will be . . .' She made a sliding motion with her hand, like something falling down a chute. 'There is a long waiting list, you see. Many waiting to rest.'

I nodded. The fan of the computer whirred and coughed. In the car, John and I had sat in silence for two hours, passing through orange hills and slipstream tolls under a sky darkening with heat. Then John drummed an executioner's roll on the wheel with two fingers and asked: So, what did you find out? I told him quietly at first, but then he began to prod me, Was that before or after the Arrow Cross took power? Was that before or after the Russians reached Theresienstadt? I was mounting a script to which he already had the cues, and we constructed it together, nodding sometimes, smiling sometimes, over the dusty roar of the motorway. An hour from Paris, I tried to ease into a further familiarity, asking, Are you OK, I mean, hearing all this . . . ? A sharp shrug. How am I supposed to react with you staring at me? I studied his face now for a reaction. Whatever it was, wherever it was, it was out of my reach. He had asked me on the road, So, what else is going on in your life? I didn't know how to answer. We didn't share a language with which I could answer, from my studies, to the documentary, to my feelings for Felix. We live in different lands. We only share a border. But haven't some of the most extraordinary events in human history occurred on borders?

The computer chimed. 'Here we are.' John's head turned. 'You are on time, Ms Butler.'

'We are?'

'Oui. Your grandmother is still here. I will print out the plot details for you. It is up to you to keep the grave in a good state if you wish to continue using the site. You must visit at least twice a year.'

'Then there's a decade's grace?' said John.

'Pardon?'

'My uncle László died ten years ago. It's been untended for a decade?'

'Just eighteen months. But this isn't a waiting list for the dentist, m'sieur.'

I felt blood rush into my face.

Silk had his first stroke eighteen months ago.

John got out of his chair, took a few uncertain steps to the window.

The conservator heaved a leather-bound book onto the desk. The pages shook under her quick thumb. 'The first man to tend the grave was the one we contacted when it fell into disrepair. Your uncle. We did not have the address of the other man, the gentleman who has been coming for the last ten years. Here is his name.'

It was a signature I didn't recognise.

József Zyyad.

I looked at John. I looked for a mirror of my own regret, my loss, my anger, this confusion. He turned his back on me.

THE GRAVE WAS GUNMETAL grey and pitted with moss and time. A Star of David had been inscribed at the top. Beneath it the writing was tidy and contained:

פ״נ

WESSELY ZUZKA

1929–1951

5689–5712

'She was younger than me,' I said. 'She was three years younger than I am when she died.'

When Silk let her die. When László let her die.

The coldness of the stone reached inside my body, gripping me from its abandonment, so that, momentarily, it was me Silk had let slip from his grasp into that cold, me who had needed him, as I needed him now, to answer for himself – but he'd slipped away from that too.

John didn't reply. He was sitting on a tomb a few feet behind me, his elbows on his knees, his body collapsed. The sun was low, burnishing his face. Unfamiliar compassion hurt my chest. His body rose and fell with a long sigh and then he looked up at me. His eyes were a paler brown than I thought they were. I realised I couldn't call to mind what colour I had imagined them. We hadn't maintained eye contact long enough in our lives for me to know. He stared at me now, for a few brief moments, the time it took for a wood pigeon to call the end of the day.

This is the most important conversation we will never have.

I do love you.

I know you love me.

We'll call it a sea change, however fleeting.

SITTING IN THE BACK of the Great Synagogue in Budapest, I enjoy the silence of three thousand empty seats. Rose marble and globe-bulb chandeliers invite my camera. I peer up at the painted ceiling, peach and gold and red geometry. The stained-glass windows are blue and orange. Outside, mulberry trees bow over a mass grave where over two thousand bodies still lie in the ground. The Jewish Museum waits at the back of the synagogue; Felix is inside, talking to the archivists. Karl is on his way.

I am writing Silk's last will and testament. The Blue Room will go to Tate Modern. I will add nothing to it: not a stone plucked from the Danube, not the airmail letters exchanged between Silk and László. The Budapest Holocaust Documentation Centre will digitise Silk's testament in partnership with the Hungarian Jewish Museum. The testament will go on permanent loan to Felix at the Berlin Jewish Museum, with the agreement that it will be exhibited in Hungary and elsewhere. The fragile paper will sit in a glass box in Berlin, where Felix will project Silk's words across the walls in saxe blue.

A guide holding up a Chinese paper fan for her group bustles in, then a man shouting, 'English tour! English tour here!' Tourists tie themselves around him, gathering in the pews near me. He rests his arms across the back of the bench, eyes pitched over the head of his audience.

'Let me ask you something . . .' The man takes off his orange skullcap, folding it in four. 'Judaism is a world religion but you can also be psychologically Jewish. I was born to a Jewish mother, so I am Jewish, there is no disputing it. But . . .'

I do not catch his question when it comes. I wonder if he does this for every tour group. I look to the stained-glass windows. Silk leans against the wall, painted in blue light.

His voice, caught on the magnetic tick and rustle of *Audio Arts Cassette Magazine*, tells the interviewer that his granddaughter has just been born.

'The happiest day of my life. There is something about being a grandfather. You think to yourself, yes, she isn't *mine*, and yet, and yet – this child might be the best thing I have ever done. My greatest creation. And through that, perhaps I can re-create myself. Holding her in my arms in the hospital, it struck me: I have never loved so fiercely, and so simply.'

After murmurs of agreement between the ageing artists there, the interviewer gambles: 'You mention re-creation. How would you characterise yourself as an artist, as a man, if such a thing can be labelled, put in a box?'

A half-smile from the dark of the synagogue as Silk replies: 'I would characterise myself as a man against labels and against boxes.'

A younger artist pushes: 'But doesn't that leave you unmoored? Isn't it essential to embrace and *own* our identities, *especially* in the face of those who might use them against us? Don't you want to make a statement?'

'Any statement I wish to make can be found in my painting.'

'But you're an abstract artist.'

'Maddening, isn't it?'

The young artist grows frustrated: 'Is your art *about* something, or not? Is there a meaning behind it?'

A small laugh. 'I'm not that complicated.'

I tell Silk now, I am Jewish historically, but history doesn't happen in the past tense. The pain you inflicted on those you loved hurts me now. The pain you felt hurts me now. I want to hear you ask for forgiveness, I want to tell you I'm rageful, I want to tell you I forgive you, that I wish it had been any other way, that I understand you weren't capable then of another way.

I wish I could have packed neat tailor's scissors for cutting back the grass; could have taken the Eurotunnel to Paris with you; could have bought flowers from the nearest Metro; could have stood beside you as you leant on your walking stick, holding speech with our dead.

I will not return home to you. But I am your granddaughter always. Your testament will bring you to the world in new ways, and in that movement, you will be taken further away from me. My grief is a private grief, but here are the demands of stones and poems and ribbons left at altars, of mass graves without names. I will go to Prague. I will buy a museum ticket and walk the silent streets of Theresienstadt, past tired men selling army surplus from barracks with smashed windows, to the cellar painted red with the Star of David, where I will pray. I will stand in the River Ohře. I will find Zuzka on the cutting-room floor. I will go to Israel, and Palestine. I will return to Dragan. My small film will gain attention as security at Jewish institutions is put on high alert, as shootings in Paris wake us up, as refugees are made to plea at barred ports, as the Mediterranean swallows lives, as a 'Beware Jews' sign goes up in north London, as tickets to the Blue Room sell out, as the UK closes its doors to Europe, as neo-Nazis attack our leaders and our citizens, as protestors take to the streets of Budapest in their thousands. Friends will watch *Testament* and say I have come to terms with your death. I have used up the terms of loss, but those bodies in the ground – death and I cannot come to terms over them. But still, I'll try, because there is no vigil for me in silence.

And yet. No words can say goodbye to you. Only this ache in my heart, this certain love, these memories, the ground we've walked, roads I built for you, lakes I filled with paint for you, rivers I have imagined were once yours. I have no words with which to tell you that missing you is a constant remainder, that your absence remains present, even today. That I would not do without it. Between us was the gift of unconditional love.

All I can do is tell our story with the terms I have, and hope they are enough. I can only say to Felix, as he sits down next to me, 'He's gone. He's really gone.'

Felix looks over the empty seats. 'Only his body.'

He offers me his hand. I touch his fingertips, feeling his instant warmth, remembering another German abstract noun. Finger-spitzengefühl. Fingertip feeling, a kind of instinct. Understanding at a touch. I reach down for my bag. Felix accepts the testament with the look of a man preparing to lift a coffin.

In the dark, I think you might be smiling.

You wrote your name on the sands when the tide was out, knowing time would come again at the flood. I stand in the breakers.

Thanks and Acknowledgements

MANY PEOPLE GAVE THEIR time and expertise during the writing of this novel.

Drs Rita Horváth and Kinga Frojimovics collected the questions of the Hungarian Committee for Attending Deportees (DEGOB) together for the first time. My thanks to you both for sharing original research with me before you published your work. My thanks to George Szirtes for translating the questions into English.

Dr Monika Flores at the Jewish Museum in Berlin gave over her afternoon to discuss curatorial practice and the potentials of uncatalogued boxes. The Royal National Institute of Blind People answered my questions.

The Holocaust Documentation Centre in Budapest carved the name of my grandmother's uncle into the memorial wall, because he was amongst the first sixty thousand. Their staff helped me find the forest in which he is buried, and talked to me about their search for answers.

The witness testimonials of DEGOB helped me understand

individual experiences. The collection of home videos in the Open Society Archives in Budapest showed me life before the Holocaust, and the last steps of forced labourers and those on death marches. The Bristol Record Office and the Weiner Library in London helped me understand a little of the life of refugees. The British Library newspaper collection let me into the Lake District, and Jewish London, in 1945. The Whitechapel Art Gallery Archive introduced me to art and politics in the East End. A shopkeeper in Prague helped me find the site of the Belgická Street hostel.

The Herrmanns answered my questions, and the Novaković and Davidović families showed me Serbia. The Frieds and Hoods introduced me to Berlin and gave me a balcony on which to write. Philosophers and translators told me their stories in Budapest. The National Trust let me pitch my tent on the shores of Lake Windermere.

The University of the West of England supported my research in Prague.

Professor Madge Dresser, Professor Tim Cole, George Szirtes and the Herrmanns all read final drafts and answered questions on histories and cultures.

The work of many historians influenced *Testament*. Thank you especially to Randolph L. Braham, Martin Gilbert, Louise London, and the *Auschwitz to Ambleside* project.

Four incredible women changed my life in the last two years. Caroline Ambrose and Dionne McCulloch at the Bath Novel Award, my agent Sue Armstrong and my editor Rose Tomaszewska. Thank you, Caroline and Dionne, for your confidence and passion, and for introducing me to Sue. Thank you, Sue, for your vision and friendship. Thank you, Rose, for loving my characters as much as I do, and helping to make *Testament* all it could be.

My grandparents gave me poetry, history and long conversations. Thank you.

My partner, Nicholas Herrmann, and my family, Ellie Baker and Rosie Sherwood, made it all possible. Thank you for your unending support and belief. Without you, this book would not exist.

Read on for more about *Testament*

Can writing help us recover from loss?
An essay by Kim Sherwood

———————

Kim Sherwood's Guide to Budapest

———————

Questions for Book Clubs

CAN WRITING HELP US RECOVER FROM LOSS — EVEN THE GREATEST LOSSES OF ALL?

An essay by Kim Sherwood
First published in the Telegraph, *July 2018*

O do not think when you think of me
As a ghost that haunts the lamenting sea
Or visits again with speechless tongue
City or field where his pain was sung,
And cannot but cling though none may know
To glades where his mortal feet would go,
Or in libraries piteously to view
The fate of the work that he had to do,
(Ah, Time will come at the flood, though I wrote
My name on the sands when the tide was out):
Think this: 'He is gone. He will not return,
Though rains may chill us and suns may burn,
Though love is lovely and beauty bright
And the moon still shines in earth's velvet night,
He has done, he has done with us all at last,
And only to us remains the past.'

from 'Testament', Sir J. C. Squire

I READ THESE LINES, FROM a poem by my great-grandfather, at my grandfather's funeral in 2011. I managed to speak directly to the coffin. I projected to the back. That was important to my grandfather, the actor George Baker.

The speaker of the poem asks us not to imagine him lingering, unfulfilled. He asks us, instead, to imagine him achieving 'a peace that never was found on earth'. That's what George would have wanted. He would refuse to be missed, as he did as a young actor, attracting notices in repertory theatre while supporting his family after losing his father in the war. George was always larger than life, even in a hospital bed. A 1957 newspaper article describes him as '6ft. 4in. tall, and the huntin' and shootin' type to look at'. He would have laughed at that, though he did ride horses, which seemed gigantic to me as a child, big enough to support his frame. George was a voice that could project to the back of any theatre; a host who taught his family a party was a production. Even in quiet moments, reading poetry or easing potatoes from the soil, you couldn't mistake George's presence. He made sure you knew you were loved, that you were special. In my lifetime, George was always present. And then he wasn't.

Grief is a raid. It takes us by surprise, sweeping certainties and confidences into capacious pockets, until we no longer know the basics of up or down, this self or that. At least, that's how it was for me. His death wasn't a surprise. George had been ill for over a year – had longed to be out of it, really: ringed into his body by its refusal to let him quit this boxing match with himself. But with all that warning, I was still shocked by the pain of missing him. The verb 'bereave' originally meant to deprive, dispossess, to snatch away by violence. That's how I felt.

If George had been there, he would have told me: *you mustn't waste time mourning, darling – get on with living*. But I didn't know how, without him. On the day of the funeral, George's sister, whom he had called every day, set up in the doorway in her wheelchair half an hour before we had to leave for church. My mother told her she could wait inside, in the warmth, that we'd tell her when it was time. 'No, no,' she said. 'Now George is gone, there's no one in charge. Can't trust anything. So I'll just wait.' That's how I felt. Stuck.

After the funeral, I went to visit my grandmother on my father's side. Marika is a historian, and she had research to do in the Rochester archive, so we made it a day trip. A morning of scrolling through microfilm, and then over the great bridge with its sway of trucks above and tide below, to a café. It was there, amongst overstuffed purple upholstery, that Marika began to tell me about her childhood.

In *East West Street*, Phillipe Sands describes the 'silence' of his grandparent's home, his sense that the 'past hung over Leon and Rita, a time before Paris, not to be talked about in my presence or in a language I understood.' That's how I felt as a child. Though Marika and I would have long talks about my art homework, or how I'd done at football, I sensed there was another, bigger conversation. A first chapter of Marika's life, marked by great loss, written in a language I didn't yet understand. When I was twelve, Marika took me to Senate House Library, another research trip. She told me I could pick any book I wanted. The book I chose was about book burning. I remember the black-and-white photograph of a fire – books at its gorged base, Nazi officers standing in relaxed poses – with the same cold in my chest I felt then. I wanted to run away from it. I wanted to understand it. I told Marika: 'I'll take this book.' I couldn't read her expression. My grandmother is Hungarian Jewish, and a Holocaust survivor.

Over a decade later in the Rochester café, Marika told me about a childhood spent hiding: hiding family jewellery inside the hollowed stomach of her teddy bear; hiding behind false Christian papers, so that Hungarian Fascists wouldn't recognise her as Jewish; hiding in basements as bombs fell.

Marika's uncle and father were taken into forced labour service, a system unique to Hungary, in which men and women deemed too 'unreliable' for the army – because they were Jewish, or Roma, or Communist – were forced to clear minefields with their bare hands in Ukraine, to work in mines in Serbia, to dig trenches in Austria. To assist the 'Final Solution', and so to assist in their own destruction.

The first sixty thousand names on the memorial wall at the Holocaust Memorial Centre in Budapest are those who were murdered or died from illness during forced labour. When Marika told me her father was in forced labour service, she added: 'He was lucky.' I didn't know what that meant. Those days with Marika in archives had gifted me an archival impulse to uncover and understand the past. So I went to the library, and began to read about the Holocaust in Hungary.

It wasn't enough. I booked a flight to Berlin to continue my research. I would stay in an East Berlin apartment that belonged to a friend of a friend. A novel had begun to grow from my research, a novel that opened with a grandfather dying. I was looking forward to being alone with the book, with myself. But sitting on the balcony as the sun set on an oven-hot day, losses swelled inside me, uncontainable: the loss of George; the loss of Marika's family; the loss felt by millions of families. I felt mad, tossed about by grief.

I went to the Jewish Museum, my notebook ready. Standing in the concrete shaft known as the Void, words spilt over the page, undirected, unmanageable. I was drowning. I felt I'd never make my way to the surface. All I could hope, all I could believe, was this: writing has never failed me. It won't fail me now. So keep writing.

But it didn't seem to help. The hole inside me deepened the more I wrote. It became clear: I had to go to Hungary.

I visited Marika, to tell her about my plans. Marika is not religious, and so I was surprised to find a small wooden cross on the dining table, printed with the words, LEST WE FORGET. It had arrived by post, part of an effort to raise funds for the Poppy Appeal. Marika wanted to bury it in the garden, a memorial for her Uncle Gyula. She had been in touch with the Holocaust Memorial Centre, who said that Gyula was 'in our database of victims.' Marika told me: 'He has no grave.'

Many people in forced labour service *were* lucky, as Marika had said. They were still being put to work elsewhere while half a million Hungarian Jews arrived to Auschwitz and other camps to be killed immediately. Marika's father survived. Her uncle did not. The officers of forced labour service kept meticulous but euphemistic records. Gyula had been buried in a mass grave in Sopronbanfálva, cause of death *végelgyengülés*: 'senile decay'. He was nineteen.

I wrote the details in my notebook. I found out which labour service companies had been marched through Sopron to Austria; I

446

went to Budapest, where I watched black-and-white home videos of death marches; I followed their footsteps to northern Hungary. I walked the damp earth of Sopronbanfálva, the trees soft with rain, the hills silent. There was no grave, no marker, no memorial. I kept writing.

The Holocaust Memorial Centre has a wall that wraps around a synagogue where the missing worshippers are represented by glass plaques on their seats. The wall is carved with names, too, the names of the dead, the names of people missed by families still today. Gyula's name is on the wall. I cried when I saw him there, not because I knew him, but because I know the absence of him in my grandmother's life.

I visited mass graves across Europe both marked and unmarked, studied the flowers, candles, scraps of cloth and twists of twine left by people like me, small mementoes with private meanings. I attended ceremonies. I waited for a moment of recovery that wouldn't come.

The last site I had to visit was Theresienstadt, the ghetto and concentration camp outside Prague. My characters survive it, but I'd been putting it off. I was scared. I went to the Czech Republic for ten days, and kept telling myself: I'll go tomorrow. Tomorrow became my last day there.

I've spent years trying to ready words for the shiver I felt inside, standing by the railway track that led to Auschwitz. I don't know if I found them that day, but I did find something else, something unexpected. Relief. There is a remarkable memorial outside the small fortress where the SS tortured people: a star of David, three times the size of me, which casts its outline over thousands of graves. Standing in the warmth just outside its shadow, I could breathe. I finished the novel a few days later.

I called the book *Testament*, after my great-grandfather's poem, which gave me comfort that day in the church. Born from loss, *Testament* has brought me closer to my family history, recovering many things I couldn't once name as missing.

I have a recording of George reading the poem 'Testament'. I've tried to listen to it since the funeral, but had to cut him off each time. I played it when I began writing this. There was George's voice, precise but gentle in its timbre – there was the familiar rush of tears – and there was relief. I listened to him read the whole poem, and for the first time really heard its opening stanzas, heard George tell me: though 'my body has gone from the fields it walked', 'The flow of my words will fill their ears'. He's been gone for seven years, but I can still hear him telling me to *e-nun-ci-ate*; I can still hear him telling me, *this too shall pass*, as he did in a letter after my first heartbreak. I miss him, but he's not missing.

There is personal grief, irrecoverable yet recoverable. But this larger grief, welled inside me for whole villages, towns, cities, civilisations – some part of me will always be in the Void.

448

A GUIDE TO BUDAPEST
BY KIM SHERWOOD

First published in Trip Fiction

D URING THE WRITING OF *Testament* I spent a lot of time in Hungary carrying out research, which allowed me to reconnect with my family's Budapest roots. I fell in love with the city, and am delighted to share the places and unique cultural calling cards that inspired me.

Water

Budapest is a city defined by its water, from the stirring swathe of the Danube dividing Buda and Pest, to the natural hot baths. Joseph Silk, one of the main characters in *Testament*, is a Hungarian artist who arrives to England as a refugee only able to see the colour blue. He is pulled in memory back to the blue waters of his youth.

If you're visiting Budapest, make sure to visit Széchenyi Baths, where old men are always ready to challenge newcomers to a game of chess, whether it's sunny or snowing.

To really feel the strength and grace of the Danube, I'd recommend crossing Margit Bridge onto Margit Island, and walking the length of this almond-shaped oasis – you can cool off at Palatinus Strand, a Communist bath – and then crossing Árpad Bridge back onto the mainland. From Árpad you can see both the green fringes of the city and its centre, including Parliament and Buda Castle.

Café Culture

Silk and his brother László both remember their father, a businessman and publisher, drinking coffee and sharing conversation with the other intellectuals of his day. Many Austro-Hungarian cafés survived the Communist years, and it's well worth seeking them out. My favourite is Central Kavéhauz, where I wrote a lot of *Testament*, a less touristy spot than the equally beautiful but busy Gerbeaud Café. Central was the haunt of countless Hungarian novelists, poets and philosophers. If you want to read some Hungarian fiction, my favourite bookshop in Budapest is Irak Boltja, which has a fantastic translation section.

The Jewish Quarter

The Jewish Quarter has changed in just the six years I've been writing *Testament*, with a DIY arts and food culture bringing new life to an area still known locally as The Ghetto. These streets are where my characters worshipped, played, and grew up. The Jewish Quarter is a mixture of some of the most beautiful sights in Budapest – walk Andrássy ut for the architecture alone – alongside heart-breaking, half-hidden histories. Make sure to visit the Great Synagogue, a stunning mixture of Austro-Hungarian and Moorish styles, and go to the garden, intended as a peaceful site of meditation, and used as a mass grave for 2,281 people, victims of the Arrow Cross (Hungarian fascists). From there, go via Dob utca to Király utca, to see the centre of the Jewish Quarter old and new. You'll find the last standing remnant of the ghetto wall hidden in an apartment courtyard, and ruin bars where apartment blocks used to stand.

Streets and homes

If you can, it's worth staying in an old apartment block, something I did to get a feel for my characters' childhood homes: the height of a ceiling, how refreshing the shadow of a stairwell is after a hot day. Many of the streets and apartment facades of Budapest are peeling; others still show bullet holes. These walls speak.

Escaping the city

In creating my characters' childhood memories, I followed them on family holidays and day trips outside of Budapest. It's worth getting the boat to Szentendre for a day, an old artist's colony at the Danube Bend, home to the Margit Kovács Ceramic Collection, an extensive yet intimate way to get to know one of Hungary's leading artists.

Home, too, to the smallest synagogue in the world, and the first to be built in Hungary after the Holocaust.

On the trail of a death march, I took the train to Györ, and then Sopron, two towns in northwest Hungary. One of the most surreal aspects of writing *Testament* was researching horror while falling in love with architectural and cultural beauty. In Sopron, climb the hills to the Communist cemetery: you are at the very edge of the Austrian border, at the foot of the Alps. The red roofs and town squares below and the dripping firs all around are magical. The ground hides a mass grave where victims of forced labour were buried, and the forest stands in silent testimony to them. Visit the synagogue in Györ, now a cultural centre because the worshippers did not survive to return to it, and marvel at the intricacy of its painted flowers and stars. It's worth risking the perilous staircase in the Bishop's Tower in Györ for a bird's eye view of the blue Danube and brown Raba meeting.

I hope you enjoy discovering the history and culture of Hungary in *Testament*, and that you get to visit this fascinating country. Final tip: if you're planning a visit to Gellért Baths in Budapest, time it so you cross Szabadság Bridge at sunset, and climb up onto its green girders. There's nothing so beautiful.

QUESTIONS FOR BOOK CLUBS

1. 'What's a man without memory? Happier.' (p. 38) Silk's unusual vision is a powerful symbol for selective blindness. As Eva's story uncovers more of his past, how is Silk reshaped for the reader, and what did you think of his choices? Who owns our legacy?

2. 'They won't fit back together.' (p. 289) How do László and Jószef show all the ways in which war, persecution and immigration tear families apart? Were you moved by their relationship and did you sympathise more with one or the other?

3. 'History doesn't happen in the past tense.' (p. 273) Kim Sherwood takes this quite literally, writing all the historical chapters in the present tense. What effect did this have on the action? How else does she play with the idea of time, for example, through film (p. 278) or the German soldier's watch (p. 122)?

4. 'Don't talk German . . . there is nothing to show [...] you are a refugee and not a Nazi.' (p. 374) Should refugees be expected to integrate into – and be grateful to – a new society after fleeing persecution? How does the situation that Jószef, László and Zuzka experience compare to refugees in Britain today?

5. What did you think of the relationship between Eva and Felix, and how does their modern-day romance as children of a peaceful generation compare to Jószef and Zuzka's?

6. Jószef mourns Dragan and Zuzka as guilty sacrifices to his survival. But how do each of them contemplate suicide in response to their own experience, and how did you respond to Dragan's statement: 'Jószef had saved my life up until that moment, and I no longer wanted it.' (p. 350)?

7. Kim Sherwood travelled widely and did a lot of research. Did you learn anything new, and how does it compare to other novels you've read about the Holocaust? Did you find the way she wove the information into the narrative effective?

8. When she meets Dragan, Eva's struck by the idea that Silk has been imitating his spark and vivacity all his life. In this novel of tragic themes, there are several moments of joy and humour. Did you find any of the characters funny, and overall, did you find the reading experience devastating or uplifting?

9. 'The little boy who thought the Lake District was his private kingdom, his reward.' (p. 427) How does setting – in the landscape of the Lake District, the ruins of Budapest or Silk's Blue Room – reflect the characters' journeys of discovery and recovery?

10. The children of Holocaust survivors have been shown to have inherited neurological trauma. In what ways do the characters of John and Eva show how trauma is passed down through generations? In your own experience, how does the third generation differ from their parents in such ways?

A NOTE ON THE TYPE

In 1924, Monotype based this face on types cut by Pierre Simon Fournier c.1742. These types were some of the most influential designs of the eighteenth century, being among the earliest of the transitional style of typeface, and were a stepping stone to the more severe modern style made popular by Bodoni later in the century. They had more vertical stress than the old style types, greater contrast between thick and thin strokes and little or no bracketing on the serifs.